Faces in the Window

Andrew and Melinda Busch

Faces in the Window

Costly Grace Series - Book One

Andrew and Melinda Busch

Bladensburg, MD

Published by Inscript Books
a division of Dove Christian Publishers
P.O. Box 611
Bladensburg, MD 20710-0611
www.inscriptpublishing.com

Book Design by Mark Yearnings
ISBN: 978-1-957497-16-7
Copyright © 2022 by Andrew and Melinda Busch

Printed in the United States of America

Dedicated to all who have risked their lives
to resist tyranny
and fight for freedom against all odds,
whether in Lexington in 1775, Berlin in 1943,
or Mariupol in 2022.
"Proclaim liberty throughout all the land
unto all the inhabitants thereof."

CHAPTER

1

Franz Maedler was on a train going home. At least, most of him was.

The pain had begun to subside, becoming barely tolerable a couple of days ago. The terror might never go away. Two weeks ago, his left foot had been shot off in Stalingrad. After two days in a field hospital in the basement of a bombed out Russian school, he was flown to Tatsinskaya Airfield with other wounded men, then sent to more civilized facilities in Kharkiv. There, surgeons removed all but a few inches below the knee. Now the train was taking him from Kharkiv to Berlin.

Partially to please his father and partially to escape him, Franz had joined the expanding Wehrmacht in 1937, shortly after his mother's death. He looked the part of a dashing officer or would have if he still had both legs. He was five feet eleven inches when standing, with sandy hair, rugged features, a solid frame, deep brown eyes, and an air of steady authority. His father's connections had gained him an opportunity at officer training, and now he was a captain in the infantry, recently in command of a battalion of the Seventy-ninth Division. Franz had been in one of the first units in Army Group South to cross the Soviet border on 22 June 1941, at the onset of Operation Barbarossa. His battalion had jumped off with 219 officers and enlisted men. It was easy to get lost in the memory of early victories now beyond his reach, like a young man recalling a warm summer afternoon at the sea when he's hauling wood on an icy December morning.

He stared out the window, taking in the open central Ukrainian steppes. He had been on the train four days already. This country went on forever. Lebensraum. "Living Space" for Germans, as promised by the Führer. Perhaps one day his children, if he should have any, would spread out here and farm in peace. Or maybe Lebensraum had turned into a sick joke, as some of his comrades had grimly whispered between battles. If Stalingrad was any indication, Living Space for Germans was becoming Dying Space for Germans, and they were the Germans who were dying.

His mind wandered to moments from the road to Stalingrad. Memories of beautiful rolling plains of wheat and sunflowers and charming Ukrainian villages competed with scenes of wrecked cities and rolling plains littered with corpses and burned-out hulks of Panzers and T-34s. Life and death, sharing a landscape. He wasn't so sure he wanted his future children to make their homes atop that graveyard.

The clattering movement of the train jolted him back to reality, sending a sharp pain through his bandaged stump. Franz shut his eyes and tightened his fists. He could do without a leg, he reasoned as the pain faded to a dull ache. He would rather have lost a hand, as long as it was his left hand, but a leg was manageable. Crutches, a prosthetic. Many had gotten along with one leg. Many had lost more. His thoughts wandered again, and faces began appearing in the window by some dark trick of his mind. Heinz, who had lost both feet and bled to death in the snow. Peter, two fingers and an eye, outside of Donetsk. Ziemann, run over by a German tank. That letter had been harder to write than most. How do you tell a family that their boy had been obliterated in an accident of his own making? "Herr and Frau Ziemann, your son fell under a Panzer IV and was unrecognizable."

Then there had been Troppen, Geldhaben, and Bauer, sharing an entrenchment when a Red artillery shell burst overhead. Troppen and Bauer hadn't made it. Marcus returned to Germany missing both legs, and Franz had not heard from him since. Franz's eyes grew heavy and cloudy. There were more faces in the window, but he couldn't make them out. Didn't want to make them out. He looked away. When he turned back, they were gone, leaving only his own reflection. He blinked, then drifted into slumber.

At first, his dreams were fitful, his drowsy mind jumping from one disconnected alarm to another. *Air raid! Terrible sauerkraut at mess! The crackle of the enemy's Mosin-Nagant 91/30 rifle. Keep your head down!* Then calm and dark, that peaceful moment of deep sleep when life seems to end for a while. Nothing.

Then, a fresh nightmare.

Franz was back in Stalingrad. Back in the rubble of the ruined city, seeking shelter with some of his men among the scattered corpses of horses and humans. Two T-34 tanks appeared, an advance guard of the Red Army probing for weakness on one of the few streets still passable to vehicles. Before the Soviet tankers could see the Germans, Franz gave the order to fire a shoulder-held anti-tank rocket. He could see the flash of the Panzerfaust, followed by the flash of a T-34 as the rocket hit its mark. Then came the third flash—the other tank firing its seventy-six mm gun. One, two, three—each flash more frightful than the last.

He woke with a start, sweat trickling down his neck. His foot throbbed, and he tried to flex his toes to fight the pain. The toes on the foot he had lost. He had heard of such cases, phantom limbs. Someone loses a foot, but the foot still hurts. *How long will this last? This is the worst of everything. The pain, but without the foot.*

Four months before, in August 1942, they had entered Stalingrad. Soviet reserves poured into battle, driven to combat by the NKVD political officers who manned machine guns behind the line, ready to shoot any who retreated. The two sides were locked in an embrace of death.

Then, in a lightning thrust on the vulnerable Axis flanks, the Soviets encircled the city and trapped the Sixth Army.

The Luftwaffe began an airlift. Supplies flew in, the wounded flew out. A couple of weeks later, Franz and his increasingly hungry ninety-three men were holding a sector of the ragged and shrinking German perimeter.

Franz thought back to the other faces in the window. Had they been his men? Would they make it out? Surely the Luftwaffe was up to the task. Surely General Paulus had a plan to break out. Surely the Führer would finally grant them permission to escape. Franz could not accept that his men were doomed.

Or perhaps he could not accept that his men were doomed and he was not. If the T-34 had misfired, he would still be with them, sharing their fate as an officer should. If its gunner had aimed better, Franz would have been a true hero of the Reich. He considered either outcome preferable to his present condition, a broken soldier staring out the window at ghosts.

~

Franz glanced out the window again. The train was passing through a frozen Kyiv, white with a dusting of snow. A medical orderly came to change his dressings and offer him morphine for the second time that day. He was young and tall. And talkative. Unlike the previous orderlies. Unlike Franz.

"Hello, sir, I'm Greiner. I need to change your bandages."

"Right." Franz grimaced.

"Have you been here before? To Kyiv?"

A pause. "Yes."

Greiner pressed on, his face animated. "Where were you wounded, sir?"

Another pause. "Stalingrad."

"My brother is there, in the Third Motorized Infantry. Will he be all right?" Greiner sounded worried, as if he had already tended to a pipeline of wounded men fleeing west from Stalingrad.

Franz had known men from the Third. For the briefest moment, he turned his eyes from the window to the orderly, pursed his lips, then returned his gaze to the city scene. He had nothing more to say. Greiner hesitated a moment, then moved on.

Passing scenes of Kyiv led Franz back to the unknown faces in the window. Not all the faces that haunted his memories were German. Ukrainian faces. Jewish faces. Men, women, children. In September 1941, before his unit had moved out from Kyiv for the advancing front, they'd received new orders. Fliers posted throughout the city had commanded all Jews to appear at the old Jewish cemetery on the outskirts of town. Franz's battalion was to provide security on Melnykova Street, a key route to the meeting spot. From his post, he had watched nervously as first a handful, then dozens, then hundreds of people, streamed in the direction of the cemetery carrying one suitcase each, some wearing unseasonable layers of extra clothing. What was this about? He was afraid he knew. In August, the Sixth Army had given logistical support when the SS massacred at least four thousand Jews in Bila Tserkva. Franz had studied the faces of the walkers. Some were confused, some frightened, some angry, some complacent as if taking a morning stroll.

Occasionally, the walkers had been escorted by German soldiers. Once, a small family group broke free from the crowd and darted into an alleyway. A sergeant from another unit gave chase. A minute later, Franz heard shots. The sergeant emerged, alone but for a young, tear-streaked girl whom he returned to the procession. She was, Franz had guessed, about six years old, with a round face, pug nose, and brown hair up in pigtails—a cute child who should have been sitting on her father's knee listening to a story instead of being dragged weeping down the boulevard. Franz had vomited into the gutter, then tried to put the scene out of his mind, along with the fact that none of the people with suitcases ever came back.

Later, he heard from a lieutenant in another battalion that the SS and a couple of police battalions had shot thirty thousand Jews in two days. Now Franz shuddered to think of it, and the little girl stared back at him from the window.

Another face hovered beside the girl's. A sad face that made Franz close his eyes and swallow hard. Mama. Every time he thought of the terrible things he'd been part of, he considered what his gentle and devout mother would have thought. If she were still living, waiting to welcome him home, what would he tell her? As much as he missed her, perhaps it was better that she had not lived to hear him dissemble about what he had seen at the front. She had always known when he was lying, had somehow seen the truth in his eyes. If his father had trained him in the virtues of National Socialism and the glories of military service, his mother had trained him in the virtues of truth and the love of Christ. Because he loved both parents, he had worked to convince himself that he didn't have to choose. But how could he live with truth and lies, love and cruelty, warring in his soul?

~

Mother and Father. Their conflict had left a deep mark on Franz, and his conscience was dredging it back to the surface.

"Franzi, come here and give me a hug." The voice was his mother's. The day was 19 May 1929. Pentecost. It was not quite true to say that Franz, sitting in the creaking train carriage in December 1942, plagued by his throbbing stump, had thought back to that day. It was always present with him.

He remembered, as if it were yesterday, the Confirmation service marking his full acceptance into the Christian church. Pastor Brammeier peered over his wire-rimmed glasses and asked the confirmands if they would renounce the devil and live according to the grace of God, unto death itself.

The talk of death had unnerved Franz at the age of twelve, but it had also seemed far away. He did not expect it could touch him. Now he was surrounded by death, and perhaps even the devil. What sense could he make of this oath in the midst of total war? After the Confirmation, Mother had hosted a party to celebrate, her face radiant. Until Father had come home from a Party meeting, shouted at the assembled guests that it was time to leave, and overturned the table holding the punch bowl. "What, exactly, are we celebrating?" he had demanded. Even now, Franz's jaw clenched at the memory of his mother's face and his own hurt.

His mind turned to the other oath he'd taken, the oath that had brought him to Russia. On the day he entered the

Wehrmacht, he'd sworn to render to Adolf Hitler, Führer of the German Reich and People, Supreme Commander of the Armed Forces, unconditional obedience and risk his life as a brave soldier. That day, Father had thrown the party. Mama was no longer alive to disapprove, and no one dared upset the punch table. Franz had basked in his father's pride and quietly swallowed his regrets.

~

Christmas Eve. West of Kyiv, the sunrise behind the train seemed to chase the locomotive. Though shrouded in clouds, the sun brought a light that lifted Franz's spirits. An orderly passed through the chilly car, giving each man a small breakfast of bread and cheese. Franz ate some and wrapped the rest in a napkin. He then turned his thoughts, for a moment, to happier things. Soon he would see Katrin, the girl who had written him so often, the girl he hoped was waiting for him. His "Sunshine." His mother and hers had been dear friends, and the two children had grown close. Fingers entwined, they would sit together on a bench in her family's garden, surrounded by the fragrance of lilac and honeysuckle, teasing out their hopes for the future. Dancing around the discussion of family, children, where they would live.

Smiling, he pulled her creased and battered photograph out of his pocket and gazed at it. Katrin was about five foot two, slender but gently curved, with luminescent green eyes and wavy brown tresses that fell just below her shoulders. *I hope I've understood her meaning.* The smile faded. That was the problem with communicating in code.

"Captain..." It was Greiner again, nudging Franz out of his reverie. "Captain, it is time to change your dressings. Is that your girl?"

After the night's rest, Franz was a bit more talkative. "Yes... Um, I hope so."

"She's pretty." Greiner raised an eyebrow. "Where is she?"

"Berlin. Grunewald."

"So you will see her soon?"

Franz looked up from the photo. "I hope." So much depended on hope.

When Greiner moved on, Franz pictured himself on holiday with Katrin in five years. The two of them together after the German victory, a couple of babies on their laps. A beautiful picture. A beautiful Frau. A woman of deep conviction. His 'little flower with a heart full of sweetness,' his own version of Erika, the namesake of the folk song that was a favorite marching tune for the Wehrmacht. He needed her tenderness in his life. He needed to hold her. He had marched too much, seen too much, done too much.

But what if she doesn't want a cripple? What if she's found someone new? The thought twisted his heart. *Maybe a handsome Luftwaffe pilot, stationed close to home?* No. She would have told him. Katrin was nothing if not honest and kind.

But maybe too kind to tell him?

Franz's mood slipped again into melancholy. His depression deepened as he stared out the window at burned-out wrecks of German military vehicles, the work of anti-German partisan guerrillas. A few seconds later, beyond the vehicles, a couple dozen bodies came into view hanging from a crude scaffold. Retribution. Some may have even been guilty, but neither guilt nor innocence mattered to those tasked with maintaining security in the German rear. Franz knew his own Sixth Army had its hand in such things on its march to Stalingrad.

What seemed like a lifetime ago, he had thought it would be different. Soon the train would reach Lemberg, known to Ukrainians as Lviv and to Russians as Lvov.

When the Germans had first arrived in Lemberg, they were treated as liberators. Now partisans roamed the forests and fields, killing any German they met. To them, the promise of liberation had been a false one.

The entire enterprise had gone wrong. But where? Maybe when General von Reichenau gave the Sixth Army a blank check to wage indiscriminate war against Jews and partisans. Maybe with the SS. Or was the fault at the very top? Franz dared not think about it anymore. Thinking led to speaking, and speaking could be fatal. In any case, what could be done? Germany had to win, if only to avoid dangling at the end of someone else's rope of retribution.

~

At Lemberg, a slender officer with salt-and-pepper hair boarded and took the seat next to Franz. The two gilt-metal pips on his braided shoulder insignia indicated that he was a colonel. The train carried a mix of the wounded and the whole, and the colonel was headed for a staff meeting in Poland. Franz didn't want to talk, but the colonel did, and he had rank.

"Hauptmann, what happened to you?"

As his phantom limb throbbed, the thought shot across Franz's mind: *I'm missing a leg. What do you think?* But he controlled his tongue. "Herr Oberst, I lost my leg under fire in Stalingrad."

"And you got out? You were lucky."

"Sometimes I don't feel lucky. I still have men there."

"Oh, of course."

Franz thought for a moment. He had hoped for encouraging words. Then he recovered and spoke. "There will be a rescue, right?"

The colonel lowered his voice and coughed a bit. "I shouldn't tell you this, but the breakthrough has already been tried. It failed."

"Will there be another try?" Franz knew he shouldn't ask the question and the colonel shouldn't answer—it was undoubtedly classified information—but he couldn't help himself.

The colonel's voice dropped to a whisper. "Everything depends on the Luftwaffe. The word is that Goering promised whatever was needed. That's at least five hundred tons a day. Seven hundred is better. The flyboys are only delivering eighty-five tons a day, and we just lost the airfield at Tatsinskaya. Paulus and three hundred thousand men are now dependent on the empty promises of an egomaniac."

"So, there is no hope?" Franz had feared as much, given the near blackout of information about the Sixth Army in official sources. Dr. Goebbels and his Ministry of Propaganda were never anxious to publicize bad news.

"I didn't say that. As you know, that would constitute defeatism." Though his words were sharp, the colonel's eyes looked at him knowingly, as a man might do who has told you a lie that isn't really a lie because you both know it isn't true. The colonel cleared his throat and spoke a bit louder, so the adjacent rows could make it out. "Thank you for your sacrifice, Hauptmann. It is courage like yours that will allow the Reich to prevail."

Franz slumped in his seat. He had fought his way from Poland to Stalingrad. For what? For military failure? Moral disgrace? He was no longer certain that Germany deserved to win. He thought again of his mother, who would have told him to say a prayer at this moment. *When things are dark, Franzi, go to the Lord.* He started to pray, then stopped, gripped by doubts. What would he ask for? And why would God listen to him? In any case, the colonel seemed ready for an end to the conversation. Franz was relieved.

As Christmas Eve drew to a close, some of the men lifted their voices to *O Tannenbaum.* In the midst of war and hardship, almost all Germans retained their love of the Christmas tree. The facade of unity was broken though, when someone started a refrain of *Stille Nacht*. Some sang the traditional Christmas carol with a mixture of reverence and wistfulness.

> *Silent Night, Holy night*
> *All is calm, all is bright*
> *Round yon virgin mother and child*
> *Holy infant so tender and mild*
> *Sleep in heavenly peace*

At the same time, the hard-core National Socialists, and those who wanted to seem as if they were, sang the approved revision that had appeared in print a few years before:

> *Silent night, Holy night*
> *All is calm, all is bright*
> *Only the Chancellor stays on guard*
> *Germany's future to watch and to ward*
> *Guiding our nation aright*

Franz, who knew both versions well, simply listened. In his current state, he could no more pick one version over the other than pick one parent over the other. So far, his return trip to Germany had been a jumble of disorienting memories and conflicting emotions. Defeated, or maybe just exhausted, he closed his eyes and slept.

CHAPTER
2

26 DECEMBER 1942

The offices at the Bendlerblock in Berlin were humming with activity. In the East wing of the massive building, the general staff of the Army High Command, the OKH, tried desperately to stabilize the situation in the East. In the South wing of the Bendlerblock, Abwehr, German military intelligence, struggled to divine the Soviet order of battle in Stalingrad, where the surrounded German defenders were barely hanging on. They also had to evaluate the situation in North Africa, guess where and when the Allies would strike next, and estimate Russian and American war production. Germany was caught between the colossus of capitalism and the colossus of communism like a walnut being squeezed by a Christmas nutcracker.

At a plain oak desk in a large second-floor room assigned to Abwehr, Major Friedrich Maedler ended a call. His comrades never had any difficulty picking Friedrich out of a crowd with his slender six-foot two-inch frame, short blond hair, and blue eyes. Possibly, they joked, the most perfect Aryan in Abwehr.

A few weeks ago, a letter had arrived from the Army Information Center in Berlin announcing his brother Franz's injury. Every day since, Friedrich had called his father to see if there was news. *No, not yet,* had always been the reply. Until now. Their father had just called to say that Franz had survived his wounds and was coming home. Franz had lost his left leg below the knee, but it could have been worse. Friedrich had sensed something different about Father as he conveyed the news. Beneath his gruff exterior and unstinting devotion to Führer and Reich lay an unaccustomed vulnerability.

Now Friedrich breathed a sigh of relief and casually swung his feet onto his desk. His eyes fixed on a photograph standing on his desk: Magda, Franz, Georg, and himself at fifteen. He picked it up and held it close. Of the three Maedler boys, Friedrich was the oldest. Franz was next, only eighteen months younger, and Friedrich had always tried to look after him. As youngsters, they fought over toys. As adolescents they fought over sports and girls. Once, Friedrich had knocked out one of Franz's teeth in a struggle over a football. In Gymnasium, Franz had tackled Friedrich and dislocated his brother's right thumb because Friedrich was sweet on the same Mädchen, Elise Grossman. Or had it been Alicia? Liza? Friedrich chuckled to himself. The fight was more memorable than the girl. For all their tussling, the brothers were inseparable. Whenever Father berated Franz, Friedrich would step in to defend or distract. They also shared a deep love of their mother.

Friedrich sighed and studied Magda's image. Dear Mother, gone nearly six years now. She had lived to see the rise of Hitler, but not the war. She had never been political; she left that for Father. In public she was the dutiful wife, but she had convictions, rooted in her faith, and she would not budge. Despite Father's persistent entreaties, she refused to join the Nazi Party. *Magda, don't you understand you are making me look bad in the eyes of the Party?*

Friedrich remembered her response, always the same, not hectoring but pleading. *Klaus, you should worry more about how you look in the eyes of God.*

The other thing the boys had shared was a brother. Georg was the last born and the first to perish for the Fatherland. He had chosen the Kriegsmarine because the sea was where his brothers were not. As the youngest, he wanted to make his own way, and service in the Navy became that way. He'd gone down in U-207 off of Greenland over a year ago. A burial offers a grave where one can say goodbye, but Georg had simply slipped into the depths of the sea. No marker, no place to visit.

Georg had been the first. Friedrich had feared for some weeks now, ever since the letter had arrived from Army Information Center, that Franz was the next. For all Friedrich knew, the maw of war might end up swallowing them all, but for now he and Franz were alive and would soon be back together. For that he was grateful. He was sure that Katrin would be glad as well, though Franz's return would pose new complications.

Friedrich had grown up around her as much as his brother had, and he, too, had grown to admire her. Franz was a lucky man, but Friedrich wouldn't interfere. They weren't in Gymnasium anymore, chasing the same girl. He had too much respect for his brother, and for Katrin. But there were days when he wished things were different.

Soon, he would have to tend to his duties. The psychological burden was large and growing, and it took a toll on his body. His chronic indigestion had worsened, and he rarely enjoyed an undisturbed night's sleep. Out the window, he watched Army staff cars come and go from the Bendlerblock. He reached for his telephone. Before he could get back to work, he had to make a phone call of his own.

"Katrin, it's Friedrich. Franz is on his way home."

~

Katrin wound her scarf tighter as she wandered through the garden. She could see her breath whenever she exhaled. *If Franz were here, he would take off his jacket and drape it over my shoulders.* She eyed their bench from a distance. It was a lonely place to sit without him, but she moved toward it and settled herself on the cold stone seat.

She might have blamed the war for the years of separation, with only a few bittersweet reunions when Franz came home on leave. But she had experienced too many separations on account of the Nazis long before the war began.

When Hitler had become Chancellor in January 1933, Katrin was fifteen, a student at a private girls' Gymnasium in Berlin. One morning in early April, she arrived at school to find a new teacher at the front of the classroom. Five teachers and the school's director had been replaced, simply because they were Jewish. Latin and Greek classes were replaced with racial studies and home economics. As Papa said, "When the Nazis came in, the humanities went out."

Katrin's Jewish classmates were relegated to the back row of the classroom, where their new teacher took pleasure in humiliating them. Soon, Katrin joined the exiles, along with a few others who refused to join the League of German Girls. One morning, her friends Leah Morgenthal and Ella Stern were absent. Katrin never saw them again.

Then there was her brother and his Jewish wife, living somewhere in Switzerland now, after the seminary Reinhard attended was closed and many of the students jailed. Katrin's best friend Edith, whose Jewish father had taken his family to England in the early days of the Third Reich. Her cousin Marion, whose father had forbidden them to associate after Katrin's father lost his position at the university for protesting the firing of Jewish colleagues. By the time Franz had marched off to war, Katrin had become far too accustomed to goodbyes.

She closed her eyes and, as she imagined Franz beside her, she twisted the simple gold band on her left ring finger. The ring had not come to her from Franz. They had no understanding yet, but in Hitler's Germany, a woman of twenty-five was expected to be married, or at least engaged.

She remembered sitting down with her mother in 1936 before leaving for her mandated year of agricultural service. Mama had handed her a small birchwood box. Inside, Katrin found the plain gold band. "It belonged to your Oma," Mama explained. "You must wear it to help you avoid unwanted attention. Let everyone believe you are engaged to that boy Franz."

This advice from her mother shocked Katrin. "But Mama... is it not a sin to lie?"

Mama gently cupped Katrin's cheek in her palm. Her bright eyes shone with tears. "Our Germany has been turned upside down, my dear child. If this small deceit serves to protect you, surely God will not hold it against you."

"Yes, Mama." Katrin had solemnly taken the ring from the box and slid it onto her finger. Admittedly, she was not as concerned as her mother. After all, with her dark hair, she was unlikely to be recruited for the Lebensborn. The very idea of being assigned to one of the SS brothels, expected to produce perfect Aryan babies, made her cheeks burn. The ring marked her as unavailable. Over the next year, when anyone asked about it, she spoke of her fiancé, son of a Berlin Kreisleiter, and their plans to build a life together. The engagement was not real, but the glow in her eyes whenever she said Franz's name was no lie.

She could hardly remember a time when she didn't know Franz. When she was seven and Reinhard and Friedrich had considered her a pesky little shadow, Franz had spoken up for her, welcoming her into whatever adventures the boys had in mind. As teens, they began drifting away from their older brothers to spend hours talking about books or faith or whatever came to mind. Katrin loved Franz's natural courage and his straightforward nature. She admired his kind heart. And, as time went on, it didn't hurt that he cut a dashing figure.

As long as Katrin had known Franz, his father had been a bitter man, angry at the world. But Franz was his mother's child, gentle and compassionate. Katrin would never forget the day he defended her friend Maria's brother Pauli, a sweet boy but slow-witted, from a pair of bullies. She had started falling in love with him that day.

Sweet Pauli, lost to them forever. Sometimes when Katrin closed her eyes, she saw his smiling face. Would Franz still defend him today if he could? Or had war made him like his father, bitter and cold?

She had removed the ring when her service was done and she returned home. After Franz went to war, she slipped it on again and she'd been wearing it ever since. Each time she looked at it, she breathed out a silent prayer that God would watch over him and bring him home to her.

Now, at last, Franz was returning, not on leave, but for good. Katrin ought to be excited. She was pleased, certainly. But she was also fearful. Would the Franz she had fallen in love with be the Franz who returned to her? His loss of a leg would not cause her love to fade. But how had his service in the Wehrmacht damaged his soul? His faith had been important to Franz, despite his father's disdain.

He once told her that he believed he could be both a loyal German and a devout Christian, to please both father and mother. Katrin had prayed that his mother's influence would win out. Had he become an unquestioning son of the Reich? His gentle mother's heart would have broken to see such a thing. *As my heart will,* Katrin thought. She shivered, chilled more by her fears than by the December weather. With a soft sigh, she slid the ring from her finger and slipped it into her pocket, then stood and headed back to the house.

CHAPTER
3

30 DECEMBER 1942

Franz was sure Friedrich would welcome him home. Though competitive, they had always been close. He was not so sure about his father, now District Leader of Wilmersdorf, a western suburb of Berlin. Perhaps his father, who mourned Georg as a fallen hero, would see Franz's loss of a leg and his evacuation from Stalingrad as an inferior sacrifice to the glory of the Fatherland. Familiar feelings of inadequacy washed over Franz.

The two *Kriegslokomotives* dragged his overloaded train inexorably toward the Potsdamer Bahnhof, with fifty-five utilitarian passenger cars trailing behind. They carried Franz and eight hundred other officers and men of the Wehrmacht back whence they had come, all without victory and some without body parts. The victory, most Berliners hoped, would yet come. The parts were gone forever.

Franz watched the city come into view, starting with the southeastern suburb of Schonefeld. After passing the Herschel aircraft factory, he watched the newer houses on the outskirts of Berlin fade into older apartments, shops, and churches. Unlike Stalingrad, Berlin was mostly intact, though Franz could occasionally see a damaged building, hit in one of the sporadic British raids. *Do unto others as you would have them do unto you.* It felt strange, somehow blasphemous, to hope that others would not be able to do unto Germany what Germany had done unto them.

Next to Franz, an SS Obersturmführer kept checking his watch. He gave Franz a sidelong glance. "Six months in the field. I'm ready to be home."

Franz grunted. He had spent eighteen months in the field, so his reservoir of sympathy was running low. The SS man had taken the colonel's place an hour after Franz awakened to find the seat next to him empty. Franz had spent most of the time since wishing he could get the colonel back. Technically, he outranked his neighbor. In reality, everyone had to be on guard when the SS was around. No Army field marshal outranked Heinrich Himmler, and it followed that no mere Army captain could pull rank on an SS lieutenant, at least not without risk.

This one was brusque, loud, and arrogant, boasting of his exploits in Einsatzgruppe VI. Franz silently laughed to himself. *Completely unique among the SS!* Like Franz, many Army officers saw the SS as fanatical, self-important, and generally devoid of normal moral constraints. At the same time, he was drawn to the man's bravado about the war. It appealed to his deep need for hope that his sacrifices, and those of his men, were not in vain.

The lieutenant resumed his monologue. "No matter what happens in Stalingrad, we are historically destined to prevail against the Slavs. As the inferior people, they will yield. It is only a matter of time." It reminded Franz of the early days, before bravado was the preserve of the ideologues. "In any case, soon we will have ended the Jewish threat forever. The Bolsheviks cannot stand if the

Jews are no longer with them."

Franz knew the National Socialist doctrine—this was a war of extermination, a fight to the death, against the intertwined monolithic enemy of Slavs, Bolsheviks, and Jews. The life of the German nation was at stake. The part about the Jews had always been murky to Franz, but he understood the part about the Bolsheviks. All the way to the Volga, he had seen evidence of the depravity of communism. As a soldier, he could not help wondering, *What sort of tyrant points guns at the backs of his own troops, preferring to kill them rather than let them retreat? No one deserves to rule who has such low regard for his countrymen's lives.* The thought involuntarily entered his mind that his men in Stalingrad would probably perish because the Führer, too, preferred to let them die rather than retreat. Not a thought Franz could fully digest, let alone express on a military train while sitting next to an SS Obersturmführer.

Franz was jolted back to the present when a middle-aged man across the aisle joined the conversation, ending the awkward silence that had developed. He wore the insignia of an Order Police lieutenant in the 101st Reserve Battalion from Hamburg, and Franz assumed he was returning home from duty in Poland. "I am leaving that business to you and my comrades," the Orpo officer said to the SS man, a tremor in his voice. "I thought we would be fighting partisans and guarding prisoners. Instead, they are sending us to do your dirty work and shoot women and children in their beds."

Again, Franz's thoughts carried him back to Ukraine. He had witnessed things, heard things that proved that the massacres of Jews at Bila Tserkva and Kyiv were not exceptions, but a new rule. People rounded up, trenches filled in. Roving Einsatzgruppen squads were equipped with special vans designed to gas people inside. Then Franz had learned of trainloads being sent to camps in Poland.

He wanted to believe this "relocation" was a more humane alternative, but in his heart he knew better. As his westbound train passed an eastbound train of cattle cars, he wondered whether they carried cattle or people, and a new sense of guilt washed over him. He began to pray, but somehow his prayers felt cold and lifeless. Unheard. Perhaps he had put himself beyond grace. He sighed and gave up.

"Are you questioning the orders of the Führer?" the SS man snapped in an appeal to the Führer Principle, the Nazi doctrine that the leader of the German nation must be obeyed unconditionally.

The Orpo man's eyes bulged with ill-concealed anger. "How do I know the orders came from the Führer and not that chicken farmer Himmler? The only orders I know came from my commander and he gave us the choice to opt out. I opted out. I've been doing transport ever since."

Franz blinked. *Opted out? I didn't know that was possible.* There was the rumor of the lieutenant colonel in the 295th infantry who had blocked the SS from killing a group of Jewish children in a barn at Bila Tserkva, but word was, that resistance hadn't lasted long.

A couple of wounded soldiers on opposite ends of the car shouted for the two men to shut up. Franz imagined they'd had enough of conflict. A Luftwaffe officer in front of him shot a glance at the Orpo man, snarling, "Do your duty. The rest of us are." A few scattered voices, with varying degrees of conviction, volunteered, "That's right," "Yes," and "Listen to him."

As the train pulled into the station and screeched to a halt, the rest of the car was simply silent. As silent as Germany.

~

When Franz arrived at the Beelitz-Heilstätten Hospital by military transport, two orderlies carried him by stretcher to a bed in a spacious second-floor room with about three dozen other officers. Every bed was full. The room had a high ceiling and large, arched windows. The sickly-sweet smell of healing and death, antiseptic and blood and gangrene, hung heavily in the air. When it was his turn, an orderly pushed him in a wheelchair to the room's one telephone, a modern desk phone with a handset resting over the dial, which sat on a short, square wooden table.

Franz picked up the handset and dialed Friedrich. His second call was to Katrin. His stomach twisted. The third was to his father.

He had been mentally practicing the call to his father since getting on the train in Kharkiv. There were so many ways it could go wrong, so many ways Father could express his disappointment. Finally, time had run out. Franz couldn't put it off for long or Father might come to realize he'd been left for the last.

"Hello?" The clipped, businesslike voice was just as Franz remembered.

"Hello, Father? It's Franz."

There was a pause on the other end, and then the voice softened. It sounded as if his father had to force the words around a lump in his throat. "Son."

Franz took a deep breath. "I am outside Berlin, at Beelitz-Heilstätten."

"How are you?"

"As well as possible. My leg hurts like the devil, or what's left of it does." Franz grimaced. "It was a long trip home."

Another pause by his father. "How long did it take?"

"Eleven or twelve days. I lost track. The train only goes a hundred kilometers a day near the combat zone in case of sabotage."

"How was it?"

"What?" Franz asked in some puzzlement. His father's

questions had thrown him off.

Father repeated himself. "The train. How was it?"

Franz thought for a moment. *I've just come home with a grievous war injury and this is what he asks?* Not "When can I see you?" or "How long will you be there?" No, it was a question about the train. After a quick mental adjustment, he managed an answer. "It was fine. I walked to Stalingrad. Anything other than walking back was a luxury."

"You know, Beelitz-Heilstätten is where the Führer went for recovery after he was wounded at the Somme."

Of course Father would know that. "Yes, there is a plaque at the entrance to the building."

"Son, when can I come see you?"

Ahh, there it was. "I have been told visitors can come starting tomorrow. Every day the visiting hours are after dinner, 14:00 to 17:00. Can you make it?"

"I will do my best."

"Thank you."

Franz exhaled. The call was over. It was anticlimactic, but also a relief. No berating for letting down the Fatherland or the memory of Georg. No digs about leaving his men behind. Maybe that would come. But not today.

Franz spent the rest of the day settling in. In the evening, an older doctor snuck around a bottle of schnapps to share with the newcomers to the ward. After a few swigs, Franz fell asleep, the first time in several days that he had not been rocked to sleep by the motion of the train.

He didn't want to go back to Stalingrad, but his dreams took him there anyway. The same three flashes—the Panzerfaust, the first T-34 exploding, the second T-34 firing. Then smoke, dirt flying, hot metal, ringing in his ears. Someone's mangled foot in the snow. Oh, right, *his* foot. Grimm, bleeding out next to him; Tiegert screaming for his mother. And then, somehow in Stalingrad though they weren't, Bauer and Ziemann. Then the family in Kharkiv he had found boiling shoe leather for dinner when he briefly ducked into their flat seeking shelter from a sudden blizzard. A tear-streaked six-year-old. And back to darkness.

~

Franz awakened at 07:00 on New Year's Eve to the sound of the daily report issued by the Oberkommando der Wehrmacht, the Armed Forces High Command, on the Reich Broadcasting Corporation, announced by the strains of *Wacht am Rhein*, the stirring patriotic song dating back to conflicts with France early in the last century.

> *They stand, a hundred thousand strong,*
> *Quick to avenge their country's wrong,*
> *Dear Fatherland, put your mind at rest,*
> *Firm stands, and true, the Watch, the Watch*
> *at the Rhine!*

The OKW report had more to say about the Rhine than the Volga. "Our brave forces continue to be engaged in heavy fighting in the Southeast of Russia." Then on to North Africa, preparations to defend occupied France, another bombing raid against Britain. Franz, who had sat up to listen, slumped back against his pillow. *Engaged in heavy fighting? Nothing about the encirclement, the flailing airlift, the failed breakthrough? The quarter of a million men on the verge of starvation, massacre, or surrender? Not even the name of Stalingrad?*

An agitated amputee five beds away noticed, too. "Tell the truth!" he raged against the disembodied voice on the radio. A Bavarian, Franz reckoned from his accent. "The devil take Goebbels and OKW. Ivan is killing us, and no one knows. Liars! Do they think they can keep it a secret forever?" A doctor quickly appeared at the man's bedside and injected him with a sedative. Others turned away, focusing on their breakfasts of cheese and bread or on the weather report and music program that followed the *Wehrmachtbericht*.

Just before dinner was served, a pair of Sicherheitsdienst officers appeared in the ward. A chill seemed to sweep over the room at their dark grey uniforms with police pattern shoulder straps, black collar patches, and black diamonds embroidered with "SD" on their left sleeves. At their first stop, they spoke in hushed tones with the angry Bavarian, who had recovered from the effects of the sedative. Franz could not hear what was said, though the Bavarian seemed to lose some of his color. The SD was, after all, the security service of the SS, founded by the coldly fearsome Reinhard Heydrich. If one didn't lose a little color when the SD came to visit, one wasn't human.

After speaking with the Bavarian, the pair moved on to another bed, and then another. As they drew closer, Franz's chest tightened.

Franz was their seventh stop in the room. "Good morning, Hauptmann," the senior of the two, a tall, thin major, greeted him. Both men flashed their SD identifications. Franz stiffened. "Good morning."

"How were things in Stalingrad?" the younger officer probed. He was average height, average weight, with medium brown hair—average in every way but the power he held over others.

"I did my duty," Franz replied. "We were engaged in heavy fighting." He needed a safe answer, and what could be safer than the wording of an OKW communique?

"Yes," said the first man, running his hand through his salt and pepper hair, "you did your duty with distinction. We have come to remind you that your duty does not end on the battlefield."

"Sturmbannführer?" Franz hoped the major would

clarify his admonition.

"We do not need to tell you that the Army is facing a difficult fight. We must be prepared for a setback." *Finally, some honesty.* "It is essential for the survival of the Reich that we remain resolute in this moment. To come back to the Fatherland and undermine the war effort with rumors and defeatism would render meaningless your sacrifice and the sacrifices of your men."

After a brief pause, the younger officer picked up the cudgel with greater directness. "You should remind your comrades that defeatism is a crime."

Franz swallowed hard. He felt trapped in his bed, surrounded by jackals.

The major's next words restored some subtlety to the conversation. "We understand that you are suffering. There is no doubt that you will continue to suffer. For this, you have the eternal thanks of the nation. Just be careful what you tell others. You are not authorized to say anything more about Stalingrad than what is released by the German State. Some of our fellow countrymen would be unable to put it into proper context."

Their concession to honesty had been short-lived. Franz nodded silently. He understood the message, but it rankled him. Whether in the train or in the hospital, truth and the National Socialist regime were not on speaking terms. After the "Heil, Hitler" salute—not required in the Army, but highly advisable when the SD was involved—the pair moved on to continue spreading their message of circumspection.

~

At 14:03, Franz looked up to see his brother. A wide grin erupted on his face. This was the sort of visitor he wanted!

Friedrich inspected him closely, eyes flicking from Franz's face to his blanket-covered form. Then he grinned just as widely and blurted out, "How did you plan to beat the Red Army with one leg?" He gently pulled Franz into an embrace, his tone shifting from jocularity to concern. "Father told me about your leg, Franz. How are you? Tell me everything. You are a hero of the Reich."

Franz still wasn't sure about that, but it meant everything that Friedrich believed he was a hero. Almost everything.

Katrin had entered while Franz's attention was on his brother. When he saw her at the foot of his bed, he almost forgot Friedrich was there. His mouth dropped open as he drank her in. Her face was radiant, her dark hair a bit tousled, and her green eyes dancing. She did not repeat Friedrich's accolades on behalf of the Reich but simply clasped Franz's right hand and squeezed it with care. "You're home, and I'm so happy. I worried about you every day you were gone, and double when I heard about the letter." Then she draped a knitted scarf around his neck, beautiful and soft in a mix of forest green and sky blue. "Your favorite colors," she said, and she gave him a kiss on the forehead. "Merry Christmas, a little late."

Franz nodded and touched her hand. "Thank you."

Friedrich pressed his brother again. "Tell us everything."

Franz didn't want to. His recent brush with the SD had had its intended effect. Anyway, the whole story was too painful. Instead, Franz shared a few safe anecdotes to appease his brother's curiosity.

~

Katrin could tell Franz was holding back. After a few minutes, he wouldn't look directly at her or Friedrich. Instead, he focused his haunted gaze on his own hands, on the bare tree branches outside the window, on the cracks in the ceiling above him. Perhaps he was protecting her. Or perhaps he did not feel able to speak freely in front of his brother. Maybe his experiences were too difficult a topic to revisit. She could see in his eyes that they haunted him, that he was struggling to reconcile his natural compassion and kindness with the hard cruelty the Führer demanded. Katrin wished she could speak with him alone, but with forty injured men in this ward, even if Friedrich were not here, they would have no guarantee that their conversation would not be overheard and reported. So she listened, her fingers interlaced with his, every so often giving his hand a gentle squeeze or murmuring words of sympathy.

Franz's voice faded to silence before he reached any real end to his story. Katrin glanced from him to Friedrich. He gave a long slow nod, then squeezed Franz's shoulder. "An old friend of mine is recuperating in Ward Three. I should go say hello." He winked. "Give you two lovebirds a little privacy." Katrin could not suppress the smile creeping across her face.

Once Friedrich had gone, she felt obligated to keep the rest of the time with Franz light and cheerful. In his letters home, he called her "Sunshine", a pet name he had given her years ago. She wanted to part the clouds that darkened his countenance, so she chattered cheerfully about the antics of her kittens, Schatz and Spaetzle, and the oversized dog who had wandered into the garden a few weeks ago and made himself at home. Father had threatened to donate him to the war effort after the clumsy creature destroyed a prize rose bush, but somehow, they had become the best of friends instead. The hound was now a beloved member of the Weber family and answered—occasionally—to the name Bruno.

As Katrin described Bruno burrowing his full bulk into the snow and then pouncing on her unsuspecting father with muddy paws, Franz's reserved chuckle escalated into genuine laughter. She felt a thrill of victory. For a little while, at least, she had chased the specter of war from his eyes.

All too soon, it was time to leave. Friedrich had accompanied Katrin on the train and would take her home again. She gave Franz one more light kiss on the forehead and a whispered "Happy New Year. I love you," then followed Friedrich out of the ward and through the maze of corridors to the door.

CHAPTER
4

Franz began his physical rehabilitation exercises the day after New Year's. Friedrich and Katrin had made two more visits since then. Yesterday, they sneaked in a box of chocolates wrapped inside the *Völkischer Beobachter*. Somehow, Friedrich's work with Abwehr brought him into close contact with a large volume of Swiss chocolates. Franz wasn't going to ask questions.

Each day, he reported to an exercise room to strengthen his good leg and his balance. Soon they would fit him with a wood prosthetic, and he would begin exercising that leg as well. Doctors expected he could return to service in six weeks. He could never go back to combat. He would sit out the rest of the war working at a desk in Berlin. There were days he could hardly face the world. He would never be whole; could he ever be useful?

Two medical orderlies took turns helping him with his exercises. One was about twenty-five, blond, and a picture of Aryan vitality. He was also severe and laconic, as if he had been asked too many times by wounded soldiers why he wasn't at the front himself. Franz wondered as much but kept the questions to himself. Some of the men suspected that Blondie was SD, keeping tabs on the wounded and their visitors. Probably a rumor concocted by bored men who disliked the SD nearly as much as they disliked physical therapy. Still, Franz had an arrangement with Blondie. Blondie told him what to do in the most economical way possible, and Franz did it.

The other orderly was about forty-five, with a bit of a pudge and thinning brown hair. He wore round wire-rimmed glasses and talked too much, like a middle-aged woman on the U-Bahn after grocery shopping at the market. He had a joke for every occasion, some of them clean, and told unending stories about his Frau's cooking, his dachshund Bärli, and his experience as an orderly in a field hospital in the last war. If anyone was SD, Franz would bet it was Pudge, but he didn't hold it against him. He had an arrangement with Pudge, too. Franz would share his chocolates and Pudge would let him go back to his bed five minutes early.

When he wasn't in physical therapy, he played checkers with some of the other men, listened to the radio, and read the newspaper. He was hungry for updates from Stalingrad but knew better than to take the news at face value, putting him in the curious position of desperately desiring information he wouldn't believe once he got it.

The nightmares came with nearly every sleep. Three flashes, a foot in the snow, a mix of doomed faces. And sleep came more often than he preferred, thanks to the morphine that doctors continued to give him for the pain. After today's dinner of sausage and sauerkraut, Franz settled in for a nap. This time, when he woke, there was a familiar face looking at him.

Not Katrin. Not Friedrich.

Father. He looked like he had aged at least ten years in the twenty months since Franz had last seen him. His face was creased, his fringe of hair almost completely white, and his shoulders were bent as if he carried a heavy load.

"You came. Finally!" Franz blurted out,

His father shrugged up a shoulder and offered a regretful smile. "Son, I have been... weighed down with work. The Party makes great demands of us all in these times."

"I've been here a week. Friedrich has come three times already. What do you want me to think?" Franz bristled, suddenly wide awake, his heart pounding in his chest. Once, he would not have challenged his father. His wounds, he supposed, gave him the right.

At one time, his father would have slapped him down with some self-assured answer. Today he waited a moment, his fingers rubbing the brim of the fedora he clutched, before responding. "I want you to think that I take my duty as seriously as you take yours." After another brief silence, his father mustered up a question. "What was it like? Stalingrad?"

Franz paused. The faces of the SD officers with their warnings about defeatism flashed through his mind. *It was hell.* "Full of Russians with guns. We called it the Cauldron." He studied his father's face. "How much have they told you about it?"

"I know what is reported by the OKW each morning," Klaus answered. "Not much more. My contacts in the Party and my old trench mates who are still in the Army share rumors, but that is all they are."

Franz scanned the room and lowered his voice. "The situation is very serious, Father... If things were going well, don't you think there would be more news?"

His father scowled, eyes darting to the end of the bed where Franz's left leg should have been. "How did it happen?"

"We were holding the line against Red armor. We got one of them. One of them got me." Franz looked down at his hands as he made the admission. He couldn't bear meeting his father's stern gaze. "And others."

"What is the country like?"

"Difficult terrain for fighting. Marshes, ravines. And harsh in winter, even in the South. The boys outside Leningrad weren't the only ones freezing."

"No, I meant for living."

Franz looked out the window, then back to Klaus. "Good enough, I guess." *If you want to live in a graveyard.*

"I would hope better than that," Klaus replied brusquely, before changing the subject. "What is it like fighting the Russians?"

"The Communists are bastards." The words burned in Franz's mouth as he catalogued the enemy's sins. "They shoot their own soldiers in the back if they don't advance. They kill their prisoners rather than take them along. When we came to Stalingrad, they wouldn't evacuate the people. I think the Bolsheviks wanted them in danger to spur their troops to action. We found mass graves everywhere. Outside Kyiv, maybe a hundred thousand, killed by the secret police. Nothing is sacred to them. They wage war on God as well as man."

Klaus nodded as Franz spoke, though Franz knew that last point would not stir him like the rest. Klaus had abandoned the church after the Armistice and had found a new religion and a new god. "The Führer is right, of course," Klaus finally said. "We cannot coexist with such a species. This is a war to the finish. The French are dilettantes. The British are, after all, Saxons. The Americans are mongrels and soft. We can live with them all, once they submit. Not so in the East." Klaus changed the subject again. "What of your men? Is it hard being away from them?"

"Yes, it is hard. Communication now is... not easy. As far as I know, they are still fighting."

Franz followed Klaus's eyes as his father looked around at the filled beds and two doctors moving from man to man. "Have they been treating you well here?"

"As well as I could expect."

"You know, the Führer was treated here after the Somme."

"Yes, I know. I saw the plaque." Franz rolled his eyes. "We talked about this before. Having taken an oath to the Führer, I can express my hope that the food was better for him when he was here."

A stiff grin teased at Father's lips but vanished quickly. "What will they do for you?"

"If I do my exercises I can be out in a couple of months. They will give me an artificial leg. I will remain in service, behind a desk."

"Hmmm. A pencil pusher. When I was in the trenches, we hated them."

Franz looked away. *Here we go. He's going to tell me I'm a disappointment.*

But to his surprise, the remonstration never came. "But now I am a pencil pusher myself," Klaus said, "and I see that every form of service to the Reich is valuable. We all do what we can. If you are smart, you can kill more Russians from behind an Army desk than from behind a Mauser."

Klaus pulled something out of the pocket of his waistcoat and gave it to Franz. It was a copy of Georg's Sterbebild.

Franz took a long look at the memorial card, gazing at the soft features of his younger brother.

"I thought you might like to have it," Klaus said, blinking rapidly. "Friedrich said you wrote of losing the other one."

Franz let his eyes skim the text.

In Fond Memory
of
Seaman Second Class
Georg Maedler
From Wilmersdorf
Who in September 1941 on an enemy patrol
in the North Atlantic
in the 20th year of his life died a hero's
death for Führer, Folk, and Fatherland.
You died too early on a distant field of glory.
Into a cold grave you sank with your
comrades.
Our beloved one, we will never forget you
Until we ourselves rest in the grave

Franz lowered the card, letting it drop onto his blanket. He felt the familiar heartache that always accompanied thoughts of Georg. He missed his younger brother. What was it all for? It was a question that kept coming back to him in a variety of forms. Finally, he raised his eyes to look again at his father. For the first time, he slipped into the informal address. "Papa. Why am I alive and Georg is not?"

"Who can win an argument with destiny? I have made peace with his loss." Klaus's right hand grabbed his own left hand, probably to prevent it from rising to stroke his mustache, a tell-tale sign that he was lying. "You and Georg have both given the sacrifice that the Fatherland required. The war is not over. Who knows how it will end for any of us? In the meantime, you are alive and must make the most of it for us all."

Looking into the sepia eyes of Georg's photograph, Franz quietly nodded. Klaus reached down to touch his son's shoulder. He lingered for a few seconds, then abruptly drew his hand back, turned, and walked out of the room.

After Franz watched his father leave, he picked up Georg's memorial card, stared at it awhile, then turned it over, set it down, and fell into a fitful sleep.

CHAPTER
5

2 FEBRUARY 1943

Over a period of weeks, Franz settled into the hospital routine. Up with *Wacht am Rhein* and the morning OKW communique. Breakfast. Reading. Physical exercises, sometimes including boxing. Dinner. Nap. Visiting hours. Checkers with Wilhelm or chess with Fritz. Supper. More reading. Circulating through the large room on his crutches and talking with new friends. Goodnight.

He was down to one nap a day. His body was healing, and the doctors were giving him less morphine. The nightmares came less frequently, though he could still count on losing his foot in the snow at least three times a week. If there were fewer flashes, there seemed to be more faces. German faces, Russian faces, Ukrainian faces, Jewish faces. All troubled. All doomed. Who were they? Some he remembered from Kyiv or Kharkiv, from Stalingrad or that village outside Zhytomyr, or the Jews fleeing the SS Einsatzgruppe that his battalion had been ordered to turn over to their fate. Some he didn't recognize. Sometimes they were silent. Sometimes they seemed to be trying to speak to him.

Visiting hours were his favorite time of day. Katrin and Friedrich came often, usually together, and Father when he could. Katrin and Friedrich would bring candy, newspapers, and books. On occasion, Friedrich would bring a new record that Franz could play on the ward's hand-cranked Victrola. His brother respected Franz's preference for Liszt and Bach and Brahms, though he threw in an occasional Wagner opera for good measure. Father came bearing only exhortations and memories. For Franz, that was enough.

About once a week, he was also visited by Pastor Matthias Hoffmann, a friend of Katrin's mother. Katrin had asked him to look in on Franz. As a pastor in the Confessing Church, the portion of the Evangelical Church that split off to protest the church's quiet accommodation with National Socialism, Hoffmann came to the hospital as a personal visitor rather than a sanctioned chaplain. On his first visit, he'd brought a catechism to add to Franz's reading collection.

Franz appreciated the pastor's efforts, but every kilometer he had marched into the Soviet Union had taken him farther from God. "Pastor," he said in their first meeting, "I am not sure I can talk with God any longer. I am not sure He wants to hear from me." Such thoughts had oppressed him for months, but this was the first time he had confessed them openly.

"Go on."

"The Bible says that God is holy and pure. I don't see how I can be of use to Him anymore." Franz knew he was leaving the heart of the matter unspoken. *How can God use me after what I have been a part of? What grace can He offer that would ever cleanse my soul?*

"Many have doubted that, Franz." The pastor's gaze did not waver as he looked Franz in the eyes. Could he see everything Franz held back? After a few uncomfortable seconds, Franz broke eye contact, focusing on his hands as they twisted his blanket. The pastor continued. "Peter and Thomas each denied Christ in his own way. Paul waged war against Him. But He brought them all back. He had a use for them. More importantly, He had love for them, no matter what they had or hadn't done."

"They weren't on the Eastern Front." Franz snapped his mouth shut. He could not say more without revealing forbidden truths about the war in the East.

Hoffmann's hand settled on his and squeezed it gently. "No, Franz, only you know what you have been through. You and God. I will talk with you whenever you want, but you cannot find what you are looking for without taking it to Him. Pray and read your catechism."

The pastor's words were a balm. On Hoffmann's third visit, Franz asked if he could take Communion. The Pastor quietly spoke the words of Institution, then gave him a consecrated wafer and a sip from a small bottle of wine he carried with him. Franz had stopped taking Communion from the unit's chaplain somewhere east of Kyiv. His soul had become numb. It was starting to feel again.

~

The radio was an ever-present feature of life in the hospital. On 16 January, OKW finally acknowledged that the Sixth Army was "fighting on all sides," another way of saying "surrounded." Franz knew it had been surrounded for nearly two months by then. After that, dispatches became increasingly grave.

Now, seventeen days later, Franz was losing a game of checkers with army Lieutenant Wilhelm Neuheisel, wounded by shrapnel in the leg and side in the Caucasus. Then the Adagio Movement from Bruckner's Seventh Symphony began to play. The abrupt change in music matched the mostly cloudy weather. Franz could hear the room grow quiet as the men noticed the solemn dirge, each at a different moment. An orderly turned up the volume. It was news from the High Command.

> *The battle for Stalingrad has ended. The Sixth Army, under the exemplary leadership of Marshal Paulus, true to its oath to fight to the last breath, has succumbed to the enemy's superiority and unfavorable circumstances.*
>
> *The sacrifice was not in vain. Although completely encircled, the Axis army tied up strong Russian forces for weeks of the hardest fighting and most bitter hardship. The German leadership thus was given time to take countermeasures, on the execution of which depended the fate of the entire Eastern Front. The Luftwaffe, after a long encirclement, despite the utmost efforts and heavy losses, was unable to guarantee sufficient supplies by air and the possibility of the German Sixth Army's relief dwindled more and more and finally disappeared. Their example will be remembered for all time.*

Following the announcement, the radio repeatedly broadcast "Good Comrades," another song typically played at military funerals. A period of mourning was announced by Joseph Goebbels.

The room remained silent. Franz returned to his bed, the checkers game forgotten. The radio had just solemnly announced the first total German defeat on land since the war began. His Sixth Army was no more. His men were dead or beyond rescue.

~

That night, Franz did not eat his supper. Few on his floor did. Nor did they talk. The new and bitter taste of unmitigated loss was radically unlike the taste of victory they had enjoyed before. *The whole Sixth Army? Swallowed up in the morass of Russia?* Who could avoid wondering if the sacrifice of three hundred thousand men had been worth it?

The next day, all of Franz's visitors came. Friedrich and Katrin arrived first, together again.

"My Franz," Katrin's mouth was turned down gently, compassion in her eyes. "How are you?" She gave him a long hug, then asked again, "How are you?"

"What is there to say?" Franz worked to drain the emotion from his words.

Friedrich clasped his brother's hand. "Are you all right?"

Franz freed his hand and crossed his arms. He welcomed the company, but not the conversation.

Friedrich tried again. "You know, the Sixth Army saved the southern sector by holding on for so long. You should be proud of your men and your role in the fight."

Franz remained quiet.

"The Führer will know what to do. We must have faith in him." Friedrich paused a moment. "Victory is made more glorious when one has to win it through setbacks."

The Führer will know what to do? If the Führer knew what to do, this wouldn't have happened. Franz's brow furrowed. *That infernal city could've been bypassed entirely. Because it had the name "Stalin" attached to it, the Führer decided we couldn't retreat.*

Friedrich nudged his shoulder. "You'll see, Franz. The Fatherland will win out in the end."

Friedrich's assurances grated on Franz. He opened his mouth to speak, but stopped short. For one thing, anyone could be listening. For another, while his faith in the Führer might be diminished, his loyalty to the Wehrmacht was unstinting, and the Wehrmacht had sworn an oath to Hitler. Besides, he knew his brother. Why bother arguing with him? Friedrich was an apple who had fallen not far from their father's tree, too much of a committed Nazi to be driven off his optimism about the Führer and the war. Better to let it go.

"I hope you're right," he finally choked out. That, at least, was true.

Katrin, as usual, focused on the human side of the equation. "Franz, you must have hope that all this will end someday. All of the loss."

Friedrich excused himself to go smoke a cigarette outside. He would need to return to work soon. The Führer and the Abwehr needed him. Katrin stayed at Franz's bedside.

Franz avoided her gaze. Hundreds of thousands lost at Stalingrad. *Nothing is guaranteed in life. Has my patience turned to complacency?* It was time for a conversation with Katrin. He felt suddenly queasy. *Really? I wasn't queasy when I was being shot at.* Then he broke his silence.

"I love my brother, but there are times I am glad he leaves us alone," Franz announced.

Katrin moved closer to the bed. "Is something on your mind?"

He grasped her hand and took a deep breath. "What are we doing, Sunshine?"

With a coy flutter of her eyelashes, she answered, "Well, we're having a conversation about Stalingrad. And maybe brothers."

Franz chuckled. Of course, she knew exactly what he meant. "You've always known how to make me smile. I never want to lose that."

She pursed her lips and asked, "What do you suggest we do about that, Franz Maedler?"

He wanted to kiss her. But not here. Not in the ward surrounded by soldiers.

Instead, he weighed his answer carefully. Should he be bold? *It's time for us to marry.* Maybe he should he be more careful, leave more to Katrin. *Is it time for us to marry?* More subtle? *Perhaps it's time to take hold of our future. No one knows how long we'll have.*

Suddenly, Pastor Hoffmann was standing in their midst.

"Pastor. Hello." Franz forced a smile. He wished the clergyman would have arrived twenty minutes later.

"Hello, Pastor Hoffmann. It's good to see you." Despite Katrin's welcoming smile, Franz thought he could see his disappointment mirrored in her eyes.

"Katrin, Franz," Hoffmann nodded a greeting. "I wanted to see how you were, Franz, after last night's news."

"I wish I could say it was a surprise," Franz replied. "We were surrounded before I was wounded. They had to fly me out."

Katrin's eyes gleamed with tears. Perhaps she couldn't stand to think of him hungry and desperate, or of how much danger he had truly been in. Franz regretted upsetting her.

She gathered herself and declared, "Then you being here is a bigger miracle than I knew."

Franz had not yet decided whether he was glad to be alive or wished he had seen the fight through to the end with his men. It was the first time he had thought of his escape as a miracle.

"Like God opening the Red Sea for the people of Israel, He opened a path in the air for you to pass through the Red Sea of Russia." Pastor Hoffmann broke into a sheepish grin, clearly amused by his own cleverness.

Yes, just like it, but different. Franz sighed deeply,

thinking about Kyiv and Bila Tserkva. He couldn't represent the people of Israel in this story. Was he one of Pharaoh's men? But they all drowned. And here he was. *Why is Hoffmann saying that out loud, anyway? He could get us all shot.*

"Franz," Hoffmann continued, furrowing his brow, "God has a purpose for your life. You must be prepared to find it."

"Didn't He have a purpose for each of the men we lost? All three hundred thousand of them?"

"Yes. But you know it wasn't God who put those men in Stalingrad." Now Franz thought the pastor was veering dangerously close to treason. But if someone was going to turn Hoffmann in, it wouldn't be him. "There is only one God, Franz. If we have followed a false god, we must expect many Stalingrads."

Katrin nodded in agreement with Hoffmann, but she also began looking around the room, tapping her foot and squeezing Franz's hand tighter and tighter.

Franz looked into the distance as he recalled the pronouncements of the chaplain who had traveled with his unit on the Eastern Front and had rallied the men's spirits by asserting that the war in the East was a holy war. In the face of all the unholy things he had seen, Franz had held onto the chaplain's assurance as a drowning man might to a lifeline. He looked back toward Hoffman. "Pastor, every enlisted man and non-com in the Army wears a belt buckle that says 'God With Us.'"

Hoffmann narrowed his eyes. "Franz, what do the SS belt buckles say?"

Franz knew the answer. He assumed Hoffmann did, too. *"My honor is loyalty"*—loyalty to whom went without saying. If God was with Germany, and if Germany was with God, wasn't it curious that the belt buckles of the SS—the beating heart of the National Socialist state, the vanguard of modern Germany—didn't proclaim it? The SS did not even allow chaplains in their ranks.

Hoffmann whispered the question that troubled Franz, too. "Is *God With Us* just a sop to Army conscripts, cannon fodder for a regime that has no use for God?" Franz didn't say a word.

Finally, Katrin whispered, "Perhaps we should continue this conversation when Franz is out of the hospital."

Franz agreed. Hoffmann made him nervous. At the same time, the words the pastor spoke were bracing, a brief gust of truth blowing in a fetid land that had too long been dominated by the half-truths and weasel words of National Socialist propaganda and misleading OKW bulletins. The contrast with the SD bullies who had commanded that he deny the truth struck him hard. Hoffman's words frightened him, but more than that, they drew him in. They made him want to continue the conversation. Just not now. Not here.

Franz asked again for Communion, and Hoffmann gave it to him and Katrin together. Then his visitors left, just in time to pass Klaus Maedler on his way in.

~

"Son, how are you?" asked Franz's father, who wore a black suit and tie to honor the state of mourning.

Franz considered keeping silent. He was already exhausted. His father had taken time to see him, though, and he deserved an answer.

"I'll live," he said flatly. *Unlike my men.*

"It is a terrible day for us all," Father offered. "Did you hear the news when it was announced?"

"Yesterday, yes. The radio was on in here. We heard the music, then the report. No one said a word."

Klaus's shrewd gaze drilled into his son. "You knew, didn't you? That this was how it would end?"

"Father, the corridor was closed on the twenty-fourth of November. We were already on one-third rations the day before I was wounded."

Klaus's eyes widened briefly at Franz's revelation. "The OKW says the Front has stabilized thanks to the sacrifices in Stalingrad. The German fighting man has proven his worth in that bloody place. Let the Reds have it. There is nothing left of it anyway."

Franz clenched his jaw. How could he answer that? *If we were going to let the Reds have it, we should have given it back before we lost a quarter million men.* Men with parents, wives, sweethearts, children, friends. His men.

"Sacrifice is part of war, son." Father greeted Franz's discomfort with disdain. "Every individual dies. Only the nation lives on. And only if it conquers."

Franz couldn't dispute the cold logic. But who could demand such a sacrifice of others?

"Father, I gave a leg, but what was it for?" The question had weighed on his mind before, and not just about his own loss. Klaus's nonchalant dismissal of so much pain forced it to burst out.

"What was it for?" Father protested. "What do you mean? We are in a fight to the finish against Bolshevism and world Jewry. We are fighting for Living Space for the German people. We are fighting to correct the wrongs of the last war. Everyone in Germany knows what we are fighting for."

"Yes, Father, I know all of that." Franz paused to reorganize his thoughts. "I'm loyal to my oath. But things on the Eastern Front are ugly. I suppose every war to the finish is bound to be that way." He inhaled, seeking common ground. "You're a man of honor. You fought honorably in the last war. This war in the East has no honor. I have seen things. Maybe you know about them. But just know

I would never have been able to tell Mother about them." Franz trailed off, not sure where to go next.

Father's eyes narrowed and he began wringing his hands. "Franz, you are a soldier of the German Wehrmacht. You did your duty then. You are doing your duty now. That is honor. Fulfilling the oath you took to the Führer, that is honor. Do not confuse honor with kindness." He paused. "Yes, the war in the East is ugly. War is ugly. When Germany wins, the result will be beautiful. Do not forget it."

Having made his point, his father abruptly shifted the line of discussion. "So, you are still seeing the Weber girl? I thought perhaps you two would have drifted apart since you went to war."

Franz's gaze darted downward. He should have expected this. "No, Father, we are still close."

"You know you can do much better," Father scoffed. "Her father was dismissed from his professorship for defending Jews. And her mother cares more about her church than her Fatherland. Neither has joined the Party."

Franz scowled. "Mama wouldn't join the Party, either. Are you saying she was an unworthy wife? Or have you forgotten?"

"I've tried to forget," Father shot back. "Do not disrespect me or your mother like that again. Do you understand?"

Franz had struck a nerve. Father had loved Mother dearly, and Franz knew it had always hurt him deeply that she would not join the Nazi Party even though it might have advanced his career. Perhaps he would have been a Gauleiter by now.

His father continued harshly. "Just be careful with that girl. She's nothing like your mother. There was only one of your mother. Keep your eyes open for a better girl from a good family. You are a war hero. You need a wife as loyal and strong as you."

Franz didn't want to argue about Katrin, who was actually just like his mother in every important way. Instead, he opted to avoid the fight. "We aren't even engaged, Father. Who knows if we ever will be?"

"And who was the man who left with the Weber girl?" Klaus seemed suspicious. "Some priest, I suppose, from the collar."

"He is a pastor who visits men here from time to time." Franz didn't think Hoffmann visited anyone else at the hospital, but his father might be less alarmed if he thought the man was just making rounds.

"I don't like it. You should tell him to stop coming."

Franz shrugged. "I like him."

Klaus frowned. "I learned in the last war, God is nowhere. I learned it again in the bitter peace when we couldn't buy bread because we didn't have enough wheelbarrows full of Marks. Compassion, love, charity—all the Christian 'virtues'—are just platitudes. They cannot feed you, they cannot keep our race pure, and they cannot win a war. Put them out of your head. Only the Party and the Führer offer hope." Father stabbed the air with a finger as he echoed his last point. "Only the Party and the Führer."

Franz didn't want to argue about this, either, but his head raced with thoughts. Father was a brave man and a German patriot. He'd spent four hard years in the trenches in France, risking everything for the Fatherland. He spoke from hard-won experience. But Franz had already tried putting his hope in Hitler and was not satisfied. And he'd just come back from the Eastern Front, where it seemed God had been banished by all involved. It wasn't the kind of place he wanted to make his home. He recalled that Mother always held her own in arguments with Father, whose realism ran headlong into what seemed to be her grasp of a higher reality.

A reality to which Hoffmann had reintroduced him, even if he wasn't sure it had a place for him.

"The Party and the Führer," mumbled Franz without conviction. He bade farewell to Klaus, hopeful that his weak concession had disguised the fact that what he really wanted was another bracing gust of truth.

CHAPTER

6

In the Reich, Abwehr had carved out a certain independent space from the other security services. Friedrich knew there was an advantage to that. Untethered from SS oversight, he and his colleagues had a freer hand to pursue Germany's interests as they saw fit.

Of course, there was also a significant disadvantage. The SS had never fully trusted Abwehr and vice-versa, and a serious rivalry had grown up between them. The former was constantly trying to trip up the latter, the latter constantly working to evade the SS noose, figuratively speaking. Or maybe not so figuratively. Behind its facade of unity, the National Socialist state was a dog-eat-dog world. High stakes games for everyone involved.

Friedrich had entered that world in 1939, joining military intelligence at the onset of the war, after earning a degree in history and languages from Berlin University. His responsibility was to keep open the pipeline of Abwehr agents in Switzerland, the cockpit of European spy intrigue. Protected by the Alps and a heavily armed population, the

Swiss jealously guarded their neutrality and their border. For now, Germans had to settle for sneaking their people across. Sometimes Friedrich crossed over himself. Swiss counterintelligence was skilled, but Friedrich had skills of his own.

He was working in a spacious room accommodating about twenty-five desks. His desk was next to one of several large south-facing windows overlooking Tirpitzufer Street and the Landwehr Canal, but Friedrich's mind was not on the scenery. Instead, he was studying a map of the Greater German Reich and Switzerland after reading a raft of reports describing the activity of agents in Zürich, Basel, Geneva, and Bern. Other reports assessed the most effective means of infiltrating Switzerland. A sense of discomfort in Friedrich's chest heralded the return of his heartburn, the cost of his life as a spymaster compounded by Germany's deteriorating situation. Returning to his desk, he pulled a packet of sodium bicarbonate from a drawer, emptied it into a glass of water, and drank.

A few days ago, in this very spot, he had listened as Joseph Goebbels' shrill voice issued a call for complete mobilization: "I ask you: Do you want total war? If necessary, do you want a war more total and radical than anything that we can even yet imagine? Now, people, rise up and let the storm break loose!"

The radio had transmitted enthusiastic cheering in the Sportpalast, but in Abwehr headquarters the only soft words of acknowledgement came when Friedrich thought he heard Deputy Director Hans Oster mumble under his breath, "Yes, people, rise up and let the storm break loose." Hans von Dohnanyi, standing next to Oster, turned to look at the Deputy Director, then stared at his shoes for a moment and walked out.

Today, Friedrich was asking von Dohnanyi's advice.

Hans had grown up in Grunewald, not far from the Maedlers, and had been an acquaintance of Friedrich for years. He was the brother-in-law of Dietrich Bonhoeffer, the well-known pastor who knew the Weber matron and trained Katrin's brother Reinhold. Now Friedrich worked with von Dohnanyi on a number of secret projects.

Friedrich took a quick look behind him. Even in familiar territory, he would not let down his guard. "Hans, the word is that things have tightened up. They have never worked harder to control the border."

Von Dohnanyi grimaced. "What are our options?"

"The fastest route is by rail." Friedrich pointed to the map. "High-speed train through Karlsruhe to Basel."

"Have them go in at the railroad border crossing?" Hans thought for a minute. "Very high security there. Extremely risky."

Friedrich shrugged. "It's all risky, Hans. There is no easy way. And who would expect it?" The element of surprise would be crucial.

"Right." Hans nodded. "But once they get off the train, they could be walking right into a trap."

"What do you suggest?" Friedrich rubbed his chin.

"Automobile to an obscure border crossing, far from a major city," Hans declared. "It will be slower, but less conspicuous and there will be less security."

"If we have to get more than a couple across, it could actually be more conspicuous than on a train. But they can spread out over several cars and not seem connected." Friedrich studied the map again. Perhaps their two insights could be combined. German lives depended on their success. "Maybe we drive them to a slower train that crosses east of Basel, Bregenz, perhaps. It is the least guarded. Everything will depend on the quality of their papers, anyway."

"All right, Friedrich. Start drawing it up. And talk to

Helmut in Section G about the papers."

"Of course."

Hans returned to his office. Friedrich folded up the maps, then locked them and the files in a drawer of his desk.

At lunch, Friedrich took a stroll. Some cafes and restaurants were closed due to the "Total War" campaign, but he found a delicatessen that would make him a Braunschweiger sandwich and a cup of coffee.

He took his bounty to a nearby park, found a spot on a bench, and started to eat. As always, he observed his surroundings for any trouble. He made note of three mothers, two nannies, nine children, a cleaning man picking up cigarette butts, an Army officer and his girlfriend, two SS men having a smoke, and a gaggle of Hitler Youths strutting, shouting, and jostling each other. Mid-February in Berlin was not exactly park season, but the sun was peeking out, the temperature nearing fifty degrees, and Berliners were ready to take advantage of the slight thaw.

For a moment, Friedrich focused on the children. He had none of his own. He had not found the right girl. He frowned, thinking of Katrin. No, he had, and she was already taken. In any case, he couldn't settle down. There was too much work to do. Moreover, his gift for deception, invaluable in his job, was not helpful in building relationships. Living a double life made trust impossible. Still, a man could dream, right?

He watched a brother and sister at play. The children, around three and five, alternated between hugging each other and pushing one another off the swings. The little boy spent long periods digging in the dirt when the nanny wasn't watching. His big sister would occasionally stop playing and beg the nanny to read to her. Every time the nanny would stop reading and close the book, the girl would scream and run away. Friedrich was close enough that he could just make out the cover of *Struwwelpeter,* the very edition Father had once used to terrify him and his brothers. Perhaps the girl had just heard the story of the tailor who cuts off the thumbs of thumb-sucking children. Friedrich smiled. Everything he was fighting for with his friends in Abwehr was wrapped around securing a worthy future for Germany's children. If he could give them that, he would be satisfied.

He finished his sandwich, got up from the bench, and walked a few more blocks to St. Hedwig's Cathedral. He hesitated on the doorstep for just a minute. Church was no place for a man who lived a life of lies. And yet, he must enter. He lay a hand on the door and pushed it open. Stepping inside, he dipped his fingers in the holy water, genuflected, made the sign of the cross, then proceeded to a confessional.

On his way, he recognized a Carmelite nun, about thirty, with short brown hair. "Hello Sister Klara Marie. How are things today?"

The nun narrowed her eyes as her mouth formed a slight smile. "About the same as ever, mein Herr. Many are called but few are chosen."

Friedrich nodded politely and entered the booth.

"Father, forgive me, for I have sinned. It has been three months since my last confession. I don't know what to do."

"My child," the priest responded, "Let me help you."

Friedrich felt a sense of relief as he recognized the gravelly voice with its distinctive Bavarian lilt on the other side of the curtain. There were some things he could only confide in Father Fellner.

"Father, I have family members that I have betrayed. I want to make amends."

"What family members?"

"They live in Friedrichsbrunn but will soon be moving to Augsburg." *Hopefully, very soon.*

Father Fellner paused, then put a question to Friedrich. "How many rosaries do you think you should say?"

Without hesitation, Friedrich answered, "Five."

With a gentle assurance, the priest concluded. "Child, say the rosaries and your sins are forgiven."

"Thank you, Father."

Relieved to have performed his duty, Friedrich stepped out of the confessional, left the church, and walked back to the Bendlerblock.

~

Friedrich's final task of the day was something for his brother. He wanted Franz to get a posting where he could be of use, so he was about to call in a favor from an old friend in the Army Personnel Office. Siegfried Koenig had been one of Friedrich's best friends in high school, but they had kept in touch only sporadically over the years. Friedrich had even courted Siegfried's sister for a time. Fortunately, it ended amicably, or this phone call would have been rather awkward. He picked up the phone and dialed.

"Sig? It's Friedrich."

"What are you up to, you rascal?" Sig's raspy voice filled the phone line.

"Working hard for the Fatherland, just like you."

"What's new in Abwehr?"

Friedrich stuck with tried-and-true material. "If I told you, I would have to shoot you. How are things in Army Personnel?"

Sig sighed. "The main problem is the personnel. They keep dying."

"Right... How is Hanni?"

"Oh, she's good." Sig paused to cough. "Engaged to a

naval officer based in Bremerhaven. He might have the safest job in the service. He's not going anywhere."

Friedrich chuckled. The British had most of the surface Navy bottled up in port. "Well, give her my best." He moved on to the real purpose of his call. "You remember my brother Franz?"

"The one in the Navy?"

"No…" Friedrich paused. Should he tell Siegfried? "No, that was Georg. He was on a U-boat. He didn't make it."

"Oh, I'm sorry."

Friedrich could hear Sig's discomfort over the telephone wire. "My other brother, Franz."

The voice at the other end perked up. "In the infantry, yes?"

"Yes. A captain. He got his foot shot off in Stalingrad and was evacuated. He's recovering now, but they'll reassign him soon." Friedrich laid out his request with precision. "He's smart and tough, a perfect fit for OKH. I wanted to see if there was any way he could be put in OKH Carpool. It's cushy, mostly low stress. Maybe after a while he can move into something more demanding. It isn't quite what he wants, but for now, it's what he needs."

Siegfried hesitated for a second. "Anyone who fought in Stalingrad and came back to tell about it deserves some consideration." Friedrich could hear his friend opening a file drawer and shuffling through papers. "Like you said, it's a cushy job and there are several people already on the list." He paused again. "But none of them went to Stalingrad. None of them lost a foot. And none of them are Friedrich Maedler's brother."

"So, you can help him?"

"I'll do what I can."

From Siegfried, Friedrich knew that assurance was as good as gold. "Thank you, Sig. Heil, Hitler."

~

On his way out of the office a little after 20:00, Friedrich ran into Hans von Dohnanyi. "Thanks for helping me work out the transportation issue. I hope we'll be able to activate the plan soon."

"No problem, Friedrich, though I may not be here when the plan is a go."

Friedrich raised an eyebrow. "Leaving Berlin?"

"Yes, for colder climes."

"What's up?"

Von Dohnanyi paused, looked away, and lowered his voice. "Making a trip to Smolensk. I need to assess the situation firsthand. Maybe help, um, change things."

Friedrich gave a curt nod. "Well, be careful, Hans. I hope your trip is... fruitful."

"Yes, I hope so too. But if it is, I just might put you out of a job. Perhaps with the right input from Abwehr, we can succeed in bringing the war to a conclusion."

Friedrich chuckled and clapped von Dohnanyi on the shoulder, then grew somber. "I hope you can, my friend. I hope you can."

CHAPTER 7

In a few days, Franz would be released from the hospital. His morning workout had readied him for a serious nap after dinner, a hospital luxury he would have to give up soon. Once he dozed off, the haunting faces returned. This time, just the faces.

Then there was another face, a beautiful face. The soft alto voice that went with it said his name. *Wait, this isn't a dream. It's real.* Franz didn't quite mean it that way. The other faces were real, too, or had been.

But this face was here, right now. Alive.

"Katrin!" Franz came fully awake and pulled himself up in bed. "I'm glad you're here."

Katrin smiled, but her eyes were sad. He wondered how long she had been watching him sleep. He hoped not too long—he could control his expressions when he was awake, but he feared that in sleep, the anguish he felt must be clear to anyone. "How are you, my Franz?"

He summoned a brave face. "Tired. Therapy was hard this morning."

"But soon you will be out and that will be done with." After a furtive glance left and right, she looked back at him with a conspiratorial grin. "I brought something special with me today."

"Hmmm. What could it be?" Franz looked at her mischievously. "More chocolate? Maybe a piece of fresh fruit from some exotic place? Maybe another copy of *Der Angriff*? You know how much I love unfiltered news from the front."

She wrinkled her nose at that last suggestion, then giggled. "Your brother is the one to get exotic treats, not I. And I have brought you something much better than *Der Angriff*." She reached into the pocket of her coat and pulled out a small grey kitten. "This is Schatzi. Of course, I know you would rather see Bruno, but he's not so easy to sneak in." The little creature purred as she handed it over.

"A cat. You're right—not as good as a dog." Franz feigned disdain before chuckling. "But very cute!" He held Schatzi in one hand as he gently stroked the kitten's head. "Where did he come from?"

"His mama abandoned him and his sister, Schnitzel, under the bushes in our garden. Bruno found them, and Papa and I are raising them." She laughed and stroked the kitten. "Papa says this one has the soul of a dog. He even likes to play fetch!"

"With a name like Schnitzel, it's a wonder Bruno doesn't eat the other one." Franz thought for a moment, his hand still idly rubbing Schatzi's head and back. "I've missed your garden... daydreaming together on our bench, planning a future together."

She squeezed his hand. "It's lonely without you. But still... it's my favorite place to sit when I am praying for you... even now, when it's cold." He followed her gaze to see an orderly coming their way, and quickly passed Schatzi back to her. She returned the kitten to her pocket. "I can't wait to walk there with you again, or just sit on our bench and talk."

"We could fill books with the words we have shared sitting on that bench."

Katrin's cheeks turned pink. "I wouldn't want anyone else to read them!"

Franz stifled a chortle. "No, I suppose not. They would be books just for us." He glanced out the window, gathered up his nerve, and looked back at Katrin. Perhaps this was the moment. "Katrin, my Sunshine, do you still love me? I miss those days in the garden too, but Stalingrad... changed me. And not just physically. Can you—do you still love me?"

She wrapped her fingers around his hand and gave it a gentle squeeze. The blush had faded, but her warm green eyes held him captive. "Franz, it's true, you're not the same man you were before. But you are still the man I love. And I still want the future we used to daydream about in the garden."

Franz broke into a smile and nodded. "We had so many dreams... The right number of children, where to live—"

"What sort of palace we would each build." As she recalled the fond memories, her face began to glow, and she laughed. "Remember that? We each wanted a big library and a music room and finally decided maybe we only needed one Schloss after all."

"Yes, the Schloss." Franz remembered their imaginary palace fondly. "Today I would settle for a house in the country with a garden. As long as it had the library."

"And the music room." A thoughtful smile lit up her face. "Strange, isn't it, how time and circumstances change things? And yet... I suppose much hasn't changed. It's more that... we see better how we might achieve what's really important, yes?"

"It is hard to see well these days. The whole world has changed. There is uncertainty everywhere." Franz lowered his voice to a whisper and drew Katrin close. "The war, the regime. I have an oath to fulfill, but I'm no longer sure how to do that without becoming someone I don't want to be." Remembering his confirmation vows, Franz added, "I've taken more than one oath. They don't tell me the same things. How can anyone make a future these days?"

Katrin glanced around, then moved her mouth close to his ear. He expected a kiss, or maybe some sweet nothings, but she spoke intently. "We must look beyond these days for the future God will give us." Her warm breath tickled his ear, but he forced himself to attend to her words. "That's what got me through those long days without you."

"Mama said something like that. I want to believe it, Katrin."

"Your mother was a wise woman. Franz, I think I know what else she might say." She dropped her voice even lower, her mouth still hovering close to his ear. "If one of your oaths is contrary to another, you must consider which will help you become the man you want to be—the man who must one day stand before God and answer to Him for his life."

Franz thought about his mother, a wise woman, as Katrin said. He could not help thinking about his father, as well. Tough, determined, a brave warrior for Germany. Two visions. Franz was serving one vision in the Army. He did not want to marry it, too. Whatever his father might say, Katrin was the woman he loved, the woman who brought beauty and truth into his life.

His mind veered for a moment from Katrin to another bearer of truth. "Have you heard from Pastor Hoffmann? He hasn't been by lately."

Her voice suddenly went shaky. "Pastor Hoffmann was

arrested. Many were."

Franz's jaw dropped. "When?"

"Just after the loss of Stalingrad. The last thing he said to me before we parted was that he would keep you in his prayers."

Franz slumped a bit, taking in the news. *He probably made another wisecrack about Jews and the Red Sea.* "It sounds like he's the one who needs prayers now." Hoffmann had been nothing but good to Franz. His arrest added yet another question mark about the regime in Franz's mind.

"And yet, I know he still prays for you." With a soft smile, Katrin added, "He knows Whom he serves. In a sermon recently, he said that, like Paul, whether in prison or free, whether he lives or dies, he is content."

Content. Franz wished he could feel that way. Instead, he felt only contention. Contentedness had eluded him in the Army. He was always striving for the next bridge, the next town. More than that, he was always in turmoil, caught between his oaths. "I will pray for him," he finally acknowledged.

Franz suddenly realized his plan for this conversation had gone far off course. He gripped Katrin's hand, looked into her eyes, and took the plunge. "Sunshine? Will you marry me?"

She gasped a little. "Dear Franzi..." Franz felt his heart sink as he realized she was not about to say the words he wished to hear. "I... I've waited a long time for you to ask me that," she confessed. "I've imagined it, practiced my answer over and over. And I *do* wish to be your wife. But... I can't. Not yet." He scowled and started to pull away, but she grabbed his hand back and held it tight. "Please, understand that I want it very much. But you say that you struggle to reconcile the oaths you've already taken. Until you know where your loyalties lie, isn't it wiser to wait before you add another oath into the mix?"

Franz sat stunned. He had heard her words, but what echoed in his mind right now was simply, "No." Were those years of friendship and love for nothing? Were the talks in the garden merely for fun? No. "Is there someone else?"

"Didn't you hear me?" Katrin sounded exasperated, but her lips twisted into a wry grin. "Mama says men need to hear something three or four times before it starts to sink in." She squeezed his hand. "Listen to me. Franz, I love you and I want to be your wife. There is no one else. But first, you need to know which path you will follow. You must not make that choice for my sake. It must be between you and God. Franz, I can't tell you which oath deserves your loyalty. You have to decide."

"What would you have me do?" Franz asked in some bewilderment, his mind reeling as he tried to understand. *What is she asking? Where does this come from?*

"I would have you think and pray and consider. Do you still have the catechism Pastor Hoffmann brought you and the old Bible you used to carry—the one your mother gave you?"

"Yes, I have them." Friedrich was not the only one who kept secrets. Franz had allowed Father to think he had discarded that Bible, but he held onto it out of reverence for his mother. It had travelled with him across the steppes and back.

"Read them. And perhaps I can give you other things to read." She glanced around. "After you are discharged." He could imagine the sort of reading material she meant. Sneaking a kitten into the ward was one thing. Forbidden literature was quite another.

Katrin bent and brushed her lips against his. For once he did not return her kiss. Instead, he turned away, giving his hurt free rein. She put a hand on his chin and gave a gentle tug, until he was looking at her again. "Franzi, know this. I love you. Nothing will change that. We have time to decide about marriage. I want..." Her voice trailed off.

He couldn't leave her with nothing. "I love you, Sunshine. I can't live without you. I would not have survived the Russian Front without your picture in my pocket." He sighed. "I don't know what you want from me or how we'll know I've passed your test. But I'll do as you ask—read, think, and pray. What else can I do?"

Franz felt a wave of contending emotions. Disappointment. *This is not how things were supposed to go.* Fear. *What if I lose her?* Confusion. *I am being pulled apart. How does she think I can solve this?* And a touch of anger. *How can she lead me to the edge of marriage and then push me away at the last second?*

She sucked in a deep breath. "Franz, your father and mother. In the last days of their marriage, were they happy?"

"No."

"Why not?"

He spoke slowly. "Father had changed in the War. And the Party drove them apart. Mother could never reconcile herself to it, and Father would never give up trying to make her."

"Is this the sort of marriage you want for us? Because I can't reconcile myself any more than your mother could."

"No." Franz understood her point, but did she actually want him to repudiate his father? The Army? The regime? This was no small thing. He had spent a quarter century trying to win his father's approval. His Army oath was an oath of honor, sealed with the blood of his brothers in Stalingrad. Turning against it would be a betrayal of them and of Georg, as well as Friedrich, still living. And turning against the regime was several steps beyond the cynicism with which he now viewed it. Such a step would not only be painful after years of training but could also be suicidal.

"Then you know why I want to wait while you figure out which path to follow. I believe in you. I believe you have your mother's heart. If..." She smiled, her gaze fastening on his. "*When* we marry, I want to bring you joy every single day of our life together."

Though Katrin's words were kind and optimistic, Franz's spirits were flagging. He drew her fingers to his lips and kissed them gently, more in the hope things would work out than in the conviction they would. In the midst of his bitter disappointment, he understood her reasons. If only his mother were here to confide in.

There was nothing more he could say. One of the many things he loved about Katrin was that she pushed him to be better. But could his war-stained soul be better? Franz tried to look on the bright side. He was on a journey with the woman he loved.

It couldn't be as bad as the one he had just completed. Could it?

CHAPTER
8

25 FEBRUARY 1943

Franz stood uneasily in front of a mirror, combing his hair and straightening his collar. His green-grey uniform was neatly pressed, his newly acquired wound badge properly affixed. The other new addition to his wardrobe was a sturdy wooden cane. He'd been issued one at the hospital, but he'd discarded it in favor of this one, a gift from Friedrich. Crafted from chestnut wood, the cane had a smooth bone grip that felt good in his hand. Maybe someday he'd be comfortable walking without it, but he was still getting used to the new leg.

It was time for him to get back into the war. He had been released from the hospital yesterday and driven by Friedrich in an Abwehr staff car to take up residence in the OKH officers' quarters. Now, he was about to head to his new front line, the battle waged every day by the Oberkommando des Heeres, the Army High Command, to try to hold the war together from Berlin.

As he looked at himself one last time in the mirror, he thought of his men left behind in Stalingrad. Would they be proud of him for his recovery? Proud that he was thrusting himself back into service, even in his diminished state? Or did their ghosts resent him, the Hauptmann who got a rare ticket out of hell while they were compelled to remain to the end?

He would never know. Franz turned, put on his officer's hat, and left for work.

~

The Bendlerblock was a vast complex, housing three of the five departments of OKH, as well as Abwehr and the Navy High Command. Franz had to ask three people to find his way to the Carpool office in the east wing. A guard at the entrance got him started, a lieutenant five turns in got him a little further, and a pretty secretary in the OKH Propaganda Office got him the rest of the way. If it weren't for Katrin, he might have wanted to get to know the secretary better. As it was, he took her directions, thanked her, and went on.

He'd wanted to work in the OKW's Defense Command Office, which oversaw operational planning and orders, or the equivalent office on the OKH general staff, which still ran operations in Russia. That's where the action would be, where he might do the most good. Franz had asked Friedrich to try calling in a favor to help him get a spot, but it hadn't worked out. Apparently, Friedrich didn't have as much pull as Franz thought.

So off to Carpool it was.

The Carpool office, Division Three of the General Army Office, maintained and allocated an inventory of vehicles for use by the three OKH departments based at the Bendlerblock, the personnel office, the general staff, and the General Army Office, a sprawling command headed by General Friedrich Olbricht. Mostly staff cars, some motorcycles with sidecars, and some trucks. The office kept track of the vehicles, signed them out and back in, made sure they were kept in good repair, ordered replacement vehicles when necessary, and made sure the Carpool always had adequate fuel. This meant keeping a large stockpile of petrol ration cards on hand. Sometimes, the staff cars took generals and field marshals to crucial meetings with Hitler, Himmler, Goebbels, or other bigwigs.

Franz arrived at his posting at 08:02 and the office was full and humming. As he stepped through the door, a lieutenant, arms piled high with a stack of files, came barreling through in the opposite direction. He shoved past Franz, who barely grabbed hold of the door frame and managed to steady himself. Where was he going? Franz raised his eyebrows and cocked his head, staring at the offender.

"Good morning, sir. I'm sorry sir." Shamefaced, the lieutenant backed up a step while Franz regained his balance.

"Good morning. I am Hauptmann Franz Maedler. I'm newly assigned to this office. Where should I report?"

"Yes sir. Colonel Muntzer's office is in the back left corner." The lieutenant's mouth snapped shut and he saluted, then scurried past.

"Thank you," Franz began, but the man was through the door and gone before he could finish. He scanned the high-ceilinged room, which held about a dozen desks, located the commander's office, and went straight to it. He knocked on the door and waited for a call to enter.

"Sir, I am Hauptmann Franz Maedler, reporting for duty." By this time, it was 08:04.

Oberst Karl Muntzer was sitting behind his desk, reading today's copy of *Völkischer Beobachter*. The colonel lowered the paper slightly and glared over it at Franz. "Maedler, you are late," he bellowed. "You are in OKH now, not keeping your own time on the Russian Front."

"Herr Oberst." Now it was Franz's turn to be shamefaced.

"People depend on us, Hauptmann. They depend on me. Important people. That means I depend on you." His face grew even sterner. "We cannot be late, we cannot be slow, we cannot fail in our jobs. An auto keeps a meeting, a meeting moves a regiment, a regiment wins a battle, the battle saves the Reich."

Franz saluted and recited the first line of the old proverb his superior officer had paraphrased. *"Diz sagent uns die Wisen"*—*"Thus say to us the wise."* Father had made him memorize the lines when he was small. The original verse was about the importance of a little horseshoe nail to the battle. "Yes, sir. I'm sorry. I won't be late again."

Still, the outburst seemed excessive. Was Muntzer more interested in convincing Franz or himself of the importance of their task? One could only guess how the colonel felt about being assigned Carpool in Berlin rather than a field command.

Muntzer took a long look at Franz, then invited him to sit down. Some of his brusqueness wore off as he gestured toward the cane. "Wounded in Stalingrad, weren't you?"

"Ja, Oberst." Franz noticed the file folder with his name on it sitting on the colonel's desk.

"It has been a long road back?" the colonel asked.

"Ja."

"I'm afraid it's going to be a long road back from Stalingrad for all of us."

"Ja." Franz wasn't sure how to interpret Muntzer's statement. *A long way back from Stalingrad to victory? A long way back from Stalingrad to sanity? A long retreat back from Stalingrad to Berlin?* Whichever was correct, Franz had just met the man and was certainly not going to pour out his heart regarding the subject of Stalingrad.

The colonel pulled out a silver cigarette case and offered

an Eckstein. After Franz took it, Muntzer pulled one out for himself, then lit them both. Franz was not a heavy smoker and had nearly given it up at the hospital, but it was difficult to go through months of combat without developing some taste for tobacco. This, of course, was despite the Führer's disdain for the stuff and the Nazi Party's attempts to stamp it out.

As the two drew drags on their cigarettes, their conversation ground to a halt. Perhaps a shared smoke was better than conversation. As the new man with the lesser rank, Franz was not obligated to introduce topics of discussion. And the colonel, for his part, seemed preoccupied, his gaze distant.

He finally broke the awkward silence. "Well, Maedler, welcome to your new Wehrmacht home. I will have someone show you to your desk."

At that, Muntzer snuffed out his cigarette, picked up the receiver on his desk phone, dialed, and issued a summons. Another fresh-faced lieutenant appeared.

"Herr Oberst."

"Olbermann, this is Hauptmann Maedler. He is joining us. He'll take Brusewitz's old desk. Show him where things are. Introduce him to people."

"Yes, sir."

"Thank you, sir," Franz saluted on his way out.

~

Lieutenant Olbermann motioned to Franz. "Captain, follow me to your desk." The assigned desk was close to halfway back in the room, with a window view of the courtyard. It was a heavy wooden desk with a medium finish, accompanied by a wooden swivel chair on wheels. A small lamp stood on one corner of the desk. Otherwise, the entire surface was bare.

"I never planned on doing desk work when I became

an officer," Franz remarked when they reached their destination.

"Of course, sir. Neither did I. Not too long ago I was swatting flies and trying to avoid dehydration in Tunisia."

"And I was trying to avoid hypothermia in Russia," Franz added. *Now we're both back in Berlin, pushing paper and keeping track of Daimlers.*

The lieutenant gestured for Franz to precede him as he continued the tour. "You know, the colonel had a nephew in Stalingrad. He still doesn't know if he is dead or captured."

That explains the softened tone and the shared smoke. Franz stopped a moment and looked out a window. He quickly turned away when he saw the faces of his men looking in. So much loss. For all he knew, he had come across the nephew. Or perhaps his corpse. He blinked a few times, then noticed the red piping on the lieutenant's shoulder straps. "What did you do in Africa?"

"Anti-tank artillery. Eighty-eights. We lost our guns in the retreat from El Alamein. What about you?" Olbermann had started walking again, with Franz following close behind.

"Infantry in the Sixth Army, when there was one."

Olbermann fumbled for words. "I'm... eh... umm... sorry, sir." The uneasy silence that followed was broken when the lieutenant found something to refocus their attention. "Umm, Captain, the message center is on the right. Requests for Carpool come through here. Sergeant Schuchart runs the center in the day, Sergeant Nonnheim at night. Schuchart!"

A stocky man of medium height in a slightly rumpled uniform came to the door of the message center. "Sir!" The sergeant saluted.

"Schuchart, meet Hauptmann Maedler. He is taking over for Brusewitz."

"Sir!"

Franz gave a curt nod, and the rumpled sergeant returned to his post.

The tour continued. The lieutenant indicated another small room with a counter, a table, and some chairs. "People come here for coffee and a smoke when they need a break."

"How often is that?" Franz was used to the whole world being the break room. An abandoned farmhouse, a tent, the shade of a tree, the basement of a bombed-out store, under a Panzer. Whatever was handy.

"Whenever you need. But don't make it too often. The colonel keeps track, as he can. 'An auto keeps a meeting...'" Olbermann began the colonel's ditty with an ever-so-slight air of mocking. Apparently, Franz was not the first to have heard it.

Olbermann soon made another stop. "Hauptmann, let me introduce you to the office bursar." The lieutenant turned to a major in an immaculate uniform. The major had a pencil mustache, pronounced sideburns, and a deeply receding hairline. He sat at a desk with three perfectly straightened piles of papers and an open ledger book. Franz could not imagine a more stereotypical accountant or Prussian officer. The nameplate on the desk read "Maj. Rudolph Kobel."

"Herr Major."

"Good morning, Olbermann." The major spoke in a mechanical monotone. "Whom do we have here?"

Franz took the initiative to introduce himself and made a shallow bow in the major's direction. "Hauptmann Franz Maedler, sir."

"Good morning, Hauptmann." Kobel looked down at his ledger book and seemed to start some sort of calculation.

Olbermann spoke up. "Herr Major, the Hauptmann is here for Brusewitz."

"Ah, Brusewitz." Franz marveled at the bursar's

ability to carry on a conversation while continuing his calculations. "Well. Hauptmann, you will keep track of petrol requisitions. When filling from the OKH supply, you are to obtain receipts for the amount and get them to me. If we need to fill elsewhere, you can request ration cards from me. I keep some here and can get more. OKH has high priority, as you might imagine." Finally looking up at Olbermann, the major instructed, "Lieutenant, make sure he knows about Brusewitz."

"Yes, sir."

"Good day to you both. I have work to do."

The two saluted, then Olbermann turned and began walking back in the direction of Franz's desk. "Do you have any questions, sir?" he asked.

"Just two."

"Anything."

"WC?" A water closet, like a breakroom, was not a feature of life in the field. It would be good to know where the nearest one was located.

"Yes, of course. The closest one is in the outer hallway, about 10 meters to the left when you leave. The toilet overflows about every seventh flush, though, so I use the one on the next floor up. It's right above this one."

"I'll keep that in mind." *Hmm. The odds are only slightly better than Russian Roulette with a revolver. Upstairs will be fine, even with the prosthetic leg.*

"And your other question, sir?"

"What about Brusewitz?"

"Oh." Olbermann, who had been too chipper for any human being at 08:37, suddenly got quiet. "Brusewitz was caught selling fuel allocations on the black market. He was court-martialed and shot last week."

Welcome to the Bendlerblock.

CHAPTER
9

27 FEBRUARY 1943

Katrin gasped softly and almost dropped the tray of pastries she was carrying to the display case. Across the street from Ulrich Rothberg's Bäckerei, two Gestapo men approached a couple. As she watched, they grabbed the pair by the arms and forced them into a car. Why, she could not understand.

Though the bakery was moderately busy, Katrin kept a close eye on the scene outside the plate glass window for the rest of the day. Uniformed SS and plainclothes Gestapo—identifiable by their black trench coats and fedoras—were out in force.

When a middle-aged man with the yellow star on his coat was arrested right in front of the bakery, Katrin knew what was happening. The number of people wearing the yellow star in Berlin had diminished steadily since 1940. How many remained, she did not know. By all appearances, after today there would be many fewer. Clearly, Berlin was in the throes of a large-scale roundup of Jews.

As morning turned into afternoon, she saw more SS,

more Gestapo. Another successful arrest, and one intended victim, a young man, who fled out of view. Not long before Ulrich let her go, two heavy transport trucks rumbled past with somber prisoners peering out the back. Pursing her lips and holding back tears, Katrin looked at Ulrich. Ulrich stared back at Katrin, clench-jawed. Wordlessly, they shook their heads.

Katrin had taken the position at Rothberg's bakery to help out after her father lost his teaching position. She had been there ever since, except for the year she spent in Bavaria. Ulrich had been a family friend for years and was like an amiable uncle to Katrin. The two saw eye-to-eye on the most important questions.

When Ulrich released her from work early to look for new shoes, she was afraid to go out. The Nazi security presence made her uncomfortable, and she didn't want to watch anyone else get picked up. She had already seen too many. Their stories would not end well. Evacuation to the East was the official explanation, but rumors that the Jews went to their deaths had penetrated Berlin. The rumors had been confirmed to her by someone who would know. The thought of it made her blood boil.

But Katrin needed shoes, so out she went into the cold. Shoes were a precious commodity in the Third Reich. In theory, each person was allotted only two pairs. When one pair wore out, certification from the rationing office was required to replace it. Then came the trouble of finding a pair of shoes that fit.

On the rare occasions she could shop for shoes, Katrin liked to visit a little store on Rosenstrasse. It was a long walk from the bakery's location on Unter den Linden Boulevard just west of the Spree River, but she was too agitated to sit still in a tram. Every time she saw security personnel, she lowered her eyes and quickened her pace. It was an involuntary reaction, one that had become instinct for many Berliners. *Keep moving and don't look them in the eye.* As she walked, another two trucks rolled by, either filled with people, or about to be.

To get to her destination, she had to cross over Museum Island. There used to be a lovely park there, full of life, but in 1939, the Fuhrer had it paved over for Party rallies. *Typical,* she fumed as she walked.

As Katrin neared the shoe shop, she heard a commotion. It sounded like an unhappy crowd, high-pitched voices shouting and chanting. As a general rule, unhappy crowds were forbidden in National Socialist Germany. She wanted to see—and was afraid to see—what sounded like a melee in the making. With the final turn that brought her onto Rosenstrasse, the commotion came into Katrin's view. In front of Rosenstrasse 2-4, once the Jewish Community Center, a few hundred women stood in the cold, chanting, "Give us our husbands back." Some SS men guarded the front door. No one could get past the women, who had the guards cornered and were blocking access to the building.

Katrin's feet were cold and wet from the holes in her shoes and she was getting blisters on her right heel. But shoes could wait. She made her way to the crowd, then stopped at its edge. She did not wish to draw attention to herself, but she wanted to know what was happening. She needed to know. Whatever their cause, she was thrilled to see someone stand up to the tyrants out in the open. It was about time. She plunged forward into the group, eagerly seeking information.

One of the wives, perhaps in her mid-forties, her graying hair covered by a kerchief, told her. "In the sweep today, our husbands were picked up and brought here. We're not Jewish, but they are. We're afraid they'll be deported with the others." Katrin took a deep breath.

A younger woman with tired eyes and a small boy in tow sidled up next to Katrin and spoke up. "First, we just came to get information and deliver food or other things to our husbands. But now we're not leaving unless they come home with us."

An SS guard shouted an order, threatening to shoot unless the women dispersed. Katrin scampered into an alley, along with many of the protesters. Another group darted behind vehicles parked on the other side of Rosenstrasse. After a few peaceful minutes, the women returned to the street and resumed their chant. The tired woman with the boy told Katrin, "They keep threatening us, but nothing has happened. We'll keep coming back as long as it takes."

Katrin looked in the woman's eyes. "How many are there?"

"We don't know for sure. Maybe fifteen hundred, maybe two thousand."

There were not two thousand protesters outside on the forty-degree day. But every few minutes another one or two would come. Despite the danger and the increasing cold of early evening, the crowd was growing.

Katrin's morbid curiosity took hold. "What do you know about the rest of the roundup? I saw several trucks and arrests on the street."

A cascade of answers came back to her. "The Gestapo went into factories and pulled out all the Jews."

"Plus any they could find on the street." The violent images from the day came back to Katrin, and she shuddered.

"My husband's brother Gad and his wife were picked up today, too. They are full Jews. They will be on trains for sure."

"Some have gone underground with their children. I don't know how long they can keep it up, but they said they would rather be free and hunted than to walk tamely onto the train."

Katrin's blood went cold. She knew of the Jews in hiding, the *Taucher,* or 'divers.' Some called them "U-boats," as they subsisted underground like submarines of the land. A hard life. A life outside the law for a normally law-abiding people. Always on the lookout, always afraid of being turned in or slipping up. Struggling to find food, a place to stay. And who could know how long it would last? As long as the Nazis stayed in power. A year? Two years? A thousand years? It was no wonder so many lost hope and surrendered to their fates.

To her astonishment, many of the women talked with Katrin, sharing heart-rending stories. Their own stories, stories of their husbands' relations. They were afraid, but they were also angry, and for this moment, their fear of losing their loved ones was greater than their fear of the regime.

Katrin had never abandoned hope that things would get better. *God always wins in the end. But how many will suffer before that end?* For the first time in years, these women had given her hope that the end might come sooner rather than later. In the grand scheme of things, this group of protestors was small. Their moment of bravery might be short-lived, undermined by natural timidity, overcome by the raw power of the state, or co-opted by clever compromises. But at least it was a beginning.

At the same time, she wanted to do more. She travelled through the crowd, offering words of encouragement and praying for the women who shared their stories and for their men inside the building. And she took notes. Among other things, it was important to record the facts for posterity. Names, addresses, events. Many were reluctant. No one knew Katrin or whether she could be trusted. What if she were a Gestapo infiltrator or provocateur? But some, in a moment of desperation or defiance, chose to trust. Perhaps her ragged shoes gave away that she was not in favor with the State.

As the women chanted, "Give us our husbands back," Katrin wanted to add her voice to theirs. Help make the regime listen. But she never did. Every time she almost joined in, she pulled back. After all, she did not have a husband in Rosenstrasse 2-4. The cause was just, but this was a deeply personal protest. She could sympathize, but she could never fully be a part of it.

She also did not want to be caught up in the backlash that might come. Already, the SS presence had been bolstered, and who could say where that would lead?

By the time Katrin slipped out of the back of the crowd, the shoe shop was closed.

~

After walking a few blocks, Katrin stepped into the first telephone booth she saw. She started to call Franz, but then stopped, letting her hand hover over the dial for a moment. Suppressing a twinge of guilt, she called Friedrich instead to see if he would meet her for a late cup of coffee. Katrin loved Franz, but sometimes she needed an older brother, and Friedrich had stepped into that role after Reinhard left for Switzerland. For all his faults, Friedrich knew who he was. Franz was still figuring it out, and Katrin didn't want to burden him with anything more right now.

"Sure, why not?" he said. "I'm ready to call it a day."

They met in a poorly lit, slightly ramshackle coffee house halfway between Rosenstrasse and the Bendlerblock. A dozen tables, populated mostly by Army and SS officers and their girlfriends or mistresses, filled the small space. Katrin had met Friedrich there before.

Katrin's heart was racing, her hands trembling slightly.

"Friedrich, you will not believe what I saw today." The words spilled out of her mouth.

"Let me guess. An SS roundup." Friedrich's flat tone indicated boredom, but Katrin thought she saw a spark of interest in his eyes. "Anyone who went outside today knows that."

"Yes, a roundup. More Jews will be deported. More will go into hiding. But more than that. On Rosenstrasse, there was a demonstration against the roundup."

"I've heard about that, too." Friedrich leaned forward and raised his eyebrows, his voice no longer affecting boredom.

Katrin continued. "There were women, wives. Blocking the door, chanting, screaming."

"And you were there?"

She shrugged up a shoulder. "I was trying to buy shoes and I stumbled across it."

"Don't tell anyone else you were there." Friedrich's tone had gone from bored to interested to concerned in a matter of seconds. "Did anyone see you?"

"No one important," Katrin assured him. "I talked with several of the women. It was a large crowd and getting bigger. The SS were only starting to beef up when I left. I don't think they expected it."

"You shouldn't take such risks," he growled. "Don't you ever think before you act?"

Katrin twisted her mouth into a frown. "You always worry about risks."

"Someone needs to," Friedrich grumbled "What would Franz do if you were arrested?"

The waiter brought two cups of coffee to the table. Friedrich and Katrin went silent until he had gone away.

Friedrich continued. "You were worried, too, or you wouldn't have called me."

"Worried and excited. For years I haven't felt so free as I did standing among those women."

His tone suddenly sharp, Friedrich rapped his knuckles on the table, and Katrin shuddered. "The feeling of freedom is a dangerous thing, Katrin. If it excites you too much, I may have to report you." He fell silent and took a sip of his coffee, then relaxed his features. "You know I wouldn't." He leaned forward again, his gaze locking with hers. "But someone else may." His voice was soft but firm, full of urgency. "You should know that some students in Munich got excited by the feeling of freedom, distributed some anti-National Socialist pamphlets, and just got caught and executed a few days ago."

Katrin's gaze went to the floor. She fell silent for a moment before whispering, "I only wanted to help."

"I'm sure you did, you and your soft heart. You shouldn't be telling me such things, at least not here." He held up an admonishing finger. "And don't speak a word of it to Franz."

The two finished their coffees and Friedrich escorted Katrin to the nearest U-Bahn at Klosterstrasse to go home. She could not get Rosenstrasse out of her mind, or what she learned there.

CHAPTER
10

1 MARCH 1943

Smartly attired in his dress uniform, Franz sat next to Friedrich near the back of the crowd in the Volkstheater Berlin. It was Luftwaffe Day, a date set aside to honor the reborn German air force, and Friedrich had acquired tickets for a special concert. Since Stalingrad, Franz's appreciation for Luftwaffe chief Herman Goering had diminished considerably, but he still loved a good concert, and Goering's failures seemed far away.

Until the orchestra suddenly stopped playing and the ushers hurriedly shepherded them to the exits. As sirens wailed in the near-freezing darkness, Franz and his brother made their way amid a throng of concert-goers and others to the modern air-raid shelter serving the Tiergarten area.

Franz had heard of the shelter but had never seen it up close. As they approached, his eyes grew wide. The shelter was a gigantic six-story structure with thick concrete walls. On the corners were square towers with flat roofs that served as platforms for giant 128-millimeter anti-aircraft guns, radar, and searchlights. He'd heard that the shelter could hold at least ten thousand people.

On their way, they passed an air defense battery preparing for action. The earnest faces of the young gunners were tense. Some of the "layers," who prepared the artillery shells for the eighty-eight millimeter gun, were mere boys of fifteen or sixteen, as were some who manned the giant spotlights which traversed the dark skies in search of the enemy. Their lieutenant, a stout, rough-spoken man of about thirty, was barking orders, commanding adjustments of the firing angles. Attempting to lighten the moment, Franz asked Friedrich, "So is this how they teach geometry these days?" It had been a small controversy when the regime took boys out of school to teach them to operate air defense batteries. Now the boys were defenders of Berlin. Friedrich just shook his head.

When Franz reached the shelter, he could see that the batteries on the roof were also swinging into action. He tensed. He couldn't see these boys' faces, but he could hear the commotion, the universal chaotic sound burned into his brain of men and boys about to face battle and death. And then he and his brother were inside, finding seats. Franz looked from face to face. Some occupants were pensive, some outright fearful. Most were stoic. Things in the shelter got still when the 128-millimeter guns roared. Someone had told Franz that when they fired, they shook apartment buildings blocks away. He believed it. The distant "ph-cha" of the eighty-eight-millimeter flak guns added to the cacophony.

"Do you think it's a heavy raid?" Franz asked his brother. He knew there had been devastating air raids in cities like Cologne in western Germany as much as a year before, while he was on the Russian Front.

Friedrich frowned. "Maybe. The British are still working out how to reach us. But our time is coming."

Franz's thoughts turned to Katrin, facing the same rain of bombs, probably in her home shelter, and held his face in his hands. Unplanned, a whispered prayer escaped his lips. "Take me instead." Whatever they were going through, he loved Katrin enough to trade his life for hers. He always would.

Then came the sound of one, two, three bombs landing somewhere nearby in close succession. The muffled explosions shook the shelter. The lights flickered. Franz started, clenched his teeth and fists, and went down on his hands and knees. The sound of the artillery and the bombs brought him to a near panic. He was, for a moment, back in Stalingrad and a dozen other battles. How many times had the eighty-eights kept him alive by holding Red tanks at bay?

A gasp arose from the crowd, accompanied by a piercing shriek from a girl who appeared no older than fifteen, still decked out in her German Girls' League uniform for the day's festivities. Four, five, six, seven explosions.

"Must be a dud," Friedrich offered sardonically. "British bombers usually drop eight."

The reflex passed. Franz sat up, embarrassed as dozens of eyes watched him. Friedrich winced and put a hand on Franz's shoulder, then offered his brother his hand to help him back up to the bench. Franz exhaled and blinked a few times, struggling to get ahold of himself.

Friedrich jostled his brother. "Where's the Luftwaffe when you need them?"

"I asked the same thing in Stalingrad." Franz looked up. "Maybe I missed it, but Goering hasn't switched his name to Meyer yet." The Air Force chief had boasted early in the war that if any enemy succeeded in dropping bombs on Germany, he would change his name.

Friedrich snickered. A few more muffled explosions

could be heard. The shelter shook slightly. Dripping sweat, Franz clenched his fists again, but he fought his fear and kept his seat. "Franz," his brother noted, "there are four meters of concrete and rebar between us and the bombs. Only the Führer's new bunker would be safer."

Franz sighed. *The Führerbunker? That's only for those who started this war. The rest of us are stuck here. Or on the roof, learning geometry. Or in a dusty cellar somewhere.*

~

Katrin Weber was playing a board game at the kitchen table with her parents when Radio Berlin abruptly advised listeners to switch over to the "wire radio" and then stopped broadcasting. Accessed by plugging the radio into a splitter box on the telephone cable, the wire radio was an emergency system that gave Berliners updates on the progress of air attacks while preventing enemy aircraft from following a radio signal to the target.

Katrin listened nervously as Papa plugged the radio into the splitter. "Enemy bomber squadrons approaching the territory of the Reich!" was the preliminary report. Next: "Enemy bomber squadrons in the grid square Gustav/ Heinrich." According to the grid markings on Papa's map, "Gustav/Heinrich" meant the bombers were headed for Berlin.

Abandoning their board game, the Webers moved quickly through their air raid routine. Katrin pushed fear to the back of her mind as she focused on each well-rehearsed step. She switched off the electricity while Mama turned off the water. Papa turned off the gas and opened windows and doors to reduce damage from pressure blasts. Mama grabbed the single suitcase with the family's spare clothes, gas masks, and key documents. Then they hurried into the back yard. Papa unlocked the cellar and urged Katrin inside with Mama. When Bruno followed, Papa tried to stop him, but Katrin pleaded with him to let the dog join them. He finally nodded, and she grabbed Bruno by the collar to guide him down the steps.

At the bottom, Katrin sat in one of the folding chairs Papa had brought down when he turned the cellar into a proper bomb shelter. New beams reinforced the ceiling, sandbags were piled around the exposed windows and walls, and tables and chairs had been brought down, as well as shovels and picks in case of cave-in. On plain wooden shelves, they had laid in a supply of candles, oil lamps, flashlights, a first aid kit, and tins of food. Next to the shelves stood a large tub of water in case of an extended stay. Another tub was filled with sand that could be used to smother any fires. The shelter might not protect them from a direct hit by a large bomb, but they should be safe from anything short of that.

Katrin folded her hands and said a quick prayer. After a few minutes, she heard the Schneider girls come running down the stairs. Bruno growled low in his throat at the noise, but Katrin patted his neck and told him to settle down. *"Ruhe,"* she soothed. "Hush. They're our neighbors." Little Sofia was whimpering, and her mother snapped at her to be brave. Papa and Herr Schneider followed them down. Except for sharing a desire not to be obliterated by a British bomb, the two had little in common. Herr Schneider was an official in the Reich Labor Service and doubled as the Nazi Party Block Warden, the eyes and ears of the regime in the neighborhood. The Schneider son, eleven-year-old Karl, trotted down the stairs next to his father.

Outside, the air raid sirens began wailing, first three long tones of the same pitch, followed by a menacing, undulating howl. Even when it was a drill, the howl chilled her blood. This wasn't a drill.

Katrin tried to distract the twins and herself. "How was

your day, girls? Did you go to the park?" She tried to sound cheerful. Frau Schneider took the girls to the swings three or four times a week, so it was a good guess.

"No," answered Sofia with a frown. "We had to go listen to boring speeches."

Silence settled over the cellar. Katrin clutched at the hem of her dress. What if Franz and Friedrich didn't make it to a shelter in time? She clenched her teeth. What about Ulrich and the bakery? *Will our shelter really hold?* Katrin closed her eyes for a long moment. *So, this is what waiting for battle is like.*

Though some Germans hated the British for their indiscriminate bombing, Katrin couldn't. The destruction visited upon Germany felt like a sort of divine judgment on the country for turning its back on God.

Soon, the sound of anti-aircraft gunfire invaded the shelter, then a whistling noise, followed by three explosions. Then another whistling noise and two explosions. Then three more explosions. Too close. The ground shook and dust fell from the ceiling. Katrin noticed the water sloshing in the tub. Sofia Schneider had grasped her mama and shut her eyes tight. Anna clung to Katrin, her eyes wide open.

Then came the sound of an immense explosion, followed a couple of seconds later by an earthquake. Katrin felt a pressure wave slamming through her body. Her limbs felt like jelly. Her ears rang. Sofia shrieked and her legs twitched. Trembling, Anna hid her face against Katrin's shoulder and wept. She thought the child might break her fingers from how tightly she squeezed them. Karl bounced in his chair, eyes bright with indignation, and shouted curses against the British. Bruno whimpered and hid under the table.

Katrin steeled herself for death. She was ready to give her life for God, for the helpless, for the beauty of Germany as it was and could be again. But in a cellar, another random casualty of a war that shouldn't have happened? Divine judgment against nations did not always distinguish. Like the rain, bombs fell on the just and the unjust alike. Even prophets were carried off to Babylon.

What about Franz? Surely, he is in a shelter somewhere. Hopefully a better shelter. I can't die before I settle things with Franz. He can't die. Dear God, I do love him. Keep him safe.

Then another set of explosions. Farther away, like the heavy footsteps of an assailant receding into the distance.

CHAPTER
11

28 MARCH 1943

Franz's shoulders tightened as he approached the imposing two-story stone house that had been his home for most of his life. This was his first visit back to the old place since leave in Spring 1941. Since Bila Tserkva, Kyiv, Stalingrad. All the way here, he had passed by evidence of the massive British air raid four weeks ago. Only two blocks away, some row houses and a butcher shop were burned out.

Once he reached the house, he stood a minute at the wrought-iron gate, then opened it and walked past the three sweet chestnut trees he and his brothers used to climb. When he got to the front porch, it felt strange to have to knock on his own door. He was not entirely sure what his father intended with this dinner invitation. Klaus had treated Franz and Friedrich to dinner at the swanky Horcher's, reputedly a favorite of Hermann Goering's, to convey the invitation to dine at his own home. Something was up.

After a quick snap of the brass knocker, a frumpy woman

opened the door. Simple and severe, her attire marked her as a servant, but Franz didn't recognize her. *Father must have hired someone new since I left.*

"Good afternoon," Franz offered.

She raised her right arm in the German greeting, "Heil Hitler," then stepped aside and allowed him to enter.

"Thank you. Let me introduce myself. I am Franz Maedler, the Kreisleiter's son."

"Ja, Herr Hauptmann. I know." Her tone brusque, she did not offer her name. "I am the housekeeper. I will take your coat. You will join your father and his guests in the parlor."

Franz handed over his topcoat, then proceeded through the foyer and past the grand staircase—*how Mother used to scold, when we raced at sliding down the banister!*—to the parlor. His parents had entertained guests there. It looked unchanged since he had last seen it. The antique red velvet Biedermeier sofa with its scrolled armrests, a gift to Father from Mother, still dominated the room. Still, it felt different, somehow foreign. Father sat there now, with an older woman unfamiliar to Franz. She was at least as frumpy as the nameless housekeeper and wore an unremarkable, floor-length brown dress. Franz bristled to see that a second woman, much younger and not at all frumpy, had claimed Mother's favorite armchair to the left of the sofa. Dressed in a snug, low-cut black dress that fell just below her knees, she wore her hair pinned up in a wreath of braids. She was around twenty, Franz thought, and a picture of Aryan health—blonde, blue-eyed, athletic. And well-endowed. Perhaps a bit shorter than Franz, though it was hard to tell with her sitting.

"Good day, Father," he said, his tone flat. He was beginning to understand Father's machinations. Klaus had invited him not to eat, but to meet.

"Good afternoon, Son." Father's face brightened. "Allow me to introduce Frau Luisa Hilgenberg and Fräulein Gretchen Fürsich. Ladies, my son, Franz."

Franz bowed stiffly. "The pleasure is all mine, meine Dame... Fräulein." He looked back to Father.

Klaus addressed the ladies. "Franz has recently returned from the Eastern Front. He was wounded in Stalingrad. We are lucky to have him here."

Gretchen gazed up at Franz, clearly starstruck. "You are truly a hero of the Reich," she gushed. "I would like to hear about your exploits."

Frau Hilgenberg lightly elbowed the girl. "Not now, Fräulein Fürsich." Gretchen quieted at the correction, chewing on her lower lip for a second before suddenly stopping, as if she'd been warned not to do that and only just remembered. "I am sure there will be plenty of time for you and the Hauptmann to become better acquainted." Frau Hilgenberg turned her attention to Franz, looking him up and down. "Your father speaks quite highly of you, Herr Hauptmann. I can see why."

Franz eyed the pair warily. "You are gracious, Frau Hilgenberg. Please do not hold me accountable for my father's exaggerations." Franz considered responding to Gretchen as well but decided against it. No need to encourage her. He loved Katrin.

Before anyone else could speak, the bell rang. The housekeeper's voice floated into the parlor as she opened the door and acknowledged newcomers.

"Thank you, my dear." Franz could make out Friedrich's voice as his brother tried to conquer the housekeeper with his charm. *Good. Friedrich is here. Surely, he can distract Fräulein Fürsich for a time and let me eat in peace.* Then Friedrich and his guest came around the corner and Franz involuntarily froze. On his brother's arm was none other than Katrin Weber. Sharing a ride to the hospital was one thing. Arriving arm-in-arm at what was clearly, at least in his father's mind, a major function was quite another.

"Hello, Franz." Her forehead wrinkled and a shadow of anxiety flitted across her features. Inwardly, Franz wrestled with conflicting emotions—sympathy, anger, disbelief. "I mean... Good afternoon, Herr Hauptmann... Kreisleiter. Meine Damen." She dipped her chin politely to each in turn.

Father managed to sputter out the most basic of introductions. "Frau Hilgenberg, Fräulein Fürsich. My eldest, Friedrich."

"Father, you know Fräulein Weber, I believe." Friedrich had mischief in his eyes.

"Yes, son, I know her." Father's voice betrayed a mixture of disgust and desperation. Of course he knew her, and Friedrich knew it. Franz could almost read his father's mind as Klaus scowled at his older brother. *What were you thinking?*

Franz wasn't sure what Friedrich was thinking, either. Was he doing Franz a favor, spiting Father by bringing the only girl Franz wanted to dine with? Or was he spiting Franz by making a play for Katrin himself? Memories of their boyhood brawl over Else Grossmann floated through his mind as he observed Friedrich and Katrin. Before Franz could puzzle out the implications, the housekeeper appeared again to announce that dinner was served.

~

Her hand still in the crook of Friedrich's elbow, Katrin walked beside him to the dining room. She would have preferred walking with Franz, but tonight Friedrich was her escort. She had trusted Friedrich when he said he suspected that it might be important for Franz that she be there. Acutely aware of Franz's discomfort and uncertainty, as well as Herr Maedler's tight-lipped anger, she almost wished she had not agreed to come. Clearly, Friedrich had not warned them of his plans.

She did not like the feelings welling up in her right now as Gretchen Fürsich stared hungrily at Franz. Katrin knew Gretchen, though not well. She had once attended school with the girl's older sister, Adelheid. If Adelheid was scheming and malicious, Gretchen was more so. Either one would report her own mother if she thought it would advance her station. Now, apparently, Gretchen was determined to land an important husband, and she was not to be underestimated. She did not even wait for Franz to offer his arm! Instead, she simply flounced across the room and took it. Even her chaperone seemed shocked by the display. And Franz? Was that a tender look in his eyes when he smiled down at her? What if Katrin's hesitation had spurred him to move on?

When everyone was seated, Klaus held aloft a glass filled with a fine French wine.

"Appropriated by the German nation," he announced. "To my son, Franz, a hero of the Reich, and all the heroes of National Socialism. Long live Germany!"

Katrin lifted her glass and repeated the one part of the toast she could speak in good conscience. "To Franz." Across the table, Franz simply raised his glass without saying anything.

Next to Katrin, Friedrich lifted his glass and repeated, "Long live Germany." Frau Hilgenberg and Gretchen repeated the full toast and tacked a "Heil, Hitler" on the end for good measure. Out of the corner of her eye, Katrin glimpsed the housekeeper, who hovered nearby, raising her arm in a salute. Then they drank. Katrin almost choked on the purloined wine. and She couldn't help wondering what happened to the rightful owners of the wine. Setting her glass back on the table, she carefully suppressed an expression of disgust.

This was not Katrin's first encounter with Klaus Maedler. When the Aktion T4 euthanasia program burst into the open in 1941, she had joined the national protests, going directly to the Kreisleiter's office with her friend Maria Bittner to demand that the program cease. "God cares for every person, Herr Maedler," Katrin had declared. "We cannot just murder people who are inconvenient to the State."

"My darling," Klaus had responded, "if they are inconvenient to the State, it is not murder." The Führer ultimately relented and cancelled the program, but the halt order came too late to save Maria's brother Paul.

As the meal was served, Klaus proceeded. "And now, how are my dear sons?"

Friedrich looked at Franz, who shrugged, then looked to Klaus. "I am well, Father. Though I can't tell you much about what I am doing. Rules of operational security apply even to Kreisleiters." He arched his eyebrows and produced a charming smile. "Especially in the company of beautiful women." Then he winked. "After all, Fräulein Fürsich here could be a spy."

Katrin barely restrained herself from laughing at the momentary look of horror that had crossed Gretchen's face at the suggestion.

Klaus glared at Friedrich as he sipped his wine. Then he set his glass down, suddenly somber. "At least tell us things are going well somewhere."

"We are having some luck getting Germans into Switzerland," Friedrich replied. "I can do some good. I have friends who can do more. We are willing to give everything for the Fatherland. There can be no greater happiness."

Klaus beamed, but Franz shot his brother a look filled with disgust. "You are safe and sound in the Abwehr offices.

What do you think you will be giving?"

Friedrich stiffened. "Brother, you don't know where I go, what I do. I might have to give everything someday."

Franz tugged at the collar of his uniform. "You're right," he grumbled. "I don't know what you do. I'm sorry I assumed too much. Maybe I'm just feeling guilty, safe at home, doling out cars while men are dying on the front."

Uneasy silence fell, lingering until Gretchen finally broke it. "Herr Hauptmann, perhaps now you could tell us about your exploits? You must have many exciting stories of your valor."

Katrin tensed. Her gaze went to Franz. He paled slightly, his shoulders stiffened, and his eyes darkened. She hoped he could feel her silent support. Gretchen was unkind to broach such a painful topic.

After a moment of silence and a swallow of wine, Franz managed a response. "Well, Fräulein, I was in many battles. It is not what you think. The newsreels don't tell the story. My men were the brave ones. I got to leave Stalingrad. They had to stay." Katrin watched as he paused and collected himself. She hardly dared breathe as she waited for him to continue. At last he exhaled, and his shoulders sagged. "It was hard," he said. "The fighting was hard. The living was hard. But we did it because we are soldiers of the Fatherland. What else could we do?"

Frau Hilgenberg's stiff smile made Katrin's skin crawl. "You must have been an excellent leader. And you do yourself great credit, deflecting the praise in deference to the Fatherland."

Gretchen nodded agreement. She opened her mouth as if to ask something more, but before she could speak, Friedrich interjected, "Frau Hilgenberg, how are you and Fräulein Fürsich acquainted?"

"Why, Fräulein Fürsich is one of my best students."

Enunciating her words precisely, the older woman looked toward Gretchen. "It has been my privilege to supervise her training."

"So, you are a teacher?" Friedrich probed. Katrin was relieved that the conversation had shifted, and the restored pink in Franz's cheeks suggested that he felt the same.

Frau Hilgenberg ate a bite of schnitzel before answering. "Yes, I am a teacher. I train Germany's best young women, preparing them to take their place in the Reich as proper German wives and mothers."

"I wanted Franz to get to know a good German girl," Klaus added. "He is a war hero. He deserves a hero's bride."

Katrin was staring down at her plate, but she could feel Herr Maedler's stern gaze as it landed on her. Her cheeks heated up under the scrutiny and she knew she must be turning bright red. She hated her tendency to blush. If Franz's professions of love meant anything, surely he would defend her.

But Franz remained frozen. Instead, Friedrich spoke on her behalf. "Father, I have it on good authority that Franz is already courting a good German girl. He needs no assistance from the Bride Factory."

"Bride House," Frau Hilgenberg muttered to no one in particular. Katrin feigned a cough to disguise a laugh at Friedrich's scornful words.

"If I believed that," Klaus snapped, "I would not have invited Frau Hilgenberg and her student. You are misinformed, Friedrich."

Frau Hilgenberg sat up straight, eyes narrowing as she looked at them each in turn, and croaked out, "Herr Kreisleiter, if we have been brought here under false pretenses, perhaps we should be on our way."

"No, no. I insist you stay." Klaus's sharp tone made it clear that he was commanding, not suggesting. "Friedrich is in Abwehr and always thinks he has intelligence on everyone. He's putting his nose where it doesn't belong."

Throughout this exchange, Franz remained silent. When Katrin finally looked up, she turned her eyes to him. What would he say? Did he want to defend her? Would he risk angering his father to do so? Or would he just let his older brother speak for him? *Does he regret proposing to me? I never should have come.*

She ought to keep quiet. Mother had told her time and again to control her tongue. But the tips of her ears were burning, and she blurted out words. "Friedrich is absolutely right, Herr Kreisleiter. Franz asked for my hand in marriage before leaving the hospital. I needed time to be sure of my answer, but I..." She directed her gaze at Franz. "I accept. I would be proud to become your wife, Franz Maedler."

~

The room grew suddenly silent. No one ate. No one drank. No one chewed. The housekeeper stopped serving. Complete, utter silence.

Except for Franz. He had just raised his wine glass to his lips when Katrin made her announcement. Suddenly his throat was burning and for a moment he was coughing, tears springing to his eyes. Once he caught his breath, he sat there, trying to process what had just happened. He had barely accustomed himself to settling in for a long courtship. He still wasn't sure what Katrin wanted from him. Now, as if from a lightning bolt, he was engaged. Nothing had changed, and yet everything had. He hadn't even risen to her defense when his father set upon her, and yet she came to him. All he could gather from within himself was a garbled "My Sunshine."

"Franz, tell me this is not true." The table shook from the impact of Father's fist, and his voice was pure steel. "Tell me."

Franz felt trapped. It should have been the happiest moment of his life, but he could not have been more terrified if a T-34 had crashed into the dining room and leveled its gun at his head.

"Franz?" Katrin's tone was tentative, pleading. Franz's Sunshine was now dangling in no man's land, exposed to his father's withering glare, the hateful stares of the Bride Frau and her charge, and the possibility of general humiliation. He was confused about everything but this: he loved Katrin and wanted her for his wife. He was not the one who had said no. He had disagreed with his father before, or quietly disobeyed him. He had never openly defied him. It was time to take a stand.

Finally, he broke his silence. "Father, it is true. I proposed to Katrin in the hospital. Now we are to be married." In the vain hope that he could quell his father's anger, he spoke again. "There is nothing more to say."

"Nothing more to say?" Klaus's emotionless tone was unaltered. "There will be much more to say, but not at this table." Klaus wiped his mouth with his cloth napkin, dropped it on the table, then stood and pointed to a pale, wide-eyed Katrin. "I want her out of this house," he growled. "She is not welcome here." Then he turned on his heel and left the room.

Frau Hilgenberg huffed and got to her feet. "Come along, Fräulein Fürsich," she said, arching an eyebrow. Gretchen stood. Before following her teacher from the dining room, she tossed her head and fired a parting shot. "I would rather marry a man who did not get out of battle by getting himself wounded, anyway." She trotted after Frau Hilgenberg without looking back.

Franz watched the dyspeptic parade out of the dining room with a mixture of bemusement and concern. Friedrich, as usual, interjected some cynical humor. "If that's Frau

Hilgenberg's finest student, I'm worried for the future of the Reich." He chuckled, looked at Franz, and shook his head. "You've really done it now."

Friedrich was, Franz figured, at least half teasing. But Father was not one to trifle with. He looked to his brother. "Don't act as if you aren't in trouble, too," he declared. He wondered still about his brother's intentions, but at least Friedrich had stood up for him—and Katrin—when it mattered. And, of course, his first act of defiance was bringing Katrin to begin with.

Friedrich waved the concern away. "Don't worry about me, Franz. I take bigger risks all the time." Franz thought his brother's overwrought spy bravado was wearing thin, but he laughed anyway.

Setting aside brotherly banter, Franz quickly grew serious. He had seen on her face that the scene upset his newly minted fiancée, and he knew he needed to attend to her. "Katrin, are you all right?" Suddenly he realized that Katrin was nowhere in sight. With a clipped urgency he normally reserved for battle, he demanded of his brother, "Friedrich, where is she?"

Friedrich swiveled his head. "Not here."

Franz followed Friedrich's glance to see Father's housekeeper standing in the dining room doorway, watching them. Under his breath, Friedrich told his brother, "I'll ask Brunhilda if she saw anything." Franz couldn't help chuckling at Friedrich's irreverent moniker. The dowdy middle-aged woman bore scant resemblance to the legendary beautiful queen, but her glare certainly made her seem just as deadly.

Franz watched as Friedrich stepped out and pulled the servant away from the door. After a brief but animated conversation, he returned. "Katrin left." In the commotion, she had slipped out too.

Franz wanted to hold her tight. They also needed to talk. He had so many questions. But given her head start and his gimpy leg, he would never catch up with her. For all he knew, she might be on the streetcar by now. Still, someone needed to try. It was broad daylight, so Katrin would be safe, but she was distraught. "Friedrich, catch up to her and take her home."

Without saying a word, Friedrich retrieved his coat from Brunhilda and darted out the door. Franz was the last member of the dinner party to depart the stone house. As he hobbled toward the U-Bahn to head back to his quarters, he wanted to be happy—no, overjoyed. Part of him was. But he could not sort out all of his feelings instantaneously.

He had imagined any number of scenarios ending happily with Katrin saying "yes" to marrying him. This wasn't any of them.

CHAPTER
12

Franz scowled. He had a stack of fuel requisitions in front of him, demanding his attention, but all he could think about was Sunday's dinner party. Five days later, he was still recovering from the shock. He had suspected his father was plotting something, but to arrange for a bride-in-training and her minder to join them at dinner was beyond the pale. Gretchen was pretty enough, in a National Socialist sort of way, but she was too young, too cloying, and too predictable for Franz.

Most importantly, he already knew the young woman he wanted to marry: Katrin Weber. And she had finally said, "Yes!" But then she had disappeared.

Katrin had not spoken to him since fleeing the party. Every day, he had tried phoning her at home but was told she had gone away for a while. Gone where? The answer was evasive. Why? Also evasive. Perhaps she was simply afraid, and reasonably so. Klaus was upset enough that perhaps it was prudent for her to leave town. It embarrassed Franz that his father might wield his power to settle a personal vendetta against his fiancée. A part of him appreciated Klaus's solicitude for his welfare. Most of him did not.

Suddenly Franz was angry. Angry at his father. Angry at Katrin. Angry at himself. He pounded a stapler to fasten the last three forms together. *Why would she leave without talking to me?* He pounded it a second time. *What does she really want?* A third. *Are we even really engaged?* Franz sat back, staring out the window at the courtyard below. His flash of anger had passed, replaced by an intense fear that he had lost something of great value and might not get it back. The workday was done, and he needed to talk to someone about all this.

He found Friedrich hunched over his desk, so deep in thought he didn't even notice his brother standing over him. Franz cleared his throat, then quipped, "So, Friedrich, are you working out the best routes for smuggling Swiss chocolate for your hungry brother?"

"I could tell you, Franz, but...."

Franz raised a hand to fend off the overused quip. "I know, I know... you don't have to say it."

Friedrich closed the file he'd been working on and put it in a drawer of his desk. "So, Franz." He cocked his head. "What brings you to Abwehr today?"

"I don't come to Abwehr. I come to my brother." He set aside the jesting tone, his voice subdued by his uncertain emotions.

Friedrich leaned back in his chair. "Should we take a walk?"

Franz appreciated that his brother recognized his need for privacy. "Yes, that would be nice."

Friedrich locked his desk drawer and pocketed the key, then the two men walked out of the room, through the long hallways of the Bendlerblock, and onto Tirpitzufer Street.

"Katrin is gone," Franz blurted out as they crossed the

street. "I don't know where. Her family could not tell me— or would not." He sucked in a breath.

"Slow down, Franz."

Franz took a minute to gather himself as they turned to walk along the stone-lined Landwehr Canal, one of Berlin's prime spots for people-watching. A pair of Hitler Youth rowing teams jostled for position as they raced. Franz was grateful that Friedrich slowed his pace without having to be asked. It was a cool spring day, in the forties. "I don't know where she is, and I'm worried for her. And us. We haven't spoken since the dinner party. I'm not even sure what I think about marrying her now. I've wanted it for so long and now it seems... awkward."

Friedrich turned to his brother. "What do you mean?"

"There is more than I told at the dinner. When I first asked her to marry me, she said 'no.' Or, as she put it, 'not now.'" Franz scowled. "She said she did not want us to end up like Mama and Papa—pulled apart by opposite ways of looking at the world. She gave me things to read and wanted me to think about where my duty lies. I told her I would, and I expected that eventually she would either accept me or reject me." He paused to catch his breath. "Then, I blinked, and she said yes. Now she is gone. What should I make of a woman like that?"

Friedrich took a deep breath and grew tense. "She is a good woman, Franz. Not perfect. Impulsive, sometimes rigid, but a very good woman. You are lucky to win her."

Franz thought he detected a touch of jealousy buried in his brother's voice. He knew he had to broach the subject. "And you, Friedrich—she was on your arm last Friday. Should I be worried?" He had framed the question as a joke, but it fell flat.

Friedrich's eyes slipped past Franz to focus on a large paddle boat in the wide, still canal. "Brother, she is your fiancée. She said, 'Yes.' Stop worrying."

Franz felt better, but only a little. Friedrich had not exactly renounced an interest in Katrin. But pressing the point would suggest a lack of honor in his brother. "What did she say after you two left the dinner?"

"Franz, she loves you. Father drove her crazy." Friedrich shrugged. "There is not much more to say than that."

Franz stopped and put his hand on his brother's arm to keep him from walking on. "Why did you do it? I mean, why did you bring her?" He had not been able to get the question out of his head since Sunday.

With a roll of his eyes, Friedrich shot back. "What, are you complaining?"

"No, no," Franz quickly assured his brother. "You rescued me from having to face Gretchen alone. Not to mention Frau Hilgenberg and Brunhilda. And now I'm engaged."

The two continued walking. "Yes, I suppose you do have me to thank for that." Friedrich flashed a cocky grin as he nearly tripped over a swan that waddled in front of him on the path. "Father told me what he was doing, and I just thought you could use some female company more to your liking. And, of course, I didn't want to come alone. I figured I might as well bring someone smart and beautiful."

"But you had to know how Father would see it."

"How should I know how Father would see it?" Friedrich shrugged again and winked.

Franz grinned, then turned serious. "Brother, tell me. You are a loyal National Socialist. You have no doubt where my allegiance lies. What should I make of her insistence that I examine my duty?"

"Your duty, her duty, my duty... it's all the same." Friedrich waved a hand through the air. "To protect the Fatherland from the vicious forces that would destroy it. I have talked with Katrin. I believe she understands this. I do not think she will ask more of you than that." He paused, his expression sobering. "Though if you want to marry her, Brother, you will need to practice keeping her quiet. Or you'll both wind up in a lot of trouble."

Franz nodded slowly. "I know. Though keeping Katrin quiet will be no easy task." One of the reasons he loved Katrin was that she had a mind of her own—she wasn't just a carbon copy of every Nazi girl in the Reich. The League of German Girls turned out a raft of Gretchen Fürsichs. Katrin's honesty, her heart, her compassion—he found them compelling. He admired and envied her faith, which seemed so uncomplicated, uncompromised. But her mouth and her convictions had gotten her in trouble before, and thanks to her impulsiveness and willfulness Franz wasn't sure where he stood. He didn't want to end up imprisoned or worse— and he couldn't bear the thought of her ending up that way. *What sort of country forces its best souls to fear speaking out?*

"Friedrich, I don't know how to tell her to be careful. If she were a careful sort, she wouldn't have come with you to the dinner." Franz finally loosed the question that bothered him most. "Do you know where she is?"

"It is not for me to say, though I know she is all right," was Friedrich's only answer. That, Franz thought, was worse than nothing. If Friedrich didn't know, he would simply say so. No need to dance around the truth. And then there was the distant look in his eyes. He knew something. Why would Katrin tell Friedrich something but not her own fiancé?

Just then, Franz looked up to notice that they were passing a battery of eighty-eight-millimeter anti-aircraft guns. "The air raid—is that the way things will be from now on?" He hoped the Luftwaffe Day pummeling was an aberration.

"You know I can't share intelligence estimates," Friedrich answered quietly. "Just make sure you always know where the nearest shelter is."

"Right. And I won't bother asking you where the Eastern Front is going to be this time next year." Franz wasn't sure he wanted to know. "We can't stop fighting now, can we?"

"No, Franz, not as long as the Führer orders us to keep fighting."

The Führer and his orders. Recalling the Führer's orders in Stalingrad, Franz wanted to release the anger that gripped him. He felt his hands balling into tight fists, and he pressed them close to his side, determined to keep control. He could not rule out the possibility that Friedrich would report him if he crossed the line. *No wonder Katrin struggles to keep her words in check. It's exhausting.* "Will the orders ever stop coming?"

"Someday."

~

Katrin gazed out the train window, watching the scenery pass in a blur as she travelled back to Berlin. The fourth of April was shaping up to be a beautiful day. She had left Friedrichsbrunn early that morning in a horse-drawn cart, headed for Thale, where she caught the 9:30 train to Berlin. Her family's isolated holiday home had proved perfect for a much-needed escape, but it was time to go home. Katrin's fingers tugged at the hem of her modest green woolen jacket and she chewed at her lower lip. *What have I done?* The question had not left her since she accepted Franz's proposal.

"You are far too impetuous, Katrin Weber," she whispered, her breath fogging the window.

Mama had spoken those very words when Katrin told her about the outcome of the dinner party, followed by, "Mark my words, that boy will break your heart."

The words echoed in Katrin's mind. *That boy... when did Mama stop calling him by name? She used to like Franz.* Lately it seemed she could not see beyond the uniform.

After bolting out the door of the Kreisleiter's house, Katrin had spent a fretful night at home before leaving for Friedrichsbrunn first thing in the morning. She had things to attend to at the cottage, but they could have waited a day or two. Yet she was afraid of Klaus Maedler. More than that, she needed time to collect her thoughts, and she wasn't ready to try to explain to Franz what had happened. What *had* she done?

She knew she couldn't marry Franz yet. She had already given him good reasons why. Those had not changed. Her convictions were clear. She could not marry someone who was not committed to doing the right thing, but she had long known that she couldn't possibly marry anyone but Franz. At dinner, Gretchen Fürsich suddenly drove home to Katrin a new reality, that she couldn't stand the thought of Franz marrying anyone but her. On top of that, Franz's father had baited her mercilessly, and she couldn't let his scheming and bullying succeed. *God forgive me!* She and Franz belonged together. She had to have faith he would eventually see the truth. Until he did, she would put off the wedding day. What a mess! But life was messy sometimes.

Katrin looked down at the book she had brought for the train, Livy's *Early History of Rome*, written shortly after the collapse of the republic. Her father had introduced her to Livy, and now she was reading it a second time. *I will trace the process of our moral decline...* Katrin absorbed the historian's words. *...until the dark dawning of our modern day when we can neither endure our vices nor face the remedies needed to cure them.* So old, and yet timeless. *Can we face the remedies that Germany needs? Can I?*

She lowered the book to her lap, sobered by Livy's

words and the character of her dark modern day, when real education could only take place outside of the classroom. Shortly after her seventeenth birthday, Direktor Heinrich Scholz had called her into his office. She had failed physical training for the second time, and the fact that she had never donned the League of German Girls uniform had not escaped notice. Membership was not yet compulsory in 1934, but that mattered little—Katrin, marked as a bad influence with a rebellious nature, was expelled.

Once, the punishment would have shamed her; instead, it lifted a burden from her shoulders. School, once a haven, had become a miserable place where physical training and National Socialist ideology held precedence over academic and religious instruction. When they heard the news, Mama frowned and muttered about the idiocy of Nazi bureaucrats, but Papa shrugged a shoulder and squeezed Katrin's hand. "You are learning more at home these days anyway." She settled happily into schooling under Papa's tutelage. Now she was twenty-five years old. Her schooling had never really ended and her life as a wife and mother had not begun.

Wife and mother. As she glanced out the window of the train on the way through a small town, she glimpsed a park with a playground. In a brief flash, she seemed to see her children at play, herself sitting on a bench watching over them. It was so fast—a blink of an eye and they were gone. The moment startled her. She was not normally given to daydreaming. Her mind scrambled to recall what she had seen. Two children? Or were there three? And where had Franz been? Franz was missing. Katrin felt a moment of panic, but quickly remembered that it was only her imagination.

She shook her head and blinked hard in an attempt to drive away the images, focusing instead on the real view rushing past. Farm fields and rustic villages gave way to city streets. The train slowed with a squealing of brakes. Before long, the small trainyard came into view.

As the train shuddered and jerked to a stop, Katrin glimpsed a familiar figure standing on the platform. She smiled, fetched her satchel from under the seat, and hurried to the door. A moment later, she took her father's outstretched hand and stepped down to the pavement.

"It is good to have you back." Papa greeted her with a peck on the cheek, then took her satchel and escorted her from the station for the short walk home.

CHAPTER
13

7 APRIL 1943

When the bell rang about a quarter past seven, Katrin laid Livy on a side table and rose to answer the door. She looked through the peephole, then swung the door part way open. Her fiancé stood on the doorstep in his captain's uniform. Her heart fluttered. He looked handsome as ever with his warm brown eyes. His mouth twitched as if he weren't sure whether to smile or scowl. Katrin felt as awkward as Franz looked. She had not seen or spoken to him since the dinner party. They had much to say to each other.

"Hello, Franz," she said shyly.

Franz tilted his head, as if to inspect her. "Hello, Sunshine. You look good. I'm glad you're back. I was worried."

Her cheeks warmed, both at his compliment and his tone of reproof. "I'm sorry," she said, ducking her head briefly. "The cottage needed tending and it seemed wise to get away for a few days. Most of all, I needed somewhere quiet to think. I... should have told you." She reached for her coat and gloves, which hung on a hook near the door, then stepped out to join him. "Would you like to walk in the garden?" It was unusually cold for April, but Father wasn't feeling well and had gone to bed early, and Mother was visiting a friend. She would be furious if Katrin invited Franz in without a chaperone.

"Yes, you should have told me." Franz's stiff bearing betrayed disappointment or perhaps agitation. Then he relaxed a little. "And yes, I would like to take a walk."

He helped her with her coat, and she slipped a hand into the crook of his elbow. Glancing up at him, her lips lifted in a soft smile. "I am glad to see you again. I missed you."

"I missed you too." His tone grew sharp. "I should not have to hear about you from my brother. If it had not been for Friedrich, I would not have known you were safe, or that you had returned. He told me this morning. All your mother would say was that you had gone away." He frowned. "I don't think she's any happier than my father about our engagement."

"She'll come around." Katrin shivered and pulled her coat close around her. A path of paving stones led them around the house to the garden. "Franz, I... well... I have apologized. I know I should have spoken to you, but... I didn't know what to say. It all happened so fast."

Franz's features softened and his frown faded. "I forgive you. And I'm sorry I was upset. But you know as well as I do that when people disappear these days, sometimes they do not return." Franz gave Katrin's hand a gentle squeeze.

She blanched at the thought. "Yes," she said, her throat tightening. "I know."

Franz stopped next to the fountain and leaned against it. He cut straight to the most important question. "Sunshine, where do we stand? You left so quickly from the dinner party that we couldn't talk. I couldn't even give you an engagement kiss."

Katrin smiled bashfully. "I know. I'm sorry. Are you angry?"

Franz hesitated. "With you? No. But I am confused. Nothing has changed but your answer. What happened?"

"To be honest, I'm... not sure. I was just so angry, I wasn't thinking. I couldn't let your father or that Gretchen Fürsich drive us apart. What I said in the hospital is still true. I want to marry you." Katrin reached for his hand. "I've known since I was twelve that I would become Frau Maedler one day. I just didn't tell you then." She pursed her lips, then continued. "When I said 'yes,' what I meant was that I know I could not marry another. I will not court another. There is no use imagining otherwise. You have my heart. But I cannot give you my hand until I know which path you will walk."

Franz cleared his throat and hesitated for a moment. "I thought I had won you. Then you fled and I thought I had lost you. Now I see it is not quite either. But closer to won than to lost?"

"Closer to won than to lost, Franzi." Katrin reached for his hand but looked past the fountain toward a row of chestnut trees. "Someday you will understand."

His thumb stroked her cheek, drawing her gaze back to him. "I understand that you are mine and I am yours. I will wait for you to be ready to give your hand."

"And I will wait for you." Katrin shuddered, struck with a sudden realization. "I'm sorry, Franz. I brought your father's anger down on you. I... I didn't mean to."

Franz shrugged. "Father has been angry since 1918. It's his burden, not yours. If he hadn't insisted on trying to fix me up with a proper National Socialist girl, he wouldn't have been so disappointed. He is accustomed to ordering people around and watching them click their heels and obey."

She chuckled ruefully. "I'm not so good at clicking my heels, and Mama says I am far too outspoken when I'm angry."

He placed a light kiss on her forehead. "That is something I love about you, Sunshine, though it can be dangerous in our world." Franz pulled her close.

Katrin grew serious again. "Do... do you think there's a danger? Your father will be looking for ways to break our engagement. What if he causes trouble for me or my parents?"

"Let me worry about my father. For now, let's enjoy being engaged. We've both anticipated this moment for years, and now it has arrived."

Katrin stopped for a moment. A big brown dog was ambling through the yard, sniffing at the bushes. She whistled, then called out. "Bruno, komm her!"

A moment later, the full-grown Rottweiler bounded toward them from over by the gardening shed. He stopped not far away and glared at Franz, a low growl emanating from his throat. Franz took a step back, but Katrin tugged him forward.

"Bruno, *ruhig!* Quiet now. This is Franz. We can trust him." Katrin held out a hand, beckoning the dog closer. "Franz, this is Bruno. You can see that he is protective, but once he gets to know you, he's quite friendly."

Franz chuckled at Bruno's ungainly form. "Here, Bruno!" he called to the canine beast, stooping down to the dog's level.

The hound strode the last couple of feet and sat in front of Franz, regarding him carefully, clearly on full alert.

Katrin rolled her eyes. "He's all right, Bruno." Suddenly she knelt beside Franz and kissed him on the cheek. "See, I like him. You should too."

The kiss must have done the trick because Bruno trotted over and planted his muddy forepaws on Franz's shoulders, sealing their friendship with a slurpy kiss of his own. Katrin giggled.

"Good boy, Bruno." Franz laughed again, wrapping his arms around the dog before gently shoving Bruno back to all fours. He wiped a gloved hand at his overcoat. "Now I look like I just climbed out of a muddy trench."

"Oh no! Do you need me to clean it for you?" Katrin did not want Franz to be in trouble on account of Bruno if he was unlucky enough to face a uniform inspection when he got back to officers' quarters. "Perhaps it will brush off once it dries." She stood up and tugged him to his feet. "Come... let's sit and talk." Their favorite bench sat empty, as if waiting for them, bathed in the fading rays of the setting sun. A carefully manicured rose bush stood at either end of the bench. A month from now, they would be dripping with blossoms.

"I see what just happened," Franz responded wryly. "You have trained your dog to make me muddy so I must stay longer. Yes, let's sit."

Katrin laughed. "Father would tell you, Bruno came by this skill quite naturally! And if it causes you to stay with me a little longer, I won't complain." She clutched his arm and together they strolled through the garden to their bench.

~

Before Franz sat next to Katrin, he pulled off his coat and draped it over her shoulders. After the Eastern Front, he hardly noticed the cold for himself, but he did worry about her. Then he settled into his accustomed spot. "How many times have we sat here, secretly imagining that we would someday be engaged?"

"More than I can count," Katrin said with a slight shrug.

He had missed this, sitting in the garden with her, their conversation ranging from light-hearted to serious and back again, always somehow returning to their mutual feelings. Now he changed gears. "Sunshine, Dietrich Bonhoeffer was arrested two days ago, along with Hans von Dohnanyi and General Oster. Friedrich told me at lunch today. He wouldn't admit it, but I could tell it shook him up."

"Yes, I know. Frau Bonhoeffer visited Mama yesterday." Suddenly somber, Katrin gazed toward a line of lilac bushes at the edge of the garden. "She is holding up well, but she lost a son in the last war. Now Dietrich and her daughter and son-in-law have all been arrested and she doesn't know why or what will happen."

"Friedrich doesn't know either," Franz offered. "Or wouldn't say."

Katrin wrinkled her forehead. "Have you read the book I lent you?"

Franz was embarrassed. "Not much, not yet. I have been busy learning my new posting." He didn't admit that part of him was a reluctant reader. Perhaps Bonhoeffer would make demands on him, as Katrin did, that he wasn't sure how to meet. "But I want to. I promised, and I will." He sensed that in those pages Bonhoeffer, like Pastor Hoffmann, offered a burning drink of unadulterated truth. In contrast, Franz had spent years splitting the difference, afraid to face the truth squarely. His mother lived only in memory. His father was a flesh-and-blood presence attempting by the triumph of his will to dominate the lives around him. And, though sometimes irreverent, his brother had chosen his father's side. But was this the best Franz could do? Katrin certainly didn't think so. He wanted to believe her.

Katrin's eyes narrowed, and she sighed. "Have you at least hidden the book somewhere safe?"

Franz winced at her scolding tone. "Yes, it's safe." He

kept it in his locker, wrapped in the dust jacket of Alfred Rosenberg's *Myth of the Twentieth Century*. An approved National Socialist text.

Appeased, she leaned against him, her head resting on his shoulder. He wrapped an arm around her and bent to kiss her head. "I wish the war would end," she said softly, "and that we didn't have to worry about such things anymore."

"So do I. I wish it had never happened. It's like being stuck in a nightmare and unable to wake up."

"Do you have nightmares about Stalingrad?" She curled her fingers around his hand. "I'm sorry if I shouldn't ask. But if you want to talk, I'll listen."

Franz sat still for a minute, his muscles tightening. He wanted to tell Katrin. At the same time, he didn't. At least not everything. She was too good. Perhaps it would be too much for her. And if he didn't lose her by his honesty, he might taint her with the cruelties of war.

She pressed his hand to her lips and kissed it. "Sometimes Papa has nightmares about the World War," she said. "Mama says they used to be much worse than they are now, and that she has helped him bear that burden. Now we are pledged to each other, and I want to help you bear your burdens as best I can. If you don't want to talk... at least know that I pray for you, my Franzi."

Franz would answer Katrin's question, but not completely. He did not want the gloom of war to eclipse his Sunshine. And he had not come to grips with his guilt— guilt about leaving men behind, even greater guilt about the fate of innocents along his road. Sometimes he could push it to the back of his mind, but never for long. How could she come to grips with it? "Yes, I have nightmares about Stalingrad. The tanks, the death, the moment I lost my foot. There are nights I don't want to sleep."

She clasped her hands together around his hand. "Does it still cause you pain? Your leg, I mean."

"Not as much as it used to. For weeks, it felt like it was still there." He grimaced. "But it still hurts. Perhaps in my mind most of all."

She nodded. "Yes. My uncle lost an arm at Verdun. He told me once that sometimes his missing arm itches terribly, but because it isn't there, he can't scratch it." She squeezed his hand. "Franz... may I pray for you?"

Since Pastor Hoffmann's visits to the hospital, Franz had begun to recover from the spiritual numbness he had felt on the march to Stalingrad. He had even told Katrin that he would pray for Hoffmann, and he had done so. The pastor had been released from "protective custody" just last week. Franz found it easier to pray for a holy man than for himself. Surely the answered prayer had more to do with the goodness of the man prayed for than with the one praying for him. Though Franz still wasn't sure how much good prayer would do on his behalf, it was meaningful that Katrin offered. In fact, he craved it. "Yes, please."

Her hands still cradling his, Katrin smiled up at him, then bowed her head. "Our Father in Heaven," she began. "Thank you for bringing Franz safely home. You know how I love him. Please give him peaceful sleep tonight, without any nightmares. And please relieve his pain. Keep drawing our hearts closer to yours. In Jesus' holy name, Amen." She kissed his hand again, then let it go.

Franz opened his eyes and looked down at Katrin. He might have been unsure of the power of prayer, but he was certain of the power of her love. Even if he still felt far from God, he felt closer to Katrin than ever.

Katrin's eyes locked with his. He wondered whether she could see the myriad of emotions that battled within him. Anxiety and doubt and the loneliness that comes from unshareable sorrow all struggled for the upper hand, but none of them could match his deep love for her. That was what he hoped she saw. "Thank you." He brushed his lips against hers in a quick kiss.

She returned his kiss and cupped his face in her hands. "I will keep praying for you, every day," she promised. "And maybe you will come to church with me? Next week is Palm Sunday. Pastor Hoffmann will be there."

Franz remembered once, long ago, when they had agreed that it was important for husband and wife to attend church together. His father, of course, would be aghast. Some of his comrades would ridicule him as only half a National Socialist or as a weakling ruled by his woman. No matter. He craved more of what Hoffmann had offered. And Franz wanted to win Katrin's hand. She had taken a step toward him by pledging herself. He would take this step toward her. He wasn't sure he would ever fully comprehend Bonhoeffer's abstractions but going to church was concrete. "Yes, I'll come."

Katrin beamed. "I'm glad!"

Franz kissed her again, then chuckled as he pulled away and touched the pawprints on his overcoat. "Well, this mud is dry now."

"I'm sure I can get it out," she said with a laugh.

~

Palm Sunday 1943 came on 18 April, a warm but overcast day in Berlin. Franz stopped by the Webers' an hour before church and the four trundled off together. He couldn't help noticing that while Katrin's father greeted him warmly, her mother eyed him warily. When they arrived forty-five minutes later, Herr and Frau Weber found a seat toward the front. Katrin and Franz claimed places in the next-to-last row of hard wooden pews.

Franz would not admit it, but he was nervous. He would

stand out in his Army uniform. This was a congregation of the Confessing Church. Most of the people he knew who belonged to such churches were proud Germans, but they weren't proud of what Germany had become. He wasn't afraid of them, but they might fear him. Ever since it reared its head in opposition to the National Socialist regime's attempt to co-opt, control, and, as they saw it, corrupt Christianity, the church had been at the receiving end of state repression. He would also stand out to any informers or agents the Gestapo had planted there. He had considered coming in civilian clothes. But Katrin Weber had asked him to come—all of him—and he would not dishonor that by hiding who he was, from the congregation or from the Gestapo. Or from himself.

As the organist began a familiar processional hymn, a boy of about ten carried the cross high down the center aisle. Acolytes followed, then Pastor Hoffman. A few children carried palm branches, or the closest facsimile available in Berlin. The cross was the focal point. Not conquest, but sacrifice. It occurred to Franz that the swastika was a cross made crooked. Mother used to tell her boys that the Devil could not create anything. He could only twist the good that God had made.

The Scripture for the day included a passage from the Old Testament, a passage from the Epistles, and one from the Gospels. In many of the so-called "German Churches," the Protestant churches that had embraced National Socialism, the Old Testament had been dispensed with as entirely too Judaic. Then again, they had dispensed with most of the teachings of the New Testament as well.

Hoffman, on the other hand, embraced the whole Book.

Franz took his small childhood Bible out of his pocket to read along.

First came the prophecy of Zechariah 9:9: "Rejoice

greatly, O Daughter of Zion! Shout, Daughter of Jerusalem! See, your king comes to you: he is just, and having salvation; lowly and riding on a donkey, on a colt, the foal of a donkey." *Rejoice, daughter of Jerusalem. Could any child of Jerusalem rejoice in these days?*

Then, from the Epistles, I John 4. "God is love; and he that lives in love lives in God, and God in him. Herein is our love made perfect, that we may have boldness in the day of judgment..." Franz shuddered. *The day of judgment may be upon us.*

"We love him, because he first loved us. If a man say, I love God, and hates his brother, he is a liar: for he that loves not his brother whom he has seen, how can he love God whom he has not seen?" Hoffmann paused. Franz felt the pastor's eyes land on him. "And this commandment have we from him, That he who loves God loves his brother also."

Finally, the congregation rose to its feet to hear the Gospel story of Christ's triumphal entry into Jerusalem.

The story of the Passion had always touched Franz's soul. In 1930, Mother had taken the boys to see the Passion Play in Oberammergau, the oldest surviving Christian drama coming out of the Middle Ages. Franz had watched it in wonder. *Greater love hath no man than this, that a man lay down his life for his friends.* Franz had thought of that verse often since being sent into combat for the first time. Many of his friends had given up their lives for him. He had been prepared to do the same. But to give up one's life for the whole world? Not just your friends, but your enemies and the indifferent? Perhaps it would be hardest to give your life for the indifferent. Yet here was Jesus, riding into Jerusalem, knowing he was about to do just that. Friends, enemies, the lukewarm. Katrin, Father, Franz. He felt a twinge of shame.

A favorite hymn introduced the pastor's sermon. "Lord, Keep Us Steadfast in Your Word" was a hearty call to the faithful to remain true.

> *Lord, keep us steadfast in Your Word,*
> *Curb those who by deceit or sword*
> *Would wrest the kingdom from your Son*
> *And bring to naught all he has done*
>
> *O Comforter of priceless worth,*
> *Send peace and unity on earth;*
> *Support us in our final strife*
> *And lead us out of death to life*

When the final verse had drifted away, Franz and Katrin sat again. Franz wondered, *If Christ leads us from death to life, what should we think about those who have led us from life to death?*

"In the name of our Lord and Savior Jesus Christ, Amen." Hoffman's voice had sometimes seemed tentative. Now, as he began his sermon, it was strong and purposeful, endowed with an unseen power.

"'God is love, and those who abide in love abide in God, and God abides in them.' This is the Word of God to man. It is God's holy promise to us, fulfilled by Christ as he came into Jerusalem, suffered, died, and rose again. It is also God's command to us.

"Are we following that command as we start this Holy Week? When we look out at the world, we see chaos and sin. Peoples are exterminated, races go into the abyss of destruction; a sea of blood and tears, inconsolable sorrow goes over the world."

Franz could no longer follow the pastor's words, and he was no longer in Berlin. He was in Kyiv, or Kharkiv, or Stalingrad, or any number of other places along his road. He looked out the window, and the faces returned. He had not seen them for a while, but there they were. His comrades left behind to their fate, or the ones who died by his side. The little girl in Kyiv and the others on their way to doom. Partisans hanging from gallows. Jews in villages across Ukraine being swept up in the nets of the Einsatzgruppen. The face, contorted by disgust, of the Orpo lieutenant on the train home. Fear. Inconsolable sorrow.

Franz did not know how long Hoffmann had been speaking when the sermon drew to a close. He only realized that he had grabbed Katrin's hand and was squeezing it tightly when she let out a sharp gasp.

"If we call ourselves people of God, let us be people of His word. Let us abide in His love." Hoffmann closed his Bible and looked to the congregation. "Let us join together now in the prayers of the church."

The people rose. Up and down, up and down, up and down. This, too, was part of Franz's childhood, and it made him think of his mother. "It is good exercise, Franzi. We are not here for amusement and convenience. We are here to show God our love and respect."

Now Hoffmann tiptoed from the rhetorical frying pan into the fire. "Almighty God, be with your people. Be with your holy church, that it may bring comfort to the oppressed and truth to all people. Let it speak always the gospel of love.

"Almighty God, be with our country in this difficult time. Forgive us for idolatry and pagan pride. Look into our hearts and give us wisdom and courage. Return peace to the world. And be with our brothers who are not with us now. In the name of Jesus Christ, Amen."

Niemöller, Bonhoeffer, hundreds more arrested since 1935. Katrin's brother Reinhard, driven into exile. Hoffmann did not speak their names but did not need to. Franz stared at his shoes, his back bowing under the weight of guilt.

Hoffmann faced the altar to prepare for Communion. As he recited the words of Institution, Franz remembered receiving Communion from him in the hospital. Franz could rush into enemy fire to take a key position, but Hoffmann had a spiritual courage that Franz envied. Surely, the pastor had been warned against speaking out as he had done, but he had stepped back into the pulpit and spoken anyway, willing to give himself for the faith he followed. "Take and drink, this cup is the new testament in my blood, shed for you for the remission of sins."

Sitting far to the back, Katrin and Franz were among the last to go to the communion rail. Franz hobbled a bit to the front of the church as Katrin held his hand. He knew it would be hard to get back up, but he needed to kneel. So he knelt and closed his eyes as the pastor placed a wafer on his tongue. Guilty hands must not touch the body of Christ. Then came the chalice of wine, which burned its way down Franz's throat. So little blood to atone for so much sin. Franz struggled to stand as Katrin helped pull him up. He could feel the eyes of many following him back to his seat. Did they fear him or pity him? He wasn't sure. When he got back to his pew, he was prepared to send a long and ornate prayer to Heaven. Instead, he felt a moment of unaccustomed peace, closed his eyes, and said, "Thank you."

The closing hymn could not have been selected by chance.

> *O little flock, fear not the foe*
> *Who madly seeks your overthrow*
> *Dread not his rage and power*
> *And though your courage sometimes faints*
> *His seeming triumph o'er God's saints*
> *Lasts but a little hour.*

Franz focused intently on the words. As the third verse began, he felt a wave of something coming over him. Was it conviction? Courage?

> *As true as God's own Word is true,*
> *Not earth or Hell's Satanic crew*
> *Against us shall prevail.*
> *Their might? A joke, a mere façade!*
> *God is with us and we with God—*
> *Our victory cannot fail.*

Then it was over. The hymnal indicated the words were written in the seventeenth century and later set to a tune called "Nuremberg." Ironic. The city that was, more than any other, a symbol of Nazi power. Home to the massive Party rallies of the 1930s, Nuremberg gave its name to the racial laws that defined the National Socialist state.

At the end, the congregation remained standing as the pastor and acolytes recessed. They stood silently a moment longer, perhaps in solemn acknowledgement. Here, in this place at this time, Franz grasped that Nuremberg the tune was aimed squarely at Nuremberg the ideological symbol. As far as Pastor Hoffman was concerned, Hell's Satanic crew was the regime whose uniform Franz wore.

Franz noticed a tear streaking down Katrin's cheek. She clutched his hand, and he wiped her cheek dry.

CHAPTER
14

20 APRIL 1943

The Führer's birthday, as always, was a day of celebration. Around Berlin, concerts and speeches were planned in his honor, though he himself was spending the day at his villa in the Bavarian Alps.

Franz had worked all morning at his post in the Bendlerblock, then joined Friedrich for lunch at the café down the block. A group of SS men offered a loud toast to the Führer "on the glorious fifty-fourth birthday of the leader of the Reich." Friedrich joined the toast, but Franz simply lifted his stein. When they broke into the Horst Wessel Song, Friedrich sang heartily. Franz remained silent. Sometimes he envied Friedrich, who knew where he stood: joyfully allied with the Nazis.

Spring was beginning to blossom in Berlin, and the brothers had been given some release time in the afternoon in honor of the day. After lunch they parted ways, and Franz took his time to walk through the Zoologischer Garten, the famed Berlin Zoo. He had loved the zoo since he was a child, and he wanted to be alone.

But the zoo wasn't as he remembered it from childhood. Every animal seemed to scream a reproach. The magnificent stone aquarium, with its large glass skylight, its square tower, and its decorative carvings of reptiles around the top of the building, brought to mind thoughts of Georg, his bleached bones at the bottom of the sea, picked clean by the cousins of the fish that darted about the tank. Heck's cattle, reconstructed from the Auroch of pagan Germany, looked and acted mean, as if cows had drunk some wicked potion to become bulky and vicious. *This is our völkisch past? Our future?* Then there were the noble lions, king of the beasts. Franz could not put out of his mind the sight of lion carcasses in the Kharkiv zoo, shredded by artillery fire and Luftwaffe bombs. They never had a chance. Like the family boiling shoe leather.

As Franz continued his walk, the whole zoo seemed to be a metaphor that brought to mind the sting of Pastor Hoffman's sermon. The zebras were lounging in the shade of a tree when Franz found them. Two SS men were leaning against the railing to the enclosure, laughing and taking pictures with a small camera. The zebras had always been Franz's favorites.

"Are they white horses with black stripes, or black horses with white stripes?" he had once asked his mother.

"What does it matter?" she responded. "They are God's creatures, and they are beautiful." Now, Franz found himself wondering: Was the zebra God's natural rebuke to Nazi racial theories?

The hippos were next. Huge, lumbering beasts, they had always fascinated Franz. When he was almost two, during the World War, Mother had brought him and Friedrich to the zoo. According to Mother, Franz had gotten out of his carriage, stared at the hippos, and, grunting and pointing to his open left hand, made it clear he wanted to take one home. From that moment, Franz carried a soft spot in his heart for the river monsters. Hippos were cunning creatures. They looked slow and harmless but were the most dangerous foes of the crocodile. They would stand on the bottom of a muddy African river with their mouths open, waiting for an overconfident croc to pass. When the opportunity arose, they would snap their jaws shut and cleave the crocodile in half. Now he watched them and wondered, *Is Germany the hippo? More likely the arrogant crocodile.*

What had Hoffman said? "Forgive us our pagan pride."

The wild donkeys of Arabia, fenced in a foreign land? *"Rejoice, O daughter of Zion, your king comes to you lowly and riding on a donkey."* The humility of Christ, such a stark contrast to the crocodiles of the National Socialist state. And what of the daughters of Zion? Who would speak for them?

Franz entered the aviary. Many of the birds were beautiful, and he loved to watch them, especially the colorful parrots. The aviary housed exotic birds from around the world. They all sang, but different songs. Sometimes the cacophony made Franz feel free; sometimes it seemed like chaos he could do without. Bird songs, ideas, opinions, all affected him the same way. Perhaps the birds needed some National Socialist discipline, some order. Maybe people did, too. But then he rebelled. What if they all sang the same song? That wasn't natural either—or right. More of Hoffman's words came to mind. *"Peoples are exterminated, races go into the abyss of destruction."*

He followed a Luftwaffe lieutenant and his girl into the Reptile House. When the girl shrieked at the sudden sight of a dozen different snakes slithering up trees and down rocks, Franz chuckled. The moment of humor quickly dissipated. An army of serpents? The old hymn answered.

"Not earth nor Hell's Satanic crew against us shall prevail."

For Franz, there was no escape. As much as he loved the zoo, it was time to leave. Not for the first time, Hoffmann had somehow bored to the center of Franz's soul and filled the hole with a dose of bitter but liberating truth which followed and tormented him wherever he went. What to do about this truth was the next question. Neither the donkeys nor the hippos could answer for him.

~

After lunch, Friedrich made the twenty-five-minute walk to St. Matthew's Church on Goltzstrasse, south of the Bendlerblock. He badly needed the confessional again. He took his time along the way, ducking into a book seller for a moment. He left empty-handed, looked over his shoulder, then stopped at a sidewalk vendor to pick up a small red, white, and black swastika flag. The flags were being distributed for the Führer's birthday, and Friedrich tucked one into the breast pocket of his suit.

Normally, he would stop at St. Hedwig's, but the cathedral had been severely damaged in the 1 March air raid. The domed roof had collapsed, the interior burned. When he reached St. Matthew's, Friedrich checked his watch, stepped inside, genuflected, and walked purposefully to a confessional. "Father, forgive me, for I have sinned. It has been six weeks since my last confession."

"My son, what have you done?"

Friedrich was relieved. Father Fellner again. The priest had been reassigned to St. Matthew's after the bombing.

"Father, I have waited too long since my last confession."

Fellner must have recognized Friedrich's voice, as well. "Yes, too long."

Friedrich took a breath, then continued. "My sins are the same. I have betrayed my family. I must have redemption soon. I should not have waited so long to come to you, but... things happened."

"You are prepared to make penance now?" The priest's tone was one of invitation rather than judgment.

"Yes, now." Friedrich's voice was soft but resolute.

"These are the same relatives? In the same town?"

"Different relatives, the same town. The circle of my sin has grown."

"Last time I asked you how many Hail Marys you thought were the right penance for your sin," the priest reminded him.

"Yes, I remember."

"What is the right number today?"

"I believe ten would be appropriate." Friedrich paused and wiped his brow. "And I would add three Our Fathers. Nothing less would be right."

"Then go and do so. Your sins are forgiven."

Saying nothing more, Friedrich crossed himself and exited the confessional. As he stepped out of the church, he met a familiar face about to enter.

Friedrich smiled. "Sister Klara Marie."

The nun stopped. "Herr Maedler, we meet again."

"How are you holding up?" Friedrich asked softly.

"God is good, and his mercy endures forever."

Friedrich stroked his chin for a moment. "Indeed. I have a feeling we will cross paths again soon."

The Carmelite nodded briskly, wordlessly passed by Friedrich, and disappeared into St. Matthews.

~

Katrin spent the Führer's birthday as she spent most days, working in Rothberg's bakery. It was, to say the least, not her favorite holiday. She had to drag herself to work today after leaving home without breakfast. "I'm not hungry," she had told Mama. A slow but steady stream of customers, most wearing Nazi Party pins, came in to pick up baked goods for the celebrations they had planned at work or home.

Katrin tried to show respect and kindness. To do otherwise would be wrong. It could also be fatal. For some Germans—the ones with the power—Hitler's birthday eclipsed Christmas. It was to be expected from people who had elevated a corporal to the place of God.

At about three in the afternoon, an elegant woman in a fur stole walked in, accompanied by a plain man Katrin took to be her driver. "Fräulein, I require a cake for an event tonight. Is your employer here?" She looked down at Katrin through critical, narrow eyes.

Katrin forced a smile. "He's in the back. Can I tell him what you need?"

"I need a two-layer cake, thirty centimeters in diameter, frosted in red with the Party emblem on the top."

This is excruciating. Katrin swallowed her revulsion and forced a smile. "I'm not sure such a thing can be done so quickly."

Drawing out her syllables, the woman responded as if Katrin were one of the "half-wits" the Nazis were fond of euthanizing. "My dear, I am quite sure it can be done. I am the wife of SS Obergruppenführer Heissmeyer." She fluttered her fingers toward the kitchen door. "Now go tell the baker."

Katrin shuffled to the back and told Ulrich the bad news.

The normally jovial baker frowned, then shrugged. "What can we do?"

Katrin shuffled out again to tell Frau Heissmeyer, "It will be ready at five o'clock."

"Excellent. I will be back at precisely five o'clock. Heil Hitler!"

Katrin managed a "Good day." Though the Nazi salute was theoretically mandatory for civilians, many in Berlin quietly resisted the regime by reverting to traditional greetings. Katrin was among them. The Obergruppenführer's wife arched an eyebrow, wheeled about, and left, her driver in tow.

For the next two hours, Katrin kept an eye on the clock, watching the minutes tick by. At 4:58, she left for home. Ulrich could hand over the swastika cake. She knew he would forgive her.

After a long ride home, she came through the door, silently hugged Papa, and sat down for a plain but fortifying supper. There was no cake. There was no commemoration of the day at all. Then, just after Katrin had finished packing for tomorrow's train trip and had gone to bed for the night, the air raid sirens went off. The Webers had to scurry back to their cellar bomb shelter. The RAF were celebrating the Führer's birthday in style.

CHAPTER
15

23 APRIL 1943

Franz had not seen his father since the dinner party. Carpool had kept him busy, and Klaus was even busier running Wilmersdorf. More to the point, Franz hoped to give his father a chance to calm down before their paths crossed again.

He couldn't put it off any longer. Klaus had called this morning to ask Franz if they could talk. Franz had responded with artificial cheer. "Of course, Father. When?"

"Tonight, after supper," was the answer. Franz had gulped—he was not expecting to be thrown into battle so quickly.

At the door of the stone house, the grim housekeeper greeted him. "Good evening, Herr Hauptmann. Your coat?"

"Good evening, Bru–" Franz nearly called her Brunhilda to her face. Friedrich's moniker was the only name by which he knew her, and it still amused him. The pause lingered in the air. *Fräulein? Condescending, given her age. Meine Dame? Inappropriate with staff.* Franz settled for an awkward "...my dear." Somehow Friedrich made it sound better.

Brunhilda, spare as ever, draped his coat over her arm. "The Kreisleiter is in the parlor." Then she made herself scarce.

Klaus Maedler was sitting on the Biedermeier couch, pouring himself a shot of Kirschwasser. "Franz?"

"Yes, Father, please." Klaus poured another shot and handed it to Franz. Son sat next to father.

"To surviving another air raid." Franz lifted his glass and opened the toasts. The British raid on the night of the Führer's birthday had been a small one, though some of the boys in the air defense batteries had been killed.

Klaus raised his glass and swallowed the contents. "How have you been, son?"

"Working hard. I have to confess I don't find my post very rewarding, though it's sometimes challenging." Franz cracked a slight smile. "As my commanding officer reminds us, without Carpool, OKH couldn't operate, and all would be lost." Since receiving his posting, Franz had feared that his father would look down on him. In the hospital, Klaus had said he could kill more Russians behind a desk than behind a Mauser, but Franz supposed that was only true if he were helping draw up operational plans or ensuring that supplies reached the front. Handling petrol disbursements for generals' cars in Berlin didn't seem to fit the bill.

Klaus set down his glass and leaned forward. "Franz, duty is its own reward. Any assignment the Reich gives you is important. Be patient."

Franz sighed and sipped his drink. "Yes, Father, I know. It is just hard to go from leading a battalion in Russia to sitting behind a desk."

"In my years in the Army, I never had as much responsibility as you have carried. They gave me a rifle and a few feet of trench, and every once in a while ordered me over the top to attack. You have led men in battle. Now, you lead men in your office." Klaus paused to make a self-satisfied face and nod at his own point. "You have given much to the Fatherland. You have nothing to be ashamed of."

Franz folded his hands in his lap and smiled. He had always struggled to feel accepted by his father, and now the older man's words worked like a salve. In a way, his father was right. There was no shame in being reassigned to a useful post after sacrificing a leg in battle. Then Franz shifted uncomfortably in his seat, his smile gone. There were many other reasons for shame. When he glanced out the parlor window, faces crowded in to remind him.

For a long moment, neither Franz nor his father spoke. Finally, Klaus cleared his throat and broke the silence, bringing them to the real subject of the evening. "About dinner the other day."

Franz raised an eyebrow. "Yes?"

Klaus stared at his shoes. "I am sorry that I stormed away. I was not a good host."

Franz sat agape. He could not recall his father ever apologizing for his brusqueness. Or anything else, for that matter. In the farthest reaches of his imagination, he could picture Klaus apologizing to a superior, a Gauleiter perhaps, or maybe Hitler. But his son? Had he been summoned to the stone house for this?

"I understand you were surprised," he finally answered. "It was not my intention to upset you."

Klaus mused for a moment. "I blame Friedrich. The imp should not have brought that girl."

"I don't know what Friedrich was thinking. I promise you I had nothing to do with that." *So far, so good,* thought Franz.

"I will not ask you what you thought of Fräulein Fürsich. She was immature. The Bride House must do better."

"She will make a fine wife for an SS Obersturmführer."
Franz chuckled at his own suggestion. A lieutenant
was about right for Gretchen. "Though he may wind up
requesting a posting to the Russian Front."

Klaus chuckled along with his son. "I will contact Frau
Hilgenberg and see if there are others more suitable."

Franz lost his smile, set his glass down, and sat up
straight, bristling. *So this is why I was summoned.* It was
certainly closer to what he had expected.

Klaus suddenly slipped into the same exasperated,
cajoling tone Mama had used when Georg resisted eating
his vegetables. "Franz, you cannot marry the Weber girl.
She is a few short steps away from a Gestapo prison and
so is her father." He emitted a long, loud sigh. "You have a
future in the Reich. Promotion, someday a generalship or a
high place in the Party. Every day you are married to her,
you will be looking over your shoulder."

"Father," Franz said stiffly, "I am engaged to Katrin. I
intend to marry her." He set his jaw.

"It is a mistake, Son! She is wrong in every way. What
do you see in her?"

For Franz, that question was easy. Katrin was pretty,
smart, and strong. She brought out the best in him and
challenged him to become better. It mattered to her to do
right. But it boiled down to one thing. "I love her, Father."
He took another sip of his drink. "If Mama were alive, Katrin
is the girl she would want for me."

Klaus was quiet. He poured another drink and took a
sip, then picked up a folder from the coffee table. It was
stamped "Geheime Staatspolizei." He opened it, scanned
the contents for a second, and handed it to Franz. "You
were at Hoffmann's church."

Franz was only half-surprised. "Are you having me
watched?"

"No, no. Not you. They just happened to see you."

"Katrin, then?"

"You realize I could have had her arrested after the dinner party? I thought about it. It would have solved many problems." Father shook his head. "But no, I haven't had her followed, either. We are watching all the Confessing Churches. They are filled with traitors. Hoffmann, for one, is forbidden to teach his drivel. And she led you there."

Franz's temper flared. "If you had her arrested, I would never forgive you."

"I know," Father snapped. "Why do you think I didn't do it? I have lost one son already. I would be at my end if I lost another. But if she truly loved you, she would not drag you to a den of vipers like that."

Franz felt his father's withering stare boring into him. "It was my choice, Father."

"Choice, yes. You need to make a choice." Klaus clenched his fists and raised his volume. "You can serve the Fatherland and the Führer, or you can follow that weak religion. Embrace the future or be captured by the past. The future is National Socialism. Hoffmann and the Webers are the past."

"Is Mama the past?" Franz wasn't sure how far to push, but he had to ask.

Klaus ignored the question and plunged ahead, but Franz saw his eyes darken and knew he'd struck a nerve. "At the beginning, we thought the Christians could be co-opted. And most of them were. They wanted to be part of the future, too. But some remained stubborn. We're ready to move on now." The Kreisleiter wagged his finger at no one in particular, or perhaps everyone. "When the war is done, the cross will be replaced with the swastika, the Bible with *Mein Kampf*. There will be no middle ground."

Franz furrowed his brow. "This is your opinion, or the

Party's?" He knew that Hitler had kept some of the Party's anti-religious radicals on a leash for years. Perhaps his father's own animus against the Church was speaking out of turn.

Klaus got up, walked into the adjoining study, and returned with a small pamphlet. He handed it to Franz. It was a Party circular dated 1942 and stamped "confidential." Written by Martin Bormann, the Führer's personal secretary and second most powerful man in the Reich, it was addressed to Nazi Party regional leaders. It was titled "National Socialist and Christian Concepts are Incompatible." *Isn't that what Katrin has been telling me?*

Franz began reading:

> *The Christian Churches build upon the*
> *ignorance of men and strive to keep large*
> *portions of the people in ignorance because*
> *only in this way can the Christian Churches*
> *maintain their power. On the other hand,*
> *National Socialism is based on scientific*
> *foundations.... To an ever-increasing*
> *degree the people must be wrested from the*
> *Churches and their agents, the pastors....*
> *Only the Reich leadership, together with*
> *the party and the organs and associations*
> *connected with it, has a right to lead the*
> *people.*

No middle ground. Franz handed the circular back to his father, sighed, and looked up at the wall. One of Klaus's prized possessions hung there, a high-quality print of a Hermann Otto Hoyer painting. Franz studied it for a moment. To the right stood Adolf Hitler in the midst of an impassioned oration. To his left, a beer hall crowd of German men and women listened in rapt attention. Franz could almost hear the man speaking, his voice ascending from a whisper to a shout proclaiming the truths of National Socialism. He had seen the painting many times, though it had not gone up on the wall until after Mother's death. For the first time, Franz took the time to read the title: *In the Beginning Was the Word*. Digging into his memory, he finally recognized that this title was taken from the first verse of the Gospel of St. John: *In the beginning was the Word, and the Word was with God, and the Word was God.* John was referring to Christ. Hoyer referred to Hitler. There was the choice. John or Hoyer. The Gospels or National Socialism. Christ or the Führer. Only one Word can be God. *Maybe there really isn't room for both.*

Klaus spoke, coming back to Franz's question. "Your Mama loved us all very much. But yes, she is the past. Her Germany is the past. The Germany of Bach hymns and catechisms and Christmas carols and church bells. This past is gone. Where have you seen this God who cares about us? Was he in Stalingrad?" Klaus opened the Bormann circular and began to read aloud. He was no longer discussing anything with Franz; he was lecturing. "The assertion that this world-force can worry about the fate of every individual, every bacillus on earth, and that it can be influenced by so-called prayer or other astonishing things, is based either on a suitable dose of naivete or on outright commercial effrontery.'"

This was always the heart of Klaus's argument. Hard-headed, challenging Franz to look squarely at the suffering in the world and daring him to say it was compatible with the Christian God. Franz looked down and folded his hands in his lap. He felt a twinge of pain in his missing leg, as if it were mocking him for daring to confront his father. Franz knew about suffering.

Klaus lowered the pamphlet, but he wasn't done. "How

many of your comrades prayed to God moments before being obliterated?"

Franz had no answer, but he knew it was many. Klaus had attained the rank of Kreisleiter partly because he had the capacity to pound others into the ground with a stream of unanswerable questions. For the moment, Franz was silenced. Cornered, cowed. As blow followed blow, he could hardly marshal his thoughts to form a response. He was a soldier, not a debater.

"Son, you cannot claim the future and follow your mother. Respect her. Love her. Remember her with honor. But let her go. Let Katrin Weber go." He finished his glass of Schnapps, then waved a dismissive hand through the air. "Forget Frau Hilgenberg. Find your own wife. But find a woman who looks to the future. Then I can give you my blessing."

Franz felt as if he'd had the wind knocked out of him. First Katrin had demanded that he choose. On Palm Sunday, he had edged closer to that choice. Now his father had clarified things by demanding a choice, too. Klaus's relentless onslaught had set him back on his heels. All the illusions that he had sustained for years—that he could honor his father and his mother, that he could follow the Word of John and the Word of Hoyer—had crumbled around him.

He couldn't walk away from Katrin. He knew that. He couldn't consign his mother to the past. But as cynical as he had become about the National Socialist regime, he couldn't just turn his back on his father or his Fatherland. Nor could he betray the solemn oath he had sworn when he entered the Wehrmacht and which bound him to the memory of his men. He couldn't deny the beauty of the forgiveness he felt at the communion rail, and he couldn't deny the ugliness in the world that seemed to mock God.

Nothing he could say would make sense of it all. But he would have to make sense of it, and soon, if he wanted to keep Katrin—and his sanity.

Franz did the only thing he could do. He stood up and said, "Goodnight, Father. It has been a long day." Without another word, he walked to the front door, took his coat from the coat rack, and, exhausted, let himself out. The last thing he heard as he fumbled down the steps was Brunhilda huffing after him, scolding him for not closing the door properly. He did not look back.

Franz could feel himself on the edge of a knife. He needed to see Katrin, to hold her and talk to her, as soon as he could.

As he walked slowly to the U-Bahn, he tried to work through his schedule in his mind. He gritted his teeth and scowled when he realized he would have no opportunity to see his fiancée until his upcoming May Day furlough a week hence. Too long!

CHAPTER
16

1 MAY 1943

Immaculately dressed in his Wehrmacht uniform, Franz stepped into the Rothberg bakery and looked for Katrin. The week since his intense conversation with his father had passed slowly, though he'd had more than enough work to keep busy. With Katrin's help, he was growing back into his faith, but his father had unnerved him, challenged him.

Franz was enjoying a short furlough and had stopped by the bakery to surprise Katrin, maybe take her on a May Day walk by the Spree River. He did not see her. The baker was busy boxing up an order of Schrippe rolls. He was a large man, tall and stocky and just round enough to suggest he had freely sampled his wares. The small shop was a pleasant place, what with the aroma of baking bread, and his mouth watered as he peered into the display case of tortes, some apple strudel, and crusty Schrippe like Mama would make for breakfast every morning. *Except Sunday, of course. It wasn't Sunday to Mama without a cake for breakfast.*

"Can I help you?"

Franz hadn't noticed that the customers had left until the stern voice pulled him away from his memories. He looked up and found himself under the cool scrutiny of the baker. Franz respectfully removed his hat, cleared his throat, and answered, "Heil Hitler," his flat tone devoid of ideological fervor. "Is Katrin Weber here?"

"Good morning. Who is asking?"

He is protective. I'm glad he's looking out for her. "My name is Franz Maedler. Katrin and I are recently engaged."

"Yes, of course." Rothberg's wary tone lightened as his brow smoothed. "Katrin has told me about you. I'm sorry, but she has taken the day off. I believe tomorrow as well."

"Is she home?"

"I don't think so. A gentleman came by to pick her up yesterday after she finished work. I believe they were going somewhere." The baker stopped and stuttered, as if he realized he had spoken out of turn. "I... I'm really not sure."

Franz winced. *Not again. Why won't she tell me when she is going away? And who is this man she left with?* "Do you know where she was going?"

"No. Out of the city, I think."

Now his mind was tied up in knots. He had to find her. They couldn't go on like this. Here, gone, here, gone. Now gone with a mystery man. This was the third time since late March that she had gone away suddenly. First, after the dinner party; then shortly after Palm Sunday, and again, now.

"Thank you." Franz took a shallow bow, put his officer's hat back on his head, and started to leave the bake shop. In the doorway, he turned back toward Rothberg. "Could you describe the gentleman?"

"Tall, slender, blond hair. About thirty. He has stopped in before." The baker held on to that last sentence, studying Franz's face, then continued. "Herr Hauptmann, Katrin loves you."

"Thank you," Franz repeated, and he left. *Tall, slender, blond, about thirty. Friedrich?* He hobbled toward the Bendlerblock as fast as he could for a few blocks, then admitted defeat, sat down on a bench at a transit stop, and waited for the next streetcar.

The trip was a torment. *What is Katrin doing? What is Friedrich doing?* Franz needed answers. When he reached his destination, he went straight to Abwehr. His mind told him he would find Friedrich at his desk. His heart somehow knew he wouldn't. When he entered the main door to the office, he held his breath. A moment later, he was deflated. Friedrich was nowhere to be seen.

Franz walked to Friedrich's desk. It was cleared of papers. No loose pens. No cup of coffee, either empty or full. No sign he had been working there recently.

"May I help you?" The voice belonged to an Abwehr officer at a nearby desk.

"Yes, I am Hauptmann Franz Maedler. Friedrich is my brother." Franz had visited his brother here several times and recognized the owner of the voice, though he couldn't put a name to the face.

The officer apparently recognized him as well. "Right. Hauptmann, it is good to see you again."

"Is Friedrich here today?"

"I'm sorry. He is out of the office. You will understand that for reasons of operational security I cannot share any details with you."

Franz paused. "Of course." *So, he is on a mission. It's a coincidence that he and Katrin are both gone.* "You can at least confirm he is on a mission?"

"I can confirm nothing, Hauptmann." The man began working on a form sitting on his desk.

Franz was stumped. "All right, I understand. If he comes

back today, will you let him know I stopped by?"

"Of course, Hauptmann." The Abwehr man looked up for a second. "If he comes back today. Good day."

With that curt dismissal, the conversation was over. Franz didn't know much more than when he arrived. There was one more place he could go.

~

By the time Franz knocked on the door of Katrin's home, it was early evening. Her mother answered.

"Frau Weber, how good to see you." Franz knew better than to greet her with "Heil, Hitler." In any case, he preferred not to.

"Franz." Her glare pierced through him. "I hope you are well. What brings you here today?"

"Frau Weber, I am worried for Katrin. I stopped by the bakery to surprise her, and the baker said she was gone for a few days. She didn't tell me where she was going, or that she was going at all, and then I was told she left work yesterday with some other man." Franz stopped to catch his breath.

Frau Weber spoke up to fill the silence. "Herr Hauptmann, Katrin is not a child. I do not always know what she is doing. You needn't worry. She can take care of herself."

Undaunted, Franz pressed on. "I know. She's a strong woman. But if she and I are to marry, I can't be running around Berlin trying to learn where she has gone and why. It makes me crazy. We are at war, and you know terrible things can happen."

She remained quiet for a moment, pursing her lips as she scrutinized him. "I know, Franz," she finally said, her voice losing its edge. "Many terrible things can happen."

For a moment, Franz looked down in embarrassment. He knew not all of those terrible things were at the hands of the enemy. He knew that Frau Weber knew that, too. And he had been part of some of those things. "Is there nothing you can tell me?"

"I'm sorry, Franzi."

When Frau Weber reverted to his childhood nickname, a flicker of regret flashed in her eyes. As Franz was about to leave the doorstep and make the long return to his quarters, Herr Weber appeared behind his wife in the doorway.

"Franz, my boy, why don't you come in? I apologize for Renate's lack of hospitality. Join me for a drink." Renate shot her husband a sharp look but stepped back from the door to give Franz a pathway into the house.

"I'm happy to join you. Thank you." Franz stepped through the door. He was too tired to want to head back right away, and he might learn something from Herr Weber.

Katrin's father led him to the study. In contrast with the rest of the house, which was reasonably tidy, the study was littered with piles of papers and books and an overflowing wastebasket. As Franz sat, Gustav poured two snifters of cognac, then extended one to his guest.

Franz thanked him. "You are very kind, Herr Weber." It felt good to sit for a while. He wished he could remove his prosthetic, elevate his leg, and rest his aching stump, but he did not feel comfortable doing so in front of his future father-in-law.

"If you are to be my son, we must become reacquainted."

Franz had seen Gustav frequently in his boyhood, whenever his mother would bring him with her to visit Renate. After Mama's death, though, he had seen little of Katrin's parents, and none at all since going off to war. Now that he was to marry Katrin, he was glad her father welcomed this chance to get better acquainted, though he would rather wait until he had found his fiancée.

"Herr Weber..." He paused, shifting in his seat. "I must plead for your forgiveness. I asked Katrin for her hand when she was visiting me in the hospital. I didn't have the opportunity to ask for your blessing. I didn't come here for this, but now that we are together, I do ask for your blessing." He inhaled, then continued. "I love your daughter very much. I cannot face life without her. It would make me very happy to know that you accept our union and wish us well."

"My wife has concerns," Herr Weber said matter-of-factly. He leaned back and studied Franz's face.

Franz rested his cheek in his hand. "I thought she might. She has not been as warm as she used to be."

"I will be honest, Franz, because we have known you for a long time and Katrin loves you. She trusts you." Herr Weber folded his hands and looked toward a photo of his daughter sitting on his desk. "My wife is worried about politics. Your father, you. What does your father think about this?"

Franz assumed that Gustav knew what his father thought. Surely Katrin would have told him. There was no point in trying to sugar-coat it. "He is opposed to our marriage. He wants me to back away."

"But you won't?" Gustav raised an eyebrow. "He is a powerful man. He has much to offer you in the Third Reich. And much harm he could do to Katrin."

"You may know my brother Georg died on a U-boat two years ago." There was a catch in Franz's voice. *Two years? Why is it still so hard to speak of it?* When he regained his composure, he went on. "Father does not want to lose another son. I will protect her."

"What about you, Franz? Where has Army life taken you?"

Franz remained silent as he wondered what exactly Gustav meant. Was he talking about the physical journey, or did he mean something deeper? For a brief moment, he looked into Gustav's eyes. Finally, he answered. "It took me to Stalingrad with many brave men, most of whom are now dead or as good as dead. Sometimes, it took me to places I didn't want to be, places I wish I could forget." He paused. *Gustav has been in war. Surely he understands.* "At times it took me far from God. But when I'm with Katrin, I feel I can come back from those places."

Franz saw on the wall over Gustav's desk a print of *The Last Supper*. A far cry from Hoyer. "You are a believer," Franz observed. "Are you worried, too?"

"My boy, we are all believers." Professor Weber spoke with an academic air of finality, treating a profound truth as just another bit of common sense. "The only question is who we believe in."

Franz leaned back in his chair. "I suppose so." An increasingly familiar theme. The Word of Hoyer, or the Word of John?

Gustav continued. "Am I worried? Franz, your mother was a good woman, and she taught you right from wrong. Deep down, you know who to believe in. When the time comes, I have faith you will do what is right." He set down his glass. "Take good care of my girl. I give you my blessing."

In an instant, Franz's mind shifted. It meant a great deal to him that Gustav saw him as a worthy husband for his daughter. But he had not come all this way for heart-warming conversation. He'd come for answers. In that moment, a thought came to him. *The cottage! She has gone there before!* Franz decided on a new approach. He would make the guess, and if he was right, he would know. "Herr Weber, has she gone to Friedrichsbrunn?"

Gustav Weber picked up his glass, looked away, and took a sip of his cognac.

It was the only answer Franz needed.

CHAPTER
17

Franz caught the early train for Thale, the station nearest to Friedrichsbrunn. He desperately needed to talk with Katrin, to feel her presence. And now he needed to know what she was doing as well.

Bad memories of the train from Kharkiv came flooding back. The pain of a leg that had only recently been detached. The vivid nightmares every time he dozed off. The faces in the window. The partisans swaying in the breeze next to the track somewhere west of Kyiv. The depressing colonel and the haughty SS man. Not knowing whether to be relieved or dismayed that he had lived, that he was out of Stalingrad when his men were trapped inside. A miasma of emotions, none of them pleasant.

Except for one. Soon Franz would see Katrin. He had held on to his care for her to the banks of the Volga and back again. That hope had kept him alive. In the ruins of Stalingrad, he had known he might have to die for the Reich and the Führer and Lebensraum, but he no longer lived for them. Only Katrin and his men.

Lately, he was confused about Katrin. She had pledged herself to him, and everything he thought he knew about her told him to believe in her pledge. He had never known a more honest or honorable woman. She was the one always prodding him to live up to his best self, to return to the God his own mother had led him to in his youth. But he couldn't ignore reality. She had acted erratically ever since he proposed. Now she was gone again, without warning or explanation. She was with a man, probably in an isolated spot. What should he think? War could do strange and terrible things to people's morals.

His mind skipped back to his friend, Rudolf Moldenhauer, the captain of another battalion in the Seventy-ninth. On leave just before Barbarossa, he got engaged to his childhood sweetheart, Margret. He told Franz that he trusted her with his life. For months, she wrote him every day. Then the letters stopped coming. Somewhere west of Millerova, Rudolf got word that Margret had married an Army colonel stationed in France. They had met when he was on leave, had a whirlwind romance, and married in Paris. Two days later, Rudy recklessly charged a Soviet position and was killed in action. Shot through the heart. *Do I know Katrin as well as I think?* He fought that fear with every ounce of his energy. *No. There must be some reasonable explanation.* But no matter how hard he tried, he could not completely vanquish it.

After a while, Franz tried to clear his mind and simply watched the towns go by, the fields, the trees. Finally, the conductor announced, "Thale-Musestieg. Next stop, Thale-Musestieg." Once Franz was off the train, he would need a driver to take him the final ten kilometers to Friedrichsbrunn. He went to the street side of the station and hailed a taxi. "Do you know the Weber cottage? Gustav and Renate Weber? I believe it's in the woods south of

Friedrichsbrunn."

A gruff, chubby driver said, "Get in."

Franz took a seat in the back of the taxi, then watched as the driver got out and waddled to the car in front of them. He leaned over, said something to that driver, and a moment later came back.

"Yes, I can take you there. It is outside of the city, so it will cost you extra."

Losing a leg for the Fatherland only gets you so far, I guess. "How much extra?"

"Two Reichsmarks." The driver took a bite of his bratwurst.

Franz rolled his eyes. "Let's make it one. You wouldn't want to be accused of gouging a captain in the Wehrmacht."

"Fine."

The car pulled out from the station. The driver was not interested in conversation. He was concentrating on the winding road and his bratwurst. Franz stared out the window, his jaw clenched tight.

Finally, the taxi pulled up to a modest white cottage with a steep sloping roof and a sun porch on the front. It was in a heavily wooded area dotted with dozens of similar cottages, mostly vacation homes where the Berlin bourgeoisie went to relax for a few weeks in the summer. The closest structure to the Weber cottage was three hundred meters away, barely visible through the trees. *A perfect place for a discreet tryst,* Franz thought.

His shoulders tightened. It couldn't be.

The driver stopped in front of the modest white clapboard cottage, which was set back from the road about fifty meters. "Seven Reichsmarks."

Franz paid, got out of the car, and started the long walk to the front door. When he reached it, he stood for a moment, nearly paralyzed. But he had come all this way to find Katrin, and he couldn't just leave. He slowly took hold of the brass door knocker, then banged it down on the door.

Nothing.

He banged the knocker five or six times in quick succession. Behind the door, he could hear a commotion, someone moving, interior doors opening and closing.

As he started to bring the knocker down again, the front door opened.

There stood Katrin Weber. She looked a bit disheveled, and at first, he thought she had been busy cleaning. But he could see the anxiety in her green eyes, especially in the way she avoided meeting his gaze.

"Franz..." Katrin's unspoken question hung in the air. A sheen of perspiration shone on her brow, and when she raised a hand to touch his cheek, he could feel it trembling ever so slightly. "I... um..."

"You left again." He stepped back from her touch, keeping his tone stiff, his gaze hard. "Do you have something to hide?"

"Hide?" Katrin chewed her lower lip. "Of course not." She slid her hand into the crook of his elbow. "It's a lovely day. Shall we walk a little?"

Franz frowned. He had seen that face before, usually when Katrin was nervous. "Maybe later. I have travelled a long way to see you and I'm tired. My leg hurts. I need to rest."

"Of course." Katrin nodded as she reached behind her to grasp the door handle. She pushed the door open again and stepped inside. "Come. You can have a seat while I get you a drink. Papa keeps a good store of Wippra here."

"Thank you." Franz walked through the door into a small sitting room with outdated wallpaper, a couple of well-used upholstered chairs, and a settee. Once the gatehouse for a larger estate, the cottage was comfortable, though darker and stuffier than he remembered. As Franz followed Katrin through the sitting room into the kitchen, he realized that all the curtains were pulled tight. Strange, for a place with no electric lighting. Katrin gestured to a seat at the antique oak table, and he sat, still on guard.

She bustled about the kitchen, first filling a bier stein, then opening the larder and producing a loaf of bread and a wedge of cheese. She brought everything to the table, then sat down across from Franz. "What brings you here today?"

"What brings me here?" Franz scoffed, outwardly disdainful but inwardly fearing the worst. "Hmm. What a question. You bring me here, Katrin. I spent all yesterday wandering around Berlin trying to find out what happened to you. All that I learned was that you had left. With a man."

Katrin studied her hands and Franz watched as her cheeks reddened. Normally he found her easy blush endearing. Today it only added to his suspicions. "I'm sorry," she whispered, then raised her eyes to meet his. "I love you, Franz."

Franz sipped his beer, then stood up. He had been reluctant to betray a lack of trust, but no longer. He started walking through the kitchen and into the sitting room. "Was the baker lying? He didn't seem the sort."

Katrin followed him out of the kitchen. "Herr Rothberg? I don't even know what he said. Please, Franz... sit down. You said you needed to rest."

Franz passed through the parlor into a bedroom and found no one there. *My legs need rest. But so does my mind.* As he stepped back out of the room, leaning heavily on his cane, he pressed Katrin with another question. "Why was there so much commotion when I first came to the door? You couldn't have made all that noise yourself."

"Commotion? What..."

Franz knew Katrin valued the truth, but somehow, her eyes told him he wasn't going to hear it from her. That didn't mean he was ready to stop trying. "Your mother would tell me nothing. Your father told me where you were only through his silence. What are you hiding? What are they hiding for you?" Franz moved into another bedroom. Again, empty.

"Please, Franz," Katrin pleaded, and she grabbed his arm. "Please trust me and let this go. I will go back to Berlin with you right now if you like."

Back to Berlin. The thought appealed to him. Get her away from here and whatever it was she didn't want to share and forget it ever happened. But he wasn't leaving until he knew the truth. "I want to trust you, Katrin. It's harder than it used to be. Too many times you have disappeared." Franz noticed a doorway in the kitchen that he hadn't yet opened. Another storage closet? Perhaps the cellar? "There are too many secrets. Your deception is making a mockery of your faith."

Katrin followed Franz's gaze to the door and then quickly looked away, and in that instant, he knew exactly where the answers lay. "You must understand that everyone has secrets these days, Franz."

He looked back at her. Whatever the door concealed could wait, but he could no longer contain himself. He had long wondered if his brother had designs on his girl. Friedrich had denied it, but Friedrich was a spy and thus a master of lies. "What about Friedrich? Does he have secrets?"

Her brow furrowed. Clearly, his question was unexpected. "Friedrich works for Abwehr. Of course, he has secrets."

"You know that's not what I mean."

"If you wonder about his secrets, you must ask him when next you see him," Katrin snapped. She glanced at the floor. "I'm sorry," she said softly. "I didn't mean to speak so sharply. Even so, Friedrich is the one you must ask about such things."

"Yes, I suppose so." Franz's tone also softened. He could only stay angry at Katrin for so long. Perhaps the mystery man had only come to the bakery to give her a ride to the train station. Perhaps Franz was too suspicious, a hazard of living in a society that deliberately discouraged trust. But there was that one last door. Almost mechanically, he reached for the door handle, turned it, and pulled the door open.

He was greeted by a steep staircase descending into a dark cellar. He blinked and took a step down, out of the kitchen, carefully steadying himself with one hand on the wall. Once his eyes adjusted, he realized he was looking into a familiar face coming up the stairs.

Friedrich, and he was holding a bottle of wine.

CHAPTER
18

2 MAY 1943

Before Franz could react, Friedrich was at the top of the stairs, grabbing his arm, guiding him back into the kitchen, pushing him down into a chair at the table. There Friedrich plunked the bottle of wine down and then took a seat himself. Katrin stood across the room, arms crossed, eyes cast downward.

Guilty. Franz thought grimly. *She looks guilty.*

"What is this, Friedrich?" Franz glared at his brother. "What are you doing here?" The bottle of wine seemed to say it all, but Franz wanted to hear it. When there was silence, he redirected his glare to Katrin.

"Sunshine?" For the first time ever, the nickname came out of his mouth dripping with sarcasm, more a curse than an endearment.

"It isn't what it looks like, Franzi," she said, her voice wobbling slightly. He had never seen her so flustered.

Franz glowered. "It isn't? Then what is it? Somebody needs to tell me."

She didn't answer. Her gaze flicked to Friedrich, sending

him some sort of unspoken message. Franz had thought he could read all her expressions, but now it seemed that she and Friedrich had their own private language.

"Franz," Friedrich started slowly, looking back at Katrin. "We didn't mean for this to happen. It isn't Katrin's fault."

"No, Friedrich." Katrin took a step closer. Her voice sounded stronger, though she still looked stricken. "I won't let you play that game with your brother."

Now Franz was really confused. Confused and hurt. Something was going on. It seemed obvious what. His brother had as much as admitted it. But Katrin denied the obvious. Was she just a liar? Someone who could not acknowledge the truth, even when the evidence was in plain view? His own version of Rudi's sweetheart? Or was there something else going on? It must be bad. Franz wasn't sure he wanted to ask anymore. "You two need to get your story straight. All I know now is that I can't trust either of you."

"Please, Franz." Another step, then two more, and Katrin was standing in front of him. "I can't explain what you have seen today, but I promise you my heart is yours. You know me better than anyone. Look at me," she pleaded, reaching for his hands. "I need you to trust me."

After a moment's silence, Friedrich snaked an arm around her shoulders. "Katrin, my love, what are you say—"

Before he could finish, Katrin whirled on her heel and slapped him hard. "I said no, Friedrich! Don't destroy your brother!"

Franz was about to give up and leave. He could not make sense of the lovers' quarrel unfolding in front of him, but he knew it was time to go. Perhaps Katrin loved him, or had, but this was too much. He stood up from the table, took Katrin's right hand, and kissed it. "Goodbye, Sunshine."

This time the nickname was soaked in regret. He let her go, glared at Friedrich one last time, and walked toward the front door.

"Franzi, please." Katrin followed him, weeping, and grabbed his arm. Friedrich remained in the kitchen. Before Katrin could say anything else, the unmistakable cry of an infant floated up from below. Katrin froze.

So did Franz. *Is this worse than I thought? Did Friedrich and Katrin have a child while I was away in Russia?* Without speaking, Franz turned and headed back into the kitchen and toward the cellar door.

"It's too steep for you, Franz." Friedrich spoke urgently and held up his hand as if to say "stop." His brother turned the door handle anyway. "Franz, don't go down there."

Franz turned back toward Friedrich. "I can manage. After all, shouldn't I meet my nephew?"

Katrin gasped, and now her hand flew at Franz's cheek, leaving behind a sharp sting. He hadn't realized until that instant that she had followed him.

Franz took a deep breath, exhaled, and stared at Katrin for a moment. He could feel his heart pounding. Would their relationship, their engagement, really end this way? He felt like he was trapped in a nightmare. Either way, he had to know the truth.

He turned to descend the steep stairs. From below came another cry, louder than the last. Franz hobbled carefully down the steps, tightly grasping the handrail. Eventually, with effort, he reached the bottom. Upstairs, the cottage had been a comfortable temperature, but the cellar was cold. It smelled musty, like cellars everywhere.

Another cry, a bit muffled. Franz waited a minute for his eyes to adjust to the dark space, which was lit only by the dull light that snuck through the kitchen window curtains and down the stairwell. By this time, Friedrich had joined him. Franz walked around the edge of the cellar, coming across a rack of wine and some cobwebs but no infant. He paused to stare at his brother, then continued his walk around all four corners of the room. As he ended his journey down each wall, he stopped and looked around the room, then back at Friedrich. Finally, frustrated and angry, Franz grabbed his brother by the lapels and shook him. "Where is the baby?" he yelled in his brother's face. "Where are you hiding it?"

"I don't hear anything." Smirking slightly, Friedrich shrugged and shook his head. *Too many years in Abwehr,* Franz thought. *Of course he heard it. So did Katrin.*

The cries seemed to Franz to emanate from behind the wall. He knocked and was sure it felt hollow—like there was a room rather than earth behind it. He knocked a few more times. Then, unexpectedly, a knock came back. Franz stepped back as adrenaline surged through him.

He turned to his brother. "What is this, Friedrich? And don't tell me you didn't hear that. Enough lies."

"We have to tell him, Friedrich." Katrin had come silently down the stairs to join them. Her tear-streaked face and strained voice told Franz how deeply his mistrust had wounded her. But what had she expected?

"Tell me what?" Franz demanded.

Friedrich stopped and rubbed his chin, his usual pose when he was trying to sort through a problem. Or trying to decide whether to come clean. Or both. Eventually, Friedrich nodded. "Yes, we have reached the end of the road. It's time to take off the mask."

The Abwehr officer, the loyal son of his father, pushed a spot about halfway up the wall. A portion of the wall opened, revealing a small room lit by oil lanterns, filled with cots and a few chairs. In the room a gasping teenage girl cradled a crying baby. To their left, a man and a woman rose out of folding chairs. A toddler clutched the woman's hand. On the other side, a small horde of children watched wide-eyed.

Franz's jaw dropped. Suddenly, Katrin was in the midst of the horde, murmuring in a comforting tone. Friedrich, meanwhile, slowly guided Franz back up the stairs into the kitchen. Franz let himself be pushed gently back to the table, though he kept looking down the stairs. His mind remained fixed on the faces of the mysterious group who had invaded the Weber cellar.

Friedrich spoke first in a soft voice and motioned to a chair. "Have a seat, Brother." His smirk was gone, replaced by grim determination and a furrowed brow.

Franz obeyed, more out of surprise than a desire to cooperate. Finally, he regained his faculties. "Who are those people?" For a brief moment, he grasped at a vague hope that they were some of the bombed-out residents of Berlin, given shelter by the Webers. But he instantly gave up on that thought. If that were true, why hide them?

Friedrich took on a serious air, his pale face tight. "Franz, we wanted to keep you out of this. You must believe me when I tell you that these people's lives are at stake. We have no choice but to trust you now."

"Trust me?" Franz smacked his palm on the table in anger. "*You* worry about trusting *me*? Really?" He let his incredulity sink in for a second, then continued. "What is this about, anyway?"

Friedrich kept his voice matter of fact. "These people are hiding from the authorities. If they are found, they will be deported and killed. All of them."

The faces Franz had seen in Kyiv stared in at him from the kitchen window as understanding struck him. "They are Jewish," he murmured. "Friedrich... what have you gotten yourself into... what have you gotten Katrin into? You will get us all killed." In his agitation, he stood again and began to pace the length of the room. He had never shared, nor even understood, the Nazis' obsessive hatred for the Jews. His mother had deplored it. When the Nazis tried to support their position with an obscure anti-Semitic tract published by Luther late in life, she had pointed out that it was an aberration, bracketed before and after by sentiments of kindness and toleration expressed by the reformer.

For Franz's part, until the Eastern Front he had never given the prejudice against Jews much thought. It had been a bombastic, if regrettable, part of the National Socialist package. Then, for a time, he had rationalized that the Jews were collateral damage in the necessary war against Bolshevism. As the war ground eastward, his mother's voice grew louder, and he found the human cost impossible to condone. *Women, children, old people—these are the enemies that threaten the Reich?* Now, he was haunted by the killing. But was he willing to violate his Wehrmacht oath for them? Turn his back on his father? Maybe even die for them? Sympathy was one thing. This was treason.

Friedrich stood to match his brother. "I will tell you who they are. They are human beings. They are Germans. And yes, they are Jews. These are not the first we've helped. My work gives me special knowledge of what is being done in Germany's name. And it gives me opportunities to help a handful of people." He pulled out a kerchief and rubbed it over his brow. "We needed a safe place to hide them. I remembered that the Webers owned this cottage, and Katrin agreed to help."

"You asked her? You're the reason she did this?" Franz stopped in front of his brother, his fists clenching and unclenching at his sides.

"You can blame me for asking her, but she—"

Franz didn't give him a chance to finish. He balled up his fists and threw a punch to Friedrich's gut with his left hand. His right swung wildly at Friedrich's face, but his brother blocked the blow. Franz lost his balance and backed away, breathing heavily as he steadied himself against the table. He should have paid better attention when Blondie tried to teach him one-legged boxing in physical therapy.

For a moment, neither said a word. Then Franz spoke. "I don't know what to believe now. Who are you, anyway?"

Friedrich had lost his breath but managed an answer. "I am who I have always been, Mother's son." He paused and looked into Franz's eyes. "In my heart, I have never accepted National Socialist doctrine. The hatred, the arrogance, the reversion to a pagan past where God has no place."

For the first time in years, when Franz looked into his brother's eyes, he thought he could see his mother gazing back at him. He felt like he was getting a glimpse of the real Friedrich instead of some impostor. The revelation left him stunned. "Why didn't you tell me? Don't you know I've felt torn apart by all this? I've tried so hard to earn Father's favor... to earn your favor. To be a man who would make you proud." He felt tears swimming in his eyes and blinked them back. Tears were unmanly, a sign of weakness. Father would have rebuked him. Slowly, he sank back into his seat. He felt dizzy, like when he was a boy after a spin on the merry-go-round. Friedrich had always liked pushing his brothers as fast as he could. This was the fastest the merry-go-round had ever gone. "I don't know what to think."

Friedrich gripped his shoulder. "I'm sorry, Franzi. I know you've struggled. Many times, I've wished I could tell you how I really felt about this band of murderers who are destroying our country, who killed our brother and nearly killed you with their arrogance. But this deception was necessary. If my own brother and father cannot see through it, I can hope the Gestapo will not."

"So, it was all an act?" Franz slowly shook his head.

"The 'Heil, Hitlers,' the verses of the Horst Wessel Song, all of it?"

"Every time I say the 'Heil, Hitler,' every time I spout the regime's propaganda, a little bit of me dies inside. I have felt for you, in your struggles. Think of how hard it is for me to keep my real thoughts, my real beliefs hidden from almost the entire world." His expression hardened. "But I am an intelligence officer, Franz. Dissembling is part of my craft. Now I am trying to turn it to good account. And I have always chosen my words carefully. I don't think you ever noticed how carefully." He arched an eyebrow. "It is surprisingly easy to deceive without ever speaking a lie."

Franz thought about it for a moment and realized his brother was right. He studied Friedrich's expression. Now that he had dropped his mask, he seemed softer... more approachable. And yet, somehow, he also seemed stronger. "What about Father? I am Mother's son, too, but also Father's. He would see this as a personal betrayal. Doesn't he matter?"

Friedrich cracked his knuckles, a nervous habit dating to grade school. Mother used to scold him for it, but he always resorted to it when particularly discomfited. "Of course, he matters. I don't want to hurt him." He pursed his lips and sat up straighter. "But he chose his side long ago. If we are lucky, he'll never know. Besides, Franz, when my life ends, it is not Father who will call me to account. I can't betray my conscience for his sake."

Franz thought for a moment, then moved on. "Bonhoeffer... he was part of this, wasn't he? That's why they arrested him."

"I wasn't alone in Abwehr. I can't tell you more without endangering you or them. But I was not—am not—alone."

"And yet you would endanger my fiancée." Franz eyed his brother, not yet ready to trust him. He picked up the wine bottle. "Are you sure all of this was an act, too?" He stared at Friedrich, silently defying him to confirm his suspicions.

"Franz..." Friedrich's voice hitched slightly. "I can assure you, Katrin's heart is yours. What you saw before you went down the stairs was a ploy—an act we planned in case the Gestapo came to the door. I kept playing the part because I wasn't sure how else to redirect you." He reached across the table and placed a hand on Franz's arm. "I'm sorry. We never intended to hurt you."

Franz chose not to press further. There was a more urgent matter to consider. "You've done this before? Hidden Jews? What happens next?"

"There was a group of five earlier this year. We got them out to Switzerland. That is our plan again. We must move this group soon. They've been here too long."

Franz shut his eyes tightly and sighed. His thoughts tormented him. "You know it is my duty to report you..." His voice faded to silence as he contemplated the unthinkable. That couldn't be the right thing. But his Wehrmacht oath required it.

"You asked me not long ago what your duty was. I said it was to protect Germany from the vicious forces that are trying to destroy her. I meant that. That is a duty we all have." Friedrich stopped for a moment to wipe his brow. His eyes bored holes in Franz. "If you report us, they will all die. Katrin will die. I will die. The vicious forces will have destroyed more of Germany." Friedrich narrowed his eyes, paused, and cleared his throat. "I know what you were part of in the East."

Franz felt sick and looked away as Friedrich continued. "The trains are not carrying Jews to resettlement. The trains are carrying them to camps where most are killed within a few hours after arrival. The old, the children, and the weak first. I think deep down you already knew that. You can never bring them back. But you can help save these." Friedrich stopped until Franz looked him in the eye again. "You asked me who I am. Now you have to decide who you are."

His brother's words felt like a fist to the gut. Franz would rather have taken a real punch. For so long, he had been numb. It was the only way to survive what he had seen. Coming home, coming back to Katrin, talking with Pastor Hoffmann and reading the Bible, the Catechism, Bonhoeffer... all of it was bringing him back to life. Right now, he longed to be numb again, because coming back to life hurt like hell. He scrubbed a hand across his face, then shoved back from the table and stood again to resume pacing. He wanted to talk with Katrin, wanted to wrap her in his arms and let her peace envelop him. He wasn't sure what he thought about the mess she had been dragged into, but he had already forgiven her for play-acting with Friedrich. In fact, he wanted to apologize for his own behavior. *Did I really say "nephew?"*

Suddenly, Katrin stood before him. She stepped into his arms and pressed her head against his chest. Her kisses momentarily calmed the turmoil in his heart. Whether she had overheard some of the conversation from the cellar or just sensed that her fiancé needed her, he wasn't sure. What mattered was that she was with him. He was only vaguely aware of Friedrich slipping back down the stairs.

"I'm sorry," Katrin whispered. "I wanted to tell you, but I couldn't."

Franz couldn't decide which troubled him more—that she hadn't told him or that he now knew. Life would have been easier if he hadn't come to Friedrichsbrunn. Finally, he spoke. "I'm sorry, too." He held her close for a moment. Then he stepped back and looked into her face. "But why?

You are risking everything. Your life, our future." This time, he kept his tone gentle, free of recrimination. He simply wanted to know.

Katrin took a deep breath. For a long moment, she was silent. At last she looked up at him, her green eyes filled with quiet strength, and answered. "I would rather risk my life and future than stand by and do nothing. God brought these people to me, to Friedrich... and now to you. Will you be able to live with yourself if you turn them over to be killed?"

Franz ignored the question. It was too difficult. Instead, he hesitated, then asked a question of his own. "Will you tell me about them?"

"About our guests?" Katrin cast a soft smile in his direction, her eyes glistening with tears. "Well, first there are the children. Thomas is only three. His family was taken in by kind people, but they were betrayed and had to flee. Now he doesn't understand why he must keep quiet." She swallowed hard and blinked back tears. "But he is lucky— he has his mother and father with him."

Lucky? Franz wasn't sure that was the right word for a child forced to hide in a cellar.

"I don't know much about Dov," Katrin continued, "except that he is eight and never speaks. His parents were arrested, and their landlady found him hiding in a crawlspace. She hid him for a few days, but she was afraid, especially after the roundup in February."

Fire flashed in Katrin's eyes, and Franz felt her passion for these people begin to take root in his own heart. "Then there's Eva. Fifteen and angry at the world. Can you blame her? She has lost everything. Her parents, her home, her brother and sister. She stepped out to buy milk and when she came home, they were gone. That was eighteen months ago. A neighbor woman took her in and hid her, but when she got engaged, Eva had to go. She was moved to another hiding place, and then another, until she came to me." Katrin's voice cracked and the tears that had been gathering in her eyes began to course down her cheeks. "I'm not sure I can tell you the rest right now."

Franz brushed a tear from Katrin's cheek with his thumb. "How did they find you?"

She shrugged. "Different ways. Friedrich brought Thomas and his parents. I learned of Dov and Eva and most of the other children through women I met at a demonstration on Rosenstrasse—maybe you heard about it."

"There were some rumblings about it at the Bendlerblock. Not something you see every day in Berlin. Feisty hausfraus in mixed marriages who wanted their husbands back on the day of the big SS roundup." Franz hadn't known Katrin had been there. Now, as it turned out, some of those feisty hausfraus had trusted her to take charge of their children. In spite of himself, he felt a flash of pride. Who would have thought that this slight young woman would have such courage and confidence? Franz's mind turned to Pastor Hoffmann and his recollection of the story of the people of Israel and their escape through the Red Sea.

His reflection was disturbed by a knock at the door. Too soft, he thought, to be the Gestapo. Though if he was wrong, they were all dead. He drew Katrin close, but she patted his arm. "It will be all right," she said, and she rapped twice on the stovepipe. Seconds later, Friedrich came up the stairs with another bottle of wine, closing the cellar door behind him. He moved past Franz and Katrin to open the door while they watched from the kitchen. On the other side was a man dressed in black—not an SS uniform or a Gestapo overcoat but the cassock of a portly middle-aged priest whose well-creased face marked a man much given to laughter.

Franz and Katrin listened while Friedrich welcomed the priest and ushered him in.

"Father Fellner," Friedrich said, his head cocked quizzically, "you should not have come here."

"I had to come. There are complications—" Fellner stopped mid-thought when he stepped into the kitchen and his eyes landed on Franz in his Army uniform. The priest raised his eyebrows, looking intently first at Friedrich, then at Franz with a tilt of his head.

Friedrich dismissed the priest's concern with a wave of his hand in his brother's direction. "Oh, yes. Father, let me introduce my brother, Franz. He's threatened to turn us in, but I don't believe it for a minute."

Franz wondered if the Father took Friedrich's remark as some sort of gallows humor. For his part, it wasn't a very funny joke, but Fellner seemed satisfied. He relaxed and continued. "We have escorts for the children, but your friend arranged the plan for vehicles. When he was arrested, the arrangements fell apart. We need a truck or a few cars. We need fuel."

Franz looked at Friedrich. "Your friend? Bonhoeffer?"

"No." Friedrich turned back to Father Fellner. "We have to move them soon. We are running out of time."

"Are the papers arranged?"

Friedrich nodded decisively. "They are all in order. Abwehr quality."

"Are there still ten?"

"Yes, Father." Friedrich's mouth quirked up in a wry smile. "Exactly the number of rosaries you assigned me. What a coincidence."

The priest chuckled, but Franz arched his eyebrows. "Rosaries?" First Friedrich was a dyed-in-the-wool National Socialist, now he was anti-Nazi. Raised Evangelical, now Catholic?

"Let's just say Father Fellner's confessional was an outstanding venue for private communication." Friedrich fixed his gaze on Franz but resumed his conversation with the priest. "Father, I happen to know someone who has access to vehicles and fuel."

Franz immediately grasped Friedrich's meaning. "Oh, no. It's bad enough that I know about this. It is worse that Katrin is tangled up in it. I haven't even made up my mind that I can look the other way. You've put me in a terrible position. And now you want me to help you?"

"With all due respect, Brother, no one invited you here." Friedrich's eyes flashed. "You made the bullheaded decision to come. Now you are here, and you don't like what you find. Did you like what you found in Kyiv, in Bila Tserkva?" Friedrich ticked off the names of places he must have known from reports crossing his desk. "That is on your head, too."

Franz clenched his teeth. Suddenly, his whole body was trembling. He knew those places intimately from memories he couldn't let go, faces he couldn't stop seeing. "No. That was never my decision, not my choice." But if that were true, why was he haunted by guilt?

"Maybe you didn't feel you had a choice then. You do have a choice now."

"You are asking me to commit treason. They shot the last man in my office who pilfered fuel coupons." Franz shifted his gaze to Katrin. "Is this what you wanted?"

"Franz..." Katrin laid a hand on his cheek. Her measured tone was soothing, her touch a balm to his heart. "Before I answer your question, I want to tell you about another child... one I could not help. Do you remember Pauli?"

"Of course. Maria's brother." *The slow one.* "He's a good kid."

A wistful smile graced Katrin's face, but she blinked

back tears. "You might not know this, but the day I knew I loved you was the day you defended Pauli from that pair of bullies." She smiled softly. "You marched in there and put your arm around his shoulder and told them to leave him alone."

Franz remembered. *Those hooligans are probably in the SA now.* "I remember. They were calling him useless and stupid."

"Franz." His name seemed to catch in her throat. Was she choking back a sob? "Pauli is dead, killed under the orders of your Führer. 'Life unworthy of life,' they said. 'Useless eater.'"

Franz looked away, blinking rapidly to keep at bay the swarm of tears that had suddenly gathered in his own eyes. The news took his breath away. He had been proud of his role as Pauli's defender and had genuinely liked the boy. *My Führer? You're acting as if I chose him.* Now Pauli somehow stood in for all the innocent victims Franz had seen since the war began. When he could breathe again, Franz closed his eyes and took a moment to feel the air go in and out of his lungs. A simple thing, for him. But not for Pauli, not anymore. Franz's guilt, his sorrow, hardened into anger.

Now Katrin's tone was calm again, if a bit strained. "You ask what I want, Franz. But this is the wrong question. You must ask whether such a Führer is worthy of your loyalty. And you must ask God what He wants. Then you must do it. Only then will you find peace." She pulled away.

He wanted to pull her back, to cling to her, to find her courage and confidence somehow coursing through him. But he let her go. Watched her walk back to the cellar door, open it, slip through, and close it behind her. He knew she loved him. But she had chosen them.

Suddenly the cottage seemed too small. Franz felt as if he were suffocating, the walls closing in on him. He had to get out, get away, be alone with his anger and his fears and his confusion. Or maybe not alone. Katrin was right. He needed to look to God. Without a word to Friedrich or the priest, he spun around and lurched toward the door, desperate for fresh air.

CHAPTER
19

4 MAY 1943

I don't want a new name!" Eva kept her voice quiet, but there was no mistaking the fury in her tone. She stood opposite Katrin and Gerta in the cottage's small parlor, arms crossed over her chest, shoulders rigid, brow furrowed. "I am Eva Levy."

"We've been over this," Katrin soothed. "It's for your safety and everyone else's." She stretched to touch Eva's arm, but the girl tossed her dark braid and stepped out of reach.

Katrin sighed. "Eva." She edged her tone with a bit of steel, the way Mama did when her children were quarreling. "Fine. If you insist, you can stay here and spend the rest of the war hiding alone in the cellar. But if you want to go to Switzerland and find your uncle, this is what you must do."

The threat instantly silenced the defiant teenager, though she did not come any closer to Katrin. Even scrunched up in a scowl, her heart-shaped face was pretty, but her eyes held too much sorrow for one so young. "You wouldn't let them leave me."

Before Katrin could reply, Gerta's hand came down on her shoulder. "Let me," she said softly. Her warm brown eyes shone in the flickering lamplight, full of understanding.

Katrin nodded.

"Eva..." Keeping her voice quiet but firm, Gerta rose from the divan and stepped across the room to the girl. Eva allowed her approach. Katrin wasn't sure if she should stay and listen or step out to give them privacy. She started to get up, but Gerta motioned for her to remain where she was.

"They've stolen so much from us," the young mother said as she cupped Eva's cheek in her hand. "And when those who wish to help us ask us to surrender our names, it seems like the drop that made the barrel overflow, yes?"

Eva nodded briskly. A tear glistened on her eyelashes, but she blinked it back.

"When my son was born, Samuel and I named him Yair." Gerta tugged Eva back to the divan to sit with her and Katrin. The teen sat stiffly between the two women, her shoulders pulled in tight. Gerta twisted in her seat and looked Eva directly in the eyes. "We were hiding with others in an abandoned warehouse, suffering the bitter cold of a Berlin winter. Just when I thought I could not survive another day, a pastor named Zimmermann came—we'd seen him before. Others had said he could be trusted, but we'd kept our distance. This time, when he offered to bring us somewhere warm and safe..." She smiled faintly at the memory. "We decided to trust him."

Eva relaxed a little, her attention riveted to Gerta's story. Katrin listened just as intently, though she'd heard it before.

"He brought us to a farm outside of Berlin. Ernst and Marta Müller welcomed us warmly. They said we were family. They gave us new names—Heinrich and Dorothea

Müller—and they said we must give our Yair a new name too. Pastor Zimmermann even provided us a baptismal certificate to write that name on. Taking new names for ourselves—that was hard enough. But to write a new name on that paper for our son..." She sighed. "Samuel was angry. He did not wish to do it. But Herr Müller told him, 'It's a piece of paper. It changes nothing—but it could help save his life.' And so Yair became Thomas. It is the only name he remembers." She smiled softly and reached to clutch Eva's hands. "One day, God willing, Yair will learn his true name. He will celebrate the feasts and he will be proud of his heritage. But first he must live. And so must you, dear Eva."

Katrin lay a hand on Eva's back and was relieved when she allowed it. Gerta's tale must have gotten through the girl's hardened shell. "Gerta is right, Eva. It doesn't change who you are. To make this work, you must pretend for a little while."

A tear slid silently down Eva's cheek, and Katrin offered her a handkerchief. "Come now, let's practice. Dov would be heartbroken if you weren't with him, you know." The little boy was the one person Eva had connected with here in the cottage. He never spoke, but somehow, she understood him.

Her face tear-streaked, Eva gave a brisk nod. "My name is Beate Kuehn," she said in a small voice.

Relief coursed through Katrin, and she smiled over Eva's head at Gerta. "Where were you born, Beate?"

"Basel, Switzerland." Eva's delivery was not enthusiastic, but her voice had grown stronger and her hostility had faded.

"Tell me the names of your parents and siblings," Katrin prompted.

"My parents are Wolfgang and Katrin Kuehn." Eva

knew her material—clearly, she had studied, despite her reluctance. "My younger brother Basil has laryngitis and that's why he can't answer any questions. Adelina is our baby sister."

Katrin nodded, satisfied. Perhaps this sullen attitude would work in their favor more than a forced cheerfulness. A moody teenager would hardly raise eyebrows. In any case, Katrin suspected that when everything was in play, Eva would find extra motivation for her performance. "Well done. Just remember that you mustn't sound as if you're reciting lines you have learned. It must be real. Speak only when necessary. As much as possible, keep your answers to yes or no."

When Eva nodded, a flash of silver in the flickering light of the oil lamp caught Katrin's eye. Eva was wearing a necklace. The pendant was hidden under her clothing, but Katrin knew what it was—a Star of David. She had seen the girl looking at it a few days ago. Katrin hated what she had to do, but it was unavoidable. "Eva, I'm sorry, but you can't take that necklace with you. If the border guards doubt your papers, they may search you or your belongings. Your necklace could mean a death sentence for all of us."

"It was Mama's." Eva's nose wrinkled and she blinked hard. Even so, one tear and then another trickled down her cheek. Katrin had never seen Eva cry, but now she seemed about to dissolve into tears. "It's all I have left."

Katrin wrapped her arms around the girl and pulled her into a hug. "I know. Let me take care of it for you. When the war is over and things are right again, we'll find one another and I'll give it back."

Eva chewed her lip. For a moment Katrin wondered whether she would choose to wait out the war in the cellar. But at last she squared her shoulders and reached behind her neck to undo the clasp. She pulled the necklace free, fastened it again, and lowered it into Katrin's outstretched hand. "Take good care of it, please."

Katrin clutched the necklace for a moment, then slipped it into a pocket of her purse. "I will give it to Friedrich when he comes. He will keep it safe."

Eva smiled sadly. "Thank you. I have to go so I can take care of Dov... I mean Basil. I should get used to that."

Katrin gently squeezed her shoulder. "Ja, Beate. Go on now—it's late and you should sleep. We have a lot to do tomorrow."

She watched from the divan as Gerta walked Eva out of the sitting room toward the kitchen. With only an oil lamp for illumination, they would descend the steep staircase to the cellar, where they would spend the night with the other guests in their cozy hiding place. The false wall Franz had discovered had been installed by Friedrich and Herr Rothberg to house the first group of refugees they had brought here. Katrin wondered how many more might find safety behind that wall. *Please, Lord,* she prayed silently. *Let Franz make his choice for you.* She felt confident that Franz would not betray them, no matter how torn he was. But what if she had gone too far? What if he couldn't forgive her? She trembled at the thought. When Friedrich returned, she would know. If he returned. She had been praying throughout the day. For now, she would let it go. They were all in God's hands, not Franz's.

When all was quiet, she lit another oil lamp and moved to the kitchen. Hidden in the pantry behind a loose brick was a packet of onion skin paper. She plucked it from the space and carried it back to the sitting room, where she settled herself at her small writing desk. She set the lamp on the desk. Mama and Papa had decided long ago to leave the cottage as it was when Grandfather purchased it, without electricity. As a little girl, Katrin had thought it a grand adventure to stay there, but these days she had to admit she preferred electric lights to the flickering glow of the lamp. Still, there was something romantic about it. She smiled fleetingly. *If only Franz were still here. But are we even still engaged?*

Prayerfully dismissing her anxiety, she opened a desk drawer and took out a fountain pen. She withdrew the pages of stationery from the envelope and riffled through them to find a blank page. Then she began to write. When Friedrich had brought the first Jewish family to her, she had recorded each of their names and a little something about them. Though it could be dangerous to keep such records, Katrin felt it necessary. Now she would add this second group to it. Time and space would not allow for more than a brief entry on each guest, the friends she had grown to cherish, but there was much she would hold in her heart.

Samuel, Gerta, and Yair Fischer—father, mother, and three-year-old son. The little boy is a friendly child with bright, intelligent eyes and a mass of golden curls. Friedrich says he looks like a cherub in a Raphael painting. His parents want him to grow up free.

Eva Levy, fourteen. Daughter of Max and Rivka. Sister to Matthias and Ruth. I pray that she will find her family when the war ends, and I hope that when I meet her again, she will have joy in her eyes.

Jakob and Jonah Bergenthal, identical twins, ten. Orphans. Their father was Jewish and their mother a Gentile. Jakob is a thoughtful boy who wants to become a doctor. Jonah loves to read.

Leah and Rachel Eisenfeldt, twelve and eleven, daughters of Miriam. Beautiful girls. Rachel believes their mother will meet them in Switzerland. Leah doesn't. They have grown up in hiding. They often quarrel, but either one will leap to the other's defense if the need arises.

Dov Hoellenstein. Our silent boy. He latched onto Eva from the beginning. We know little about him, but the landlady who brought him to me said his father had been teaching him to play the violin.

Alina Tillinger, six months, daughter of Hannelore and Michael. Her Jewish father is probably in a labor camp. Her mother asked me to get Alina out of the country.

They had come as strangers. Now they were family. With the oil lamp running low, Katrin laid down the fountain pen. As she slid the pages back into their envelope, Gerta glided silently into the sitting room and returned to her spot on the divan. Katrin laid the envelope on the desk and moved to sit with her friend. "Gerta, are you all right?"

Gerta cleared her throat. Her fingers played with the fringe of her worn blue shawl. "I hope we are not too late. We should have left Germany years ago. My father tried to warn us, but we didn't want to go. We didn't believe things could get this bad." She dabbed at her eyes. "Katrin, we have no home. Our child has no home. We have shuffled from hiding place to hiding place like hunted animals." Blinking back tears, Gerta caught her breath and collected herself. Her red-rimmed eyes met Katrin's. "I am not so different from Eva. I just want to be myself again. To walk safely in the streets, to use my true name without fear, to light the Shabbat candles, to teach my son what it means to be Jewish."

Katrin's thoughts went back to early April, when she had asked Gerta what was needed to observe Passover. Of course, she could not get everything, even with the extra ration coupons Friedrich had provided to help feed her guests, but she had managed a couple of chickens, some bitter herbs, and enough apples and nuts for Gerta to make the sweet mixture she called charoset. And Ulrich had secretly baked unleavened bread.

The day after attending the Palm Sunday service with Franz, Katrin had traveled back to Friedrichsbrunn with Friedrich. They meant only to deliver the food and then to leave their Jewish friends to prepare their private celebration. But at a nod from Samuel, Gerta had taken Katrin by the arm and said, "Please. Stay. Eat with us."

And so they had gathered around the long table with Samuel at the head. When Gerta lit the candles, she covered her face and sang words in a language Katrin could not understand. Eva whispered a translation in her ear. "Blessed are You, Lord our God, King of the universe who has sanctified us with His commandments and commanded us to light the holiday candle." As Gerta continued in her deep alto voice, Katrin let the song soak into her, filling her with peace. The world may be in turmoil beyond the cottage walls, but God was here among them.

Now Katrin saw that her friend needed the words of strength that had been spoken that Passover night. She did not remember everything, but she could make a start. She looked at Gerta and reached to clasp her hands. "This is the bread of affliction that our fathers ate in Egypt."

Blinking back tears, Gerta gave a quick nod and responded, "Whoever is hungry, let him come and eat." She paused for a moment, sucked in a deep breath, and then continued. "We were slaves to Pharaoh in Egypt, and the Lord our God took us out from there with a strong hand and with an outstretched arm."

Katrin closed her eyes and spoke the words that had been inscribed on her heart. "Blessed is He who keeps his promise to Israel."

Gerta nodded. "In every generation, they seek our destruction and the Holy One, blessed be He, saves us from their hand. The Egyptians made us suffer and put hard work upon us. And we cried out to the Lord, the God of our fathers. The Lord heard our voice and saw our suffering."

Gerta's eyes glowed with new hope now. Her voice no longer trembled. "When the Lord will return the exiles of Zion, we will have been like dreamers. Then our mouth will have been filled with laughter, and our tongue with joyous song." The words, reminders of the ancient past, seemed written for today.

Katrin spoke up again. "You have redeemed us from Egypt."

Gerta smiled and, with a confident voice, announced, as Samuel had a month before, "You have freed us from the house of bondage. You have saved us from the sword and delivered us from pestilence. Your kindness has not forsaken us; do not abandon us, Lord our God, forever."

The Passover Seder was one of Katrin's fondest memories with the group at the cottage. It was a celebration of life, freedom, and God's unfailing love. Surely all but the youngest at the cottage had grasped the significance of the celebration to their lives. They were subsisting in a land of slavery and death and were about to undertake their own perilous exodus to find a new home, trusting in God to watch over their path and hold back the Angel of Death.

Katrin's guests were on the run, their lives hanging in the balance. But they were a proud people, a chosen people, and even now under the Nazi yoke, they had a freedom Hitler could never take away. The Führer wanted to blot out their names, their faces, their stories. But Passover held a promise that he would not succeed. There would always be a remnant, and as long as they remembered what God had done for them, they could never be defeated.

Eyes shining, Gerta squeezed Katrin's hands. "Don't forget us."

"Never." Katrin embraced her friend. Then she arose

and, taking the envelope from the desk, slipped out of the cottage through the back door. No one would see her on the path into the woods. The night was dark, but Katrin knew the way well. She had walked it many times as a child, enjoying the fragrant garden. The scent of honeysuckle and lilac hung in the night air, a pungent fragrance that tickled her nose.

Not far into the woods stood an old, gnarled oak tree. When she was small, Papa had helped her climb onto the lower branches, much to Mama's dismay. Near the base of the tree was a hollow just the right size to conceal one of Mama's old canning jars. Once it had held her childhood treasures. Now it would hold these names.

Katrin pulled out the jar, removed the lid, and stuffed the envelope inside. Then she tucked the jar back into the shadows. The tree had stood guard for centuries in these woods. Now it would safeguard the treasured names of this small remnant while Katrin did her best to get them out of Germany alive.

CHAPTER
20

3 MAY 1943

After bolting from the Weber cottage, Franz limped into the village, where he found a driver to take him to Thale. On the train to Berlin, he stared silently out the window as his stump shot through with pain.

The scenery made little impression on him. His mind was either exploding in a dozen directions at once or nearly blank. On the way to the cottage, he had been enveloped by uncertainty, anxious about what he might find; now he was terrified, and perhaps convicted, by what he did find. Sometimes he saw the faces, starting with the little girl in Kyiv. Then a family in Bila Tserkva who had been returned to the Einsatzgruppen by his men while he watched, after they had nearly succeeded in slipping through the perimeter. Then the faces of children he didn't know, hiding in a cellar, Katrin in their midst, her green eyes silently pleading. Then Pauli Bittner, a new addition to the photo album of Franz's shaken mind, taken because his life was deemed unworthy. Then the young Soldat, Ziemann—still handsome, before he fell under the tank—imploring Franz to do his duty. He wanted to, but what was his duty? It was not as clear as he once thought.

Then the faces were gone, leaving him alone to sort through his dilemma.

Father or Mother. His oath to Adolf Hitler or his confirmation oath. Hoyer or St. John. Georg or Friedrich, a development he had never anticipated. Career or Katrin. Safety for himself or safety for the people he loved most in the world. Everything in his life had been reduced to this moment.

Once Franz had reached Berlin, he went straight to his barracks and a dreamless sleep. When he awakened, the nightmare of the previous day remained with him. Now it was the final day of his furlough. Franz strolled along the Spree River he had hoped to enjoy with Katrin. Only he was alone, exhausted, and desperately seeking clarity. His stump still ached, but he ignored the pain. Or to be more precise, he embraced it as a fitting complement to his mental anguish. He would seek solace and wisdom where he and Katrin had attended services on Palm Sunday.

When he reached St. Luke Church, he found a pew about two-thirds of the way back. The sanctuary was empty. He sat and inhaled deeply, then slowly exhaled, his hands folded and squeezing each other tightly. He closed his eyes, tried to expel extraneous thoughts, and began to pray. *Herr Gott, I need your wisdom.* Franz paused while his mind replayed the scenes of Katrin urging him to choose, Katrin disappearing behind the cellar door. *Send your Holy Spirit to help me make sense of this. Help me choose what is right.*

Franz no longer needed convincing that the Nazis were not the saviors of Germany. He had seen their lies, their injustices, the blood on their hands. What they had done to his country and his countrymen. What they had done to him, to his soul.

But what could he do about it? What should he do? That was the question. He might deplore what he saw around him, but he could only control his own actions. What did his honor require? What was his obligation? Was betrayal ever the right answer to malfeasance by those in power?

He suddenly looked up to see a familiar face. Pastor Hoffmann had seated himself in the pew in front of Franz and had turned about to face him.

The pastor smiled. "Franz Maedler."

Franz cleared his throat. "Pastor, hello."

"It is good to see you. And it did my heart good to see you here on Palm Sunday."

"Katrin invited me." Franz relaxed a bit. "I'm glad I came."

Pastor Hoffmann studied Franz intently. "You're looking much better since the hospital, Franz."

"Thank you, Pastor. Your visits meant a lot to me. I'm not sure I ever told you."

"You didn't have to." Pastor Hoffmann shifted in the pew. His penetrating eyes pierced Franz. "Herr Hauptmann, is everything all right?"

Not sure how else to start the conversation, Franz had hoped the pastor would ask after him. Now that he had, Franz was momentarily flummoxed. He wiped his brow, took a deep breath, and began. "Pastor, I need your guidance." He looked behind him to make sure no one else was in the church. "I should not share the details, but lives are at stake. Can I trust you?"

The minister rubbed his clerical collar. "I think you know you can, Franz, or you wouldn't have come. In the hospital, I trusted you with thoughts you could have used to send me to prison."

Franz thought back. *If we have followed a false god, we*

must expect many Stalingrads. "True enough."

"Go on."

"Katrin and my brother have asked me to do something that would defy the state and break the sacred oath I took when I joined the Wehrmacht."

"And lives are at stake?"

"Yes. About a dozen, I think. Plus ours."

Hoffmann paused for a moment and raised his eyebrows.

Franz grimaced. "I know what you're getting at. But doesn't Scripture say to obey governing authorities?" He struggled to recall the verse from Romans that his unit's chaplain had repeated whenever anyone blanched at their orders. "For the powers that be are ordained of God. Whoever resists the power, resists the ordinance of God: and they that resist shall receive to themselves damnation."

Franz fidgeted on the pew and glanced up at the vaulted ceiling. The sun shone in through the lofty windows, bathing the bright white sanctuary in light. He remembered the feeling of comfort the chaplain's recitation had given him. To be freed from responsibility! God decrees that all we must do is obey those in authority! But the comfort had been temporary.

Pastor Hoffmann frowned. "Yes, Franz. We are to obey lawful authority. Have you read the rest of the chapter?"

Franz shook his head.

"Do you still carry the small Bible you had in the hospital?"

Franz nodded and pulled it out of his pocket.

Hoffmann directed Franz to find the passage in Romans 13. "Read it. And don't stop reading until you reach the end. Out loud."

When Franz read it in St. Luke, it sounded different than it had in the chaplain's harsh tone. The importance of obedience was matched by the importance of right and wrong. *Do that which is good,* and he will praise you. But *if you do that which is evil, be afraid,* for he bears the sword not in vain. He is God's servant, a revenger to execute wrath *upon him that does evil.*

Hoffmann interrupted. "Paul assumed that government's laws upheld the right and that violation of them advanced wrongdoing. But what was right was not malleable, it was the North Star." The pastor waited while Franz absorbed the point. "Authorities should enforce what is right, but they must not redefine it based on their self-serving whims. Right is defined by God."

As Franz resumed reading, the next verses clearly laid out his obligation: "Owe no man anything, but to love one another: for he that loves another has fulfilled the law. You shall love your neighbor as yourself. Love works no ill to its neighbor. Therefore love is the fulfilling of the law."

The pastor again interjected. "God's law, to which the state has a duty to conform. If the state does not conform, it is not lawful authority."

Franz pushed on. "It is high time to awake out of sleep: for now is our salvation nearer than when we first believed. The night is far spent, the day is at hand: let us therefore cast off the works of darkness, and let us put on the armor of light." He gently closed his Bible, set it on the bench, and drew a deep breath. When he was younger, he had been inspired by the Nazi slogan, "Germany, awake!" *I wasn't awake. I have been asleep, morally and spiritually. The night is far spent. The hour has come for me to awaken.*

"Franz, have you read the Catechism I brought you?"

"Yes, Pastor. But Luther called for obedience to civil authority on the basis of the Fourth Commandment. Civil rulers are like fathers and deserve the same respect." Those who despised authority, rebelled, or caused unrest would find no favor or blessing. Like the verses in Romans, this passage had also been underlined by the Nazis. He could not help but hesitate to defy rulers—or his father.

"Franz, don't forget that Luther was heavily influenced by Paul's letter to the Romans. His writings on the state parallel Paul's argument." Hoffmann adjusted his glasses. "The same section of the Catechism contained this admonition: It is just as important to preach to parents and rulers on how they should treat their children or their subjects, because..." The pastor drew out his words for emphasis. "...God does not want scoundrels or tyrants in authority."

Franz had read it recently and picked up the argument where Hoffmann had left it. "Instead, they should remember that they owe obedience to God and that one of their most important tasks is to raise children, or citizens, to honor God and to serve Him." The two sets of duties—parent and child, ruler and citizen—were intertwined and mutually obligatory.

The pastor leaned toward the soldier. "Franz, let me ask a question. Are the governing authorities following this instruction?"

Franz silently shook his head. The Nazis weren't. Neither was his father.

"Alright, let's look at this a different way." Pastor Hoffmann shifted in his seat. "Who were the biggest villains in Scripture? Who, not counting Christ Himself, were the biggest heroes?"

Franz catalogued the heroes. Some were kings, like David or Solomon, but no small number were men and women of faith who defied unjust authorities. Prophets—heroes—spoke the truth when kings did not want to hear it. Moses was the hero, Pharaoh the villain. Shadrach, Meshach, and Abednego the heroes, Nebuchadnezzar the villain. Daniel the hero, Darius the villain. The early

Christians the heroes, emperors like Nero and Diocletian, villains.

"Yes." Hoffmann gripped the top of the pew tightly. "Time after time, the villains were political authorities who wanted to be treated like gods. The heroes were the ones who refused to bow down to them. Even Luther defied the Holy Roman Emperor: 'Here I stand, I can do no other.'"

Hoffman's line of discussion brought Franz back to his father's Hoyer painting, with Hitler treated as The Word himself. *You shall have no other gods before me.* The Führer, to whom Franz had sworn allegiance, was not only a liar, a tyrant, and a fool, conclusions which Franz had already reached. He was squarely in the company of Nero, Nebuchadnezzar, Darius, and Pharaoh.

"So Franz, do you see? When the state demands that we do evil or look away while it does evil, we must obey God rather than men, as Peter said in Jerusalem." Pastor Hoffmann rubbed at his neck. "Does that describe your situation?"

This time, Franz did not hesitate. "Pastor, it sounds like all of Germany's situation." *Love does no harm to its neighbor.* How many neighbors had been harmed? Neighbors in the foxhole next to Franz. Neighbors across the street, hauled away in the middle of the night. Neighboring countries devastated and under a yoke, their people sent to Germany to labor, sent to camps, or left hanging in the breeze for daring to resist. The faces he had been seeing for months? He saw them again. Each one was a neighbor who had been harmed.

The pastor homed in on the fundamental question facing Franz. "If your obligation is to love your neighbor, what does that mean for you?"

Franz knew from the Catechism that Luther had declared that the Fifth Commandment prohibition on murder was violated not only when we do evil, but when we could save others from harm and fail to do so.

Hoffmann took a deep breath, then spoke slowly and firmly, enunciating each syllable. "If you see anyone who is condemned to death or in similar peril but do not save him although you have means and ways to do so, you have killed him."

Franz blanched. *You have killed him.* This assertion was as straightforward as it could be. It was more than a condemnation of his past—it made a demand of his present, utterly lacking in ambiguity. Those were hard words.

Franz could say nothing for a moment, while Hoffmann studied his pained face. Then, "Pastor, have you read Bonhoeffer?"

"He was my teacher," Hoffmann replied with a smile.

Franz scrunched his face. He had tried reading *Discipleship,* but it was a sophisticated theological work by a brilliant theologian. He had managed to plow through no more than a third of it. "I'm a soldier, Pastor, a practical man. Not a scholar. *Discipleship* is hard reading, but I am taken with Bonhoeffer's words about 'Cheap grace' and 'costly grace.' It's the heart of his argument. I want to be sure I understand."

Hoffmann was quiet. He looked to the ceiling, crossed his arms, inhaling and exhaling several times. Finally, he asked a simple question. "Do you want grace?"

"Pastor, I want to be able to ask God for forgiveness, to be forgiven, to be absolved and at peace."

"Have you felt that forgiveness since you came home?"

"Not at first. I started to when you came to the hospital." Franz nodded. "At the Communion rail on Palm Sunday, I felt peace for the first time in years."

"Franz, was that all you felt?"

He shook his head. "No, Pastor. I felt as if the Lord was

summoning me, calling me." He had quietly thrilled to that call to a deeper relationship with God, to live out his reviving faith in a meaningful way. But he had also feared it and tried to control and submerge it. Pastor Hoffmann raised his eyebrows. "Franz, I think that is what Bonhoeffer means by 'costly grace.'" The minister then recited his teacher's words from memory. "Costly grace is the treasure hidden in the field; for the sake of it a man will gladly go and sell all that he has. It is the call of Jesus Christ at which the disciple leaves his nets and follows him." He paused briefly, then finished the quotation. "Such grace is *costly* because it calls on us to follow, and it is grace because it calls us to follow *Jesus Christ*. It is costly because it costs a man his life, and it is grace because it gives a man the only true life."

Franz took a moment to absorb the words. Though he had once acted as if he did not know what Katrin wanted from him, deep down he had known all along. Katrin wanted him to live by "costly grace." What should he do? Luther had given Franz a characteristically blunt answer, Bonhoeffer a characteristically elegant one. But they were the same answer.

"Pastor, thank you." Franz reached over the pew to take the Pastor's left hand in both of his. Hoffmann had never told him what to do, never made demands. He had quietly, methodically, led Franz to his own conclusions.

Hoffmann looked Franz in the eye. "Will you be all right? Do you have the answer to your dilemma?"

"Yes, Pastor. I have the answer. And I will be all right." Franz's mouth curled upward at the corners. "My soul will, at any rate."

"I'm glad you came." The pastor squeezed Franz's hand, stood, and slowly walked to the aisle.

"Pastor—" Franz called after him in a stage whisper.

"Please pray for me. And for Katrin and Friedrich."

Pastor Hoffmann turned back toward Franz. "You know I will, Franz." His eyes seemed to brim with new tears. "As I have been."

Left alone in his pew, Franz knew what he had to do. The Bolsheviks were evil, the British ruthless. But he could no longer justify and excuse the Nazis. Indeed, he could no longer obey them. Friedrich was right. The vicious band that most threatened Germany was the National Socialist dictatorship itself.

For a moment, Franz was back in the East, writing a letter. "Herr and Frau Ziemann..." Then he was reading a letter from Father explaining that Georg was dead. Then he was standing on the side of the road in Kyiv, retching into the gutter after a sergeant killed a little girl's family. For what? He was no longer merely disillusioned. He was repulsed. It was no betrayal of Germany to oppose the regime. The regime itself was a betrayal of Germany—including Georg, including Ziemann and the rest of his men, as well as the Germans hiding at the Weber cottage, hoping desperately to avoid the Kyivan girl's fate.

Franz would not look the other way when he could stop a murder; he would embrace the costly grace God had invited him to. Perhaps he would never have come fully around to this incendiary conclusion if he had not been forced into the stark choice he now faced. But here he was.

Franz uncrossed his legs and planted both his feet, one real and one artificial, on the floor. He looked up at the cross above the altar. *Greater love hath no man.* He suspected that the Gestapo wouldn't call it love.

Tomorrow would be a new day. Back to work at the Bendlerblock. Back to work in Carpool. Back to work where there were vehicles and fuel.

CHAPTER
21

Friedrich had returned to Berlin, leaving Katrin to prepare the guests for transport, and was back at his desk in the Bendlerblock. Though he worked hard to hide it, he felt emotionally spent by the confrontation with Franz, the constant need to bury his feelings toward Katrin, and the general stress of being on the verge of a major operation with innocent lives at stake. At the same time, an unaccustomed relief had washed over him when he had shared the truth with his brother. All his cards were now on the table.

He expected that Franz was back at work, too. Friedrich had gotten Franz placed in OKH Carpool in anticipation of just the sort of emergency they now faced. He had expected to spin some story to get Franz's help without giving up the true nature of the requisition. Now Franz knew everything. He had vehicles and fuel but couldn't be manipulated into making them available. He would have to want to help.

Friedrich studied the family picture on his desk. His chest tightened. Poor Franz. His problem wasn't that he had no compass. His problem was that he had two compasses, and one was broken. Would he follow the right one?

Ever since Franz had stormed out of the cottage, Friedrich had turned that question over in his head. He had grown to manhood with Franz, spent countless hours with him, mourned Mama and then Georg with him. Yet their lives as brothers would come down to this. Friedrich would walk to the other end of the Bendlerblock, and at the end of his walk he would either find a co-conspirator or be arrested.

After a harrowing journey through the long corridors and columned halls, Friedrich stopped at the door to Carpool for a moment. Sending a silent prayer heavenward, he squared his shoulders and prepared for whatever he would find on the other side of the door. He wondered briefly how it could be more nerve wracking to face his own brother than to plot treason. At last, he pushed through the door and strode to Franz's desk.

In the background, the radio conveyed the latest bulletins from OKW. "The Luftwaffe has completed its redeployment from Africa to strengthen the defenses of the Reich in higher priority regions." Friedrich knew the Luftwaffe had evacuated Tunisia because the Axis position was on the verge of collapse. *More Germans killed by Nazi arrogance.* But he would ruminate on Africa later.

"Good morning, Franz," Friedrich offered, as coolly as possible. He could not act as if anything was different.

Franz looked up and closed the file he was working on. His eyes were calm, his jaw set. To Friedrich, he appeared at peace but resolute. As if he had made a decision. That could be good or bad. "Friedrich," he said. "Could we take a walk?"

"I generally like a walk, but it all depends on where we would be walking." Friedrich hadn't been arrested—yet— but he remained on guard in case Franz was leading him into a trap.

Franz pushed back from his desk and reached for his cane. He said nothing more until they had left the Carpool offices. "I missed breakfast. Let's go to the cafe. I could use the fresh air."

"We eat there all the time. There's a food stand in the Tierpark that you should try." The cafe was a popular location for those who worked in the Bendlerblock. A place Friedrich preferred to avoid today.

Soon they stepped outside onto the Bendlerstrasse. They turned left and headed toward the Tierpark, talking about trivial matters. As they waited to cross Tiergartenstrasse, Franz asked after Katrin. "How's my girl?"

Friedrich looked both ways for traffic. "She's fine, Franz. You will have to talk to her soon." He spared Franz the detail that she had wept for her fiancé after he left the cottage.

The pair crossed the street and soon plunged into the woods of the Tiergarten, following a path that led to the small food stand Friedrich had in mind. Here amid the linden and maple trees, he felt at peace.

The brothers returned to trivialities while waiting in line. "Have you been busy today in Carpool?" Friedrich asked. He glanced at Franz frequently as they waited their turn, trying to read him. Franz's furrowed brow suggested a headache. Or it could be anxiety. But that didn't tell Friedrich much—his brother was bound to be anxious no matter what choice he'd made.

"No more than usual. I won't bother asking how things are in Abwehr." Friedrich allowed himself a chuckle at Franz's reply, using it to cover up his own nerves. The tension was growing. *Franz is taking too long to show his hand.*

They carried their sausages to an isolated bench where they could speak more freely. Franz took a bite, then leaned in.

"I'm in," he said quietly. Even in this peaceful place, unfriendly ears might be listening.

Friedrich smiled—and breathed. He lay a hand on Franz's shoulder as unexpected emotions crowded in on him. Relief, brotherly pride, fear for Franz's safety.

"So, what do we do next?" Franz asked with a wry laugh. "I'm afraid I'm not as practiced at sneaking around as you are."

"Well, we need either one truck or four cars. You're the carpool man. What can you do?"

"A single truck would be easiest to explain. Four cars will raise questions. I'll need a requisition form and a reason my boss will believe."

"A single truck it is." Friedrich paused for a moment, the wheels turning in his head. This group was bigger than the last and would have to be split up. "I'll drive it to Friedrichsbrunn, pick up the group after dark, and drive them close to the border, where they'll catch trains."

Friedrich paused. How many times had he and Franz plotted together as boys, dreaming up childish mischief? It felt good to be conspiring again. "I'll drop them in four groups at different stations along the line to Bregenz." He was concerned about the train. They had used it before, but one never knew what would come of nosy conductors, SS men sharing the compartment, or other random dangers. And this time, there were more children. He would try to limit the risk by keeping their time on the train to a minimum and by utilizing a sleepy border crossing. "And I will arrange the requisition. Better if it doesn't come from me."

Friedrich knew the risks. Last year, Hans von Dohnanyi had organized Operation Seven that saved fifteen Jews by getting them to Switzerland under the guise that Abwehr was sending them to South America as German agents.

Von Dohnanyi was under arrest now, and it was unclear how much the Gestapo knew.

"Bregenz is small, not so well-guarded." Franz leaned in toward Friedrich, keeping his voice low. "It's good, but how will you get them into Switzerland? I thought the Swiss were sending back anyone who enters illegally."

"For now, they are letting in children under sixteen and their parents, but no one knows how long that will last." Friedrich scratched his head. No one could be quite sure what the Swiss were going to do from day to day. "To be safe, my friends have created papers for them that are perfect forgeries of Swiss papers. It'll create fewer questions on the German side, and hopefully the Swiss will think they belong there and leave them alone. If the Swiss catch them, then they will officially be refugees under the current policy." He shrugged. "It is better to ask forgiveness than permission."

Franz nodded, then stuffed another bite of sausage into his mouth. "I asked forgiveness," he said thoughtfully. "From God. Yesterday. I should ask you and Katrin too."

"I can't speak for Katrin, but you don't owe me any apology. You've done me no wrong. Well, except for slugging me." Friedrich, who had finished eating, fished for his napkin.

Franz raised an eyebrow and almost smiled. "I'm not apologizing for that. You deserved it."

Friedrich laughed, then grew serious. "Two days ago, you were debating whether to turn us in."

"I know."

Friedrich's eyes narrowed. "What happened, Brother?" He looked around, scanning for threats. "Not that I'm complaining, mind you."

Franz finished off his sausage. After he swallowed, he wiped grease from his face and hands. "I had a lot of thinking to do. About my oath, my duty. I went back to St. Luke, and Pastor Hoffmann was there. We talked."

"Go on." Friedrich locked eyes with Franz.

"Someday I'll tell you everything." Franz paused briefly. "We discussed our Christian duty to obey lawful government, and how that duty ends when government becomes unlawful in God's sight. We talked about how not stopping a murder is the same as being a murderer."

Friedrich nodded.

"Have you read Bonhoeffer's *Discipleship?*" Franz asked.

The question caught Friedrich off guard. He shook his head. "By the time it was published, I was already diving into my National Socialist cover. I couldn't risk being seen with it."

Franz went on. "I haven't read most of it, either. But what I have read stuck with me, and Pastor Hoffmann helped me understand. It is not enough to stray from God and ask forgiveness. You have to drop your nets and follow Him. I've dropped my nets."

Friedrich stroked his chin. "This is how you decided?"

"The condensed version." Franz sighed. "I'm not proud of how long it took me to get there."

Friedrich smiled and put his hand on Franz's back. "Where you end up is more important than how long it takes." His brother was a good man whose sense of honor had been manipulated to serve dishonorable forces. But now that was over and the brothers were united. Friedrich returned to the practical issues at hand. "What about fuel?"

For a moment, Franz furrowed his brow and chewed his lower lip. Then his brow smoothed. "I can get you an Opel Blitz. If you start with a full tank, you'll need to refill three times to get there and back. I can arrange enough ration cards. I just hope I don't end up like the fellow I replaced. He was shot for selling fuel on the black market."

Friedrich winced. "Be careful, Brother. None of us have any margin for error." He looked around, then back at Franz. "Can we do it tomorrow? Katrin needs a day to get everyone ready, but we shouldn't wait any longer. Keeping that many supplied is difficult. You already showed how vulnerable they are, and with warmer weather the cottages nearby will start filling up. And with Oster and von Dohnanyi under arrest, our support system in Abwehr is crumbling."

"Do you have their train tickets?"

"They'll buy the tickets themselves when they get to the stations." Friedrich smiled. He imagined Franz was trying to work out how bereft Jews on the run would pay their fare. "With Reichsmarks, like everyone else." It was a beautiful thing to work for an agency that had a slush fund for "irregular operations." The Abwehr was one part of the Wehrmacht that was expected to do things under the table. After the fact, there could be the devil to pay. The Gestapo was always on the lookout for ways to trip up Abwehr, and indications had dribbled out that von Dohnanyi and Bonhoeffer had been charged with misuse of funds. But for now, the money was in Friedrich's pocket.

A smile slowly crossed Franz's face as he balled up his trash and tossed it into the nearby rubbish bin. "No time like the present."

The men rose from the bench, but Friedrich reached out to grasp Franz's arm before they started the walk back to the Bendlerblock. "Franz... there's one more thing." When Franz looked at him, Friedrich couldn't meet his eyes. "Katrin is going, too. One of Father Fellner's chaperones is too sick to travel. There's no one else. I'm sorry."

Franz stood still, clenched his fists, and took a deep breath. Then he exhaled slowly. "No time like the present."

CHAPTER

22

Franz sat at his desk in the Bendlerblock, tapping his fingers on his desk and attempting to work.

It was a spring day in Berlin with temperatures in the sixties. Neither hot nor cold. Neither sunny nor raining. Just in between. In contrast, Franz's days of in-between had reached an end. Today, he would cross the line into opposition. If things went well, he would help save some lives. If things didn't, he might lose his own. Katrin and Friedrich were also hanging in the balance. There was no more splitting the difference. The thought sent his heart racing. It also sent a thrill of freedom through him.

Friedrich had told him that an unusual requisition would be his signal to spring into action. In the meantime, he tried to focus on his other tasks. More than once, he closed his eyes for a brief moment of prayer. The wait was excruciating, and pressure built in his chest throughout the day.

At last, in the late afternoon, the moment came. A requisition from Abwehr, delivered by courier, dated two days ago and signed by Captain E. Fredericksmeyer. It was for one transport truck and fuel enough for a trip to near the Swiss border and back. The reason was listed as classified emergency transport of intelligence assets.

Carpool was first and foremost for the use of Army High Command—people who went to meet with Hitler to make big decisions about the war and their immediate staff. Abwehr and OKM occasionally tapped into Carpool, but only as long as OKH needs were otherwise met. And only if approved by Colonel Muntzer.

Over time, Muntzer and Franz had formed an almost-familial relationship. Muntzer's nephew was still missing in action, and Franz had determined the nephew's unit had been stationed a few blocks away from his own when he had lost his foot. After his first day in Carpool, when he arrived at Muntzer's office at 08:04, Franz had always been on time, a punctuality that his superior equated with respect. Moreover, he took his job seriously: "An auto keeps a meeting, a meeting moves a regiment..." On more than a few occasions, Muntzer invited Franz into his office to share a smoke and ask him about Stalingrad. Once it was a smoke and a glass of schnapps. It turned out Muntzer and his wife had no children. His nephew had been the closest thing.

Franz could never quite tell where Muntzer stood on the war, the Nazi Party, Hitler. And he never felt it wise to press. The colonel put on an impressive show of dedication and military bearing but in private moments did not seem so sure. Franz had genuinely grown to like the man, which made what he was about to do nag at his conscience. But not nearly enough to outweigh the need to prevent the murder of Katrin's Jewish guests.

He strode to Muntzer's door and knocked, mustering as much confidence as he could.

"Come." The colonel's voice was distant, preoccupied.

"Herr Oberst, we have received a special requisition that requires your approval." Franz thrust the form at Muntzer.

"I see. Abwehr." The colonel put on his glasses and scanned the form carefully while Franz worked hard to mask his nervousness. *I've been shot at by T-34s and lived to tell about it. This is nothing.*

Muntzer ticked off the key elements of the request. "Truck. Swiss border. Forty-eight hours. Classified." He set the form on his desk and took off his glasses. "This is quite unusual."

"We get them from time to time." Franz affected a tone of disinterest. "Remember it was, what, maybe six weeks ago? They needed a staff car because one of theirs broke down."

"Right. Can we spare the truck?"

"Yes, sir." Franz had checked this morning to assure an Opel Blitz was available. If another OKH request had come in for it, it would have gone missing.

"I need to make a call."

Franz watched as Muntzer dialed his telephone. He pieced together the conversation based on Muntzer's half.

"Put me through to Abwehr. Fredericksmeyer."

There was a pause on the other end, then a muffled voice.

"Captain Fredericksmeyer... Oh, I see. This is Muntzer. OKH Carpool. We have received a requisition from Fredericksmeyer, and I need to verify it..." He wiped his forehead. His frustration was beginning to show. "I see. Well, who is in charge of the operation? ... Of course, I understand." Muntzer sighed and leaned back in his chair. "I have taken enough of your time."

The colonel looked stumped. He pulled out a cigarette and lit it, this time not bothering to offer one to Franz. "Fredericksmeyer left for Spain two days ago. He cannot be reached. The requisition form was lost in a shuffle and delivered to us late. There can be no delay. And the mission is a classified intelligence mission so no one can tell me who is in charge now." The colonel took a drag on his cigarette. "Maedler, I need you to go to Abwehr and verify this."

"Yes, sir." A smile creased Franz's face. Without knowing it, Muntzer had set a wolf to guard the sheep.

Franz retrieved the requisition form, saluted, and opened the door. Muntzer returned the salute. "And Maedler, remember to close my door."

Twelve minutes later, Franz reached Friedrich's desk. Except Friedrich wasn't there. He was sitting two desks down, behind a nameplate that read "E. Fredericksmeyer." So, today, Friedrich was Fredericksmeyer. Franz marched over and took a seat across from him. "Were you just on the phone with my boss?" he ventured.

Friedrich shrugged. "Maybe."

Franz looked around the room. "Where's Fredericks-meyer?"

"Spain." Friedrich picked a telegram off of the desk and handed it to Franz. ABWEHR EYES ONLY***EF DEAD-***REQUEST INSTRUCTIONS***STATION BARCELONA 04.05.43

Franz cocked his head, his eyes widening, and handed the telegram back to his brother. "Muntzer wasn't satisfied. He wants verification."

Friedrich shrugged. "No one here can give it by name without compromising operational security. Standard procedure."

"Of course." Franz rolled his eyes. "Can someone send a note *not* by name?"

Friedrich took a packet of sodium bicarbonate from his jacket pocket, poured it into a glass of water, shook the glass, and gulped the contents. He pulled a blank piece of paper out of Fredericksmeyer's desk, jotted down a note, and handed it to Franz. *05.05.43. Oberst Muntzer: Abwehr verifies E. Fredericksmeyer requisition order. Urgent. You will be responsible for mission failure if not approved.*

Franz looked at Friedrich, raised an eyebrow, and let a modest smile crease his face. "Thank you, Brother. I will call Fredericksmeyer's number to let you know when it is settled."

"Thank you, Hauptmann." Friedrich winked, and Franz left the room.

Exactly twelve minutes later, he returned to Carpool. Again, he knocked on Colonel Muntzer's door.

"Come."

Franz opened the door and stepped through, suppressing a cough. Muntzer was still smoking, though it looked like a new cigarette. The door was closed, the windows shut, and Franz entered to a cloud of smoke. "Sir, I went to Abwehr and received verification. They are quite anxious to get moving." He handed the note to Muntzer, watched his eyes follow the text, and waited for his reaction.

The colonel lost some color as he read. "Who wrote this? It isn't signed."

Franz attempted an innocent expression. "They won't sign for the same reason they won't tell you over the phone. If you ask me, they take this quest for operational security a little too seriously. But they are spies, after all. It's the best I could do."

Muntzer shook his head. "Your brother is in Abwehr, isn't he?"

"As a matter of fact, yes." Franz's mind raced to address this latest question without giving anything away. "I stopped by his desk to see if he could give me any greater clarity, but he wasn't there."

"And the person who wrote this?" The colonel cocked

his head quizzically.

"Seems to know what is going on. Whatever his name is." Not untrue, but Franz hoped the questions would end soon. He lacked confidence in his ability to dissemble like Friedrich.

Muntzer thought out loud, shaking his head and muttering under his breath. "This is all highly unusual. Highly unusual. But it is Abwehr, so what should I expect?" He shifted in his seat. "And Maedler checked it out, at least as far as anyone can check anything out in Abwehr. There could be German agents at risk... Responsible for mission failure if not approved." His head stopped wagging and he plucked his pen from the desk. After one last look, he signed his name below Fredericksmeyer's and handed it back to Franz.

Franz had to work to hide his relief. "Thank you, sir. I will process this immediately."

After saluting through the cloud of smoke, Franz took the approved requisition to Major Kobel and held it up for him to see. "Major, the colonel has approved a special request from Abwehr. They will need a full tank here and ration cards for three refills. They will be assigned an Opel Blitz."

"Let me see that, Captain." Kobel squinted and spun his mustache while he read over the order. "This request is two days old. Why are we just getting it now?"

Always a stickler for detail, that Kobel. "Apparently it got lost in their paperwork machine. Now it's a rush."

"I see that." Kobel hesitated a minute, then did a quick calculation with paper and pencil. When he was done, he took a key from his pocket, unlocked the cabinet by his desk, and counted out petrol cards. "Tell them not to lose any of these, or they'll be walking home."

"Yes, sir. Thank you." After he saluted and spun around,

Franz sighed. *Almost there.*

Franz's final stop was a visit with Sergeant Schuchart at the message center. Schuchart, as usual, was a bit rumpled. "Sergeant, the colonel has approved a special requisition. We need an Opel Blitz fueled up and ready to go within the hour." Franz handed Schuchart the order.

"Sir, most requests come through the message center. Why didn't this one?" Schuchart was no detail-monger like Kobel, but he was a practical soldier who was bothered by discrepancies.

Franz took a step toward the sergeant. He lowered his voice but grew more intense. "It's Abwehr. It's classified, it's urgent, and it came directly to me for processing. The colonel has approved it and will be held responsible if there is any delay. That means you will be held responsible if there is any delay." Franz pointed his index finger at Schuchart's chest. "Am I understood?"

Schuchart took a step back and looked away. "Yes, sir. Perfectly."

Franz didn't like throwing his weight around, but in this army, the best defense was a good offense. He softened his tone. "Sergeant, thank you for your help. I know you only want to make sure everything is done properly. But German lives are at stake." True enough.

Schuchart relaxed in turn. "Yes, sir. I will call the order down right away."

As soon as Franz knew the call had been made, he returned to his desk and called the building operator. "Abwehr, please. Captain Fredericksmeyer."

The phone rang twice before someone picked it up without speaking. That should be Friedrich.

Following his brother's instructions, Franz said as little as possible. "Fifteen minutes." Click.

At 18:07, Franz made his way to the Carpool garage.

When he arrived, he confidently told the attendant, "Sergeant Schuchart called down a few minutes ago for an Opel Blitz. I am to hand it over to the driver personally. It's for a classified operation. No out-take paperwork. Orders of Colonel Muntzer. I will see to its return."

The attendant, a callow youth, gave way without contest. "Yes, sir."

"Show me where it is, give me the key, and make yourself scarce."

"Yes, sir." The spindly young private took Franz to the back of the garage, where a two-year-old Opel transport truck sat, newly washed and filled with petrol. "Keys are in the ignition." Then he turned and ambled out of the garage, fumbling with his cigarette case. He seemed happy to take orders. Probably just relieved to be posted in Berlin instead of Russia or Africa.

Franz had kept his nerves bundled up tight all day. Now he felt like shouting or sprinting, doing anything to release his energy. He had succeeded. Then he sobered up. He was the most exposed of any of them, at least for the moment. He was the only one with fingerprints on the operation so far. Fredericksmeyer hadn't really approved the requisition; he had died in Spain yesterday. Franz had received the requisition and gotten Muntzer's blessing. The Abwehr verified it, but the verification was unsigned. Franz had procured the verification and convinced Muntzer. Franz had even finagled his way into taking the dispatcher's place and handing off the truck to an Abwehr officer no one else had seen, a serious breach of protocol. If someone started poking around, that would add up to a lot of unanswered questions.

Franz said a prayer. "Lord, you've brought me to this. I want to do the right thing. Please let this work." Short and to the point.

Two minutes later, Friedrich entered the garage and made his way to the Opel Blitz. Though he often worked in civilian clothes, he had donned his uniform for the drive.

Franz took a long look at his brother. "Here are the petrol ration cards. Be careful."

Friedrich took the cards, tucked them in the inside pocket of his jacket, and embraced Franz. "Thank you, Franzi." He stood back and winked. "We couldn't have done this without you." With that, he climbed into the driver's seat.

Franz turned to walk back to his office, then turned again to face his brother. "Friedrich..." His voice cracked, and he swallowed hard against a lump in his throat. "Give Katrin my love. Go with God."

CHAPTER
23

5 MAY 1943

Friedrich had been driving for an hour. Two more hours remained before he reached Katrin and the cottage guests, those ten lives trusting him to help them reach safety. He breathed a prayer that all would go smoothly tonight. No prying eyes. No mechanical break-down. The latter was less likely than the former. The three-ton Opel Blitz 3.6 was the motorized workhorse of the Wehrmacht. With a six-cylinder, seventy-five horsepower engine, it was powerful enough to pull artillery, haul ammunition, or carry a load of people under its canvas cover. But even a workhorse could go lame.

The cottage guests would split into four groups. Friedrich would drop one near the Buchloe station. The next he would deposit near the Kaufbeuren station, and the last two near Kempten, closest to the border. Everyone would catch the first train to Switzerland through Bregenz except the second group at Kempten, which would take the second train. Four groups, three stations, two trains. Even if something went wrong, they couldn't all be caught at once.

Friedrich's chest burned, but there wasn't much he could do about it. The scope of the operation made him nervous. The previous group had been a family of five. This was more complicated. His mind focused on everything that would have to go right. First, he had to make it to Friedrichsbrunn without mechanical trouble and without being delayed by the authorities.

Once he got to Friedrichsbrunn, he would drive the truck up to the cottage, potentially drawing attention by belching noise and fumes all the way down the gravel road, in order to load his passengers. The truck was designed to seat two in the cab and ten soldiers with gear in the back on two seats facing each other. Friedrich and Samuel would sit up front, leaving Gerta, Father Fellner and his associate Estella, Katrin, and eight children in back.

After they boarded, Friedrich would drive for hours, again hoping for no mechanical failures or checkpoints. Then he would find a safe spot to drop each group. They would have to buy their tickets, show their papers, board the trains, show their papers again, and endure two or three hours on the train, with no control over who might be seated near them. Friedrich had tried to minimize their exposure, but there were still a million ways it could go wrong.

Then, while he was driving the Opel back to Berlin, his charges would be trying to cross into Switzerland through SS border controls without breaking down into a puddle of overwrought nerves. On the other side, the minders would turn the children over to Katrin's brother Reinhold, whose church would take them in and help them blend into Swiss life. Their task completed, they would return home.

When Friedrich and his Opel Blitz reached the cottage in Friedrichsbrunn, it had been dark for half an hour. After he turned onto the dirt road, he had to pass three cottages before reaching the Webers', a few hundred meters further on. He shifted down and slowed to twenty-five kilometers an hour to limit the noise. About a hundred meters from the Weber cottage, he turned off the headlights and slowed to a crawl.

At last, he came to a stop in front of the sanctuary, exited the truck, and walked toward the front door.

It was now or never. A dozen lives were hanging in the balance, and he did not intend to fail them.

~

Katrin bit her lip as she watched out the front window. Behind her in the small sitting room stood the entire coterie of passengers. She had spent the last few days drilling them on their new names, details they would need to know if they were asked questions, and basic rules of safe behavior. *Don't make a scene. Don't act as if anything is wrong. Don't stare at soldiers or SS men. Say as little as possible. Don't use your real names, even if you think you're alone.*

After Friedrich had left for Berlin, Katrin had walked into Friedrichsbrunn each afternoon in order to be standing by the pay phone at the marketplace at five. Today he had called with a short, simple message. "21:15. Truck." She hurried back to the cottage. They had spent the last few hours cleaning and removing all signs that the little cottage had hosted guests. The cots had been dismantled, their parts hastily reassembled into a row of wine racks. The bedding had been carefully folded in the linen closet.

Shortly before nine, Father Fellner arrived with his associate, who went by Estella, a woman of about thirty with short, brown hair. As he passed through the door, Father Fellner gently touched Katrin's arm. "We must trust God. He will see us through."

She responded with a tight nod, trying to settle her nerves with deep, calm breaths. While she was helping the guests prepare for their departure, she had been able to distract herself from the fear that had settled like a stone in her gut. Now the work was done and there was only the waiting. Katrin had reconciled herself to the dangers inherent in hiding her guests; the dangers involved in crossing the border with them were far worse.

A tremble passed through her. If only she had refused! The thought of capture by the SS terrified her—not the prospect of death but being tortured and wasting away, starving and filthy, in some place like Dachau. But she was even more afraid of looking into Eva's eyes and telling her that she and Dov were staying in Germany because Katrin couldn't go through with it. She lay a hand on Dov's head and mustered a silent prayer. *Please, Father. Help me trust you.*

So here she was, waiting for Friedrich. When she heard the truck at 21:16, she turned to face her guests. The small sitting room was filled with nervous, wide-eyed people. She could not show her fear. "Our transport is here. We must go quickly and quietly. Say nothing. Once I open the door, we have two minutes to get to the truck and get in." Her eyes scanned the group. Then, with a simple "Go!" she pushed the door open and stepped aside.

Katrin watched as Samuel went first to assist Friedrich in helping the children into the back of the truck. Then the older children filed past Katrin, one by one. Father Fellner, Gerta, and Estella were next to leave, shepherding the little ones while Katrin locked up the cottage.

~

Friedrich met Katrin in the yard and handed her freshly minted Swiss papers. Together, they followed the last group to the back of the truck and watched as they scrambled in. Friedrich nodded to Estella as she passed by. "Sister Klara Marie."

She nodded back. "Herr Maedler."

After seeing the final passengers aboard, Friedrich hung back awkwardly, avoiding Katrin's eyes, uncertain what to do with the wave of longing that passed through him. Katrin was radiant. Strong, kind, passionate. His arms itched to pull her into a hug, but he squeezed them to his sides instead. Katrin didn't feel anything for him. Whenever she said Franz's name, Friedrich could hear the love in her voice, see it in her eyes. Shoving his hands in his pants pockets, he bent close so he could whisper in her ear. Her skin smelled of lavender. "Katrin, your fiancé did well. He sends his love." In the moonlight, he could see a smile crease her face. He stepped back quickly, turning his attention where it belonged. "Get in. We need to leave."

Samuel helped Katrin into the truck, then moved around to climb into the passenger seat. Once the passengers had tied shut the canvas flaps across the back, Friedrich bounded to the driver's seat and started the Blitz. There were another seven cottages before they would loop back to the main road. Altogether, ten opportunities for suspicion. Most did not have electricity, and several seemed altogether empty, but a few had lights on or smoke escaping their chimneys. They could only drive. And hope.

Once he had made his way to the Reichsautobahn 9, Friedrich picked up some speed. A speed limit of eighty kilometers an hour had been imposed on the Autobahn. The Blitz was straining at sixty-five. Few private cars were permitted, though bicycles were recently allowed because traffic was so light. During the long, tedious ride Friedrich briefly heard raised voices in the back. It was to be expected that tensions would flare, but they were lucky the disturbance didn't happen when they were stopped in a city. Halfway to Kempten, he found a station where he could trade in some ration cards for petrol. Friedrich hoped for a quick and uneventful stop, but after he handed over the ration coupons, the drunk attendant began asking questions.

"Where are you ... you go-going with that truck?"

"Abwehr business," Friedrich responded with assurance. "You are best advised not to ask."

"Right... And I'm Heinrich Himmler." The attendant let out a loud belch and stumbled backwards a bit.

Friedrich clenched his teeth, then growled out, "Friend, it is unwise to mock Himmler. I'll show you my papers."

"I'm not your friend..." The drunk noticed Samuel in the cab. "Who's that in the truck?"

"He's with me. Abwehr business, remember?" Friedrich pulled out his Abwehr identification and held it open.

Easily distracted, the attendant refocused on Friedrich, to the extent he was capable of focusing at all. "You don't look like the fellow in the picture. Do I have to call the police?"

Friedrich was part worried, part bemused. He had run many operations, including this one, in which forged documents with fake identities were essential to success. Now he was showing his real documents and this man didn't trust them. "Look closer."

The man squinted and belched again. "Ummm, okay... No, wait. Your eyes are different. I'm calling the police." The drunk turned and staggered back toward the station—and his telephone.

Now Friedrich's anxiety was mounting. When the man had nearly reached the door of the station, he called out, "What's your name?"

The drunk almost toppled as he swiveled around to face Friedrich. "Kleiner."

"First name?" Friedrich demanded.

"Why?" He reached out to steady himself against a light

post. "Did I win something?"

"I need it for my report."

The drunk stood up straight and seemed to pay closer attention. "What report?"

"Herr Kleiner, the report where I explain that your obstruction prevented me from completing my classified mission for the Fatherland. For the Gestapo to interview you, they will need your first name, too."

Kleiner slumped to the ground and leaned against the door of the station, silent for a minute. Then two. Friedrich dared not leave without knowing that he had diverted Kleiner from his dangerous, inebriated path. "Helmut," the man finally muttered. "But never mind. I believe you."

Friedrich smiled and nodded. "Vielen Dank, Herr Kleiner. We will be on our way. Have a pleasant evening."

~

For much of the drive, neither Friedrich nor Samuel had spoken. Samuel slept some, and Friedrich did not want to disturb him. In any case, Friedrich was too preoccupied with the mission to make conversation. Samuel had been awakened at the gas station by the attendant's drunken blustering. Once the Blitz was on the road again, they talked for a while.

"Some of the others said you were Abwehr, but I didn't believe it until you showed up in uniform." Samuel's voice held a slight tremor.

Friedrich sighed. He had been the one to bring Samuel, Gerta, and Thomas to the cottage but had never shared anything about himself with them. He briefly glanced over at Samuel.

Samuel was staring at him, eyes wide, forehead puckered in confusion. "Why have you helped us?"

"You, your wife, your boy, those children—you deserve to live. I do it because it is right, and I do it to honor God and to redeem Germany." Friedrich stopped talking for a moment to concentrate on a Mercedes staff car that was passing the Opel, going at least a hundred kilometers per hour. When the scofflaw had passed, he resumed. "Katrin told me your story. The many escapes, the false identities, hiding places. You have done well, keeping your family alive. Now it is my turn to help."

"Katrin is your girlfriend?"

Friedrich was quiet for a moment. "My brother's fiancée." And he wished them all the best. Never mind the ache in his own heart.

"Your brother, the one in the cellar in the Army uniform?"

"The very one."

Now it was Samuel's turn to be quiet. Friedrich imagined that all of this might be a bit too much for him to digest. "Samuel, in this world, many things are not as they appear."

Samuel didn't answer right away. Maybe he was wrestling with what to say. Finally, he agreed. "Many things." Then he nodded back to sleep. Friedrich drove on in silence.

As the truck neared the rural town of Buchloe, he reached over and gave Samuel a gentle shake. They still had ninety minutes before the train arrived. Friedrich would wait until there was no traffic and then he would drop the Fischers off as close to the train station as seemed safe. They would walk the rest of the way, buy their tickets, and wait on the platform. By the time they found a bench, there should be seventy minutes until the train arrived, if it was on time. It would undoubtedly be the longest seventy minutes of their lives.

About two hundred fifty meters from the station, around a bend that kept them hidden, Friedrich pulled over. He looked to the front. Nothing. He looked to the rear using the mirrors on each side. Nothing. The moment had come.

Samuel placed a hand on Friedrich's arm. "The Talmud says, 'Whoever saves a life, it is as if he saved an entire world.' Thank you."

Friedrich clasped Samuel's hand and nodded. Then he checked the mirrors again and motioned to Samuel, who jumped down from the truck. Suddenly, around the bend came an army motorcycle with a sidecar driving toward them. Friedrich's heart skipped a beat, and he froze in place. He looked in the mirror to the right; Samuel had not quite made it to the back of the truck and stood plastered against the side next to the rear wheel, keeping completely still. Friedrich glanced at the motorcycle. *Just keep going, keep going.*

He sighed as the motorcycle stopped across from the cab of the truck. As the driver pushed his goggles up onto his helmet, Friedrich rolled his window down.

"Is everything all right?" the motorcycle driver shouted, though he was only a few meters away. A side effect of riding a motorcycle

"Yes, fine," Friedrich answered. "I've been driving all night and pulled off to get a few minutes of sleep. Thanks."

"What?" the driver shouted. Friedrich would have to speak up. Meanwhile, the soldier in the sidecar stared at the truck.

Friedrich raised his volume a few notches. "I'm fine! I drove all night and pulled over to rest!"

"Oh. That's smart. Just be careful." The driver pulled his goggles down and sped away. Friedrich realized he had been holding his breath. Now he exhaled as he watched the right-side mirror. Once the coast was clear, Samuel hurried around to the back end. Half a minute later, Friedrich saw Samuel, Gerta, and Thomas step off the road with their suitcases. He shifted into second gear, stepped on the accelerator, and left the Fischers to their fate.

~

Twenty kilometers and twenty-five minutes later, the Opel approached the train station in Kaufbeuren. Soon, Friedrich would let off Rachel, Leah, and their minder, Sister Klara Marie, also known as Estella. Recruited by Father Fellner, the nun had hidden Jews in the past and had eagerly accepted this assignment to get innocent children to safety. Like the children, she carried false Swiss papers created by Friedrich's Abwehr friends. She had a thick Berlin accent, but in this business, you took what you could get and made the most of it. Her story was that she had met a Swiss student, fallen in love, married, and became a Swiss citizen with Swiss children. Estella would return to Germany at a different crossing and was in the risky position of carrying two sets of papers: the false Swiss documents and her real German papers, sewn into her clothes.

Friedrich would not leave these groups on the road, which had more traffic than in Buchloe. As he passed the station, he found an undeveloped area across the tracks where he could pull off unobserved. South of the station, he turned left and followed a narrow dirt road into the wild. Farther than he would have liked—a little less than a kilometer—but there wasn't a safer alternative.

This time, Friedrich got out himself. It was his first chance to stretch his legs since the encounter at the gas station. He strode to the back, said, "Open up," and waited for someone to loosen the canvas flaps. Then he stuck his head inside the back of the truck and, in a stage whisper, called, "Monika! Iris! Estella! It's time."

He hated using the children's false identities. They had names. They had stories. Each had a purpose, like the children he had studied at that Berlin park on a cold day in February. Calling them by their real names would have been one more small way to defy the tyrants who denied their humanity. And yet, they must embrace their false identities or this whole exercise would be in vain.

When they were all out, Friedrich gave them a quick refresher of the instructions they had drilled. "You will leave immediately. Follow the dirt road to the main road, turn right, and walk to the station. Remember everything you have learned. And children, say as little as possible."

Without further ado, Friedrich turned, walked back to the truck, and climbed in. Soon he was on the road again, with one more destination before heading home.

~

In the back of the truck, Katrin tried to keep her mind off the upcoming ordeal. She had spent most of the drive trying to sleep or keeping the children calm by telling stories, as she often had at the cottage. Somewhere after the petrol station, she had exchanged pleasantries with Estella, but it was in both their interests not to know much about each other, so the conversation was short. Now, Estella had been dropped off with her pair. Father Fellner, the only other remaining adult, started going over instructions again with Katrin. She knew the back story, but had never done this before, and the Father wanted to make sure she was ready.

Katrin listened for a while before her mind drifted. She needed the drill, but she could not help thinking about Franz. He had only just discovered her secret, Friedrich's secret. He had only just made the choice she had demanded of him. Would she even see him again?

Her long-held dream of marriage and children and a long life with Franz had never seemed so fragile. *Trust God,* Father Fellner said. Surely, God would not bring her and Franz and Friedrich and Eva and Dov and baby Alina to this moment only to abandon them. *Yet God owes me nothing.* That she was loved and at the same time a grain of sand upon the seashore of the universe was a mystery that brought her peace. She would do what was right and leave the results to her sovereign God.

~

In Berlin, Franz couldn't sleep. His mind was racing. *How far have they gotten? What if someone saw them leave the cottage?* He rolled over. *What if they were stopped at a checkpoint? Friedrich can talk his way out of almost anything. But what if they look in the back?* He rolled in the other direction. *What if they don't make it across the border? What if Friedrich doesn't come back? He's my brother and I just found out who he really is. I want to get to know him better. What if Katrin doesn't come back? I would die. I might die anyway, if any of this can be traced back to me. What if I say something wrong and betray them all?*

Franz gave up on sleep, got up, and began pacing his room. *Was it one group at Buchloe and two at Kempten, or two at Buchloe and one at Kempten? I wish I knew where Katrin was getting on.* Katrin. He saw her face, her bright green eyes.

Pacing didn't calm his mind, so he sat at his small writing desk. He opened his Bible to Psalm 107. One of Mama's favorites. "He maketh the storm a calm, so that the waves thereof are still. Then are they glad because they be quiet; so he bringeth them unto their desired haven."

Lord, guide them to their desired haven. Keep them safe, all of them.

He slipped the Bible into the pocket of his jacket, hung it back up, then lay back in bed. If God could bring peace to the storm, He could bring it to Franz.

His last conscious thought before he fell asleep was, *I did the right thing, but there is no guarantee that it will succeed.* At that moment, he somehow felt closer to Katrin than the hundreds of kilometers that separated them. *We just have to leave it in God's hands and trust to his providence.*

~

Thirty-seven kilometers down the road from Kaufbeuren, Friedrich closed in on the railway station in Kempten, where the last two groups would board trains that would, he prayed, take them to freedom. Once he let them off, he would refuel and then head back to Berlin. Only after arrival would he learn whether the border crossings had been successful.

Kempten was the largest community of the three. Driving into town, they passed the Cambodunum ruins, remnants of the Roman imperial outpost. *What will we leave behind for future generations?*

When Friedrich found a safe place to leave the main road within a reasonable walk of the Kempten Hauptbahnhof—a secluded corner of a huge park west of the station—he repeated the procedure of quietly calling the passengers who needed to get off. It wasn't really necessary, as they were the only ones left, but with each name, he offered a silent prayer.

"Rudolph, Martin! Beate, Basil, Adelina! Minders! End of the road!"

The children got out first, with Eva cradling the baby. Then the adults. Katrin would go first with Eva, Dov, and Alina. Fellner and his two charges would follow. It was better for three to have to wait hours for the next train than four, including a baby. Anyway, the unflappable priest had more experience at this, so he was the best suited to bring up the rear of the operation. He was the only chaperone who would use his real papers. It was quite believable that a priest would accompany two war orphans to their surviving aunt and uncle in Geneva.

Friedrich took a moment to look at them each in turn. He quickly repeated the admonition he had given at Kaufbeuren, then turned to Father Fellner. "Father, it has been an honor. Take care of yourself. I don't know what I would do without your confessional."

Fellner chuckled. "Yes, you are always welcome, my son."

"I will gladly say another ten rosaries if this works."

Friedrich could see the priest's eyes moisten as he said, "Have faith."

"I do. God bless you." Friedrich and Fellner grasped each other in a tight handshake. When they finally let go, Friedrich looked to Katrin. His heart heavy with feelings he could not express, he settled for, "Are you all right?"

"No, I'm not." Her voice was tight. Katrin glanced at Father Fellner before continuing, and her hand stroked Dov's dark curls. "But I have to do this."

"Please be careful, then... for my brother's sake."

"Friedrich..." Katrin glanced downward, then looked back up, her eyes locking on his. "In case the worst should happen, please... tell Franz I love him."

If the worst should happen, Franz will never forgive me... and I will never forgive myself. Giving a brisk nod, Friedrich turned away. He climbed back in the Opel Blitz and started the long drive home, watching his last passengers in the mirror until he couldn't see them anymore.

CHAPTER
24

6 MAY 1943

In Wagon Four of the morning train rumbling toward Switzerland, Gerta and Thomas sat next to each other with Samuel behind. Their boarding at Buchloe had been blessedly uneventful, but two SD men had boarded at Kaufbeuren and picked seats directly across the aisle from Samuel. As soon as he noticed them, Samuel faced a dilemma. He had a copy of *Völkischer Beobachter* in hand, but he could only hold it up for just so long without arousing suspicion. How long did it take an average person to read that rag, anyway? On the other hand, it was the only barrier between him and evil, and he was almost physically incapable of lowering it.

Finally, decisively, he folded the paper, set it in his lap, and looked out the window. He had picked a window seat so he could turn away from the other occupants of the wagon. Some people could spend an entire train trip staring out the window.

If he hoped to divert the attention of the SD officers, he was disappointed.

A voice called from across the aisle. "How old are you?"

Samuel kept looking out the window, pretending he didn't hear.

The voice persisted. "You, by the window, how old are you?"

Samuel finally pulled his gaze back inside and glanced across the aisle. "Excuse me?"

The SD man sitting closest to him looked frustrated, "How many times do I have to ask? How old are you?"

"Thirty-seven." Samuel returned his gaze to the window, but the man was not finished.

"You look younger. Still, you aren't above fighting age. Everyone but the boys and the old men are in uniform. What is wrong with you?"

Samuel thought for a moment before answering. "I have a uniform at home. For the army reserves, along with my rifle. I'm Swiss."

"Swiss, huh?" the officer jeered. "It's a good thing you speak German we can understand. You'll need it." The mouthy one's seatmate guffawed at that.

Samuel sat up straight, clenching his teeth and fists. Switzerland was a free, prosperous, and peaceful country. It had done Germany no wrong. Did the Nazis think they could just march in someday and subjugate it, as if it were Belgium? *Say as little as possible.* But then he thought if he really were protected by Swiss citizenship, he wouldn't let it pass.

"We have mountains, you know," he said. "And every man is in the army. But we aren't spread from Russia to Tunisia. We're all in Switzerland. We are armed. We are trained. And if you come to my country, most of you won't go home alive."

The SD men sat in stunned silence. No one dared speak to them that way.

Enjoying the spectacle and feeling empowered, Samuel

recalled a story he had heard from a Swiss friend. "Before the last war, a German Field Marshal was invited to observe Swiss Army maneuvers. He told his Swiss counterpart, 'The German Army has twice as many men as the Swiss Army. What will you do if we invade?'" Samuel paused for effect. The SD men stared at him hard. "Do you know how our general answered? 'If that happens, we shall each have to shoot twice.'" Samuel took a moment to chuckle before adding, "If you could invade Switzerland, don't you think you would have done it already?"

Now the SD men were clenching their teeth and glaring at him. They had moved from shock to undisguised hatred.

When Gerta turned around in her seat to glare at him, Samuel knew he could expect a tongue-lashing once they had reached safety. For now, her carefully controlled frosty tone made it absolutely clear that she would brook no argument. "Dear, why don't you leave these men alone? I am sure they meant no offense."

"This is your Frau?" the mouthy one asked menacingly. "You should listen to her. You are still in the Reich."

The seatmate leered at Gerta. "Your Frau is beautiful. You wouldn't want anything to happen to her while you're temporarily detained at the border."

Samuel's first instinct was to wrap his hands around the seatmate's throat, but he restrained himself. That would be the end of everything.

Once he regained his composure, he turned to the SD men. "You're quite right. There's no need for harsh words." He unfolded his *Völkischer Beobachter*, opened it wide in front of his face, and stared at a page he had already read twice.

~

Kempten was the final stop the train would make before Bregenz and the border.

The station in Kempten was in the center of town, so it was a full kilometer walk from the park where the Opel Blitz had deposited Katrin, Eva, Dov, and Alina. Katrin and Eva took turns carrying the baby. Stopping to catch her breath, Eva told Katrin, "She's so heavy." Fortunately, they only had to carry one suitcase.

Katrin hoped that it was clear that the harried family of four was in mourning. She was dressed in black, as were the two older children. Katrin had complained to Father Fellner that she was too young to have a fourteen-year-old, but he had assured her that it was a simple thing to add ten years to her age. So today she wore her hair up and sported a headscarf and the kind of thick glasses worn by thousands of frumpy middle-aged hausfraus. Surely no one would notice that the lenses had no prescriptive correction. *It's this border crossing that will add ten years to my age.*

Katrin's group of four was the largest group coming from the Weber cottage and the only one with an infant. To compensate, they had a short wait for their train after being dropped off and the shortest time on the train before crossing the border. Still, it was a lot to handle.

The train to Bregenz and on to Switzerland was scheduled to arrive in Kempten only twenty-one minutes after the family arrived at the station. Eva handed Alina back to Katrin and demanded water. Since Dov didn't speak, he couldn't complain, but he squinted and grimaced, which was much the same thing. When Katrin took Alina back, her arms ached, and she was grateful they did not have long to wait. She stepped up to the ticket counter.

"Papers?"

Katrin pushed her fake glasses up the bridge of her nose and handed the papers to the clerk, a thin man in his sixties with greying hair slicked back from a receding hairline.

"Returning to Switzerland?"

"Yes. Zürich."

The clerk examined the papers. "You arrived third May? That was a short stay."

"Yes. We came for my cousin's funeral."

The clerk nodded and offered his condolences. Then it was back to business. "What class?"

"First."

He stamped the tickets, then passed them back through the window. "One hundred forty-four Reichsmarks for a compartment for four. Take anything in Wagons One through Three. The baby will sit on a lap."

Once on the train they went into the second wagon, where they found a private first-class compartment of four seats. Shortly after the train jolted to life, the DRB conductor entered to collect tickets, and the children quieted. He was a jovial fellow in his mid-forties and liked to talk. Leaning against the frame of the compartment door, he told of his own three children, who were about the ages of Katrin's three. He then asked them each their names.

Eva answered, "Beate."

Then silence. Dov said nothing. Eva put her arm around him. Still silent. Katrin looked up at the conductor, who had cocked his head a bit and raised his eyebrows. "You'll have to excuse him. He has laryngitis and the doctor ordered him to conserve his voice." She then turned to the boy. "Basil, it's all right. Can you just tell him your name?" Dov took his cue, shook his head, and contrived a convincing cough. Katrin smiled inside. She had trained him well.

Lingering, the conductor asked Eva if she had a favorite subject in school.

The fourteen-year-old volunteered, "Math." In truth, she had not been in school for a few years. Katrin wished the conductor would move on.

He didn't. "Do you ski?"

"No," the girl replied.

The conductor crossed his arms. "Doesn't everyone in Switzerland ski?"

Katrin intervened. "Sir, I don't permit my children to ski. It's far too dangerous."

"Oh, that's too bad. I take my family skiing every winter. What do you do for fun?"

The question made Katrin groan inside. What fun could Eva have in hiding, having lost her parents and not knowing whether she would see her next birthday? What could she say?

To her relief, Eva met the challenge. "We like the cinema, sir. And ice skating." Once, that had probably been true.

Satisfied, the conductor straightened and excused himself. "Meine Dame, Kinder, I must continue my work. Good day."

"Thank you, good day." Katrin breathed a sigh of relief. One advantage to being Swiss was that, at least for the next few hours, no one would expect her to say, "Heil Hitler" in every conversation.

She glanced out the window at the bucolic Bavarian countryside. It was beautiful but rushed by so quickly. *Maybe like life itself,* she mused. "Lord, thank you for the beauty," Katrin whispered. "Please let it last."

CHAPTER
25

6 MAY 1943

Franz Maedler yawned. A stack of carpool requests awaited his attention, but he struggled to concentrate. He had checked DRB timetables, and a train that passed through Buchloe, Kaufbeuren, and Kempten was scheduled to pull into Bregenz at 11:07. There was a good chance that it was Katrin's train.

He glanced at his watch. 11:04. His stomach twisted. *How does Friedrich ever get any work done?*

Walking past, Olbermann must have noticed that he was troubled. "Are you all right, sir?"

Franz nodded. "Just feeling a little queasy, Lieutenant."

Olbermann smiled. "Too much bratwurst last night?"

"Something like that." Franz turned away and went back to work.

~

Until five years ago, Bregenz had been a city of the free and sovereign nation of Austria. After the Anschluss of 1938, it had been incorporated into the Greater German Reich, along with the rest of Austria. Now Bregenz was the final stop on this route from Germany to Switzerland. Passengers would get off to show their papers and be stamped for exit, then get back on. After crossing the border, they would stop again on the Swiss side and repeat the process for entry. Hopefully.

Passengers were processed in order of wagons. A single line moved past a desk manned by an SS Sturmbannführer who was responsible for border control. Katrin and her charges would be the first through. The Fischers would be next. Finally, Estella and her pair. Friedrich had explained that by spreading the groups out, he hoped to minimize suspicions by the authorities as well as keep the children from seeing and reacting to each other in line.

When Katrin's group reached the desk, she didn't wait for the SS officer to demand their documents. Taking the initiative, she held them out and declared, "Here are our papers."

Was that too bold? Would the SS man notice the perspiration she had to wipe from her brow?

"Yes." The officer looked coolly at each member of the family in turn, then opened the documents of Katrin, Beate, Basil, and Adelina Kuehn. Katrin watched as he inspected them carefully. Father Fellner had explained that he would be looking for imperfections in the mass-produced German entry stamp that forgers could rarely duplicate. Katrin tried not to fidget as he raised his head and narrowed his eyes to look her over.

"Names."

Katrin answered with confidence. "Kuehn, Katrin; Kuehn, Beate; Kuehn, Basil; Kuehn, Adelina."

"No, you must each say your own names."

"Kuehn, Katrin. The baby is Adelina." She turned to Eva and Dov and nodded her head, silently encouraging them to remember what they had been taught.

"Kuehn, Beate."

Then one cough, followed by another. Dov had gone straight to the medical condition.

"What is your name, boy?" the SS man demanded, leaning forward to peer down at the child.

Dov emitted a series of hacking coughs.

"Sir, I must apologize. My son has laryngitis." She laid a hand on Dov's head. "The doctor instructed him not to strain his voice. His name is Basil."

More coughs wracked the child. Thank God he was acting the part.

Seemingly satisfied, the SS man settled back in his seat. "What was the purpose of your visit?"

Katrin recited the story she had memorized. "My cousin was in an air defense battalion in Duisburg. He was killed during the British raid on 26 April. My aunt and uncle had him brought back to Schongau for the funeral. We came for that."

"What was his name?"

"Gebel, Otto." Katrin had been told by Fellner that a Corporal Otto Gebel of Schongau had indeed died in Duisburg a week and a half ago.

"Where was the funeral?"

"In Schongau."

"Yes, where in Schongau?"

Alina began to cry. For the last few minutes, Eva had held the baby. Now, the girl passed her to Katrin like she was a hot potato. Her heart thudding in her chest, Katrin took the baby, whose cry quickly crescendoed, then turned to the SS man. "Excuse me." She hushed Alina, swaying the child in one arm while she reached into her pocket with her free hand. She pulled out a memorial card and handed it to the officer. "It was in the city cemetery of course... with a mass at St. Sebastian's... A very moving service. Here is

Otto's Sterbebild."

The SS man took a moment to read the card. Included was a striking picture of Otto in his corporal's uniform, taken at a slight angle to emphasize his chiseled features. Katrin presumed it was a picture of the real Otto Gebel. Abwehr officers were nothing if not thorough in their craft. She felt sorrow for the grieving parents and guilt for appropriating their grief for her own purposes. But at least they had their son's remains to bury on German soil. The vast majority of Wehrmacht enlisted casualties were simply interred on the battlefield—or left unburied in the Russian snow or the sands of North Africa.

Alina kept crying. The waiting line grew restless. A passenger behind them shouted "Quiet your baby!" Another demanded, "Sturmbannführer, can you keep the line moving?"

"Frau Kuehn, what's wrong with your child?" To Katrin, the SS man sounded more irritated than concerned.

Alina wailed louder. She was supposed to be fed every three hours, but Katrin had last fed her four hours ago. She winced. Poor child, but Katrin had expected a diversion at roughly this point in their journey might prove useful. "Sir, she is hungry. I'm very sorry. I need to give her a bottle."

The SS major took one last cursory look at the papers. *He can't let anyone think he is being hurried along by an infant.*

Then there were four quick stamps in succession.

"Next."

~

There had been no further words between Samuel and his SD tormentors for the remainder of the tense trip, but Samuel couldn't forget the implicit threats they had made against him and Gerta. As the line inched forward, he felt like his heart was going to explode. He carried both suitcases while Gerta held Thomas's hand. Just before they reached the front, the mouthy SD officer reappeared, walked up to the desk, and whispered something in the ear of the SS man who held the exit stamp that meant the difference between life and death.

As Samuel handed over their papers, the SS man motioned to another officer, an Obersturmführer who stood behind him. The lieutenant approached the desk, leaned over, and received instructions of some sort from the major. Then he barked out a command. "Frau Mueller, you will come with me. Leave the boy with your husband."

Fear showed in Gerta's eyes as she turned to leave with the SS lieutenant, who was joined by the SD officer. As they walked out of sight, Samuel could barely contain the terror and anger welling up in him. If they were to have any hope of coming through this, he must remain calm. As long as their papers held up, the Nazis wouldn't jeopardize Germany's relations with Switzerland. Would they?

Samuel redirected his eyes toward the Sturmbannführer at the desk. "Is something wrong?"

The SS man studied Samuel's face. "I don't know, Herr Mueller. Is there?"

Samuel struggled to remain collected. "Most families have been permitted to go through together."

"Yes, well...." The SS man looked at Samuel's son. "What is your name, boy?"

"Thomas Mueller."

Samuel was glad Thomas got to keep the name he had known all his life. His son would not have to remember a new identity.

"How old are you?"

Thomas proudly held up three fingers.

The SS man returned his attention to Samuel. "Herr Mueller, why did you come to Germany?"

Samuel focused his mind on their story. "My mother lives in Bad Saulgau. We were visiting her. She had not yet met Thomas."

"I see." The SS man stared at Samuel. "What is your mother's name?"

"Freda. Freda Mueller. She is a widow." Friedrich had warned Samuel this part of the backstory was thin. A Freda Mueller lived in Bad Saulgau and she didn't have a telephone, so the SS couldn't call her. Hopefully, they didn't develop a deep enough interest in the Muellers to seek in-person verification.

The SS man bore in on Samuel. "There are price-gougers around Bad Saulgau. A couple of years ago, they were selling Christmas geese for sixty Reichsmarks. Do you know anything about that?"

He's trying to throw me off balance. "No, of course not. I just told you I haven't been there since before my son was born."

"When did you enter Germany?"

"30 April." His account matched the stamp. A perfect stamp.

"You know, you don't have a Swiss accent."

Remembering his recent conversation with the SD men on the train, Samuel responded, "I've been told I am lucky my high German is so good."

The SS officer motioned to the corner. "Herr Mueller, step to the side for a moment. You and your son can wait there."

The seconds ticked off the large clock that hung on the wall behind the desk. Seconds turned into minutes. With each tick, Samuel fought the urge to run into the next room to save Gerta. Was she being interrogated? Tortured?

After an eternity, Gerta emerged from the room, her two escorts walking her to the desk. She appeared shaken but unharmed. The SS man at the desk motioned for him to approach with Thomas. Samuel was prepared for anything. *Will they let us through? Will they take us away?*

Stamp. Stamp. Stamp. "Herr Mueller, Frau Mueller. Thank you for your patience. I hope you enjoyed your stay in the Reich." The Sturmbannführer handed their papers back with a smirk.

As they walked away from the desk, the SD man called after them, "If you ever come back, be more careful what you say."

Back on the platform, Samuel resisted the urge to embrace his wife. They couldn't afford to show just how relieved they were. "Are you all right?"

Still holding onto Thomas, Gerta slapped Samuel in the face with her free hand. "Next time, *Walter*, think before you speak." Gerta wiped away a tear, then composed herself. "I'm fine. Mostly they took turns asking me the same seven questions over and over. Then they told me you had been found out as a Jew and I could only help myself and Thomas by admitting it. They told me they would... do things if I didn't cooperate." She shuddered. "But it was all talk. I think they meant to scare us, because of what you said on the train."

Samuel smiled faintly as he rubbed his stinging cheek. "My brave Gerta. Let's get back on the train. Our new home awaits."

CHAPTER
26

6 MAY 1943

Jakob and Jonah Bergenthal were the last to board a train, shepherded by Father Fellner. Fellner was using his own real papers, while the boys used forged German identity papers combined with a forged Swiss legal document allowing them to cross the border under Fellner's care.

Father Fellner had never liked the Nazis. They were impious tyrants. He hadn't actively resisted, though, until the Provost of St. Hedwig's, Bernhard Lichtenberg, died on the way to Dachau in late 1941. Lichtenberg had publicly opposed the euthanasia program, then sealed his doom by praying "for the Jews and for the poor prisoners in the concentration camps."

Fellner had grown close to Lichtenberg in his ministry at St. Hedwig's, and the death of the Provost drove him to make a choice of his own. In National Socialist Germany, one could die just for praying. One must either stop praying or start acting. He could not stop praying, and so, slowly, carefully, he began building a network of Germans who could no longer close their eyes to what was happening around them. It was small enough to keep its secrets but large enough to make a difference. Estella was part of that group. Fellner's network had drawn the attention of Friedrich Maedler when it crossed over with Friedrich's own network in the person of Reinhold Weber, who had become a conduit into Switzerland.

Now Father Fellner was escorting the Bergenthal boys across the border. After watching the first train of the day depart Kempten, the priest and the children walked into town, stopping in a coffee shop where Fellner drank several cups of coffee while treating the twins to hot cocoa. "Remember," he told them in hushed tones, "the story is that your parents are dead. You know how you felt when you lost your mother. You must feel like that again."

Jakob nodded solemnly. Jonah stared into his cocoa.

When the time came, the group crossed the street to the train station, bought their tickets, and boarded the train without difficulty. The National Socialist state notwithstanding, Kempten was Bavarian, and Catholic clergy still received a certain amount of deference from most people. Including some Deutsche Reichsbahn clerks. That hurdle cleared, Fellner led the boys to a third-class wagon, where they settled in for the short trip to the border.

~

Bringing up the end of the line, Father Fellner, Jakob, and Jonah were among the last to be processed at Bregenz. Though it was nerve-wracking, Fellner preferred it this way. The fellow at the desk would be tired and the remaining passengers would be pressing to leave the station.

He only wished he'd known whether the other groups had made it. He wouldn't know until he made contact with Reinhold in Switzerland. In his worry, he walked right past the processing desk when the people in front of them were cleared.

"Father! Priest! Your papers!"

Fellner heard the shout, stopped, and returned to the desk. "Pardon me, Sturmbannführer. Heil Hitler. I am very tired. I have been travelling with these boys and I can tell you it is not easy. Plus, standing in line for so long..."

The officer scowled. "Are you complaining to me, Priest? When you have spent ten hours stamping papers, then you can complain."

"Of course. I'm sorry. I meant no disrespect. It's just that..."

"Papers," the SS man growled.

When Fellner produced them, the Sturmbannführer scanned them, as he had hundreds of others that day. Germans crossing into Switzerland demanded extra attention.

He started with the Father. "Your name?"

"Peter Fellner."

"You, boy?" He pointed at Jakob.

"Rudolph."

"You?" Now it was Jonah's turn.

"Martin."

"Their family name is Ronke," Fellner added.

"Yes, I can see that. Why are you travelling to Switzerland with these boys?"

"Their Father died in the Army last year. Their mother was killed when Berlin was bombed in March. They came under my care then."

The SS man stared him down. "You haven't answered my question. Why are you going to Switzerland?"

"Oh, yes. Right." He found the words. "The boys have an aunt in Sankt Gallen. She is their next of kin and wishes to take them in."

The SS man frowned. "They are German boys. Their father gave his life for the Reich. They should stay in

Germany. Someday they can fight to avenge him."

I believe their father would prefer they leave Germany as soon as possible. "That is not in my hands, Herr Sturmbannführer. Their aunt procured legal representation and received a decree of adoption. According to the agreements between Germany and Switzerland, it is binding." Fellner thought for a moment how else he might calm the SS officer. "And, of course, the aunt is Swiss-German. There will be no race-defiling."

"Let me see the paper."

"Of course." Fellner handed over a perfect replica of a Swiss court decree countersigned by the German vice consul in Zürich. The SS man had likely seen thousands of personal identification papers and could spot all but the very best forgeries. A Swiss court document would be unusual, which could prove either a blessing or a curse.

The officer beckoned the Obersturmführer standing behind him. "What do you make of this?"

The lieutenant's forehead wrinkled with puzzlement. "Can we call the consulate in Zürich?"

The major agreed and dialed an operator to be connected. After a minute, he shook his head and hung up. "I can't get through."

The lieutenant shrugged. "I don't know, then."

"Wait." The major focused on Fellner. "You came from Berlin with the boys."

"Yes."

"But you only got on this train in Kempten." The major raised his eyebrows.

Fellner saw where this was going. "Yes."

"How is that?"

Fellner tried to control his fear by speaking slowly and methodically. "We came by train from Berlin to Kempten a few days ago. Then we stayed at the Church of St. Lorenz until the legal affairs were settled. Today, we got on the train again at Kempten to complete our journey."

"Is that true, boys?" the major asked.

Jakob and Jonah nodded.

The lieutenant, who had remained at the desk with his superior, seemed unconvinced. "Rudolph Ronke, what happened to your parents?"

"They died in the war."

The SS man glowered. Father Fellner groaned inwardly at the boy's vague answer. It wasn't what they were supposed to have practiced, and he doubted it would be enough to satisfy the SS. He lay a hand on Jakob's shoulder. "The boys are still getting over a terrible shock."

The lieutenant ignored him and pressed the point. "How did they die?"

Father Fellner could see the wheels turning behind Jakob's eyes. Katrin had drilled the twins, but no child should have to pass this sort of test to live.

"Papa was shot by the Reds. Mama died when we were bombed."

Having watched his lieutenant reach a dead end, the major returned to his previous line of questioning. "So, Priest, you will not mind if we contact the church to verify your story?"

"If you feel you must."

The last passengers waiting to reach the desk were still on hold, and none too happy. When the grumbling turned into raised voices, the major called out the Sturmmann, with his MP-40 submachine gun at the ready. The passengers quieted.

The major picked up the receiver of his desk telephone and called an operator. Father Fellner had bluffed his way through many trials and had to rely on faith again this time. *Father, please let this work.*

"Operator. Heil Hitler. I need you to connect me to the Church of St. Lorenz in Kempten.... Yes, Heil Hitler. This is Sturmbannführer Karl Pregler. I am at the border control station in Bregenz. I must speak to the priest in charge."

The major leaned back in his chair, propped his feet on the desk, and glued his eyes to Father Fellner.

"Hello Father, Heil Hitler.... This is Sturmbannführer Pregler at the Bregenz border control. There is a man here with two boys trying to cross to Switzerland. His papers say his name is Peter Fellner. He is a priest. He says he and the boys stayed at the church for the last several days. I need to know if this is true...." He frowned. "Yes, yes, I see. Yes, that is what he said. You understand there will be grave consequences if you have misled me.... Very well. Heil Hitler."

The major turned to his subordinate. "He checks out."

Father Fellner said a quick prayer of thanks that he had been close friends with Father Dietz for nearly two decades. St. Lorenz didn't have a telephone until Dietz had one installed recently. A little bird had told him he might need to take a phone call like that.

Just as Father Fellner thought the ordeal was over, the major remembered the consulate. Apparently, he distrusted the clergy. Maybe the call would go through this time.

It did. "Heil Hitler. This is Sturmbannführer Pregler at Bregenz border control. I need to speak with the vice consul.... Yes, of course... Vice consul, this is SS in Bregenz. Did you certify an adoption decree for two German boys being taken by a Swiss woman in Sankt Gallen?... Yes, Rudolph and Martin Ronke... Yes sir, I see. Thank you, sir. Heil Hitler." The SS man stamped the three sets of papers, handed them to Father Fellner, and waved them past as he called, "Next."

Fellner sighed internally. As it turned out, Hans Bernd

Gisevius, German vice consul in Zürich, was also a member of the Abwehr resistance circle. The little birds had been busy.

~

Franz watched Friedrich as he pulled the Opel Blitz into the Carpool garage at the Bendlerblock. Friedrich had called him from a payphone outside Berlin to tell him when to expect the return of the Blitz.

Friedrich climbed out of the truck unsteadily. Franz reached up to help. "Brother, you look terrible."

Friedrich offered him a wan smile. "You try driving this thing when you haven't slept in thirty-seven hours." When his boots were on the ground, he handed the key to Franz, who pocketed it and embraced his brother.

With false seriousness, Franz asked, "Should I inspect it for scratches and dents?"

Friedrich lightly slapped the back of Franz's head with his open hand. "I'm going home."

Franz grabbed his brother's upper arm to keep him from walking away. "No, you're not, not until you tell me your story." Maybe Friedrich would need an enticement. "Schnitzel and beer?"

Friedrich stroked his chin for a moment. "Hmm. No beer. Schnitzel, if it can be quick."

The brothers started walking out of the garage to find somewhere to eat. Franz couldn't wait until they got there. "Were there any problems?"

"None at my end. Every group got off without a hitch." Friedrich shrugged. "But I don't know anything after that."

They approached the attendant's post at the garage exit. Franz held his palm to Friedrich's chest to stop him. "Let me handle this."

Franz strode up to the post and got the attention of the spindly private who had checked out the truck a little over twenty four hours before. "I'm returning the Blitz." He extended his arm and held out the key.

The private looked him over. "I remember, from yesterday. It's hard for me to check it in without paperwork."

Franz scowled. "I told you, there isn't going to be any." He lowered his voice to a whisper. "This was for an Abwehr mission." He paused. "I shouldn't even be telling you that much." Franz shook the key.

The attendant's eyes grew wide.

"Just clean it up, fill it up, and pretend it never left the garage." Franz shook the key again.

Wordlessly, the private slowly extended his arm. Franz dropped the key into the boy's cupped hand, raised his eyebrows, and nodded. The private closed his hand around the key and slowly nodded in return.

When Franz rejoined Friedrich, his brother smiled and patted him on the back. "You learn quickly, Brother."

Franz exhaled loudly. "Survival is an excellent teacher."

They left the garage and turned onto the street. Both men looked around them. A few pedestrians in front, a few behind. Some military.

Franz lowered his voice. He needed to know about Katrin, but what could he ask that Friedrich would be able to answer? Something simple and broad. Any information would be a gift. "How was Katrin?"

Friedrich sighed. "Resolute. Brave. As always."

Franz had hoped for more, but he savored the spare description as if it were a single Swiss chocolate, the last in the box. Then, a practical matter. "I kept an ear out in Carpool in case anyone was digging, asking questions about the requisition."

"And?

"Nothing so far. And now that the truck is back, no one will waste time thinking about it." The waiting was killing

Franz. "When will you know? Whether they made it, I mean?"

"If they got through, the chaperones will be back in Berlin tomorrow. I'll hear."

If they got through... Such a little word. Yet so much hung on it. "Friedrich, what did their faces look like?" Franz now had a particular interest in faces.

Friedrich paused for a moment. "Before they got on the truck, mostly afraid. When they got off, expectant, maybe resigned. They were about to walk into life or death. I think most of them, the ones old enough to understand, had accepted that it would be one or the other, and there was not much they could do except to play their parts well."

Not terribly unlike Stalingrad, Franz thought. Or what it must have felt like crossing the bottom of the Red Sea with Pharaoh's army at your back.

CHAPTER
27

7 MAY 1943

Friedrich stepped through the doors of the Abwehr offices in the Bendlerblock with trepidation. He had slept like the dead, but now his heart was pounding. If the ten guests at the Weber cottage had made it safely to Switzerland, the operation would be a success. If not, it would be a failure. If Estella, Father Fellner, or Katrin failed to return, it would be catastrophic. Within hours, he should know.

At the next desk, his colleague Karl called to him. "A courier from the Swiss Embassy brought you this." He tossed a plain envelope toward Friedrich. "I don't suppose you know what it's about?"

Friedrich arched an eyebrow as he took the envelope. "It could be anything."

True. Friedrich had frequent dealings with the Swiss.

He reached into a desk drawer for the NSDAP letter-opener that had been a gift from his father and sliced open the seal. Inside he found a hand-written message. "Normal place 11:00." He still wasn't sure what it was about, though he now knew who had sent it. It did not come from the ambassador, Hans Frölicher, noted for his pro-Hitler tilt. The young Swiss attaché, Üli Kastler, facilitated communications between Swiss intelligence and Abwehr, sometimes without the knowledge of Frölicher. The message had come from Kastler.

~

At 11:00, Friedrich was at the normal place—the Invaliden Cemetery north of the city center. The cemetery dated to the War of the Austrian Succession in the mid-1700s. Filled with mature trees and scores of graves marked by everything from simple crosses and plain tombstones to ornate statuary, it was the final resting place of a host of German military heroes. These heroes included General von Scharnhorst, who fought Napoleon, whose carved marble sarcophagus was topped with a statue of a sleeping lion; Field Marshal von Schlieffen from the last war; and the "Red Baron," Manfred von Richthofen, the famed pilot. More recently, several Nazi favorites had been buried here, including Fritz Todt, the Reichsminister for Armaments, and Reinhard Heydrich, laid to rest last year in an elaborate state funeral.

On his way to von Scharnhorst's sleeping lion, the designated meeting spot, Friedrich paused at Heydrich's grave. He clenched his teeth. What a grotesque inversion Invaliden represented! Georg had no state funeral. His bones were picked clean at the bottom of the North Atlantic. Franz's men had no state funerals. Their corpses lay scattered across Ukraine and Russia, or they were the walking dead in some Soviet POW camp. The Jews had no funerals. Either their ashes floated into the sky, or they dug their own graves, into which they unceremoniously fell with an SS bullet in the back. The ones who sent them there— the Heydrichs, the Todts, and the rest—were honored and glorified. It disgusted him.

As Friedrich stood staring at Heydrich's grave, a familiar voice from behind asked quietly, "Did you know him?"

Friedrich waited until he heard the man step closer. "Only by reputation." Then, after a brief pause, "Good riddance."

"You're not wrong," said the voice. "Hello, Maedler."

"Kastler." An awkward silence hung between them for a moment. "Kastler, you called the meet."

His Swiss counterpart answered slowly. "There... is a problem."

Friedrich was not going to give anything away before he knew what the Swiss knew. "Go on."

"Some people were detained at the border, trying to come in from Bregenz."

Friedrich responded nonchalantly. "That must happen all the time."

"They have Swiss papers. Immaculate Swiss papers." Kastler paused. "But they aren't Swiss."

Friedrich was still reluctant to reveal anything. "Why is this my problem?"

"There are children. They might be Jews and would qualify as refugees. The woman is not their mother. We were about to send her back when she claimed that she was on an Abwehr mission. She was desperate and insisted we contact you first, as per protocol." He paused. "None of this makes sense."

"I see." Outwardly calm, Friedrich winced inside. *Katrin?*

Kastler continued. "The border guards didn't know what to do, so they called Bern. Bern called me."

"Where are they now?"

"Still being held in Rorschach. But if this is not resolved soon, it will be out of my hands." The Swiss attaché handed Friedrich a manila envelope with a document inside. "Here is the border control report. Bern sent it overnight by teletype."

Friedrich opened the envelope, pulled out the one-page summary, and began reading.

> *Three persons travelling on Swiss papers.*
> *Estella Becker 33, Monika Becker 12, Iris*
> *Becker 11.*

Friedrich breathed. *Not Katrin.* His initial wave of relief was instantly followed by a feeling of guilt over his relief. Estella could still be in danger. He resumed reading.

> *Questioned by border control. Claimed*
> *home is Winterthur. Answered basic*
> *questions about Winterthur but unable*
> *to answer questions requiring local*
> *knowledge. Fr. Becker asserted her group*
> *was detained by Gestapo at Bregenz and*
> *questioned at length. Eventually released*
> *and allowed to continue. Border control*
> *officer considers this doubtful.*
> *Unable to confirm husband Matteo*
> *Becker stated in papers. When police went*
> *to address given in Winterthur, a Matteo*
> *Becker answered but had not heard of Fr.*
> *Becker or children. After being confronted*
> *with these facts, Fr. Becker claimed*
> *children were German Jewish refugees.*
> *She produced her own German papers and*
> *claimed status as Abwehr agent. Please*
> *advise.*
> *Rorschach Border Station*
> *6 May 1943*

Friedrich looked up at Kastler without saying a word. Estella was resourceful, he had to give her that. But if he couldn't straighten things out with the Swiss, she would be doomed. And she would just be the first. Kastler, staring at the tomb of Heydrich, got to the point. "This is another of your operations, isn't it? Who sends twelve-year-olds on real intelligence missions?"

Friedrich took a moment to respond. "It would make good cover. But yes, the children are Jews."

Kastler sighed. "We will send the woman back to Bregenz, Maedler."

"We want her back. But she has to be able to come back on her own. The Gestapo would kill her—or worse."

Kastler shrugged. "Bern thinks this is too hot to handle. With von Dohnanyi in prison, who knows how much has been revealed about our past coordination."

"Not much," Friedrich countered. "The crossing on the German side would have been much harder if the Gestapo knew everything."

"It sounds like it was hard enough," Kastler scoffed.

Friedrich gave a sharp laugh. "Your own border control officer didn't think it happened."

"Nevertheless. And for all I know, this is the tip of the iceberg."

Friedrich said nothing.

Wide-eyed, Kastler asked, "There *are* more, aren't there?"

"None you need to worry about."

"That is not comforting, Maedler."

In 1942, von Dohnanyi had arranged to transfer money from Abwehr's slush fund to grease the deal with the Swiss and pay the expenses of the escaped Jews. Friedrich could offer the same. He had an additional prize that he could dangle in front of Kastler. Abwehr was not the only German security service operating in Switzerland. Their primary goal was to gather information for the war. The

Swiss didn't like them there but considered their presence comparatively benign.

Compared to the SD, that is. They came to Switzerland too, out of uniform, to infiltrate German émigré groups, to compile lists of Swiss to be arrested after an invasion, and to prepare the Swiss-German community for incorporation into the Greater German Reich—as they had done in Austria and the Sudetenland. There was even an SS center in Stuttgart, the Panoramaheim, set up to recruit, train, and coordinate a Swiss-German fifth column. That, the Swiss could not tolerate. As luck would have it, SD-Ausland had recently shared the identity of two operatives in Switzerland who had been in close proximity to ongoing Abwehr operations.

Friedrich put everything on the table. "What if I can arrange ten thousand Reichsmarks for expenses and give you two SD hyenas? The woman will return to Berlin on her own. The children will find a home through the refugee groups."

"Hmmm." Kastler nodded, his lips pursed. "Richthofen is here, isn't he?"

Friedrich had hoped for a less ambiguous answer, but at least it wasn't no. "This way. Follow me." Friedrich led Kastler to the grave of the World War I ace, who was so famous his tomb simply said "RICHTHOFEN."

"He shot down how many planes? Eighty-some?"

Friedrich knew the answer to that. The Red Baron had been his childhood hero. "Exactly eighty."

"He shot down eighty planes, but one day his luck ran out." The man paused. "One day, Maedler, your luck will run out. Today, make it twenty thousand Marks and two SDs. We will take care of the children. And if the woman ever comes back, we will send her to the Gestapo."

Friedrich nodded. "Understood. And make sure our

fingerprints aren't on the SDs."

~

It was afternoon in Rorschach, Switzerland. Katrin sat next to Father Fellner on a bench on the train station platform. Nearly twenty-four hours had passed since Estella and her charges should have arrived. Katrin didn't know how much longer they could wait, but she didn't want to ask. Were they stopped trying to get out of Germany? Trying to get into Switzerland? Did they even make it onto the train?

At a little after 13:00, a stiff man in a nice suit carrying a briefcase walked out of the station with two young girls. Katrin watched them long enough to be certain they were Leah and Rachel, then looked away. Who knew what complications could be caused if the girls saw her there. But they were alive!

A few minutes later, Katrin spied a familiar face. It was Estella, walking down the platform with her suitcase. For the first time since the journey began, Katrin could breathe easy. Everyone had made it safely across the border.

Father Fellner's broad smile stretched ear to ear, and he rose to greet her. "Estella!" The smile she returned was weary, but she quickened her steps toward Katrin and the priest. "From now on, I will call you Sister Lazarus, for you have returned from the dead! The girls?"

"Accepted as refugees. They went with someone from the Organization for Immigrant Children." Behind Estella's smile, her voice cracked. With the sigh that followed, it seemed that a heavy load of stress had fallen away from her.

Katrin embraced the nun, then backed up half a step and grasped her hands. "Are you all right? What happened? We were so worried."

Estella looked both ways. The joy seemed to drain from her face as she recounted her experience in hushed tones.

"There weren't three seats together on the train, so Leah had to sit a few rows up. I should've sent Rachel." Estella shook her head slowly. "Leah is so precocious, so open. She was sitting next to Gestapo, and she talked too much." She took a deep breath. "When we got off in Bregenz, they took us to a room and grilled me about everything—my story, things Leah said, jokes she told. Jokes you can tell in Switzerland, but not in Germany."

Katrin bit her lip. *Of course it was Leah... I should have worked harder with her.*

After a long pause, Estella continued. "I was sure they would take us away. But our papers held up, and God gave me the words I needed. I think they were afraid of an incident with Switzerland. They finally let us go."

Father Fellner stroked his chin. "What happened here?"

Estella took a deep breath. "The Swiss started asking questions about Winterthur. Questions I couldn't answer. They left us for a while, and when they came back, they put us in a holding cell. I begged them not to send me back to the Gestapo but to contact Major Maedler at Abwehr." A smile creased her face. "We waited a long time, then the girls were taken out and I was given my German papers and told to leave within twenty-four hours."

Father Fellner's eyes brightened. "Give thanks to the Lord, for he is good."

Estella finished the Psalm. "And His mercy endures forever." She looked at Katrin, then back to Fellner. "Father, how are the others?"

"You are the last. All came through safely, by the grace of God."

Estella exhaled loudly and visibly relaxed.

Father Fellner put a hand on her shoulder. "I will soon go back the way I came. You and Katrin should not tarry here."

Estella looked up at the priest. "Father," she said weakly. Katrin worried she was about to collapse.

Fellner eased her down on the bench. "I know, Sister. I know." He made the sign of the cross, first over Estella, then Katrin. "May God bless and protect you both."

CHAPTER
28

8 MAY 1943

Franz had thought about Katrin almost every waking moment since she disappeared behind the cellar door at the cottage. Not yet married, their fates were intertwined. Without Katrin's courage, he might never have found his own. Without his contribution, the escape could not have happened. Yesterday afternoon, Friedrich had confirmed that every Jewish refugee had made it to Switzerland and every minder had returned safely to Germany. His Sunshine had returned. Franz felt a desperate need to see his fiancée, to hold her close and hear her voice. The last week had seemed like a century.

After he left Carpool in the late afternoon, Franz stopped by the bakery unannounced for the second time in two Saturdays. As he entered the shop, his heart skipped a beat. Katrin was there. She looked uncertain until he broke into a big smile, which she returned with a grin. "Good afternoon, Sunshine." Franz doffed his officer's hat, sweeping it in front of him in a broad gesture. "I have come to collect on a walk along the Spree I had expected last week."

Carrying a tray of freshly baked strudel, Herr Rothberg joined Katrin behind the counter. He regarded Franz warily.

"It's all right, Ulrich," Katrin assured him. "Everything is fine."

As the baker began restocking the display case, he nodded toward the door. "Take the rest of the day off," he told Katrin. "Enjoy your walk."

"Danke." Katrin turned to Franz. "Just a moment," she said with a shy smile before turning away again. She traded her apron for a light jacket, then stepped around the counter and stood on tiptoe to give Franz a quick kiss. "I'm ready now."

As the two stepped outdoors, Franz crooked his arm and Katrin took it. He eased into conversation. "It's a nice day to walk, yes?" Though the sky was cloudy, it was nearly seventy degrees and there was no rain.

"A beautiful day." Katrin smiled for a moment. "When I was a child, on a day like this at the cottage, I would shed my shoes and socks and wander barefoot in the woods."

Franz chuckled at the thought. "You should try that now."

She laughed too. "I don't think it would be quite as pleasant here." Suddenly serious, she lowered her voice. "I'm sorry I hurt you, Franz." She stopped walking and pulled him toward her. "I have always loved you. I wanted to say 'yes' in the hospital. I wanted to marry you right away." Katrin looked into Franz's eyes. "What I told you in the hospital—that I didn't want us to end up like your mother and father—it wasn't untrue. But it wasn't the whole truth. Because of the path I am walking, I couldn't marry you if I didn't know you were committed to doing the right thing."

"I know. You did what was necessary to keep me safe... and yourself." He thought of the faces in the cellar. "And them." Franz paused as a woman and child approached. He waited for them to pass, then lowered his voice, too. "You wanted me to choose. For a long time, I didn't know what you meant. Or imagined I didn't know. Now I've chosen."

Katrin slipped her hand into Franz's and started walking again. "How do you feel?"

Franz squeezed her hand. "Scared. And brave. And free. All at once."

Katrin nodded solemnly. "That is how I felt, walking past the SS into Switzerland... What helped you choose?"

Franz gathered his thoughts. "I did what you suggested. I read, I thought, and I prayed. I spent an afternoon at St. Luke's, talking with Pastor Hoffman."

Her face darkened suddenly. "He was arrested again, Franz. I found out last night."

Franz took a deep breath. Of course they arrested Hoffmann. A regime built on lies can never tolerate truth. He exhaled slowly and pulled Katrin into an embrace. No one passing by would spare a second glance for two lovers by the Spree, holding one another close. "Hoffmann will not stop speaking the truth. That's why they fear him. I'm afraid it means they won't let him go again." He shuddered. "I could not stand their lies any longer. And I could not stand the faces."

"The faces?" Katrin cocked her head slightly.

Franz looked to the side. "You know about my nightmares. I haven't told you about the faces I see in the windows when I am on trains, in church. Faces whose pain I witnessed." His voice grew even quieter. "Faces whose suffering can sometimes be laid at my feet. German faces... Ukrainian... Jewish... Pauli... each one my neighbor, hurt by the regime."

She nodded slowly. "You're hurting too," she finally said softly. "Maybe you need to feel that hurt." She pressed close to his side. "Franz, you have made your choice. I am ready to marry you without reserve. I love you with all my heart."

Franz leaned down to plant a kiss on Katrin's lips. After all the waiting, all the disappointments, all the false starts, he had found himself, and so had found a wife. "Have you been thinking about our wedding?"

She laughed. "No need. You remember I had our wedding planned by the time I was twelve, don't you?"

"That's right!" Franz answered, then teased, "Weren't you still playing on swings then?" It felt good in the midst of the whispers and subterfuge to dream with her about a pleasant future.

"That has nothing to do with it." Katrin's eyes glowed, and she seemed to relax. "I've been thinking about our honeymoon. There's a ruined castle in Bavaria that I want to see again. It's close to where I did my agricultural service."

Franz nodded his approval. "A castle would be nice, and Bavaria is beautiful. But we have to get married first. Whom should we invite to the wedding?"

She thought for a long moment, her forehead wrinkling. "I'm not sure. My parents. Herr Rothberg. Friedrich and Father Fellner." A shadow filled her eyes. "My brother can't risk returning." She sighed. "Everything is more difficult than when I was a little girl."

"I'll have to invite Father. It would be an unforgivable slight to exclude him." A paradox. Klaus hated the very idea of this wedding but would be offended if he weren't invited. "He won't come, of course."

"Hmph." Katrin scowled. *Even with a frown on her face, she is beautiful,* Franz mused. "He might if he thought he could sneak Frau Hilgenberg in with some other candidate to take my place."

"That won't be allowed. Perhaps he will send Brunhilda in his stead."

Her scowl faded into a genuine smile and her eyes lit up. She truly was his sunshine. "Well, I suppose she could tend the coat check." She laughed, but quickly grew serious again. "I'm sorry, Franz. I shouldn't worry. God will make a way for us."

Franz's smile disappeared as three SS men walked past in a hurry to somewhere. Or someone. He stopped walking, leaned down, and whispered in her ear. "Katrin, what are we doing, chattering about wedding plans? We just committed treason. I could be executed. So could Friedrich. You might get lucky and be sent to Sachsenhausen."

She froze, her jaw slack and her eyes wide. After a moment, she shuddered slightly. "You're right. Franz... I think... maybe we should forget about a fancy wedding... or a honeymoon. Maybe we should just be married quietly."

Franz started walking again, with Katrin still on his arm. "No. I want you to have the wedding of your dreams. And I like Bavaria. But small is better than big, and sooner is better than later."

"Bavaria would be lovely." She looked up at him. "But Franz... I don't need Bavaria. I only need you."

"You will always have me, as long as I live."

~

Franz hadn't called ahead. He hoped that his father was home tonight and not entertaining his Nazi bigwig friends. Like Friedrich, he didn't wish Klaus ill. He still loved him, in the same way, he supposed, that a parent continues to love a delinquent son. Unlike Friedrich, Franz had no taste for deception, though he had recently discovered he had some skill for it. He had found it in him to act decisively against the regime. Somehow, he could confront head-on the differences he had with his father.

As he stepped up to the front door, he swallowed hard and whispered a quick prayer. Once he felt settled, he took a deep breath and knocked. A minute later, Brunhilda stood in the open doorway.

Franz had learned that it was futile to attempt to trade greetings or small talk with Brunhilda, so he cut to the chase. "Is my father available?"

"One moment, Hauptmann." The woman closed the door. *To my own house!* A few moments later, she opened the door and invited Franz inside. "You may sit in the parlor. The Kreisleiter will join you in a moment. May I take—" She must have suddenly realized he wasn't wearing his overcoat, because she sputtered, "Never mind," then turned and walked away. *Yes, she could handle the coat check.*

Franz limped to the parlor, sat down, and inspected the Hoyer print with new eyes. *Not a Party. A grotesque cult and their idol.*

Soon, Father came in and sat across from him. "Good evening, Son. It's good to see you. Why do I have such good fortune tonight?"

Franz hesitated. It had taken Father twenty-seven years to warm up to him, twenty-seven years to show him affection and genuine respect. Was he really going to throw that away now? *Maybe I should wait to talk with him. Maybe I can ease into this somehow.*

No. No more splitting the difference.

"Father, I have something to tell you…" He paused again.

"A promotion? A transfer to the OKH planning division?" Father raised his eyebrows in anticipation. Franz frowned and shook his head. "You've found a good girl?" It had been only a few weeks since their last conversation on this topic. Klaus seemed to have an exaggerated sense of how quickly Franz could find a new girl, fall in love, and settle down. But the suggestion left an opening for Franz to take the leap.

"Yes, Father. I found a very good girl and we are to be married." Klaus's dour face brightened. Until Franz continued. "Her name is Katrin Weber, and we are to be married as soon as we can arrange it."

His father instantly deflated as he glowered at his son. Before he had a chance to object, Franz continued. "I know what you have said. I respect you and I have given your point of view due consideration before making my decision. We hope you will attend the wedding"—his one moment of dissembling—"but if you choose not to, I understand."

Speechless, Klaus stared at him. He started breathing so heavily that Franz feared he might be having some sort of attack. "Father? Are you all right?"

Klaus went on the offensive, assailing Franz in a commanding voice. "I thought I made it clear that this is unacceptable. Perhaps I was not clear enough." He stiffened and glared at Franz. "Under no circumstances will I permit you to marry that girl. What about your future?"

Franz bit his tongue. "Father, your concern for my future means a great deal to me, but your path is not my path."

"What do you mean by that?" Klaus snapped.

This time Franz would not wilt silently in the face of his father's barrage. Drawing in a deep breath, he began carefully. "You have taught me many things. You taught me to stand up and fight for what I believe. You have done that all your life. You taught me courage, to be brave when my comrades need me. You taught me what it means to provide a home for your family. I admire these things. This is part of your path—the best part of your path—and I intend to make it my path, too.

"But after that, our paths diverge. Bormann is right. I did not want to see it at first, but he is right. You are right.

National Socialism and Christianity are not compatible." Franz inhaled, then exhaled, steeling himself. "We do have to choose. You made your choice. Now I have made mine."

Klaus's face grew red and his whole body stiffened. "Stop, Franz. Stop now."

"I can no longer be silent, not in my own house. I cannot pretend to be something I am not." Franz looked up at the Hoyer. "There is only one Word—"

"I'm warning you, Franz," Father growled.

"—and it isn't the Führer."

When Franz finally fell silent, he realized he had said much more than he intended. He didn't know what to say next.

After a long, awkward silence, Klaus rose to his feet, eyes bulging, and began to speak with controlled anger. "Franz, never repeat what you just said outside these four walls. This is exactly what I am talking about. That girl has filled your head with nonsense, and she is going to get you killed."

"She has filled my heart with love, Father. There is no other way to live."

Again, silence. Then Klaus sat back down as a change came over his expression. He softened, his face sagging slightly. To Franz it seemed that he was reconciling himself to an outcome he despised but could not alter. "Son, I cannot change your mind. I will no longer try."

When Franz was ready to leave, Klaus escorted him to the door and opened it himself, though Brunhilda had stepped forward to do her job.

"Good night, son. Heil Hitler."

"Good night, Papa." Franz walked through the cool night to the U-Bahn with the bittersweet realization that his relationship with his father had changed forever.

CHAPTER
29

13 MAY 1943

Katrin's heart was overflowing with joy. Warmth had returned to Berlin, and it had reached an unseasonable eighty-five degrees across the city. More importantly, she and Franz now stood side by side as partners. She hadn't meant to pull him into any of this. In fact, she had tried to keep him out and had nearly lost him over it. But here they were. At last, he had chosen his mother's path. Soon they would be married. Perhaps they would even honeymoon in Bavaria, though that seemed more dream than probability.

After a busy day at the bakery, she was home. Mother had cooked a meal of sausage and potatoes, and Herr Rothberg had sent a loaf of bread with her to contribute to the family meal. There were perks to working at his bakery. It wasn't a fancy meal, but it would keep body and soul together.

After supper, Katrin retired to her room to read, Bruno at her feet. A few weeks ago, Papa finally agreed to let the behemoth stay in the house. Mama washed dishes while Papa sat in his study, his nightly custom, listening to Greater

German Radio. Mostly, he listened to get early warning of an air raid. He also wanted to hear the bulletins, though he frequently scoffed at them. No matter how flawed the official radio was, there was no other source of news except for rumors, which were usually even more unreliable, and foreign broadcasts, which could earn one a jail sentence. Occasionally, like many Germans, Father would tune in to the BBC anyway, with the windows closed and the volume down low.

Katrin lay down the *Discourses of Epictetus* when she heard the newest OKW communique wafting through the house. After the first few words, Father turned up the volume.

> *...gret to inform the German nation that, facing superior forces and cut off from all means of escape, Army Group Africa has ceased military operations. The soldiers of Army Group Africa fought with honor and skill to the end of their resources and are owed the gratitude of the German nation. The sacrifice they made for Führer and Fatherland will never be forgotten.*

When the communique ended, Gustav turned the radio back down so that Katrin could hear only music and garbled words. *Hmm. The Stalingrad of the desert. At least they got to surrender to the British and the Americans rather than the Soviets.* Katrin hoped for the defeat of the National Socialist regime at the earliest possible moment. Every bit of bad military news brought her a bit of inner gladness. But then she would invariably reflect on the human cost to her neighbors and friends. *There were probably boys from my neighborhood, from my church in the Afrika Korps, drafted into the Army and dying alone in the sand or surrendering in humiliation. I can hate what they fight for, but I cannot hate them.*

When she began reading again, Epictetus declared that a man of virtue was "sick and yet happy, in peril and yet happy, dying and yet happy, in exile and happy, in disgrace and happy." It reminded her of a verse in 1 Peter: *If ye be reproached for the name of Christ, happy are ye; for the spirit of glory and of God resteth upon you.* Peril and death and reproach swirled all around. How long could she remain untouched?

Katrin tried to read more but couldn't concentrate, so she told her parents goodnight and went to bed. She had to be back at the bakery bright and early.

~

BAM! BAM! BAM!

The loud banging invaded Katrin's dream, forcing her awake. She glanced at the alarm clock on her nightstand. It was 4:55, and the sun was about to rise.

BAM! BAM! BAM!

The banging continued. In National Socialist Germany, that was never a good sign. Katrin sat up, swung her feet over the edge of her bed, and then did not move. She would let Papa answer the front door.

BAM! BAM! BAM! BAM!

"Gestapo! Open up!"

She tiptoed to the bedroom door, opened it a crack, and peered out as Papa, dressed in pajamas and a bathrobe, padded his way to the stairs and then down. Katrin crept into the hall so she could hear what was going on.

BAM! BAM! BAM!

Bruno was downstairs now, barking madly. Father opened the door. Before he could speak, Katrin heard a stranger's gruff voice. "Geheime Staatspolizei. Katrin Weber lives here."

"Yes, she's my daughter. What is the matter?" Papa's voice wavered slightly.

"She needs to come with us."

From upstairs, Katrin strained to hear her father's quiet response. "That can't be right." *Was Papa really trying to argue with the Gestapo?*

"Just get her."

In a pained voice, Gustav called up "Katrin! Sweetheart!"

Bruno was still barking and growling at the visitors.

A second angry voice from the doorway commanded, "Get your dog under control, Herr Weber, or I will shoot it."

Her heart frozen, Katrin quickly slipped on her robe and came down the stairs and to the door. The robe was modest, but she blushed. Two strangers stood just inside the doorway, tensely poised, like Schnitzel ready to pounce on his sister. Katrin could see their car idling in front of the house. Trying to ignore the fear that gripped her, she started cataloguing the agents' characteristics. They were, she thought, in their early to mid-thirties. One was tall, the other medium height and stocky. Both wore double-breasted suits and fedoras. That was as far as she got, her mind too rattled to notice anything more. Father had Bruno by the collar. He wrestled the snarling hound into the kitchen and closed him in before returning to his daughter's side.

The tall one spoke first. "Katrin Weber?"

His frosty tone turned her blood to ice. "Yes, I am she."

The stocky one pulled a silver Gestapo medallion from his pocket. He had a slightly nasal voice. "Katrin Weber, you are under arrest. You have five minutes to dress and gather any necessities."

Katrin saw no way out. Panic loomed, and her hands shook. Speechless, she returned to her room and put back on the dark blue dress she had worn the day before. As she pulled on her shoes, suddenly Mama was standing there with her jacket. Her eyes were wet, but she didn't say anything. Katrin slipped the jacket on and grabbed the purse she had hung over the bedpost before going to sleep six and a half hours ago. She balled her hands into fists to try to stop their trembling.

Followed by her mother, Katrin went back downstairs and stepped into the foyer. She could hear Bruno frantically barking and clawing at the kitchen door. She gave her parents each a hug and a kiss in turn. Gustav pulled her back and gave her a long kiss on the forehead. "Dear girl... I love you."

Renate, still blinking back tears, couldn't manage any words.

Gustav made one last hopeless appeal on his daughter's behalf. "She works in a bakery, for goodness' sake. She has done nothing."

The tall one responded curtly, "That is for us to determine, Herr Weber." At that, the stocky agent took Katrin by the arm, turned her around, and roughly handcuffed her. In a matter of seconds, she was in the Mercedes 260D, sandwiched between the two agents. A third sat behind the wheel. Katrin turned to look out the back window. Her parents had come outside and were standing on the sidewalk, watching in dismay. As they receded into the distance, Katrin realized she had never felt so alone. *Herr Gott, be with me.*

~

Franz had just sat down at his desk. It was 08:01 and his phone was already ringing. When he picked it up, he didn't get a chance to speak. He recognized the voice on the other end as Gustav Weber's, but it wasn't the strong, confident voice that had offered Franz a drink just last week. It was shaking, thin, frightened.

"Franz, my boy, they've taken her."

Franz's heart skipped a beat. "Herr Weber?"

"Ja, ja, it's Gustav. They've taken her."

Franz could guess who "they" and "she" were, but he needed Gustav to calm down, and he needed to make sure he understood the problem. He lowered his voice and cupped his hand over the receiver. "Who took whom?"

There was a deep breath on the other end. "The Gestapo. They've taken my little girl, my Katrin."

No, God. Please, no. Franz closed his eyes for a few seconds and inhaled slowly. "When did this happen?"

"Just before five. I've been calling since then, but you weren't at your desk."

"What did they say?"

Gustav started talking too fast again. "Not much. Just that she was under arrest. Franz, they gave her five minutes to get dressed, then she was gone." He finally paused to catch his breath. "You have to do something."

Franz clenched his fists. Now he was angry as well as worried. But he needed information. "Did they say where they were taking her?"

"No. They told us nothing. No charges, not where they were taking her. Nothing."

Franz frowned. His Sunshine! "How was Katrin? What did she say?"

"She was scared. I saw it in her eyes." Franz heard a catch in Gustav's voice. "But she stayed calm, collected her things, and kissed us goodbye."

She is a strong woman. "All right, Gustav. You and Renate must try to stay calm yourselves. I will do everything I can."

"I won't be able to calm down." Gustav sucked in a breath. "I've been losing my mind for the last three hours. But I will let you go so you can find her and get her out.

Promise me."

Franz wished he could promise. He knew Gustav had called him out of desperation. Katrin had been sucked into the vortex of the National Socialist terror machine, and there wasn't much a Carpool desk-jockey could do for her. But he had to try, and he knew a certain Abwehr agent he could trust. "Gustav, I will do my best. You know I will."

There was a long pause at the other end. "Then go do your best. And may God go with you."

~

Both Franz's heart and his leg were aching by the time he hobbled the length of the Bendlerblock. This conversation could not take place over the telephone. *How did this happen? Was Katrin betrayed by someone we know?* The possibility that his father had something to do with it gnawed at him. Klaus had promised he wouldn't, but what if he had?

On the other hand, Katrin had been doing plenty of things to arouse suspicion on her own.

As he approached Friedrich's desk, he pulled up and caught his breath. His brother was there, thank goodness, immersed in this week's edition of *Das Reich*. When he peered over the top of his newspaper, Franz spoke in urgent but measured tones.

"Brother, we need to take a walk." Franz lifted his eyebrows and clenched his jaw.

Friedrich frowned and lay the paper down, then stood and began walking toward the door. Franz hoped his brother would be perceptive enough not to ask questions until they were out of the building. He was.

When the pair reached the exit, Franz pushed the doors open for both of them. He nodded to the guards on the way out, counted fifteen paces, turned toward Friedrich, then spilled the news. "The Gestapo has Katrin. Gustav just called to tell me."

Friedrich visibly paled. "Oh no. God, no."

Fear was taking root deep in Franz's chest, the kind of fear he had not felt since Stalingrad. "We have to help her, Friedrich." There were many good reasons to be afraid, not least that he himself was now deeply implicated in her schemes. But only one thing was driving his fear: His Sunshine was in unspeakable danger.

Friedrich sighed deeply, as if collecting himself. "Franz, what exactly did Gustav tell you? Did the Gestapo mention a charge or where they were taking her?"

"No. They just arrested her and took her away." Franz knew that most people who had a loved one arrested never found out where they had been taken. They would just receive a notice sometime later that the person had been transferred to a concentration camp or had died trying to escape.

Friedrich stroked his chin. "All right. First, we must find her and get her out. Then we have to get her to safety."

"We need to narrow down the possibilities." Franz furrowed his brow. "Grunewald is natural. It is her home district."

Friedrich nodded. "Alexanderplatz or Prinz-Albrecht-Strasse, if they suspect something bigger."

Franz blanched. Either Berlin's central police headquarters or the notorious national headquarters of the Gestapo. Fortunately, Prinz-Albrecht-Strasse was rarely a prisoner's first stop. "Wilmersdorf, maybe, if... if Father..."

"Hmmm. Wilmersdorf." Friedrich caught on quickly. "Yes, we should add it to the list, just in case."

Franz spoke slowly. "Friedrich, it has to be you. I'm just a mid-level officer in Carpool. You are in Abwehr. As part of the security apparatus, you have standing to make inquiries." He paused. "And you know how to talk your way past anything." Franz desperately wanted to rescue his fiancée. Extracting Katrin was not something that could be done with brute force. It would require a level of subterfuge at which Franz was a novice but Friedrich an expert.

"I know." Friedrich looked down.

"I'll be ready to do whatever is necessary to get her to safety once you get her out. Just hurry, Brother. And keep me informed." Franz was ready for the conversation to end so that Friedrich could get started. The Gestapo arrested an average of fifty Berliners a day. If they didn't locate Katrin quickly, she would become lost in the ever-growing mass of humanity imprisoned by the Nazi State. Moreover, once questioning began, it was impossible to know how quickly the inquisitor might turn to "intensified interrogation," the Gestapo's euphemism for what they did when they lost patience. Franz could hardly bear to think about it.

He looked at Friedrich's face and knew he had to say one more thing. "It's not your fault. I don't blame you. She chose this and so did I. Just hurry."

Friedrich breathed another sigh, grasped Franz's arm, and turned toward the nearest U-Bahn stop.

~

Friedrich's heart and mind were in turmoil. Rarely did he allow himself to entertain his own fondness for Katrin for more than a brief moment, but the thought of her in the Gestapo's clutches tore at him. He had to find her.

Grunewald, Wilmersdorf, Alexanderplatz, Prinz-Albrecht-Strasse. Navigating this maze of jurisdictions would be no easy task. He would have to get an answer from the bottom up by methodically eliminating possibilities one by one.

He started with the Grunewald Gestapo office. After making his way to the 1854 blond brick two-story building, Friedrich walked in the front door. He scanned a large roomful of occupied desks in front of a few smaller offices, then glanced at his watch. It was 09:27 when he approached the front desk. "Heil Hitler! To whom am I speaking?"

"Heil Hitler. Night watch commander."

Friedrich looked back at his watch. "Why are you still here?"

The man at the desk shot him a sour look. "Because my replacement is an hour and a half late."

Friedrich stifled a chortle. "Name?"

"Who are you?" Gestapo personnel generally held tight to their names, and this one was no exception.

"Friedrich Maedler, Abwehr." Friedrich presented his identification.

"What do you need?" The man eyed Friedrich with a mixture of annoyance and suspicion.

Friedrich put on his most authoritative voice. "I am afraid one of our agents may have been picked up in some sort of sweep, and I am trying to locate her."

The Gestapo man snorted. "I am not authorized to release that sort of information."

Incredulous, Friedrich pressed on. "Well, who is? Aren't you the night commander?"

"Yes, but I only make and process arrests. I am not authorized to share privileged information."

Friedrich rephrased his question. "If she landed here, she would have just been brought in within the last few hours."

"Fine, but I can't tell you anything."

Friedrich raised his voice half a notch. "You realize you might be endangering an Abwehr mission."

In a faux-apologetic tone, the Gestapo man remained unyielding. "I'm sorry. You will have to talk to the Inspector. He's not here yet. My hands are tied."

Night commander, right. More like a night clerk. "Can you

at least tell me how many were brought in this morning?"

"Five."

"Thank you for your time. Heil Hitler." Friedrich turned toward the exit. He would have to return later.

Wilmersdorf was next. It was his home district, and he knew someone there. But he would have to be more discreet. The night commander in Grunewald may not have noticed or cared that his last name was Maedler, but the same would not be true in Wilmersdorf. He did not want to set foot there unless he knew for sure that was where Katrin was being held. He would call his boyhood friend, Ludwig Deutmann, and try to set up a meeting.

Deutmann had worked his way up the ranks of the Wilmersdorf Gestapo as a detective at the same time Friedrich had advanced in Abwehr. Of course, Deutmann also knew Franz.

After leaving Grunewald Gestapo, Friedrich stopped at the first pay phone he saw.

"Operator, connect me to Wilmersdorf Gestapo—Yes, Heil Hitler. Put me through to Deutmann. Just tell him it's a friend."

A minute later, a familiar voice came on the phone. "Hello, who is this?"

"Deutmann!"

"Is that you, Maedler?"

"You aren't a Gestapo detective for nothing," Friedrich joked.

"What are you up to?"

"Just checking in on an old friend."

Deutmann was dismissive. "Uh huh. How many times have I heard that?"

"Ludwig, we should have coffee sometime soon."

There was a pause on the other end of the line. "Sure. How about next Tuesday?"

Friedrich shook his head, though Deutmann couldn't see it. *I'm not waiting that long.* "How about in an hour?"

"I don't hear from you in months and now it's an hour?" Another pause. "I can make it in an hour and a half. The coffee shop next to Prager Platz."

"See you there."

Friedrich got himself to Wilmersdorf, though it took a while. Wilmersdorf was next door to Grunewald, sharing the southwest quadrant of Berlin, but bomb-damaged rails and roadways complicated travel. Friedrich found the coffee shop around the corner from the bombed-out Prager Platz and sat to wait for Deutmann. The shop was bright, with large front windows and seven or eight small tables sporting two chairs each.

Finally, Ludwig Deutmann appeared and took a seat across from Friedrich. Friedrich stared at him for a moment. "You're seventeen minutes late, you Gestapo slug."

Deutmann shrugged. "Who's counting?"

"It's been too long, Deutmann."

"Yes, too long." Deutmann nodded and smiled. "I suppose I should expect all this cloak-and-dagger from you Abwehr types, but what's the matter? I assume something is the matter."

Friedrich took a sip from the hot cup of roasted chicory coffee he'd ordered when he first arrived. Germans had taken to calling the stuff Horst Wessel coffee, because like the deceased Stormtrooper namesake of the Nazi anthem, the beans only marched with you in spirit. "You would not be wrong. But you should get some coffee yourself."

Deutmann got up, walked to the counter, ordered himself a cup of Horst Wessel coffee, and returned. When he sat back down, he arched his eyebrows and tilted his head. "So... how are things?"

Friedrich frowned and rubbed at the back of his neck.

"Well, they've been better."

"What's the matter?"

"You know, Franz is engaged, and Father doesn't like the girl. She got picked up this morning and I'm worried that Dad got carried away. Have you heard anything?" At this point, Friedrich didn't know what, if anything, Klaus had done. He was only fishing for information.

His line grew taut. There was a long pause as his friend frowned. Of course, Deutmann knew exactly who Friedrich's father was. "I can't tell you much. I really shouldn't tell you anything. But several days ago, the Kreisleiter called the Inspector. I don't know exactly what they talked about, but I was there. As soon as the call ended, the boss assigned a few of us to look into this girl. Welter, Weller, something like that."

"Weber?"

Deutmann stroked his chin. "Maybe... I think so."

"You don't know exactly what they talked about, but you know something," Friedrich prompted, staring him down.

Deutmann flinched. "Fine. The Kreisleiter thinks she's a subversive. He told the Inspector to find something on her."

Friedrich's heart fell. "So, do you think she is at the station in Wilmersdorf? I want at least to be able to tell Franz." He studied Deutmann's expression.

Reaching into his pocket, Deutmann pulled out a packet of cigarettes. He offered one to Friedrich, but Friedrich shook his head. Then he took one for himself and lit it. "No. Three days ago the case was sent to Grunewald. I'm not sure why, but it seemed the boss didn't want the arrest to come here. She's from Grunewald anyway. In any case, it's not our problem anymore."

"All right, thanks, Deutmann. I owe you." Between the coffee and the situation, Friedrich's heartburn was raging. How much longer would he have to pretend to be someone he wasn't, even to his friends?

"You're right you owe me."

Friedrich groaned inside. If his father was driving this, Friedrich couldn't just get Katrin out and have her lay low for a while. Klaus wouldn't let this go. Friedrich and Katrin would both have to leave Germany.

An hour and fifteen minutes later, Friedrich walked back into the Gestapo station in Grunewald and up to the desk that had been occupied by the night watch commander. It had a new occupant, though from the looks of it, he wasn't any fresher than the last one.

"Heil Hitler! Are you in charge?"

"At the moment." He looked up at Friedrich. "Who are you?"

Friedrich affected an air of confidence. "Maedler, Abwehr. I was here earlier. I need to know who you picked up this morning."

The new occupant of the desk rolled his eyes. "Of course you do. I'm not permitted to give out that information."

"The night watch commander said I could get that information if I came back later."

The Gestapo man rolled his eyes again. "What did you say your name was?"

"Maedler."

"Well, Maedler, he might have said *you* could get the information." The Gestapo man spoke slowly. "I doubt that he said *I* could give it to you."

"Can I speak to the Inspector?"

"In fact, you have to speak to the Inspector if you want that information. Unfortunately for you, he is unavailable today."

Friedrich scowled. "All day?"

"All day," he said flatly. "He is at a conference at the Reich Security Main Office."

Friedrich sighed deeply. "I see. And no one here can give me this information?"

"No." The Gestapo man turned away and started shuffling through a stack of papers. He looked up. "Do you have any idea how many come every day asking about their people?"

Friedrich fumed. "I have no doubt you are highly efficient at arresting enemies of the Reich and have filled your cells to capacity. I am also trying to do my job for the Reich. We have an agent who is due to go on a mission, and we think she was accidentally picked up this morning."

"Herr Maedler, come back tomorrow."

He bristled. "Major Maedler."

"Major Maedler, then. Come back tomorrow."

Friedrich played his trump card. "Do you really want to be responsible for a failed Abwehr mission?"

"Nothing can be worse than what will happen to me if my commander finds out I have violated procedure." The Gestapo man slid his finger across his throat.

Friedrich turned to leave but halfway to the door he pivoted back toward the desk. "He doesn't need to know. After all, we're all on the same side here."

"He's not going to know because there's not going to be anything for him to know."

Friedrich turned away again, but stopped at the door and turned back, ready to make one more attempt.

"Yes?" The Gestapo man emitted an exasperated sigh and rolled his eyes a third time.

"The night commander was willing to tell me that you picked up five. Can you at least tell me if any of them were women?"

"Yes. Some were. Now go. Come back tomorrow."

Friedrich gave a full-throated "Heil Hitler" and left. He wanted to shout. Nothing less would satisfy his frustration.

Deutmann's revelation pointed to Grunewald as her original destination, but he had nothing more than that and time was wasting.

Another hour, and Friedrich had entered Alexanderplatz, called the "Red Castle" because of its red brick exterior. There were certain to have been some new prisoners deposited in Alex over the last twenty-four hours. One may have been Katrin, either directly or transferred from Grunewald.

An SS man met him at the front of the large prison with an angry face and a low, grumbly voice. "Heil Hitler."

"Heil Hitler. I am Major Friedrich Maedler, Abwehr. I need to speak to someone in Intake."

The SS man squinted. "Why does Abwehr need to speak to Intake?"

"Your name and rank?"

"Obersturmführer August Ohser." The lieutenant slouched.

"I see. Obersturmführer Ohser, this is a matter of highest national security. Just bring me someone from Intake." Friedrich spoke rapidly and his baritone voice had risen half an octave.

"Wait."

Ohser disappeared. A moment later, another Gestapo officer came out. His face was set in a stony scowl and his bushy eyebrows bunched together under his furrowed brow. "Heil Hitler," he said, his tone a mix of annoyance and boredom. "What is this about?"

After his encounter with the SS man, Friedrich wanted respect. "To whom am I speaking?"

"Intake."

"Yes, I know that. Name and rank."

Raising his bushy eyebrows, Herr Intake gave nothing. "As I said, what is this about?"

Friedrich relented. "If that's the way you want it. The duty logs will tell us who was on Intake at this time. I am with Abwehr, and we are worried that an agent might have been picked up this morning by mistake. It is of utmost importance that I find her. Her mission is to begin tomorrow."

The Gestapo man stared into Fredrich's face. "We don't make mistakes."

Friedrich looked the Gestapo man right back in the eyes. "You are, of course, quite right. You do not make mistakes. But surely you can agree that sometimes your informants do." It was an open secret that the Gestapo sometimes had difficulty sorting out legitimate reports from the avalanche of denunciations made by jilted lovers, angry teenagers, and irritated neighbors.

"We brought in seventeen last night and today. You say it is a woman?"

"Yes."

"There were five." Intake held up a hand with fingers displayed.

"Names?"

"I cannot release that information. How do I know you are actually Abwehr?" The man paused briefly, then added, "And why should I care?"

What do I have to do to get these people's attention? Friedrich pulled out his identification and showed it to Intake. "If you want further proof that I am Abwehr, I will have Admiral Canaris stop by and introduce himself." Friedrich was bluffing, but Intake didn't know that.

"Fine. I'll be right back." Herr Intake retreated to the offices in the rear. Friedrich waited. And waited. And waited. The clock was ticking. Ten minutes passed. Twenty. *What if he just doesn't come back?* Friedrich had not yet figured out his Plan B, but he would need one soon.

After twenty-five minutes, Intake returned with a piece of paper with names scrawled on it. "Bruning, Ruth. Findahl, Christa. Schaub, Larissa. Stumpfegger, Barbara. Weidt, Ilsa."

No Katrin Weber. "You are sure they are the only ones?"

"Well, one was just put in a holding cell and hasn't been logged yet."

Friedrich pressed the man. "How old?"

"I would guess forty."

"Thank you. Heil Hitler."

Friedrich could strike Alex off the list. That meant Grunewald. But there was no point going back until morning. If the mandarin at the Grunewald front desk wouldn't give out names, he certainly wasn't going to release someone on his own authority. Friedrich would have to wait until tomorrow. Katrin would have to wait until tomorrow.

For now, Friedrich made his way to the Bendlerblock to put in an appearance. His office mates were used to his comings and goings. He spent the next hours studying maps and train schedules before heading home. More than once, his normally disciplined mind drifted. *I asked her to be part of this. I will never forgive myself if something happens to her. I have to get her out.*

CHAPTER
30

15 MAY 1943

After a fitful sleep, Friedrich arose early and prepared himself for combat. Not physical combat with weapons, but mental and moral combat armed only with his wits and his prayers.

At 09:03, he arrived at Gestapo Grunewald. A block from the front door, he unobtrusively crossed himself, a habit he'd picked up from Father Fellner. He was prepared to go to whatever lengths necessary to free Katrin. Precious time was slipping away.

When he entered, he saw the second man from yesterday.

"You again. Maedler, right? Abwehr?"

"Good memory." Friedrich forced a smile. "Then again, it was only yesterday."

The Gestapo man frowned. "You want the inspector."

"That's right."

Still frowning, the man got up and a few minutes later returned with his superior. The inspector was around 50 years old, short, and robust without being rotund. He adjusted the wire-rimmed glasses on his face.

Friedrich took the initiative. "Major Friedrich Maedler, Abwehr. Heil Hitler!"

"Major, I understand you have made quite a pest of yourself."

"I don't know what your... *clerk* told you, sir." Friedrich shot a cold glare at the subordinate. "One of our agents was mistakenly picked up. She is to go on a key mission for the Reich tonight, and I must secure her release. We believe she may be here."

"Identification, Major?"

"Of course." Once again, Friedrich showed his Abwehr papers. There was no way to do this without leaving evidence of his involvement everywhere.

The inspector looked over the documents, then handed them back. "And this can be verified?"

"By Admiral Canaris, if necessary." The bluff had worked once. Hopefully again.

"Whom do you need?"

Now we're getting somewhere. "Weber. Katrin Weber."

"One moment." The inspector looked through every sheet on his clipboard, rubbed his head, and started again at the top. When he got to the second page, he murmured, "Hmm, that's what I thought." He looked up at Friedrich. "To release her, I would have needed better evidence than you have given me. But it doesn't matter. She was transferred a few hours ago."

Friedrich scowled. "Alexanderplatz?"

The inspector shook his head. "Prinz-Albrecht-Strasse."

Friedrich's expression remained frozen in place, but he felt tied up in knots. He took a deep breath. He would be going into the heart of the beast. And Katrin had already been there for several hours.

~

Katrin was lying on a narrow cot topped with a thin,

stinking mattress. She wanted to sleep, to make her waking nightmare go away for just a little while, but she couldn't.

This was her second prison cell in two days. After being picked up, she was driven a short distance to the Grunewald Gestapo headquarters, where she was processed and put with eight other women in a holding cell meant for five. One had been arrested for illegal dealing in ration coupons, two for making defeatist remarks at work, one for spreading anti-National Socialist propaganda, one for belonging to a resistance group, and one for race-defiling. Two said they were unsure why they had been arrested and wouldn't share their guesses. Katrin didn't blame them. She kept quiet herself. Any one of her cell mates might be an informer. None had been there long. Last night, the resistance girl and one of the mystery women were taken out and had never returned.

Early this morning it was her turn. Katrin, the other mystery woman, the race-defiler, and six men had been shackled and loaded into a Green Minna for another drive. Five of the men and the race-defiler were taken to Alexanderplatz. Katrin's drive ended only when the police van pulled up behind national Gestapo headquarters at Prinz-Albrecht-Strasse 8. The terror of Berlin, this imposing sandstone building was where the Gestapo sent prisoners with secrets they would learn at any cost.

Katrin had been in her ground-floor cell for about three hours. At least she thought it had been three hours. Maybe it was more. Probably less. Though May had brought warmth to Berlin, the cell was chilly. And lonely. In Grunewald, at least, she'd had company. Here the small cell was all hers. A narrow window close to the ceiling let in some natural light. Lying on the cot, Katrin looked up at the window to pick out as many details as she could, a trivial exercise to keep her mind busy.

It's cloudy. A flock of robins just flew by. A plane in the distance, maybe coming to land at Tempelhof. The sound of a truck, maybe an Opel Blitz like Friedrich used. The engine sounds the same. A crow perched outside the window. A carrion bird. It's a good thing I don't believe in omens.

The game didn't last long. She didn't have much to work with. Katrin's mind turned elsewhere.

Will anyone ever know where they took me? I want to see Franz. Her heart ached. *I want to see Mama and Papa... Reinhold... Friedrich. What have I gotten myself into?*

She was deeply afraid, more afraid than she had ever felt. But she also realized she had to wrestle her fear to the ground. She mustn't lose hope. *Herr Gott, be with me. You know, I wouldn't mind an angel or two to lead me out of here, like you gave Peter in Herod's prison. Is it wrong to ask for such a miracle? Father, please, help me to remain strong.*

When the lock to her cell door clicked and the door swung open, hope surged in her, but there was no angel. Only a uniformed guard who barked, "Come." Katrin stood and walked to the man. He grabbed her upper arm and dragged her down a long corridor to the right. Then down a flight of stairs. Then back to the right, down an equally long corridor.

They stopped in front of a windowless, solid steel door. The policeman opened the door and led Katrin into the room.

~

Franz was on edge, unable to focus on the stack of requisitions in front of him. All day yesterday, he waited for updates from Friedrich. Every so often he got one, but they weren't satisfactory. Always as short as possible, with no definitive answers. *No news Grunewald. Not Wilmersdorf.* At least his father hadn't been involved. *No news Grunewald. Not Alex. Grunewald in morning.*

After work last night, he had gone to Katrin's home to tell Gustav and Renate what Friedrich had found, or not found. He was to marry Katrin, and it was his responsibility to comfort her parents and keep them informed.

Renate had let Franz in the house warily, as before. Gustav joined them in the sitting room. Franz told them their daughter, his fiancée, was still missing, but they were narrowing down the possibilities. Friedrich had ascertained that she was probably at Gestapo Grunewald. Cold comfort.

Renate had glared at him throughout his report, chilling him to the bone. Gustav wiped his brow and spoke gently. "Thank you, Franz. Keep trying. Don't give up." As Franz solemnly nodded, Renate's dam burst. She stood up and her head swiveled toward Gustav. "Thank you for what?" Then back toward Franz. Again, louder. "Thank you for what? His friends have taken our daughter and we will never—"

Gustav interrupted firmly. "That's enough, Renate."

"—see her—"

"That's enough," Gustav insisted, slamming his hand down onto the armrest of his chair.

Franz stared at the floor as an uncomfortable silence filled the room. He had known this would be hard. He hadn't known how hard. "Frau Weber," he began slowly, "they are not my friends." He looked up into Renate's eyes. "And I am not theirs. I cannot tell you more, but please know that I could be next." *What could I say that would make her understand?* He sighed deeply. "And please know that I am still my mother's son."

Renate collapsed into her chair and wept. When Franz drew near, she grasped his arm and clung to him for a long moment. Finally, she straightened her shoulders and released him. "Go, Franzi," she had said, her voice thin and shaky. "You can't look for her if you are here."

Now, sitting at his desk in the Bendlerblock, Franz waited for the phone to ring again. When it did, he snatched up the receiver partway through the first ring. The caller didn't identify himself, but it was Friedrich's voice.

"Listen to me. She's at Prinz-Albrecht-Strasse. I'm going there now." Franz paled. *Prinz-Albrecht-Strasse? My Sunshine.* He had wanted news, but not this.

"Did you hear me?"

Franz snapped out of his shock. "I heard."

"Are you ready?"

"Just tell me what you need." When—if—Friedrich sprung Katrin, it would be Franz's turn to be a hero.

"I will. Franz, if this doesn't work... Farewell."

"Farewell." Franz echoed. He swallowed hard as he hung up, stunned by the finality of Friedrich's goodbye.

~

The cold, musty room was lit only by a bare low-wattage bulb hanging from the ceiling in a corner behind her. At first, Katrin could hardly see anything as her escort pushed her down into a wooden chair. He handcuffed her to it, told her to wait, and walked out of the room, closing and locking the door behind him.

Katrin looked around, but it took several minutes for her vision to adjust. She could tell it was a large space, about five by seven meters. The desk in front of her was the first thing to emerge clearly, then the chair behind it.

When her eyes began to make out items on the desk, she took a deep breath. Beside a lamp she saw a riding crop, a pair of pliers, a soldering torch, and a device that looked like the medieval thumbscrews at the castle museum her class had visited in fifth form. Her heart started racing.

She looked away. As her eyes wandered around the room, she noted an empty bathtub against the left wall and, in the corner behind the desk, something that looked like a chain pulley attached to the ceiling. Katrin clenched her teeth and shivered. How long would she be able to hold out?

Her eyes darted involuntarily to the opposite corner from the pulley. On the floor lay a woman's slip and a single high-heeled shoe. She gasped and closed her eyes tight. Terror engulfed her.

Katrin opened her eyes, looked straight down at the front of the desk, and tried to collect herself. *Herr Gott, please get me out of here somehow. Please.*

She had to stop thinking about what she had seen. She closed her eyes and began to rehearse the advice Friedrich had given in case she was ever picked up.

Say as little as possible. Don't try to answer broad, open-ended questions. Make them narrow their inquiries. Be brave. They are bullies, and you will have better luck if you go on the offensive and put them off balance. Remember that they usually don't know as much as they claim to. Keep to the truth as much as you can. Lies are harder to remember and easier to disprove. They will repeat their questions; you must answer the same way each time. Clear your mind before it begins. Concentrate. It will be exhausting, but don't let them wear you down. If you show weakness or let them trip you up, all will be lost. Then it will get worse, much worse. Then you must simply try to hold on as long as you can and buy time for the others to find safety.

Katrin had never liked the last part. She especially didn't like it now. She clung to the hope that if she followed Friedrich's formula, it wouldn't come to that.

A key clicked in the lock. Her heart pounded. When the door opened, three men entered. One was a tall, ungainly man, about forty, wearing a dark suit. He sat across from Katrin and dropped a thick file folder on the desk between them. The two other men wore grey SS uniforms and took up positions standing to the side. One of them unlocked the handcuffs. A young woman about Katrin's age followed them in, closed the door behind her, and sat at another small table with a stenographer's machine. When her eyes met Katrin's gaze, she smirked.

The Gestapo man behind the desk turned on his lamp, which was brighter than any Katrin had ever seen. He flipped the lamp up to shine in Katrin's face. She was nearly blinded by the light, and she turned her head and squinted so her eyes were almost shut.

"Fräulein Weber, welcome to Prinz-Albrecht-Strasse. Do you know why you are here?" His voice surprised her—it was a rich baritone that would have been put to better use in the church choir than in this dark place.

"No, I don't." Katrin worked at regulating her breathing, keeping her tone even and respectful. "May I be informed of the charges against me?" Katrin knew the Gestapo was permitted to hold people for any reason it wanted or no reason at all, but if she knew the charges, she could at least prepare a defense.

Stringbean ignored her question. With the bright light shining, she couldn't see what he was doing, but she heard him leafing through papers for a moment. "Let's see. Expelled from Gymnasium. Father fired from university, never joined the Party, and criticized the firing of Jews. Brother involved with seditious religious organization, married a Jew, and fled the Fatherland. Protested T4 program. Employer's file says he is 'politically unreliable.' Refused German greeting on Führer's birthday. Observed at Rosenstrasse demonstration this past February." *So, someone did see me there.* The file fell back to the desk with a soft thud. "Not the profile of a loyal citizen of the Reich. What are you up to these days?"

Friedrich's voice sounded in her head. *Make them*

narrow their inquiries. The question was too broad. "I'm not sure what you mean."

"I see." Stringbean paused. "We'll get back to that. Maybe we should start with more history. Why were you expelled?"

That one, at least, was easy, though her answer would be incomplete. "I failed physical fitness twice."

"Is that all?"

Katrin shuffled in her seat. "It's the reason the director gave me."

Stringbean moved rapidly to another topic. "And why did you never join the League of German Girls?"

"It was not required at the time. My interests were more academic." Katrin blinked at the light.

The Gestapo man scoffed. "More academic. I see. So, you did agricultural service next?"

"Yes. I worked on a farm outside Feldkirchen for the mandated year." For a brief second, Katrin's mind filled with the peaceful image of a Bavarian pasture.

Stringbean's next question yanked her back to the interrogation room. "So, you served the Fatherland when it was required and did not serve when it was not required. What should that tell me about your loyalties?"

"Again, I don't know what you mean."

"It's not hard, Fräulein." Stringbean affected a tone of impatience. What would a reasonable person conclude about your loyalties?"

Silence. *Perhaps we should find a reasonable person to ask.* She cast off the thought. *No, too confrontational.*

"Sometime soon, Fräulein."

Still, it was time to go on the offensive. "Do you come to work even when there is a holiday and you aren't scheduled?"

The inquisitor drummed his fingers on the desk. "No."

"What would a reasonable person conclude about your loyalties, if you come to work only when it is required of you?" Katrin pursed her lips.

The SS men behind her chuckled. Stringbean took his losses and moved on. "Hooligans in Wilmersdorf are posting treasonous flyers on people's backs. We have reports that one of them is a girl about your age, brown hair, green eyes, short. Sounds like you, no?"

This she could answer honestly. "Sounds like many people. But *sounds like* doesn't mean *is*. I know nothing about such hooligans."

"Well, soon we will have a sketch, and then we will see...." He changed gears again. "You know Pastor Hoffman?"

"Yes."

Stringbean pressed on. "And you attend services at his church?"

"Yes."

"How would you describe his reputation?"

She tilted her head. "From whose point of view?"

Coldly, Stringbean answered, "Let's start with mine."

"I suppose you wouldn't like him much." Katrin squirmed and blinked some more.

"And why is that?" His voice sounded closer, as if he had leaned forward, but the bright light still obscured his face, and she could not judge his distance from her.

"He is a churchman, and it's hardly a secret that the Gestapo does not appreciate the Church."

"And why do you think that is?"

Her mind raced. It took every fiber of her being to keep from blurting out the answer— *Because you are tyrants and enemies of God.* The words would condemn her in the eyes of the State. Yet if she refused to answer, would she be denying Christ? *Herr Gott, give me the words. Make me wise as a serpent and subtle as a dove.* Finally, she took in a deep breath and exhaled slowly. "Sir, you are in the Gestapo, not I. You can answer that question better than I can."

Stringbean seemed stumped. He shoved back his chair with a screech, then she heard him pacing for a couple of minutes before he sat down again.

Katrin wished he would turn off the light. She still couldn't bring herself to open her eyes fully or look in his direction. She found it unnerving, being unable to see her interrogator. *How long, oh Lord?*

CHAPTER
31

15 MAY 1943

At 10:30, Friedrich strode up to the doors of Prinz-Albrecht-Strasse 8. Once an art museum, the five-story Wilhelmine structure had been taken over by the Gestapo in 1933. Now there were offices, interrogation rooms, and thirty-nine solitary prison cells. Passers-by sometimes reported hearing screams from upper floor windows. Six SS men armed with submachine guns guarded the entrance. The one to the immediate right of the door demanded identification, which Friedrich provided. His appearance of confidence belied his churning guts. This wasn't some obscure outpost. It was the national headquarters of the secret police.

Once he obtained entrance, he found the prison commandant's office. There was an outer office, with a secretary and another guard, and then the commandant's personal office. Friedrich went in, showed his identification yet again, and told the secretary, "Fräulein, I must see the commandant. It is a matter of the utmost importance."

"May I ask who you are?"

"Friedrich Maedler, Abwehr. It's urgent." Friedrich sighed and set his jaw. He didn't know what he was walking into. If Katrin had already been broken, he might never walk out.

The secretary picked up the phone and dialed. Friedrich could hear the commandant's phone ringing on the other side of the door. "Sir, you have a visitor from Abwehr. He says it is urgent." Friedrich heard a muffled answer through the door, and, with an ever-so-slight delay, words coming from the telephone receiver. "Tell him to wait."

~

The respite didn't last long. When Stringbean resumed, he led Katrin through all the same questions twice more. Or was it three times? Her head was starting to ache. Now he shuffled through the dossier again. "Your neighbors, the Schneiders, tell us that your family has a cottage in Friedrichsbrunn. Did you visit the cottage around the thirtieth of March?"

"Yes."

"And again in mid-April, and again around the first of May?"

Pausing, she wanted to appear as if she were thinking about the dates he'd given. Finally, she nodded. "Yes, that sounds right."

"That is quite a few visits in a short time, isn't it? What was the purpose of your visits to the cottage?"

She and Friedrich had discussed the possibility she would have to answer that question. She felt her cheeks warm as she thought of the answer they had agreed she would give if they needed to divert the Gestapo. "I was there with… a male friend. My parents would not have approved, so we went to the cottage instead."

"And the name of this friend is?"

"Friedrich Maedler."

The Gestapo man looked through her dossier again. "Really? Friedrich Maedler? But you are engaged to Hauptmann Franz Maedler." She could almost feel a salacious stare coming from the other side of the table. "Perhaps your parents would not have been the only ones to disapprove."

"Yes, we considered that."

He shrugged. "Or perhaps there was no secret tryst. Parents from a cottage on the same road reported that two children out playing after dark the night of, let's see, fifth May, told them that a 'big army truck' stopped in front of your cottage and 'a bunch of people' got in. Can you explain that?"

The Albrecht boys... it had to be. Of course, they were sneaking around. But they are known for their active imaginations. Katrin kept her tone light. "Children often spin wild tales. I know I did when I was a child."

"Why do I feel like you are not being honest with me, Fräulein?"

"Why do I feel like you have already made up your mind about me?" she retorted, and instantly regretted it.

Suddenly the riding crop whistled through the air and slammed on the desk half a dozen times. The sound of the *thwacks* reverberated through the room. Katrin gasped. "Do not trifle with me, Fräulein!" The whip clattered to the desk and Stringbean's chair creaked under his weight. "Your papers say you travelled to Switzerland right after your last visit to the cottage. Why?" Stringbean was talking faster.

"I went to visit my brother Reinhold." True enough, but once they checked the border control logs, they would see there was no record of her exit. *This is getting worse.*

Stringbean pressed on the subject. "The traitor? You had state permission for this travel?"

"How could I have crossed without it?" Katrin shrugged and tried to keep her hands from shaking. They would find no record of that, either.

"Excellent question." Then Stringbean tossed something onto the desk in front of Katrin. "Perhaps you have an explanation for that." It was the Star of David pendant Eva had given Katrin for safekeeping.

Katrin swallowed hard. They must have found it in her purse—in her nervousness, she had forgotten to give it to Friedrich. Fortunately, she had not been searched at the border. But now Stringbean had found it. *Oh Eva, I'm so sorry.* "It belonged to an old friend. I forgot I had it."

"An old friend? Does this friend have a name? You are quite good at talking without answering questions."

"Her name was Eva." Katrin wanted to reach for the necklace but feared what would happen if she did.

"And when did she give it to you?"

Despite Friedrich's advice, this time she had to lie. "Years ago, before her family left Germany. 1933, I think. Maybe early 1934." She felt perspiration forming on her forehead.

"And you've been carrying it around in your purse ever since?" Stringbean's voice rose in apparent disbelief.

"I promised I would keep it close, to remember her by. I put it in my purse and forgot it was there. I've had that bag for years—you can see how worn it is." That much was true. The purse had belonged to Katrin's mother before it belonged to her.

"So, you have a soft spot for the Jews..." Stringbean trailed off and let Katrin dangle for a moment. "You were on Rosenstrasse."

Katrin struggled to stay calm. "I was on my way to buy shoes and I saw the commotion. I was curious."

"And what did you find?"

She blinked. "I'm sorry, Sir. I'm not sure what you mean."

He cleared his throat. "I mean how would you describe the demonstration on Rosenstrasse?"

"It was a gathering of women understandably worried about their husbands and sons."

"We had to call out the SS to control it. And you were part of it."

"I only observed. I did not join in." Katrin felt the walls closing in on her. She wasn't sure how much longer she could avoid letting his questions trip her up.

Stringbean continued pressing. "Of course, many women there would have jumped at a chance to get their Jews out of Germany, wouldn't you agree?"

She shrugged. "I suppose." She suddenly noticed how dry her mouth had become. She longed for a drink of water.

Her interrogator paused for a moment. "And I suppose that some of them told you that?" His voice rose, but Katrin knew it was not really a question.

"I did not speak to such women at the demonstration, sir."

"No one who wanted to get out or to help a relative hide or get out?"

"No." Another lie. *Forgive me, Father.* She wished she knew how much they already knew. Did they have Franz or Friedrich in custody? Had they found the secret room in the cellar? At least Samuel and Gerta and the others had already made it to safety.

"I see." Stringbean took a deep breath. "You know, our agents searched the cottage. In the cellar they found a false wall, a hidden room. Shoddily made. Easy to detect, when you have been at this as long as we have."

Katrin struggled to put on a brave face. "A childhood hideout. A clubhouse of sorts. My brother and I played there when we were young."

"A childhood friend, a childhood hideout, children who can't be believed. This is starting to sound very strained." Suddenly, one of the SS men behind Katrin grabbed her arms, wrenched them behind her, and slapped the handcuffs back on. She grimaced as pain shot up her shoulders. Stringbean must have given them a sign, though she hadn't seen it. "The walls are thick in this room, Fräulein. Your cell is directly above us. You probably didn't even hear the girl who was here before you. Now, let's start again. What was the purpose of your visits to the cottage?"

She struggled for breath. *Help me, Father. Please. I don't know if I'm strong enough.* "I went with Friedrich. We didn't want Franz to find out." The truth, even if she was implying a falsehood.

"And what about the truck? Do you really want me to believe that the children hallucinated an army truck and a crowd of people?"

"I don't know about the truck. I do know that last year, some neighbor children tried to convince their parents that an American soldier parachuted into the woods near there. They let their imaginations run away with them."

Stringbean returned to the topic of the cottage. "Who built the hidden room, this so-called playroom?"

"My brother and I, with our father's help... when we were young."

"So perhaps you would like us to bring your father in to ask him about it?" She could practically hear him smirking.

Katrin's mind was frantic. *No, not Papa.* Again, Friedrich's words came back to her, calming her. *Remember that they usually don't know as much as they say they do.* Perhaps they knew about the room, or perhaps Stringbean had merely assumed there was a room and wanted confirmation. But she had made sure no sign remained of their Jewish guests. "Papa would only tell you what I have already told you."

"The report by the agents said the construction looked new." The Gestapo man stopped for a moment. "You are a Christian, right?"

Katrin took a deep breath. "Yes, I am. You know that."

"What does the Bible say about lying?"

"That it is a sin."

"You should reflect on that."

A sin... and yet Rahab lied to protect the men of Israel when they came to Jericho, and her life was saved because of it. She took a steadying breath. She could not stray from her story now. "I don't know why the agents say the construction looked new. Perhaps like you, they had already decided what they wanted to find, rather than looking for the truth."

The Gestapo man raised the volume of his baritone voice a few notches. "I will tell you what the truth is, you little tart. You were hiding Jews, probably some from Rosenstrasse, maybe others. Then you moved them. I don't know how, I don't know where, and I don't know who helped you, but I am going to find out." Katrin heard the squeal of pipes and then the sound of water filling the tub. Stringbean must have given another sign. Now he continued. "Your friends, whoever helped you, whoever got you into this mess, you don't owe them anything. You are here and they are... not here. They have abandoned you. I want names and I want details. All the details."

Jesus, help me. Katrin felt an unexpected sense of peace spread through her, dispelling her terror. She would not believe his lies.

"There is nothing more I can tell you." Whatever Stringbean may threaten, she was not alone in this moment.

"Oh, I am quite certain there is more you can tell me.

And you will." The Gestapo man stopped his questioning, and for a time, there was only the sound of the water filling the tub.

~

For half an hour, Friedrich sat quietly in the outer office, his legs crossed and his hands folded in his lap. His mind spun with worry about Katrin. When he noticed himself crossing and uncrossing his legs repeatedly, he concentrated on keeping them still. Finally, the secretary received a call, hung up, and said, "Sir, you may go in now."

Friedrich sprang to his feet and hurried through the door.

Sitting at the desk in front of him, he found a serious-looking, square-jawed man in the grey uniform of an SS Obersturmbannführer. "Heil Hitler! Herr Kommandant, I am Friedrich Maedler, and I am here on urgent Abwehr business."

"And what could that be?" The commandant's voice oozed skepticism.

Friedrich continued. "You have one of our agents. She is to go on a mission to Switzerland tonight. She must be released."

"Must be?" He stiffened and raised his eyebrows. "Are you in charge of this prison, or am I?"

Friedrich struck a conciliatory tone. "You are, sir. My apologies. But it is a matter of extreme national importance. The success of the mission depends on her."

"All right." The commandant sat back. "Who is this woman?"

"Her name is Katrin Weber. She lives in Grunewald but has a cover identity and is to infiltrate by train this evening. She will make contact with several of our agents there with urgent new instructions from the Bendlerblock."

Recognition flickered across the commandant's face. "I

know who she is. Her file came across my desk. Do you have any evidence, other than your own words?"

Friedrich stiffened. "We are a secret intelligence organization. With all due respect, sir, we do not print and frame certificates declaring who our agents are and what they are doing. Neither does the Gestapo. You must understand this."

The commandant was silent.

"I do have something." Friedrich pulled from the inside pocket of his coat the set of false Swiss papers Katrin had used to take the children across the border. "These are her cover papers." He tossed the booklet onto the desk. "Frau Katrin Kuehn, from Zürich." The commandant thumbed through it, and Friedrich thought he could see the man give a slight nod. It was risky to share the papers. If the Gestapo checked on border crossings made with those papers, they would see that she crossed with children. There would be more uncomfortable questions. But it couldn't be helped. This commandant was a tough bird and clearly needed something more than Friedrich's earnest charm.

Friedrich noticed the pile of paperwork on the commandant's desk. "Sir, you are a very busy man. You have a heavy responsibility for the defense of the Reich. I do not want to be forced to take this to the highest levels. It would not be a good use of anyone's time." He leaned forward. "And surely I need not emphasize that when crucial operations go badly, it is not a good thing to be held responsible."

The commandant bristled. "What are you suggesting?"

"Herr Kommandant, you have the power to release this woman to do her duty for the Fatherland or to hold her here despite being informed of the possible consequences, ensuring the failure of this operation and endangering German intelligence agents. Which is preferable?" This was getting to be an old trick, but Friedrich only had to make it work one more time. The key was confidence.

The commandant narrowed his eyes and stared at Friedrich. "We have evidence that she harbored Jews. Something about some cottage in Friedrichsbrunn."

Friedrich scoffed. "That's ridiculous. There are hardly any Jews left. She has a cottage in Friedrichsbrunn where she and I go sometimes to, let us say..." He raised an eyebrow. "...practice our tradecraft. It is nothing more." He felt a twinge of guilt at this lie—and that a part of him wished it were true.

"You are Friedrich Maedler. I saw from Fräulein Weber's file that she is engaged to Hauptmann Franz Maedler. You know him?"

"My brother."

The commandant smirked. "Is he aware of her intelligence activities?"

"Only recently."

"And your... 'tradecraft' sessions?"

"No," Friedrich said with a sly smile, "Or I think I wouldn't be here." *Dear God, how have I reached the point where I can lie so effortlessly?*

The commandant guffawed. "And you are both sons of the Kreisleiter of Wilmersdorf?"

"The one who accidentally set this fiasco in motion, yes. I will take responsibility for ironing things out with my father."

"Hmm." The commandant put his hand on his forehead. Friedrich narrowed his eyes. *He doesn't want to get in the middle of this family squabble.*

Friedrich sensed that now was the time to push. He stood, picked up the commandant's phone receiver, and prepared to dial. "Should I ring Admiral Canaris?"

"No, no, Maedler. All right." The commandant handed

the false papers back to Friedrich. "They're interrogating her now. Come with me. If she hasn't implicated herself, you can have her. If she has… it will become more complicated."

Friedrich's heart sank at what Katrin might be going through. He followed the commandant out of his office complex and into the hall. They reached a guarded and locked door that separated the entrance to the prison from a long row of cells. Beyond the cells, they reached a stairwell, then turned right at the bottom of the stairs. *Can't he walk faster?* Another long hallway brought them to a heavy steel door. A few seconds later the door swung wide.

Friedrich entered quickly and counted an interrogator at a desk, a stenographer, two SS men, a bathtub filling with water—and Katrin, in a blue dress, sitting in a chair with her arms behind her and an incredibly bright light shining into her turned face.

The commandant entered next and asked the interrogator, "Has she given you anything?"

"Not yet," Stringbean grumbled. "But she will."

The commandant nodded in the direction of Friedrich and announced, "Weber, Katrin. You are released into the custody of Abwehr." Turning to Friedrich, he added, "Maedler, you will have to sign her out." The commandant was canny as well as tough, taking every precaution to cover his National Socialist posterior. Friedrich half-walked, half-ran to Katrin's side and reached to turn off the light as an SS man unshackled her. She looked harried, frightened, and more beautiful than ever.

She blinked several times before she seemed to see him. "Friedrich?" she said weakly, and a wan smile flashed across her tense face.

The tall, blond Gestapo interrogator stood to object, but was cut off by his superior. "It's decided. Let her go." While everyone else in the room focused on the commandant,

Friedrich noticed Katrin stand and scoop something up from the desk in front of her. As he led her from the room by the hand, he heard someone turn off the water.

Against all odds, they were walking out of Prinz-Albrecht-Strasse 8. Whether they could stay out would be a problem for the next day. For the moment, they could breathe. It had been a very close call.

As they exited the building, Friedrich thought he heard a muffled scream from an upper window. He shuddered and ever-so-slightly squeezed Katrin's hand.

CHAPTER
32

15 MAY 1943

The call from Friedrich had put Franz into another level of turmoil. It was bad enough that Katrin was under arrest, but Prinz-Albrecht-Strasse? To make matters worse, he had to continue working as if everything were all right when he wanted to march into Gestapo headquarters. He was glad when Colonel Muntzer invited him to meet just before noon. When he got to Muntzer's office, the colonel was sitting behind a desk with a glass in his hand and a bottle of Polish vodka in front of him. He had clearly already started.

"Maedler, come in. Sit down."

"Thank you, sir."

Muntzer pulled a clean glass from his desk. "Join me?"

As much as he wanted to escape the realities of the moment, Franz needed to keep his wits about him. "No, thank you, sir. It's a bit early for me."

"Fair enough." Muntzer poured himself a glass. "How are things going? With the leg, the girl? Katrin, yes?"

"The leg is as good as can be expected, sir. And we are to

be married soon." Franz could only hope the last part was still true. He could hardly tell the colonel she was a guest of the Gestapo. Or could he? Muntzer was a human being. Franz wouldn't have to tell him the whole story. And he was about to burst from holding everything so close to the vest. "Actually, sir, I'm worried for her. There has been some mix-up and she was picked up by the Gestapo yesterday. I just found out this morning."

Muntzer looked away and sighed. "Oh. I'm sorry." He looked back at Franz. "I'm sure it will be sorted out."

"Thank you, sir."

Muntzer looked away again, muttering under his breath. "Bastards." But then, as always, he turned the conversation to Stalingrad. "Maedler, have you heard of any of your comrades?"

This was a bitter topic for Franz, but he knew Muntzer meant no harm. It was a bitter topic for him, too, and Franz was his closest connection to his nephew. They would share their bitterness. Three months since the battle ended, a little more information was available. "It seems most died. Most of the rest are missing. Notices for POWs have been trickling out through the Red Cross. Of course, it is hard to make contact..." His voice trailed off.

"I'm sure." Muntzer sipped his vodka. "Thank you, Maedler. Are you sure about the drink? I bet you could use it."

"I'm certain, but thank you, sir."

"Well, I should get back to work."

That was the colonel's gentle cue for Franz to go back to work himself. Such a contrast to their first encounter. Franz got up to go.

"Hauptmann," Muntzer called after him, "your girl will be fine."

Franz prayed that the colonel was right. "Thank you, sir."

~

A few minutes after Franz returned to his desk, Friedrich arrived. His expression betrayed nothing. "Franz, come with me. Now."

Franz left with Friedrich without stopping to get Muntzer's permission. Enough time had passed for his brother to go to Prinz-Albrecht-Strasse and haggle for Katrin's release. Either he had succeeded or... not. With each step he took toward the building exit, the tension grew. The brothers blew through the doors and past the ever-present guards to the sidewalk.

Friedrich remained silent. Franz wanted to know something, anything. "Friedrich?" Silence. Franz could hardly breathe. He feared the worst.

Two blocks away, Friedrich took a sudden turn down an alley and rounded a corner. Franz turned the corner a step behind his brother. Suddenly, standing in front of him, was Katrin. Franz felt alive again. He hobbled to his fiancée and lifted her in his arms. After spinning around twice, he set Katrin down and buried his face in her hair. "Sunshine! How are you? Did they hurt you?"

Katrin gently pushed away, stepped back, and looked up into Franz's face. "No, Franzi, I'm fine. They didn't hurt me, much." She paused. "I may have sore arms for a while." Franz studied her expression. Her eyes were glazed, and the stress of the morning was written across her face, but she had never looked more beautiful to him. He embraced her again and ran his fingers through her hair. His lips pressed against hers in a hungry kiss. Wrapping her arms around his neck, she returned his kiss, then rested her head against his chest.

Friedrich's practical voice interrupted the tender reunion. "Brother, we have only a few minutes to talk. I bought her a respite, Franz, nothing more. She can't stay in Germany, and after this, neither can I. We need a car and petrol coupons. Today."

Franz nodded.

"Here's the plan. Listen carefully."

Franz kept an arm around Katrin's shoulders, but turned to face Friedrich, mustering all the attention he could.

"Katrin and I have to go underground for the rest of today. I had to tell a fistful of lies to get her out, and there's no way to know how long it will take them to unravel it all. As soon as possible, we will go to Switzerland. I will travel as Berthold von Schemmel, a German businessman negotiating a business deal in Zürich. Katrin will go with me as Katrin von Schemmel..." He paused and his eyes flicked away from Franz for a moment. "...my wife."

Franz frowned. Three weeks ago, he would have feared this plan was another sign Friedrich had designs on Katrin. It still bothered him. But it was a sensible way to get a man and woman out of Germany together. "Go on."

"I will get you an emergency requisition for a staff car and petrol, like before. But do it tonight, after Muntzer leaves. He may get suspicious if he gets another emergency req—"

"It won't work," Franz cut in. "I might get Nonnheim to accept the car requisition without Muntzer's signature, but petrol coupons come from Kobel." He scrunched up his face. "He'll be gone, too, and Nonnheim doesn't have access to his fuel cabinet."

Friedrich rubbed at his forehead. "Fine. When does your accountant take inventory of the petrol cards?"

"Every Friday without fail. Nine o'clock sharp."

Friedrich nodded. "Good. It's already done for the week. Tonight, stay at work until the coast is clear. Get the cards yourself, then give the requisition to the dispatcher. It won't hold up under close scrutiny, but it probably won't need to." His fingers began tapping his chin. "I'll get a good lock pick to you along with the requisition. You'll have to drive us to Stuttgart, and we'll catch a train from there."

Franz tried to keep up with his brother's rapid-fire instructions.

"Franz, I'm having papers made for you, too," Friedrich assured him. "They should be ready in three or four days. An Abwehr courier will bring them. The day you get them will be your last day in Carpool. After work, buy tickets for an overnight train to Zürich. We'll meet you there. The accountant won't notice the missing ration cards until you're gone."

Franz nodded, though he was still digesting the plan. Friedrich grabbed his brother's arm. "Do you understand?"

Franz mustered another nod. Words failed him, but Katrin's presence at his side was a comfort.

"Good. This time, you'll pick up the car from the garage yourself. Here's an address." Friedrich handed Franz a small piece of paper with *Reinhardtstrasse 13* written on it. "Memorize the address and flush the paper. When you get the car, drive there. We'll be waiting for you."

Franz took a deep breath. This would be even riskier than the truck. He wrapped his arms around Katrin and dipped his head for one more kiss. "Sunshine... I love you."

She smiled, her eyes tired and soft. "I love you too, Franzi."

Franz started walking away, stopped, and turned to look at Katrin again. Neither one spoke. Franz covered the distance between them and planted one more kiss on her forehead. Then he turned back and kept walking until he reached his desk.

~

At 13:48 Franz's phone rang. It was Friedrich, though he didn't identify himself. "Hello, janitorial services? The toilet in the second stall of the third-floor restroom in the North wing is overflowing. Can you send someone to fix it right now?" Franz suppressed a grin and answered, "I'm afraid you have the wrong number." As soon as he hung up, he began the journey. When he reached the appointed stall, a man he had not seen before exited, brushed against him, and inconspicuously passed him a bulky envelope. In the stall, Franz took a lock pick and requisition form out of the envelope, secured them in his pocket, then flushed. The envelope, he tossed in the refuse bin.

Franz returned to his desk, where for the rest of the day he tried every imaginable trick to make time go faster. Nothing worked. Finally, he watched the clock reach 17:00 as a few desks emptied. At 18:00, more desks emptied, including the one that belonged to Major Rudolf Kobel, the office accountant, who went home to his Frau and his Dobermans. Franz fidgeted. His moment had almost arrived. This morning, Friedrich had pulled off his assignment. Franz was anxious to execute his own. At 19:25, he watched as Colonel Muntzer left his office and walked out of the room. By 19:45, only Franz, Lieutenant Olbermann, and the overnight dispatcher, Sergeant Nonnheim, remained. When no one else was around, Nonnheim would handle routine requests by himself.

"What are you doing here so late, Hauptmann?" Olbermann asked.

"Same as you. Catching up on paperwork." Franz pasted on a smile, but he didn't feel good lying again. 'Are you almost done for the night?"

"Yes, sir. Another ten minutes should do it."

"Lucky. I have at least twenty."

At 19:57, Olbermann picked up his things, let out a triumphant sigh, and left.

Franz knew that Nonnheim was a man of military

precision who stepped out for a smoke at exactly 20:00 every night. He would be out from seven to twelve minutes, depending on whether the pretty secretary in the Propaganda Office was working late.

At exactly 20:00, Nonnheim departed dispatch, leaving Franz alone.

Franz walked coolly to the bursar's desk, sat in his swivel chair, and turned it to face the cabinet. He pulled out the tool Friedrich had given him and inserted it into the cabinet lock. It was not an ordinary, low-grade cabinet lock, but was especially enhanced. Petrol coupons were, after all, the Reich's equivalent of paper gold.

When the tool caught in the mechanism, Franz tried to turn it. It wouldn't budge. He took it out, put it in again, and tried once more to twist it. Nothing. Franz stopped and took a deep breath. *I know it is a sin to steal, but please God, help me!* A third try came closer. He could feel movement inside the lock, but still no success. He had already spent at least three minutes trying to open the cabinet. If necessary, he could stay through the night and try again during Nonnheim's next cigarette break, whenever that came, but he was rarely in the office that late. It would look suspicious. He took another deep breath and tried again. Jiggle, jiggle, *CLICK*. The cabinet door swung open.

Franz had done the math, and he started counting out petrol coupons. Just then he heard a voice. "Hauptmann Maedler, what are you doing?" He turned sharply, sat up straight, and saw Colonel Muntzer staring at him from half a room away. "Maedler?"

Franz was frozen, caught in the act. The colonel must have come back without Franz noticing. Now he was really leaving to go home for the night. There was nowhere to run. Even Friedrich couldn't spin a story to explain this away. Franz's only hope was to tell Muntzer everything and throw himself on the colonel's mercy.

Out of genuine respect for his superior, he stood. "Sir, I'm desperate. I told you this morning about my fiancée. She was released, but the Gestapo isn't done with her. I am to drive her to Stuttgart, where she'll catch a train to Switzerland. She has help and papers. She just needs a car and fuel. And a driver."

Muntzer was silent, his face inscrutable.

"I don't know what you believe, sir." Franz's words tumbled out, carefully chosen but hurried, urgent. "We've never discussed it. But I believe if a man can stop a murder and does not, he becomes a murderer. There has been too much death."

Muntzer pursed his lips and closed his eyes for a moment. "Hauptmann, if you are discovered, I can't protect you... but I didn't see anything. Now, I have to get home to my Frau."

"Yes, sir. Thank you, sir. Thank you."

Muntzer began to leave. In the doorway, he stopped and turned back to Franz. "You don't look well, Hauptmann. Take tomorrow off and report to the infirmary in the evening. That's an order." He paused for a moment, and Franz wasn't sure if he imagined a catch in the man's voice when he added, "Be careful, son."

It was now 20:08. Franz finished counting out coupons, closed and locked the cabinet, and returned to his desk. At 20:12, Nonnheim returned. *The secretary must be working late tonight. Thank goodness.* As soon as the sergeant had settled in, Franz took the emergency requisition to him.

Nonnheim looked puzzled. "Sir?"

Franz mustered his confidence. "This just came from Abwehr. Highest priority."

Nonnheim cocked his head. "The colonel hasn't signed it."

"The colonel has left for the night."

"We aren't supposed to send anything out that isn't for OKH unless Muntzer signs it."

Franz raised his eyebrows and stood straighter. "Who is in the office right now?"

Nonnheim stuck his head out the door and looked around. "You and I, sir."

"That's right. What is your rank?" Franz, of course, knew the answer.

Nonnheim looked away. "Sergeant."

"What is my rank?"

"Captain, sir." Nonnheim's eyes returned to Franz's.

Franz prepared to strike the decisive blow. "That's right. What does that make me?"

Nonnheim paused. "The commanding officer at the moment."

"That's right." Franz took out a pen and signed the requisition where Muntzer normally would. "Now order up a staff car. They will take it in five minutes."

"Yes sir."

~

Reinhardtstrasse 13. What is at Reinhardtstrasse 13? Franz tried to puzzle it out as he drove the Mercedes staff car through the dark streets of Berlin. If he'd lost his right leg instead of his left, he might not have been able to drive. Practicing on Carpool vehicles, he had spent weeks learning to depress the clutch with his prosthetic, but he had to sit closer to the wheel to manage it. When he got tired, he could shift without using the clutch by floating the gears down and matching the RPMs and the car speed. A complicated endeavor, but he was more or less used to it now.

Unter den Linden past Rothberg's bakery. North on Friedrichstrasse. He chuckled. When they were children, his older brother tried to convince him that Friedrichstrasse was named for him. Franz had believed it until he wised up at ten. *Then west on Reinhardtstrasse.*

When he found the address, Franz thought it must be a mistake. Friedrich hadn't told him what to look for, and he had destroyed the paper with the address, so he couldn't double-check. But he had no better option, so he parked the car on the street, walked up to the front door of the five-story modern white stone and glass building, and entered the Caritas Psychiatric Asylum of Central Berlin.

At the reception desk in the lobby sat a Carmelite nun. She looked up, saw Franz, and greeted him. Her eyes lit up as if she recognized him, though he had never met her. "Good evening. Can I help you?"

"Um, I don't know. I hope so." He cleared his throat. "I'm looking for my brother, Friedrich Maedler. I understand he might be here."

A soft smile creased the nun's face. "Wait just a moment." She looked in a registry and announced, "Herr Maedler is in room twenty-seven. Follow me."

Franz was thoroughly confused.

When they reached room twenty-seven, the nun opened the door. Franz walked in to find himself looking at Friedrich, Katrin, and the priest from the cottage, Fellner. The nun entered behind him and closed the door. It was a sparsely furnished room, with a single bed, a small dresser, and a chair. Franz's heart lifted, and he grinned broadly at Katrin, who responded with a demure smile.

Friedrich spoke first. "Franz, welcome. You remember Father Fellner?"

Franz nodded. What was going on here?

"And this is Sister Klara Marie." He glanced at Katrin and lifted an eyebrow. "Though some know her better as Estella. We can trust her."

Franz nodded to the nun, then took a few steps to Katrin

and gave her a kiss. "I have the petrol cards. The car is in front."

Friedrich got right to business. "Were there any problems?"

"Other than Muntzer seeing me counting out ration coupons? No." Katrin gasped and Fellner's mouth fell agape, while Friedrich remained impassive. Franz held up the coupons. "He saw me and let me go. He's a good man. He's weary of death and has no love for the Gestapo." Franz remembered a detail that could affect Friedrich's plan, whatever that was. "He also ordered me to take tomorrow off."

Friedrich noticeably relaxed. "Good. We won't have to drive through the night." He winked at Katrin.

What are they up to now? Franz wondered.

Friedrich continued, "In that case, we'll stay here tonight and leave first thing in the morning."

Katrin looked to Father Fellner, then to Franz. She took a deep breath, started to speak, and stopped. Then she started again. "Franzi, there is a chapel here. It's not fancy, but..."

It took a moment for Franz to understand her meaning. Then he wasn't sure he'd heard right. "Wait.... Here? Now?"

"Yes, now." Katrin bit her lip. "I don't have a wedding gown or shoes and we haven't been able to invite any guests." Then she smiled, and Franz's heart swelled. "But as I said before—all I need is you, Franz Maedler."

Franz sank into the chair, folded his hands, and thought. *Katrin deserves better than this. But it's what she wants. But I will be in Switzerland, too, in a few days. We could at least have a nicer wedding there. But no one knows how long any of us will be around. Here we are, together tonight... Yes.* "Yes, Sunshine, tonight. Here." He thought for another second. "Who will marry us?" In better days, they would have asked Pastor Hoffmann, but who could know where he was... or even if he was.

"I would be honored, if you're willing," Father Fellner said solemnly.

Franz looked to Katrin. He doubted either the Catholic or Evangelical church would recognize it. The state certainly wouldn't. But the important thing was that it be recognized by God. Franz would let Katrin decide. She knew Fellner better, anyway. He gave her a slight nod.

Katrin reached to squeeze Franz's hand. "The honor would be ours, Father."

Father Fellner looked from Katrin to Franz, his eyes sparkling. "Well, then, let's have a wedding."

"Good. It's settled." Friedrich smiled. "Franz, I shall attend you. The Sister has volunteered to be Katrin's witness." He scanned the room. "Now means now."

The group trickled out of the room. Fellner first. After a couple of minutes, Katrin and the nun. Then Friedrich and Franz. There was little risk at this time of night, since patients were locked in their rooms and there was a skeleton staff. Still, better safe than sorry.

When they had all gathered in the chapel, Father Fellner stood in the front with his back to the altar. Facing him stood Franz on the right, Katrin on the left. Friedrich and Sister Klara Marie sat in the first pew.

The chapel was small, not a grand church like Mama might have preferred for the occasion. But simple as it was, Franz sensed that it was a holy place, worthy of a supreme act of faith in a dark time. The heady fragrance of incense filled the air, making him slightly dizzy. Katrin's hand gripping his only intensified the effect.

~

Katrin shivered with anticipation and joy as Father Fellner smiled from in front of the altar. "Franz and Katrin, do you come here of your own will and with ready hearts to receive one another in marriage?"

She turned to look up at Franz as they answered in unison, "Yes."

"Will you love and respect one another," Fellner continued, "and be true to one another until death separates you?"

"Yes." Again, they answered in unison. Katrin wondered whether Franz could hear her heart pounding. The long-awaited moment had finally arrived. This was not the wedding she had dreamed of, but to her it was perfect.

When they had spoken their vows, Franz removed the engagement band from Katrin's left ring finger. He looked into her eyes for a moment, then gently took her right hand and slid the ring on it. It was now a wedding ring.

Father Fellner kept the customary homily short. "A cord of two strands is easily broken, but a cord of three strands is strong. If you invite God into your marriage, He will give you the strength to overcome together whatever trials you may face." Then he reached out his right hand and placed it on the couple's joined hands. *"Ego vos in matrimonium conjugo.* I now join you in marriage. What God has joined together, let no man put asunder. Franz, you may kiss your bride."

Franz gathered Katrin in his arms and kissed her without reserve.

Katrin returned the kiss whole-heartedly, though her joy was tinged with sadness. *If only Mama and Papa could have been here.* She didn't mind giving up the elaborate ceremony, but she would have liked to share the joy of this moment with her parents. With Franz's mother. She leaned into his embrace, wrapping her arms around him, only vaguely aware of the happy voices surrounding them.

"I love you, my Franzi," she whispered.

"I love you, too, Sunshine."

The first voice to break through the moment was Friedrich's. "I'm sorry, Brother, but I couldn't arrange a banquet on such short notice."

"What, no party?" Franz laughed.

Friedrich smiled back. "I can only do so much. There will be time to celebrate in Zürich."

"Nevertheless, you get points for creativity." Franz chuckled. "This is probably the first wedding ever held in a psychiatric asylum."

"Brother, the whole country is now a psychiatric asylum. But the patients are running it."

Franz laughed, but Estella frowned. "Do not insult my patients. They are troubled, but they are not evil."

Friedrich rubbed at the back of his neck, his cheeks flushing at Estella's reaction. "You're right. It was a bad attempt at a joke. I'm sorry, Sister."

Father Fellner spoke up. "And now, I must go."

Katrin dropped Franz's hand and stepped up to the priest. She threw her arms around him and kissed him on the cheek. "Thank you, Father, for everything. I hope we will see you again."

Blushing slightly, the priest patted Katrin on the shoulder. "You will, my dear. Of that I am sure. Friedrich, Franz, be careful. Estella, you too. We'll talk soon." With that, the priest disappeared through the chapel doors.

Friedrich was next. "I will take my leave now, as well. I can sleep in the entry hall. Be ready to leave at 05:45 sharp." He gave Katrin a peck on the cheek. "Until tomorrow, Sister." Then a hug for his brother. "Congratulations, Franz. You are a lucky man."

Estella was the last in the chapel with the newly married couple. "I must go back to the desk. You can return to room twenty-seven for the night. God bless you both."

And then they were alone in the chapel. Katrin slipped her hands into her husband's. "It wasn't the wedding we expected."

"No, it wasn't. But we will always remember it. And we will have stories for our children." A day of high highs and low lows, of terror and chaos and joy.

"Our children," she echoed. Heat filled her cheeks, and she giggled. "Come, Franz. Let's go back to our wedding suite."

Without another word, Franz led Katrin through the chapel doors, down the asylum halls, and back to room twenty-seven.

CHAPTER
33

16 MAY 1943

The light of early dawn colored the sky. Before Friedrich had retired for a night of bad sleep on the entry hall sofa, he had made one phone call. He usually contacted Üli Kastler by courier, but there wasn't time. He had to use Kastler's private number.

"Kastler here."

"The normal place. 05:15."

Now, Friedrich waited at the von Scharnhorst tomb at the Invaliden Cemetery, a modest walk from the asylum, hoping his contact had recognized his voice. For all he knew, Kastler had a dozen contacts with a dozen "normal places." But the young man had not become the intelligence attaché to Switzerland's embassy in Berlin because he was slow on the uptake. At 05:15, he arrived.

"Maedler."

"Kastler."

The Swiss intelligence officer glared at Friedrich. "Do you always call people at home in the middle of the night? This is risky, not to mention annoying. It had better be good."

"It is," Friedrich assured him. "We have three people crossing over. Two tonight, one next week. I'll give you the names on their papers."

"More SD?" Üli raised his eyebrows. "I thought we were even."

Friedrich shook his head. "I need your assurance that they can pass to your side of the border without difficulty and take up residence in Switzerland."

"Oh. More Jews?" Kastler's tone was dismissive. "Really, Friedrich—"

Raising a hand, Friedrich cut him off. "Not this time."

"Well, what then?"

"My brother, his wife, and I. I'll make it worth your while. I know a lot."

Kastler wrinkled his forehead. "That's an enticing offer, but I'll have to pass it by Bern."

Friedrich shook his head again, more vigorously this time. "There's no time. We leave Berlin in twenty minutes."

Kastler narrowed his eyes and squinted at Friedrich. "Are you under suspicion?"

"My sister-in-law was picked up by the Gestapo two days ago. I got her out, but it was a close call. They'll be back. Many lives are at stake, including mine and my brother's. They'll put the pieces together. We have no time."

Kastler took a long pause, then sighed. "This may be the day your luck runs out, Maedler... but not if I have anything to do with it. Go. I'll make it work. But you'll still have to get yourself out of Germany."

"Thank you, Üli. We'll be entering Switzerland as the von Schemmels." Friedrich clapped Kastler on the back. "Perhaps we'll meet in Zürich in better times."

"Perhaps, Herr von Schemmel."

~

Franz and Katrin were waiting in the entry to the asylum

when Friedrich got back at 05:47. Franz glanced at his watch. "You're late." He soaked in the view of his bride, winked at her and twisted one of her curls around a finger, then swooped in for a kiss. Her eyes flashed as she stood on tiptoe and stretched upward to return the gesture. "On second thought," Franz added, stifling a yawn, "my watch must be wrong—you're early. Come back later."

But Friedrich was all business. "Let's go. If all goes well, we'll be in Stuttgart by 14:30. The train leaves at 16:05." He pulled out a set of documents and handed them to Katrin. "Frau von Schemmel." Franz winced. His wife was about to leave with his brother. *It has to be this way. It's only for a few days,* he reminded himself.

Katrin glanced at Franz, then handed her genuine papers to Estella. "Here, take these and burn them." Lost papers were a premium item and could usually be re-used by switching out the photo. But soon, no one would want to be Katrin Weber. The three quickly embraced Estella, then walked out the front door to the Mercedes staff car.

Franz would keep his true identity for now, assigned to drive an industrialist and his wife as a special courtesy from the Armaments Ministry. Friedrich and Katrin would sit behind him. His heart ached at the thought. Katrin was only as far as the back seat and he already missed her.

The Mercedes Type 320 Pullman was a lovely car, fit for a field marshal. Six seats, drink coolers, and a removable sunroof. The gentle hum of the engine was soothing. Too soothing. Twice, Franz nearly nodded off. Once Friedrich, sitting directly behind him, kicked the seat to start him to life. The other time, Katrin leaned forward, pulled on his ear, and whispered, "Wake up, Franzi." It was enough.

Franz recited in detail his adventure obtaining the ration coupons. "...And then, he turned and walked out. The dispatch sergeant didn't want to give me the car, but I pulled rank and he gave in."

Friedrich recounted how he had learned Katrin's prison location and gone to the commandant to demand her release. "I picked up his phone and threatened to call Canaris."

"What would you have done if he called your bluff?" Franz asked.

"I don't know. I would've thought of something." They all laughed. *Yes, knowing Friedrich, I'm sure that's true,* Franz thought.

He turned his head and snuck a glance at Katrin. "Sunshine, you had a close call, too." He wasn't sure she was ready to talk about it, but he guessed she needed to.

Her eyes darkened. "Keep your eyes on the road, husband."

"Ja, meine liebe Frau."

Katrin was silent for a long time before finally saying, "It was too close." Her voice held a slight tremor. "I'm grateful Friedrich came when he did. I'm not sure how long I could have held out if..." Her words faded away.

For several minutes, no one spoke. Anger burned within Franz. Anger at the Gestapo, at himself for not being able to protect her, at Friedrich for pulling her into his project, even though it was the right thing and it was Franz's project now, too. The next moment, his anger turned. "Friedrich, was Father a part of this?"

Again, an uncomfortable silence. Franz set his jaw.

"Friedrich? I want to know the truth."

A sigh filtered in from the back seat. "When I was trying to find Katrin, I checked in with Deutmann. You remember Deutmann. He is at Gestapo Wilmersdorf now. Apparently, Father called the inspector there last week, and as soon as he was off the phone, the inspector assigned agents to look into Katrin. But she wasn't picked up by Wilmersdorf. They wound up handing the case to Grunewald."

Franz said nothing but gripped the steering wheel so hard his knuckles turned white. Friedrich reached from behind to grip his shoulder. "Franz, you are married. You have a beautiful bride. Soon this will all be behind us. Father has to live with himself in his own prison of bitterness. Let it go."

"I pity him," Katrin said softly. "I pray God will help me forgive him."

Franz gripped the steering wheel tighter and drove on in silence.

The hours went by and the Mercedes passed through Leipzig, then Nuremberg. Franz had last visited Nuremberg when Father brought him to the Party rally in 1937. It was a grand spectacle, with marchers, flags, speeches, bonfires. Mother had just died, and Franz was about to join the army. Klaus had taken Franz, against Mama's wishes, every year from 1933 to 1936, as well. Franz thought back to the rallies with regret now. He should have seen through the spectacle to the ugly reality. Everyone should have. Now Germany was reaping the whirlwind.

On the other side of Nuremberg, the group stopped for lunch at a small cafe on the side of the road. It was another trying moment for Franz. There were only three other tables. One was empty, another had a pair of Party leaders in their brown uniforms, and the last seated four SS men. Franz could not show any affection toward Katrin. He was supposed to be her driver, Friedrich, her husband. As they ate, he compensated by glancing at her every few minutes. She didn't seem to notice. Her eyes kept drifting nervously toward the SS men.

Franz was relieved when Friedrich elbowed her and whispered, "You mustn't look at them so much. You'll draw their attention."

Then it was back on the road. The kilometers kept going by. Franz was tense. Soon he would have to let go of Katrin. Too soon. It was almost unbearable. Add that to the dangers inherent in the situation, and he had good reason to be on edge. Since the cafe, Franz sensed that Katrin was also on edge.

They were almost to Stuttgart when Franz made a detour. He wanted to do something for his wife. Something that would make their first day of marriage a little bit closer to what she had dreamed of and then given up.

As Franz brought the car to a stop, Friedrich recognized the place. "I'll stay with the car. Fifteen minutes, Brother. Don't dally."

Franz got out of the car, walked around to open Katrin's door, and helped her out. "Take a look." He made a broad gesture toward the castle ruins ahead of them. No one else was in sight, so he took her by the arm and walked her to an arch in the ancient stone wall. "After you, Sunshine."

The two walked through the archway into the grassy castle courtyard. Franz spotted some dog-violets growing against the castle wall. "Wait here," he said, and stepped away. A minute later, he returned to Katrin with a bouquet of the purple wildflowers.

Katrin held the flowers to her nose and inhaled deeply, then smiled up at Franz. *"Danke schön."*

Happy to have pleased her, he shrugged up a shoulder, then waved a hand toward the ruined walls. "Burgruine Hofen. Built around 1250, I think... brought down in the Thirty Years War. I came here as a boy."

The couple walked hand-in-hand the length of the narrow castle interior until they stood at the small arched back gate, looking out over the Neckar River.

"It's beautiful," Katrin breathed out. "So peaceful... you can almost forget the troubles going on outside."

"Yes. Many troubles have come by this castle and gone. It's a good thing to remember."

She twined her fingers with his. "Franz..." Her voice faded into silence.

Beneath his calm façade, Franz's heart pounded. Katrin didn't have to say anything more. They were both on the edge of a knife. He glanced at his watch. "It's time to go." Franz held Katrin close and gave her a long kiss.

She clung to him for a moment, but finally allowed him to walk her back to the car. When they got in, she folded her hands in her lap and said nothing more the rest of the drive.

At the train station, Franz got out, opened Friedrich's door, then went around to open Katrin's door and offer his hand. He got the suitcase out of the trunk and carried it into the station behind them. The suitcase and its contents had been Father Fellner's contribution from the parish donation closet. Franz walked with them and watched as his brother stepped up to the ticket counter. "Heil Hitler. Two tickets to Zürich please."

"Papers?"

Friedrich handed the clerk two sets of documents.

"Herr and Frau von Schemmel?"

Friedrich answered with an air of bored superiority. "That's right."

The clerk looked up. "What is the purpose of your trip?"

"It's for the Armaments Ministry. I am to meet in Zürich with representatives of Tavaro and Oerlikon-Bührle."

The clerk examined the papers, then glanced at Franz in his Army uniform carrying the von Schemmel luggage. "Very well. And the lady?"

"She is my wife. But you already knew that. She is accompanying me. Does there have to be another reason?"

Franz struggled with conflicting feelings. On one hand,

Katrin was *his* wife. He hated hearing his brother claim her, even knowing it was a ruse. On the other hand, he wanted to chuckle. It was vintage Friedrich, affecting insufferable haughtiness to make a bluff work.

The clerk looked back at Friedrich. "Of course, sir. Class tickets?"

Friedrich's tone grew more impatient. "What do you think? First."

Katrin touched his arm. "Darling, be kind to the poor man. He is only doing his job." As much as he resented the need for it, Franz was impressed at how smoothly Katrin moved into her role.

"Of course," the clerk said. "That will be 228 Reichsmarks."

Franz stifled a chuckle at Friedrich's next gambit. "The Armaments Ministry has a DRB account. Put it on that."

"Yes, sir. Here are your tickets."

The three found seats inside the station and waited for the train. The next twenty-five minutes passed slowly. None of them were in the mood to talk. The station was crowded, making private conversation impossible. Franz was grateful Friedrich played the role of a distant husband, more interested in his newspaper than his supposed wife.

Then the moment Franz had dreaded arrived. The loudspeaker was malfunctioning and about every third syllable was garbled, but they were able to make out a nasal voice announcing. "Zürich, track five. Freudenstadt, Tutlingen, Singer/Hohentwiel, Zürich, track five."

Friedrich stood up. "Time to go." The three walked quickly to platform five. The train had just pulled in. Friedrich walked ahead to the correct wagon and waited for the other two to catch up. When they did, Franz handed the suitcase to his brother and shook hands with him formally. He leaned over and told Friedrich, barely above the noise of the locomotive, "Take good care of her, Brother. And yourself." His brother nodded.

Friedrich helped Katrin into the railway car, then followed her up the steps. As she turned to say a last goodbye, Katrin mouthed the words, "Please come."

Her words broke Franz's heart. But he couldn't, not yet. He tried to smile. "I will see you soon." A moment later, he watched the train pull away from the platform and roll into the distance.

~

The drive back to Berlin was excruciating. Franz's stump hurt. He wanted to take the prosthetic off, but driving the car without operating the clutch was difficult and he had little practice doing it. Even more, this was the first time he fully understood the term "heartache." He always considered it metaphorical. He thought he had experienced it when Mother died, and then Georg. But this was worse. His chest literally hurt.

He could scarcely remember a time before he loved Katrin. Like her, he had thought about their wedding day, dreamed about it for years. Now it had finally happened, and he felt terrible. It wasn't supposed to happen this way.

As day faded into night, Franz mulled over everything that had brought him to this point. All along the drive, he remembered the faces. Sometimes he saw them through the windshield. It was as though he was back in Kyiv, driving on Melnykova through the crowds being herded to Babyn Yar. The little girl, her family.

He and Katrin and Friedrich had done the right thing, but Franz felt ashamed that he hadn't come to it sooner. At the same time, he couldn't entirely let go of the uncomfortable feeling that he had stepped outside of the German national community and was dangling in no-man's-land. Most of his men wouldn't have understood. And what about Father?

He had respected his father and even loved him. Even when he parted ways with Klaus, he didn't consider him an enemy. But Father had put National Socialism above Franz and handed Katrin over to the tender mercies of the secret police. Why shouldn't he see Klaus as an enemy? Katrin's voice echoed in his mind so loudly he almost turned to see if she was sitting there after all. *I pray God will help me forgive him.* Franz wanted to say such a prayer, too. But it wasn't possible. Not yet. He had struggled for years to find moral clarity. Now he faced a new moral struggle, learning to forgive the unforgivable.

By the time he got back to Berlin, it was a little after one in the morning. He was physically and emotionally exhausted. The infirmary was closed, so he lay down in bed, still in uniform. By now, his wife and brother would either be safe in Switzerland. Or not.

~

Friedrich had selected Stuttgart as the jumping off point for several reasons. If the Gestapo had already put out an alert for them, security would be beefed up at the Berlin stations first. It would also not be unusual for an industrialist from Stuttgart to travel to Switzerland. Not least, Friedrich had pressed his luck in the last operation, sending four groups across in one day at Bregenz. It was time for a new crossing.

At first, Katrin and Friedrich had the compartment to themselves. For a time, Katrin stared out the window. Her usually cheerful features were shadowed, her brow furrowed. When Friedrich touched her shoulder, she shrugged away from him.

"Katrin, he'll be all right." Uncharacteristically, he wasn't sure what else to say. They had brought his brother—her husband—into danger, and now he was dangling, the last one out. Friedrich knew his guarantee could prove hollow.

"You should have insisted he go into hiding," she said.

"It isn't safe for him to go back to work."

Friedrich tried to sound convincing. "There are risks, Katrin, I know. But if he went into hiding now, they would know something was wrong. He might never make it out of Berlin. As it is, the accountant won't find out about the missing petrol coupons until Friday. He'll have his papers before that. He'll be with us—with you—before they know anything is wrong."

"But they'll know that we're gone. Are you so sure they won't turn their eyes on him when they can't find us?" Katrin shuddered.

"For now, they think you're on an Abwehr mission. And I have left word with Canaris that I'm on a mission. That's all he knows. It should take the Gestapo a few days to unravel the truth, maybe more, and Canaris won't make it easy." Friedrich paused and looked past Katrin out the window. "It is in God's hands now. It always has been."

A tear that had been hovering on the rim of Katrin's eye escaped to track its way down her cheek. "I know," she said. "But after everything, we are finally married. I couldn't bear to lose him now." She fished in her purse for a handkerchief and dabbed the moisture from her eyes.

"Katrin, I know it's hard. But we have to compose ourselves. We haven't made it across yet, either." Friedrich stared at the passing farmland. "We all chose to do our duty, come what may. Franz too."

"You're right." She folded the handkerchief and put it back in her purse. "I'm very tired, Friedrich. I just want to sleep for a bit. Do you mind... may I rest my head on your shoulder?"

"Of course, my dear Sister."

Katrin shifted in her seat, laying her head on Friedrich's shoulder and closing her eyes. Within minutes, she was sound asleep, and she did not awaken until the train pulled into Tutlingen. Friedrich tried to push out of his mind how pleasant it was to feel her there.

From Freudenstadt to Tutlingen, a grey-headed air defense general and his young wife shared the compartment and a bit of polite conversation with Friedrich while Katrin slept. From Tutlingen to the border, Friedrich and Katrin were alone again.

Katrin awoke in better spirits, and she and Friedrich spent the remainder of the trip to the border rehearsing their parts. When the train reached Singer/Hohentwiel, it was about an hour before sunset. This was the last station in Germany, where passengers travelling to Switzerland had to get off and go through border control.

As they approached the SS checkpoint, Friedrich took out their papers and prepared to hand them to the control officer. In his other hand, he carried the suitcase. Katrin still gripped the bouquet of purple wildflowers Franz had picked for her at the castle, though they had started to wilt.

When they stepped up to the desk, the SS officer looked at them and demanded, "Papers."

"Yes, of course. Here they are." Friedrich handed them over. He was prepared for a grueling questioning.

The Sturmbannführer then glanced at a paper on his desk. Friedrich surmised it was the list sent periodically to alert border control of people they must not let cross. He wondered if he and Katrin appeared on it yet. The officer looked back at the documents. "Names?"

Friedrich looked the SS man in the eyes. "Berthold von Schemmel."

Katrin followed. "Katrin von Schemmel."

"Explain your trip to Zürich."

"I am to meet with representatives of two Swiss companies to promote trade with the Reich. My mission is approved by the Armaments Ministry." Friedrich grinned.

"The Ministry paid for our tickets."

The SS man demanded, "What companies?"

"Tavaro and Oerlikon-Bührle." Both were doing a lucrative arms business with the Reich.

The SS man took a third look at the papers and studied them closely. Friedrich wasn't sure what he was looking for. "Herr von Schemmel, you travel to Switzerland often."

"Yes, my work requires it."

"But your wife has not joined you until now?" The SS man turned his piercing gaze to Katrin.

Friedrich reached for Katrin's free hand. "This time, she insisted. I think once she sees it, we will practically be living in Zürich."

The major noticed Katrin's bouquet. "Frau von Schemmel, those are pretty flowers. Where did you get them?

Katrin smiled up at Friedrich. "My husband, sir."

"Well done, Herr von Schemmel."

Friedrich wrapped an arm around Katrin's shoulders and kissed the top of her head. "She deserves flowers. She is a remarkable woman."

The SS man looked at the couple and stamped their papers.

Friedrich took a step, turned around, and asked the Sturmbannführer, "Can someone help with our bag?"

The major called out, "Obersturmführer Hengst, help the man with his suitcase."

"Thank you so much." Friedrich doffed his hat and smiled.

What could be better than getting the SS to help with the luggage while one was sneaking out of the country? But the feeling only lasted a moment. Friedrich would feel no real satisfaction until his brother had joined them. Franz was still inside the vast prison called Germany, and he had a target on his back.

CHAPTER
34

17 MAY 1943

Franz awoke from a deep sleep at 06:00. He was roused in the middle of a dream. He and Katrin had been together, wandering the ruins of a castle. They stretched out a blanket on a grassy riverbank and were about to sit down with their picnic basket when the morning wake-up call pierced the idyllic scene.

He sat on the edge of his bed for a long moment, blinking his eyes, wishing he could return to the half-remembered dream. Instead, he had to get cleaned up and head to the infirmary. He should have gone yesterday but got back too late. As long as he went before reporting back to duty this morning, it should be fine.

When he arrived at the infirmary, there was a long line waiting to be seen. Finally, an orderly called his name and directed him to an examination cubicle. A moment later an army doctor walked in holding a clipboard.

The doctor regarded Franz. "Good morning, Hauptmann."

"Good morning." Franz yawned.

"What's the matter?"

Franz cleared his throat. "Late Saturday I began to feel ill. My commanding officer ordered me to take yesterday off, and I'm glad he did. I was throwing up all morning and afternoon. I started feeling better last night and I think I can go back to work today. Can you clear me?" He could hear his mother's voice: *What tangled webs we weave when first we practice to deceive.*

"Where are you assigned?"

"Carpool."

"And when was the last time you vomited?"

"About 17:00 last night."

The doctor made a note on his clipboard. "And you feel better now?"

Franz nodded. "Yes, much."

The doctor made another note, then took a thermometer from the breast pocket of his white lab coat. "Open."

He shook the thermometer, then placed it under Franz's tongue. After three minutes, he checked it. "You have no fever and you last vomited more than 12 hours ago. I will clear you for duty. There's a stomach bug running through the Bendlerblock. You'll be fine now. Some are taking longer." The doctor wrote something on a small pad of paper, ripped off the page, and handed it to Franz.

So far, so good. "Thank you, Herr Doktor."

As Franz walked out of the infirmary, he saw Major Kobel waiting to be seen. He nodded to Kobel, who looked tired and a bit green. "Herr Major."

Kobel nodded back wordlessly.

~

As soon as Franz entered Carpool at 08:32, he went straight to Colonel Muntzer's office.

"Come."

Franz entered.

"Welcome back, Maedler. But you are late."

"I was... not feeling well enough to go to the infirmary until this morning. I went early, but the line was long. Sir, I am cleared to return to duty." He handed Muntzer the doctor's note.

The colonel glanced at the paper. "So, your, um, illness is resolved?"

"Perfectly, sir."

Muntzer looked up from the paper to study Franz's face. "Good. Let's hope you are now immune."

Franz entirely agreed. "Yes, sir."

"Get back to work." Muntzer looked back down at the work Franz had interrupted.

"Thank you, sir." Franz moved toward the door but turned back when Muntzer said his name. "Yes, sir?"

"There's something else." Muntzer wrinkled his forehead. "An Abwehr courier came by at 08:01. He had something for you and said he was under strict orders not to give it to anyone but you. I told him you were sick. He wouldn't identify himself. Do you know what that's about?"

"No, sir. No idea." *What tangled webs, indeed. This war has made liars of us all.*

Franz found it hard not to dwell on his bad luck. The most likely explanation for the courier was that his false papers were done early and were being delivered. The courier had arrived when many others were settling in for work. Less conspicuous. Franz and Katrin could have been celebrating together tonight. Now they would have to wait until Friedrich's friend felt it was safe to try again.

Someone had turned on the radio in the office, and Franz found the music selections soothing. Mostly classical, with some opera recordings thrown in. The military communiques were cryptic. That meant things were not going well. Franz wondered how many men in the office still believed in the cause. How many ever really did. After Friedrich revealed himself, Franz realized he couldn't be sure of even the most ardent National Socialists.

Most, he imagined, were bound to the Fatherland more than the Führer at this point. When success was easy and cheap, they could imagine the two were conjoined. Franz had. No longer. But most would still see what he had done as treason, a betrayal of the Wehrmacht and Germany if nothing else. It hurt to know that, even though they were wrong.

Franz kept waiting for the courier to return, but nothing. Muntzer had told him Franz was ill. He probably wouldn't come back until tomorrow. Just one more day.

He was finally free from work at 18:00. He felt the need for spiritual nourishment. He would have gone to St. Luke, but with Hoffmann arrested, he expected its doors would have been chained shut. *Or perhaps they turned it over to the Reich church and defiled it with their twisted cross.* He grimaced. Such a sight, he could not bear.

Instead, he took the long walk across the Spree River to Marienkirche, one of the oldest churches in Berlin. Entering the church, he was faced with the faint remains of a fresco, painted during a time of plague and countless wars, portraying people of every station engaged in a dance with Death. Now war had brought the uncertainty of life to the forefront of every mind. Franz wondered how much of the dance remained for him.

A few other visitors were scattered about the pews. An older couple on the right about a third of the way back. Pensioners. A middle-aged man in a suit in the very back on the left. Probably a businessman or a bureaucrat. All seeking their own peace. Franz sat toward the back, far from the others. For a long time, he did nothing. He didn't pray, didn't bring out his Bible, didn't think. He just sat.

Finally, he pulled the small Bible from his pocket. He

opened it to a familiar verse. *We must obey God rather than men.* He read some verses in the Psalms, calling for God's peace and protection. He closed the Bible. Then he closed his eyes. After a time, he got up to return to his quarters. On his way out of the church, he turned to glance again at the fresco, only to find familiar faces fixed on the figures: Ziemann, the girl from Kyiv, the babushka stirring the pot of shoe leather. Then they were gone.

In the officer's mess on Tuesday morning, Greater German Radio played *Wacht am Rhein*, as usual, then reported that British air pirates had destroyed two concrete dams at Edersee and Möhnesee in western Germany. The communique assured listeners that the British would be amply paid back. In Poland, the criminal uprising by Jews in Warsaw had been put down through the bravery of the SS. Olbermann, sitting with Franz for breakfast, muttered something about hoping the Jews would get what they deserved. Franz instantly flashed back to scenes of Kyiv, Bila Tserkva—and fearful faces peering at him from the hidden room at Katrin's cottage. "Yes, Olbermann, I hope they get what they deserve. I'm sure at least some of them will."

After mess, he arrived at work with anticipation. Surely the courier would try again today. But he didn't come at 08:01, as he had yesterday. Nor at lunch. Nor after lunch. More routine requisitions to process. Every few minutes Franz looked up to see if a stranger was coming through the door. At 14:00, one appeared. He wore the uniform of an Army lieutenant and reported directly to Muntzer's office. A few minutes later, Olbermann went into the colonel's office, came out with the stranger, and saw him to Major Kobel's desk, empty since yesterday.

When Olbermann walked by on the way back to his own desk, Franz stopped him and asked, "Who's he?"

"Oh, that's Lieutenant Mühlen. Kobel is sick and will be out another day or two. Mühlen is taking his place."

"All right." Franz tried to appear indifferent, but suddenly the room was spinning.

At 16:30, a gaggle of military police materialized around Mühlen. Franz had just turned back from watching the commotion behind him when he looked up and saw another stranger in the doorway, in plain clothes. *The Abwehr courier?* Franz watched the man hover in the doorway a moment, then turn around. Things had gotten too hot.

That night, Franz couldn't eat or sleep. He could sense the walls closing in. Twice he had missed the chance to receive his new papers. He wanted to escape now. He wanted to live. He longed to be with Katrin. But he had no choice but to let things play out.

The next morning came and went. No papers, but no more police, either. Maybe it was nothing.

A little bit after 13:30, five military police, an officer and four enlisted men, entered the room. Two enlisted men took up positions by the main doors while the officer and the other two enlisted men walked directly into Colonel Muntzer's office without knocking. A minute later, they came out with the ashen-faced colonel.

Muntzer called for quiet and attention.

"Men. A discrepancy has been found in the accounting of the petrol coupons. There will be an investigation. Every man here is to cooperate without reservation. To my right is Major Jaeger of the Feldgendarmerie. He will conduct the investigation."

Franz froze in his seat. A stone settled in the pit of his stomach.

Attention shifted to Jaeger, a tall, heavyset man in his forties with receding reddish-brown hair, a mustache, and a professional bearing. "Thank you, Colonel. We will interview each person here. No one may leave until our interviews are complete."

Colonel Muntzer stayed in the outer room while the Feldgendarmerie set up shop in his office. One at a time, the men in Carpool went into the office, then came out. Franz tried to tamp down his anxiety. When he was called, he pretended for a moment that he was Friedrich, comfortably swimming in a sea of dissembling.

Jaeger was curt. "Name and rank?"

Standing at attention in front of Muntzer's desk, Franz was equally curt. "Maedler, Franz. Hauptmann."

"What are your duties?"

"I process requisitions, assign ration coupons when necessary, and communicate with the dispatcher to release vehicles." Franz took a deep breath to calm himself.

Jaeger scribbled notes. "So, you work closely with the bursar?"

"Yes."

"We are fifty 5-liter ration coupons short. Do you know anything about this?" The major looked up from his notes and stared directly into Franz's eyes.

The bursar wasn't supposed to count them until Friday. How do they know? Franz swallowed hard. "Are you sure?"

"Yes. The replacement bursar is, thankfully, quite rigid in his approach. He insisted on counting them and checking the figures against the ledger as soon as he started in the office."

"I see. Perhaps there was a mathematical error?"

"We can't rule that out," Jaeger conceded. "But we are familiar with Major Kobel's work, and he's usually quite precise."

Franz shifted in his seat. "I suppose it's possible that the major accidentally counted out the wrong number to someone."

"As I said, the major doesn't make such mistakes." Jaeger spoke firmly.

"Well..." Franz shrugged. "If you discount human error, the other explanation is that someone took them. But the coupons are kept in a locked cabinet."

"Who has keys?"

"Only the bursar. And the colonel." Franz swallowed hard on the last one. Muntzer had spared him. He didn't want the colonel to get in trouble for something he had done. But Muntzer *did* have a key, which the military police either already knew or would soon know. If Franz didn't admit that, it would cast more suspicion on both Muntzer and him.

"If Kobel had taken the ration coupons, he could have simply adjusted the ledger to match," Jaeger pointed out, continuing to stare at Franz. "Since last Friday at 09:30, have you been aware of anyone being alone in the office?"

"On Saturday, I was alone for a brief time while Sergeant Nonnheim went out for a smoke. As soon as he got back, I gave him an emergency staff car requisition and left. Then he was alone." Franz paused for a moment to gauge Jaeger's reaction. There was none. "I don't know when someone else came in, but it might not have been until morning. I don't know about Sunday. I was out sick."

"How brief a time is a brief time, Hauptmann?"

Franz knew the exact answer to that question—twelve minutes and nineteen seconds. But such precision would only raise more questions. "About ten minutes."

"And then you left for the night?"

Franz wiped his forehead. He found the major's persistence disconcerting. "That's right."

"And Colonel Muntzer was gone by then?"

Franz replayed the confrontation in his mind. *I didn't see anything.* "Yes. That's why I had to sign the requisition myself."

"Do you know when he left?"

"No, I didn't see."

"Thank you."

~

After he was dismissed by Jaeger, Franz watched from his desk with rapt attention. When Jaeger finished interviewing the men, he called Muntzer back. Twenty-five minutes later, the colonel emerged. His face had regained none of its color.

When Jaeger stepped out of the colonel's office, he scanned the room, then approached Muntzer. Franz instinctively got up to join his commander. Reaching Muntzer, Jaeger stopped, looked him in the face for a few seconds, and asked, "Who is next in command?"

"Kobel, but he's not here." Muntzer's voice shook, and he avoided Franz's gaze. "Maedler is next."

"Who is after Maedler?"

Franz kept a stony expression, but his heart skipped a beat. This was not good.

Muntzer paused. "Olbermann."

Jaeger nodded. "All right, put Olbermann in charge for now."

Muntzer furrowed his brow and called out, "Men, Lieutenant Olbermann is in command for the time being." The room quieted again.

Jaeger called to the lieutenant. "Olbermann, we will be back for Nonnheim as soon as he is on duty. Do not let him leave." Then he turned back to Franz and Muntzer.

"Oberst, Hauptmann, I am placing you under arrest on suspicion of *Kreigsverrat*. If you come quietly, there will be no need to injure your dignity." *Kreigsverrat*—"war treason," or aiding the enemy—was a catch-all charge covering everything from statements of political opposition to black market offenses. Article 57 of the Military Criminal Code made Kriegsverrat a capital offense.

Franz closed his eyes and nodded silently. A feeling came back to him, his chest tightening just as it had in Stalingrad as he realized a T-34 had pointed its gun directly at him. A few moments later, Jaeger and his subordinates escorted him and the colonel from the Bendlerblock.

~

When Franz arrived at Tegel military prison, he knew he was guilty of the charges—and more. He doubted that Jaeger knew it. For now, the investigators suspected but could not prove that Franz, at most, might be guilty of black-market dealings with the army's petrol cards. It was a serious offense, but no one had yet suggested that he was part of a broader conspiracy to help Jews or other fugitives escape. He would try to keep it that way.

Franz spent the next two days alone in a small cell, sometimes sitting, sometimes pacing the short distance from the door to the opposite wall. His meals were tasteless, his days spent in silence. He was beginning to wonder if the Feldgendarmerie investigators had forgotten him. Compounding his unease, he still didn't know if his wife and brother had made it to safety.

Finally, the door opened, and a guard led him to meet with investigators in a small, windowless room with whitewashed walls. Major Jaeger and a Feldgendarmerie captain waited.

Jaeger greeted him. "Hauptmann Maedler."

"Sir."

The military police major began softly. "How are you? It's been a few days."

Franz gazed into the distance. He thought he would actually rather face the T-34. "Fine, sir. But I would like to clear my name and get back to work."

"All in good time, Maedler. Do you have anything to add to your previous statement?"

"No, sir." Franz turned back toward the major.

Jaeger looked down at a notepad. "According to your statement, you would have had an opportunity to break into the cabinet when Nonnheim left for about ten minutes."

"If I wanted to, I suppose so." Franz shrugged.

"And then he came back, and you left for the rest of the night."

"Yes."

Jaeger squinted. "How do you suppose someone would get into the cabinet without a key?"

Franz tried not to squirm. "I guess someone would need a lock pick."

"Where would someone get such a thing?"

"I really don't know." Until Friedrich had given him one, Franz hadn't known. Thank goodness he had thrown it out of the car on the drive to Stuttgart. "Maybe a criminal gang?"

A knowing look flitted across Jaeger's face. "Were you aware that Sergeant Nonnheim was in trouble with the law before being reformed by the Party?"

"No sir, I had no idea." *Nonnheim? He's always so squared away.*

"Is there any reason for us to discount the possibility that you and Nonnheim were working together?"

Franz paused, took a deep breath, and answered. "I hardly know Nonnheim. I don't usually work nights. It was a fluke that we overlapped last Friday. You can ask Colonel Muntzer about our schedules."

"We have. That's what he said, too."

Franz relaxed and sighed.

Jaeger pressed in another direction. "How would you describe your relationship with Colonel Muntzer?"

Franz raised his eyebrows. "It is a good relationship," he said. There was nothing more he wanted to say.

The captain who had joined Jaeger finally spoke for the first time. "Good enough to keep secrets for each other?"

"I don't know what you mean." Franz's shoulders tightened.

The captain leaned forward and continued. "Are you more like his subordinate or his son?"

Franz wasn't sure where this question had come from, but the captain had, hopefully inadvertently, hit the bullseye. He couldn't let his affection for Muntzer show. Truthfully, at this moment, he wished Muntzer *were* his father, but for both of their sakes, he could hardly admit that. "There is no doubt in my mind that Colonel Muntzer is my superior officer and I am his subordinate. My first day at Carpool he reprimanded me for being four minutes late."

"One last thing." Jaeger reclaimed control of the questioning. "Nonnheim said that last Friday, just before you left, you were acting strange."

Franz's pulse raced. "In what way, sir?"

"Pushing through a requisition that should have been signed by Muntzer but wasn't."

"Yes, sir." Franz had to stick with the story, or all could be lost. The last thing he wanted was for them to begin sniffing down that trail. "It was an emergency Abwehr request. I was told it was urgent. I was the senior officer present, and I assumed neither Muntzer nor Nonnheim would want to be held responsible for the failure of an Abwehr mission."

Jaeger and his colleague looked at each other and nodded. "That will be all. Thank you, Captain."

The next day, Franz was released and returned to the Bendlerblock. Could it be, despite everything, that he would sneak through? When he came back to the office, the colonel had not returned and no one had seen Nonnheim, either. But Franz was focused on waiting for the Abwehr courier to arrive. Presumably he, whoever he was, had discovered that Franz had been arrested. It might take him a while to learn about Franz's release.

Three days later, at exactly 08:01, a non-descript man in a dark brown suit, brown leather shoes, and a tan necktie slipped through the door as the Carpool staff were trickling in. He walked directly to Franz's desk and handed him an envelope labelled "special instructions from Abwehr... Eyes only... F. Maedler, Carpool." The man said only, "Good morning, Hauptmann." With that, he turned and walked briskly out of the office.

Franz's heart skipped a beat. *Katrin, we are so close. If you made it.* As soon as he could, he left for the restroom. He always went upstairs, as Olbermann had recommended months ago, though climbing the steps was a challenge. When he got to a stall, he closed the door and opened the envelope. Inside, he found papers for Franz Kleist, a Berlin resident and mid-level functionary for the Armaments Ministry, traveling to assist Herr von Schemmel in his negotiations with the Swiss. He also found a cryptic unsigned note:

Herr and Frau von Schemmel in Zürich. Initial negotiations with Swiss successful.

Franz felt a load of worry fall off him. It was the first word he had gotten to confirm that Friedrich and Katrin had made it. He tore the note into small pieces, flushed them down the commode, stuffed the new papers into his pants pocket, and returned to the Carpool office.

He counted the minutes until he could leave. Tonight, he would board a train to Zürich.

Sometime around 15:30, Olbermann returned from a meeting with a long face. He made straight for Franz's desk and started speaking so fast he was unintelligible.

Franz held up his hand as if directing traffic. "Slow down, Olbermann. I can't understand you."

The lieutenant took a deep breath, blinked, and started over. "Herr Hauptmann, I just heard from a friend in the military police. He's at Tegel. They've court-martialed Nonnheim and the colonel!"

Franz took a minute to digest the news. *The wheels of justice turn quickly in the Wehrmacht, if you can call it justice.* His palms were sweating. His escape from punishment could mean that others would be punished for a crime they didn't commit.

"Sir?" Olbermann's voice brought Franz back. "They're going to be shot!"

CHAPTER
35

Franz slumped in his chair. *Shot?* He knew that his predecessor Brusewitz had been shot, but from what he had heard, they'd had irrefutable evidence against him. The evidence against Nonnheim and Muntzer was circumstantial. After all, they weren't guilty.

But fuel supplies in the Reich were dwindling, and with the collapse of the thrusts toward the Caucasus and the Middle East, there was no improvement in sight. Clearly, the authorities were cracking down. Franz had been so focused on what would happen if he were caught that he hadn't thought about what would happen if he got away.

How could I imagine they would let this slide? That they wouldn't find someone else to pin this on, if not me? His guts twisted inside him.

For months, his choice had been abstract—which oath to honor, which God to follow. Three weeks ago, it became more concrete: Do I help a group of people who have never harmed anyone? Tonight, it could not get more concrete or more painful.

He desperately wanted to get out, to go to Katrin and hold her in his arms. He was willing to do almost anything to make that happen.

Almost, but not anything.

She was so close he could smell the fragrance of her hair, feel her hands in his. He had done his duty, helping twelve people escape to freedom—the ten Jews from the cottage and his own brother and wife. If God willed that he should escape to his loving wife while others were ground up in the National Socialist death machine, who was he to argue? Many had already died, and many more would follow.

But he couldn't rationalize walking away. *I told Muntzer that I believe if you can stop a murder and don't do it, you become a murderer. If I let him and Nonnheim die for my actions, what would God call me, other than a murderer?*

When Franz got off work, he returned to his quarters, changed into civilian clothes, and took a walk to the train station. His heart was unsettled, his mind racing. He found a bench outside the main doors and sat there.

Costly grace. *It is costly because it costs a man his life, and it is grace because it gives a man the only true life.*

Franz could save his life today by boarding a train and leaving two other men to die. But such a life would not be worth living. It was one thing to stray from God and be a part of unholy things before coming back. It was quite another to come back to God and then coldly, knowingly do an unholy thing anyway. *Love your neighbor.*

Franz sat paralyzed. He couldn't leave the station. He couldn't get on a train. Two trains left that could have taken him to Switzerland. There was one more, at 22:30. The last of the night.

Still on the bench, Franz hoped against hope that God would give him some sign that freed him to get on the train.

He thought about Nonnheim. He had been truthful when

he told Jaeger he barely knew the man. But Nonnheim had parents, siblings, dreams. The pretty secretary. And no one should die for another's crime.

His thoughts turned to Colonel Muntzer, whose demanding Prussian exterior hid a man with a good heart. A suffering heart. The father Franz wished he had. Clearly, Muntzer had not betrayed Franz, or Franz would be in Tegel and Muntzer would not.

Franz opened his little Bible. John 8:32. *Then you shall know the truth, and the truth shall make you free.* As much as anything, it was his love for truth that had turned him against the Nazis. He could lie to keep the innocent alive, but not to send them to their deaths.

He sat on the bench, holding back tears, until his watch showed 22:33. Franz pulled out a pen and some paper from the small bag he had brought with him, and started writing.

The first short letter was to Friedrich. It was not easy.

> *25 May 1943*
> *Dear Friedrich,*
>
> *I am not coming to Switzerland. I cherish our friendship and our brotherhood. I want you to know how much I admire your courage and your brains. I am proud of you. I hope I have made you proud, too.*
>
> *Katrin is a special woman. You promised me you would take care of her. I expect you to keep your promise. Someday, you may admit that you have fallen in love with her.*
>
> *Forever your Brother,*
> *Franz*

The next letter would be even more difficult. Franz lowered his pen and took a deep breath.

25 May 1943
My beloved Sunshine,

I am sitting at the Potsdamer station. The last train to Switzerland just left, and I am not on it. I cannot come to you.

I cannot go into details, but things were discovered missing. Others have been blamed. I cannot let them die for something I did.

You will never know how much I treasure your love, your kindness, your goodness. When I was lost, you helped me find the way. When you think of me, think of our walks together, our talks in the garden, our wedding night, the castle. I will love you to the end of time.

We did what had to be done. We have been loyal to our Fatherland and to the Father in Heaven whom we share. I have no regrets, except that it took me so long to see the truth.

Stay close to Friedrich. He has promised to look after you.

Promise me that you will find happiness. We will see each other again.

With a full and breaking heart,
Your Franzi

When Franz stopped writing, he felt as if his life had already ended. He took a moment to dry his eyes and collect himself. Then he got up, hobbled to a metal trash barrel, set his false papers on fire with his cigarette lighter, and threw them in.

~

The next morning, Franz returned to the Carpool office for a few minutes. He placed the two letters into an envelope, sealed it, and wrote "F. Maedler Abwehr. Eyes-only" on it. He said goodbye to Olbermann, Schuchart, and Kobel, who had returned to duty after his fateful touch of the flu. They didn't understand, and Franz couldn't explain.

Then he left the office to visit two other destinations in the Bendlerblock. First, he made the long walk to Abwehr. He soon spotted the nameless man in the brown suit who had brought Franz his papers the day before. Today he was wearing a maroon tie. When he saw Franz, a quizzical look came over his face.

Franz handed him the envelope and said, "Get this to my brother."

The man cocked his head and looked Franz over. "He is on a mission."

"Please. It's very important."

"I understand. I'll do what I can."

Franz thanked Brown Suit, nodded, and left.

Thirteen minutes later, back in the East wing, he arrived at the Feldgendarmerie headquarters, which was also conveniently located in the Bendlerblock. He approached the first person he saw. "Is Major Jaeger here?"

"One moment. Can I tell him who you are and the purpose of your visit?"

"I am Hauptmann Franz Maedler. I am here to turn myself in."

~

Jaeger and Franz sat in a small room in the back of the Feldgendarmerie offices.

This would be a tricky interview. Franz would have to confess to taking the petrol cards without saying why he needed the cards or who had helped him. He had to do it without Friedrich's smooth assurance. Worse, he had struck blows for truth, and now he would have to cover them in deceit, or many others might pay with their lives.

The military police major began. "Maedler, before I was drafted into the Feldgendarmerie, I was a detective in Frankfurt. I've seen criminals turn themselves in. But I have never seen anyone turn himself in after someone else had been convicted." He shook his head. "I don't know whether to believe you."

"Why would I lie, sir?" Franz cocked his head.

"Perhaps it is a misguided attempt to save Muntzer?"

"As I told you, sir, the colonel is simply my superior officer."

Eyes narrowed, Jaeger studied Franz. "Then why?"

"It's really quite simple, Major. I cannot live with myself if innocent people die for my mistake." Franz felt good. *Finally, a truth I can utter.*

Jaeger arched a bushy eyebrow. "Mistake?"

"Crime, then."

"Did you act completely alone?"

"Yes, sir." Franz shifted uncomfortably in his chair.

"You realize it might go easier for you if you identify an accomplice."

Franz shifted again but worked to sound resolute. "There was no accomplice."

"How did you do it?"

"I acquired a lock-pick and learned Nonnheim's routine. I knew he would be gone for at least seven minutes. It only took four." Franz was exaggerating, but Jaeger wouldn't know the difference. It would have been four or five minutes if the pick had worked right the first time and Colonel Muntzer hadn't interrupted him.

"Where did you get a lock pick?"

Thinking back to his earlier interview with Jaeger, Franz answered wryly, "From a criminal gang, sir."

Jaeger shook his head. "Why? You're a hero of the Reich. Led a battalion against the Reds, fought in Stalingrad."

Franz fell quiet for a minute. Of all the obvious questions, he had not prepared for that one. He could have talked for a long time on the subject of how he became disillusioned, tired of the lies and murder, tired of complicity in things he knew were wrong. But the answer he wanted to give was justification for a treason much bigger than stealing a couple hundred liters of fuel and would raise more questions than he wanted to answer. Vice, on the other hand, the Nazis would understand. They wouldn't feel the need to look deeper. So, he swallowed hard and took another uncomfortable dive into dissembling. *How does Friedrich do it?* Perspiration dripping from his forehead, Franz straightened in his seat and drew a breath. "Sir, I have developed a gambling problem since returning to Berlin. I needed a lot of money fast."

"We checked your locker when you were in Tegel and didn't find anything but some clothes, the *Large Catechism*, and an Alfred Rosenberg book. Do you still have the petrol coupons?"

A Rosenberg book? Surely they looked between the pages, but apparently, they didn't look close enough. "No, I sold them the next day."

"That is the real reason you weren't in the office?" Jaeger was putting the pieces together, just as Franz had hoped.

"Yes, sir."

"Do you still have the money?"

"No." Franz struggled for an explanation, his gaze darting everywhere but Jaeger's face. "I lost it at the tables." Untraceable. Impossible to disprove.

"To whom did you sell the coupons?"

"I don't know his name," Franz demurred. "He was on a street corner in Alexanderplatz. I didn't know him."

Jaeger walked to the door, opened it, and called, "Finnemann! Bring your things."

When Finnemann came in, he was lugging a large sketch pad and a set of pencils. He set up his things and waited. The authorities really were taking this seriously. They wanted to track down the fictional buyer, too.

Jaeger asked, "Hauptmann, can you describe your petrol customer?"

Franz was exhausted from the questioning. Now more creativity was required of him. "Major, it was dark and I was tired. I had spent all day trying to find a customer."

The major leaned forward and half-whispered. "Do your best."

"I'll see what I can do." Franz paused, gathering his thoughts. Friedrich was not the only imp in the family. "Thin face, wider at the top than the bottom. Broad, high forehead. Long, thin nose. High cheekbones. Light, thin eyebrows. Narrow slits for eyes, eyes far apart. Thinning, short blond hair with traces of red. Medium to medium large ears. Thin lips."

"What color eyes?" The major's tone was tinged with expectation.

"Blue."

Finnemann put the finishing touches on the drawing, then held it up for Jaeger. "Sir?"

The major studied the sketch, then turned to Franz.

"Maedler," he said drily, "you have given us Reinhardt Heydrich."

Exactly what I had in mind. Franz feigned shock. "Oh no, sir, that can't be right. Heydrich is dead."

Jaeger stared at Franz for a moment, then looked back to Finnemann. "Thank you. You may take your things and go."

~

Ninety minutes later, Franz was back at Tegel. The hardest thing, of course, was knowing that he had signed his own death warrant, but he hadn't expected it to be so difficult to confess in a way that kept others alive. It was easier to lie outright than to tell half a truth. He had given up not only his life but his reputation. He would die as a thief and a gambler who had stolen from his own army to feed a pathetic addiction. It was his final sacrifice.

The Reichs Court Martial two days later in Charlottenburg was short. A military prosecutor presented the evidence. Jaeger testified. Franz confessed in open court. The presiding general took a few minutes to berate him. "You have betrayed the men you left behind in Stalingrad," the general said.

Verdict, guilty. Death by firing squad. Then back to Tegel.

Had it been high treason against the State, he would have been shipped to the Plötzensee prison and executed by guillotine. The executioner there was famous for wearing tails and a top hat for the occasion. Franz's affair would be more pedestrian. No one could tell him the appointed day, so he treated each day as if it were his last. He found himself praying more than ever and longing to hold Katrin again. The knowledge that he would soon be reunited with his mother gave him a measure of peace.

Daily, Franz and the other prisoners were given a few minutes to walk around the small exercise yard. One day, he saw Major Jaeger walking through the yard to the prison. Their eyes met and Jaeger walked over to him. Most of all, Franz wanted to know what had happened to Colonel Muntzer and Sergeant Nonnheim.

"They were released, Maedler. Nonnheim is back at Carpool."

Franz breathed a sigh of relief. "And Muntzer?"

"He got command of an infantry regiment in Army Group Center." Jaeger said it as if it were an honor.

Franz winced inside. Muntzer had been reassigned to the Russian Front, probably as punishment for letting his office get out of control. *At least he has a better chance there than in front of a firing squad.*

CHAPTER
36

10 JUNE 1943

Y ou have a visitor."

The words woke Franz from an afternoon nap. He wasn't sure he liked naps. Frittering away the last hours of life and all. On the other hand, there wasn't much else to do in Tegel. Franz couldn't even pace the floor, as his prosthetic had finally been confiscated, as property of the State. He sat up and looked around his spare cell with its peeling pistachio green paint, his eyes fixing on the short, stocky guard who had just interrupted his rest.

"Maedler, you have a visitor."

Balancing on crutches, Franz got up, walked out the cell door, and was escorted by a guard to a visiting room. Waiting for him, seated in a chair, was the Kreisleiter of Wilmersdorf.

Franz was taken aback. He had neither heard nor seen anything of his father since visiting him a month ago, before his arrest. He assumed that Klaus had washed his hands of his derelict son. Now, here sat his father in front of him. He couldn't help feeling the same trepidation he felt when he was twelve and his father was about to reprimand him for sneaking one of Mama's strudels.

Klaus wore a modest grey suit. He had left his ostentatious brown uniform at home.

Franz entered the room cautiously, eyed Klaus, and slowly sat in the empty chair across from him. No one said anything for a while. Finally, Klaus opened the conversation.

"Hello, Franz." He sounded more exhausted than combative.

Franz waited a moment before responding, a moment laden with tension and resentment. "Hello, Father."

Another silence.

"Franz, what did you do, son?"

Franz responded sharply, "You know what I did." *Actually, you don't know, but be glad you don't.*

Father cocked his head and lowered his voice nearly to a whisper. "Why?"

"I'm sure you know that, too." *Father would have asked for all the reports on the matter.*

Father reached to place his hand over Franz's, but Franz pulled away. "If you needed money, you should have come to me."

Franz looked down, refusing to meet his father's eyes. "I was embarrassed."

"Franz..." Klaus let out a heavy sigh. "Look at me, son. I need to tell you something."

Begrudgingly, Franz raised his head and fixed his father with a stubborn glare. "Yes?"

"Your brother went on a mission in Switzerland and has not been heard from." Father's eyes bored in on Franz.

He's gauging my reaction, wants to see if I know anything. "I'm sure he's fine."

"Are you?" Klaus shifted in his chair. "You know the Weber girl disappeared at the same time Friedrich left."

Now it was Franz's turn to bore holes in Klaus with his eyes. "Are you sure she didn't end up in another Gestapo prison? I know what you did."

Klaus shifted again and looked away.

"You don't even try to deny it. I loved you, Father. I didn't see eye to eye with you, but I loved you. And you delivered my w—" Franz caught himself. His marriage to Katrin had to remain a secret for now, for the safety of all involved. "My fiancée up to Gestapo torturers."

Klaus continued evading Franz's gaze, but finally spoke. "It is my understanding she wasn't harmed."

"If you know that, then you know the only reason she wasn't harmed was that Friedrich got her out just in time." He wasn't revealing anything Father wouldn't already know from the reports on Katrin.

Klaus took a deep breath. "Son, I was trying to save your future."

"Well, look at me now." Franz's tone dripped with sarcasm. *If he wanted to save the future, he should have picked different heroes.*

"The Gestapo suspects something," Father hissed. "Perhaps Katrin pulled Friedrich into some plot. They had evidence she was harboring Jews. Do you know anything about that?"

Franz crossed his arms. "No."

Father went on, leaning forward in his chair. "And he claimed, apparently falsely, that she was an Abwehr agent. That is how he got her out. Franz, she was seducing him. She confessed it!"

"I don't believe it." Franz shook his head. He knew better, though he certainly couldn't explain it to his father. "Maybe she was an Abwehr agent. I have met some surprising Abwehr agents."

Klaus scratched his chin. "Are you sure? Franz, how

would you not know things like this about your girl?"

"I have learned, Father, that things in this world are often not what they appear to be."

"I am going to ask you directly: Do you know where Weber is?"

Franz slouched in his seat. "All I know, Father, is that she is not here with me."

Klaus paused. "You know they could suspend your sentence and pull you out of here if you had information that proved useful."

Franz didn't hesitate. "If they were willing to do that, they would tell me themselves. And if they seriously thought I had information, they would pull me out and send me to Prinz-Albrecht-Strasse." He set his jaw. "It doesn't matter. I've nothing to tell them."

"Not even to clear Friedrich's name? The SD is hunting him in Switzerland now."

"Father, I can assure you that, as far as I know, Friedrich did nothing wrong."

Klaus looked away. Far into the distance. "I have held them at bay, Franz. I will tell them you don't know anything." He got up to go but hesitated. "Franzi, you are going to die." He had not used the nickname since Franz was eight. He stepped toward Franz as if to offer an embrace, then stopped himself. "I'm sorry about the girl." He turned toward the door.

Franz looked at his father. Katrin was right. He was pitiful. His strength, which Franz had always admired, had been eaten away by his steadily growing losses and moral confusion. Sycophants were not strong, no matter how much power they held over others. Klaus had made Hitler and National Socialism his god. But it was a false god, and it was already beginning to fail.

Then Franz thought about other times. The family trip

to the Chiemsee when he was nine. Walks to the park with Father, Friedrich, and Georg. The first memory barely imprinted on his brain, when he was two and his papa appeared at the house after walking all the way home from France. Mama, Friedrich, and he had crowded around Father, laughing and crying tears of joy. Father wasn't happy then, or almost any time after, no matter how much happiness people enjoyed around him. He had squandered his life in bitterness. Franz couldn't hate him.

Driving Friedrich and Katrin to the Stuttgart rail station, Franz had not been ready to forgive his father. It was now or never. *Owe no man anything, but to love one another.* If God, who is holy, could forgive Franz, Franz could forgive Klaus. Before Klaus reached the exit, Franz stopped him. "Papa?"

Klaus stood quietly in the doorway.

"Papa, I know."

Klaus cleared his throat, but neither spoke nor turned around.

"Papa, I said that I *had* loved you." He swallowed hard. "I'm sorry. I *do* love you."

Klaus turned, looked at Franz with moist eyes, and nodded.

~

The days dragged as Franz awaited his end on this earth. One afternoon, the key turned in the lock and the door swung open, revealing the same short, stocky guard. Franz's heart skipped a beat. *Maybe this is it. It has to happen someday. No matter how long I wait, it will seem like a surprise.*

Instead of summoning him for the long walk to meet his doom, the guard stood aside to admit a thin-faced man with a clerical collar. Franz nodded at his guest, though he remained on guard. He had not forgotten the other army chaplain's eager exhortations to fulfil his Nazi vows.

"Hauptmann Maedler," the chaplain said, "I am Reverend Harald Poelchau."

Franz relaxed. He had heard of Poelchau. Outside the prison walls, he was called "Doctor Tegel" for the way he ministered to the families of prisoners. Franz smiled.

"Do you mind if I sit and talk with you awhile?"

Franz shook his head and scooted over to make room on the cot. Reverend Poelchau sat beside him.

The chaplain began with a prayer over Franz.

When he was done, Franz looked up. "Pastor?"

"Yes, Franz?"

"I am sentenced to die."

Poelchau was silent for a moment. "I know. Are you ready for death?"

Franz thought for a moment. "I am not ready to leave my wife. But I am ready to face God. In Stalingrad I was not." He looked at the cell wall. "I took part in things that make me ashamed, Pastor. My wife helped me see that I had to make a choice, that I could not follow both the cross and the swastika."

"And I suppose you are here because you chose the cross."

"I could not undo what was done. But I could take responsibility for what came next."

Poelchau nodded thoughtfully. "Then you are a man of courage, Hauptman."

"Is it courage to look in a mirror and see the truth?" Franz asked. It was not a rhetorical question.

"It takes courage to act on the truth you see."

Franz studied his hands as he collected his thoughts. "I think I have done what was right. In the end, my conscience gave me no choice. But Pastor, my conscience does not feel clean. The ledger is not even. And even when I began trying to do what was right, I was bathed in lies, violated oaths, put others in danger—"

"Franz, the ledger will never be even." The pastor looked squarely into Franz's eyes. "You must understand this. You cannot clear the ledger yourself. All you can do is to follow what God commands in the time that you have. That is all any of us can do."

Franz was quiet for a minute before responding. "For a long time, I just wanted forgiveness. But then I saw that forgiveness without following God was meaningless. I decided I wanted costly grace, not the cheap imitation."

The pastor smiled. "I will tell my friend Bonhoeffer that you have read *Discipleship*. He is here in Tegel, you know."

"I read as much as I was able." Franz chuckled, then grew solemn. "It is Sunday, I think, and I have not been to church for many weeks. Are there words you can share?" Earlier, Franz had heard the pealing of church bells.

"This is not just any Sunday, Franz. It is Pentecost, the day the Holy Spirit came down to the apostles and empowered them to spread the Word throughout the earth. Only Easter itself is a greater symbol of the triumph of Christ over His foes." Poelchau thumbed through the Bible and read aloud the account of Pentecost found in Acts.

As he listened, Franz pondered his Pentecost confirmation. *The Holy Spirit doesn't always come in a mighty rushing wind, but in a breeze that blows over and over until it finally prevails.*

The pastor circled back to their conversation a few minutes before. "You have said you wished to follow God, to have costly grace. Christ speaks of this in John 15. *This is my commandment, that ye love one another, as I have loved you. Greater love hath no man than this, that a man lay down his life for his friends. You are my friends, if you do whatsoever I command you.*" He closed his Bible and lay a hand on Franz's shoulder. "You have heard His command and you have obeyed. The cost is great, yet His grace is even greater."

It was not the first time Franz had reflected on that verse. He thought back to the moment in St. Luke when he finally determined what God required of him. "Pastor, are you able to give Communion?"

"Yes, Franz. Are you prepared for this sacrament?"

"I think so."

The Reverend led him in the prayer of confession. "Almighty God, I, a poor, miserable sinner, confess unto you all my sins and iniquities with which I have ever offended you and justly deserved your temporal and eternal punishment." For a moment, Franz saw again the faces, not in a window but in the inner recesses of his mind. "But I am heartily sorry for them and sincerely repent of them..."

Poelchau pronounced the absolution: "Upon this your confession, I announce the grace of God unto you, and in the stead and by the command of my Lord Jesus Christ I forgive you all your sins in the name of the Father and of the Son and of the Holy Ghost."

All your sins. You cannot clear the ledger yourself. You can only feel a sorrow beyond measure and throw yourself on the mercy of God.

Then the chaplain spoke the words of Institution. When he was done offering the body and blood of Christ, Poelchau proclaimed, "May this gift strengthen and preserve you in the true faith unto life everlasting."

Life everlasting. Soon I will know what that's like. In that moment, he let go of this world and hovered, suspended between the earth he had forsaken and the eternal life he had not yet reached.

~

It was 18 June. Franz had been at Tegel for three and a half weeks. He had gotten little sleep the previous night. Nights were often noisy in the prison, and last night had been no exception. Mostly just the tramp of prisoners pacing like caged animals in their cells. Sometimes a distant shout or scream.

The sun had already been up for a couple of hours. It was almost the first day of summer, and sunrise came early. Soon a guard would bring breakfast. Last night's supper had been an indistinguishable mess resembling porridge; breakfast would probably be more of the same. He was just glad to get something.

As the door opened, Franz was, for a brief second, confused. There were two guards and no food. Almost as quickly as he felt confusion, he registered understanding.

"Come."

He grabbed his crutches, got up, and was escorted none too gently by the guards. When they turned him to enter the courtyard, he knew for sure.

Pastor Poelchau joined him at the door. "Franz, are you ready?"

"As ready as I can be." He had known this moment would surprise him, and it did. Was this the end? It seemed so anticlimactic. Then Franz thought back to the Communion Poelchau had given him, and the one before that at Hoffman's church. Those were, he supposed, a pale imitation of the Communion with Christ he would soon know. "I'm ready."

The guards walked Franz to a post that stood a few meters in front of a stone wall. When they had secured him to the post, a squad of three men with rifles followed an officer into position in front of Franz. The officer called out, "Blindfold?"

"No." He would not hide from death. What was the point?

"Cigarette?"

"No." Franz cracked a wan smile. "The Führer says it isn't good for you."

Pastor Poelchau opened his Bible. "In the name of the Father, and of the Son, and of the Holy Spirit."

Franz's mind wandered. He could see Katrin as if she stood next to him. Under his breath, he muttered, "I'm sorry, my Sunshine."

"For God so loved the world..."

He thought of Friedrich and Georg in happier days.

"...that He gave His only-begotten Son..."

I hope Muntzer makes it in Russia. He isn't really cut out for combat.

"...that whosoever believeth in Him..."

Then he was looking into the hidden room at the cottage. Ten lives.

"...should not perish..."

Katrin again. She was so beautiful. *Couldn't we have had just a few more days?*

"...but have eternal life."

The officer ordered the men to a firing stance.

Franz looked up at the walls of the courtyard. Window after window. And, on the third story, four windows from the left, he saw faces.

The little girl from Kyiv. And Mama. And they smiled.

HISTORICAL
NOTE

This is a work of historical fiction. As with all such works, we have woven our characters and their story into the framework of real events—in our case, terrifying events of war and oppression.

We relied on a wide variety of sources. Two indispensable books were The German War by Nicholas Stargardt and Berlin at War by Roger Moorhouse, which illuminated topics ranging from air raids to restaurants in wartime Berlin to Gestapo prisons to Jewish fugitives. Jews in hiding were also the subject of Mark Roseman's A Past in Hiding: Memory and Survival in Nazi Germany, which included information on attempts by some in Abwehr to help a limited number of Jews get out of Germany.

Nazi Culture, an anthology edited by George Mosse, included some key insights, especially the section on religion. Among other things, Mosse's collection reproduces the Martin Bormann circular to Nazi regional leaders that we quoted as well as the Hoyer painting "In the Beginning Was the Word." Two excellent general histories were Karl Dietrich Bracher's The German Dictatorship and William Shirer's classic The Rise and Fall of the Third Reich.

Henry Friedlander's book The Origins of Nazi Genocide:

From Euthanasia to the Final Solution provided some insight into the T4 euthanasia program. Similarly, Hitler's Willing Executioners: Ordinary Germans and the Holocaust, by Daniel Jonah Goldhagen, provided information on the use of Order Police battalions. For Dietrich Bonhoeffer's theology we relied heavily on Discipleship (translated into English and retitled The Cost of Discipleship). Hoffmann, Poelchau, and Franz would have used Luther's German-language translation of the Bible, which is closer to the King James English translation than to other, more recent, English translations, so we used the KJV, though shorn of its more Shakespearean aspects. Selections from Luther's Large Catechism are quoted from The Book of Concord, edited by Robert Kolb and Timothy J. Wengert (2000). The hymns used on Palm Sunday were found in the German hymnal Lutherisch-Kirchen Gesangbuch. Though published in 1980, the selections would not have been much different than in earlier editions. English verses were taken from The Lutheran Service Book (Concordia Publishing House, 2006), pages 655 and 666.

For information on ranks, uniforms, and insignia, we relied on a variety of online sources and the book Nazi Regalia, edited by Jack Pia and published as part of Ballantine Books' Illustrated History of the Violent Century. Also helpful were Barbarossa and The Road to Stalingrad, volumes in the Time-Life series on The Third Reich. A wide range of online sources were consulted. Particularly helpful were H.G.W. Davie, "The Influence of Railways on Military Operations in the Russo-German War 1941-45," published in the History of Military Logistics; William L. Skiles, "Protests from the Pulpit: The Confessing Church and the Sermons of World War II," in Sermon Studies; and Emily Greenhouse, "The Perfect Nazi Bride," The New Yorker, 27 September 2013. Details about Franz's trip home were mined from the first, portions of Pastor Hoffmann's sermon in chapter 15 were found in the second, and Frau Hilgenberg's Bride School was derived from the third. We relied on a variety of online sources for historical weather data.

Not least, we found some inspiration in the films The Invisibles and A Hidden Life.

You have found in these pages a mix of real and fictional characters. Hitler, Himmler, Goering, Goebbels, and Bormann were, of course, all too real. So were the Abwehr men Canaris, Oster, and von Dohnanyi; von Reichenau and Paulus of the Sixth Army; Bernhardt Lichtenberg of St. Hedwig's; and the pastors Bonhoeffer and Poelchau. The Munich students referenced in Chapter 9, the so-called "White Rose" movement, were real, as was their fate. Hans Bernd Gisevius, the German vice consul in Zurich, was a real member of the Abwehr resistance circle and one of the few members of the anti-Hitler conspiracy to survive the war. The Maedlers, the Webers, the rescued guests at the Weber cottage, Father Fellner and his network, Pastor Hoffman, the baker Rothberg, the officers and men in OKH Carpool, the Swiss intelligence attaché Üli Kastler, and a variety of secondary characters were fictional.

Similarly, the narrative of our characters is fictional, but the events surrounding them are not. The German defeats in Stalingrad, Kursk, and North Africa, the massacres of Jews in Kyiv and Bila Tserkva, the battles and starvation in Kharkiv, the scene found at the NKVD prison in Lemburg/Lviv, the air raids in Berlin on 1 March and 20 April, the Total War speech by Josef Goebbels, the women's demonstration on Rosenstrasse, Operation Seven by elements of the Abwehr, the communists sticking posters to people's backs in Wilmersdorf, and the bomb taken by von Dohnanyi to Tresckow in Smolensk were all historical events. Likewise, the Nazi Bride Schools, St. Hedwig's,

Marienkirche, Invaliden Cemetery, Borchardt's Restaurant, the giant air raid bunker at the Tiergarten, the paved-over Pleasure Garden, the castle in Stuttgart, and the church of St. Lorenz were real places. The memorial cards for Georg Maedler and Otto Gebel were modeled on a variety of real Sterbebilder. Not least, the book Struwwelpeter, featuring the rather severe tailor, is a very real and horrifying German children's book originally published in the 1880s and reprinted in the 1930s.

To add an air of authenticity, we have occasionally interjected a German word or phrase, or the ranks as they were found in the Army (Heer), the SS, and the Gestapo. We have also reverted to the German spelling of some names and titles—that is, with an umlaut in place of an E. We have used kilometers, which are 1.6 to the mile, but have converted Celsius temperatures to Fahrenheit and people's height to feet and inches. We have generally used the German style of dates, i.e. day month year or day month, and have mostly stuck to 24-hour military time. In support of Ukraine and those who defend her against Russia's present-day colonialism and aggression, we chose to follow Ukrainian spelling conventions throughout.

We are aware that we cannot fully understand or convey the horrors of the time. We are also painfully aware that the stand taken by our heroes was the exception, not the norm. Far too many Germans, including Germans professing the Christian faith, were shamefully silent or even complicit. But some did stand at the moment of truth—some sooner than others—and more than a few of them lost their lives doing so. Our aim is to honor them, to give them a voice, and to remind readers that such people existed, not to suggest that they were typical. In this world, it seems, the need for such heroes is never far from the surface.

About The Authors

Andrew Busch is Crown Professor of Government and George R. Roberts Fellow at Claremont McKenna College in Claremont, California, where he teaches courses and writes on American government and public policy. **Melinda Busch** is author of four Arch Books for children; The Maiden and the Toad, an illustrated re-telling of the fairy tale classic; and contributions to each of the Whitstead fantasy anthologies.

Andrew and Melinda both grew up in Boulder, Colorado, were introduced years later by their former junior high school mathematics teacher, and married in 1995. They have three grown children, two grandchildren, three dogs, and a home in Southern California.

CPSIA information can be obtained
at www.ICGtesting.com
Printed in the USA
LVHW111210191122
733278LV00025B/1416